MONTGOMERY COLLEGE LIBRARY
ROCKVILLE CAMPUS

WITHDRAWN

NO ROOM FOR MAN

NO ROOM FOR MAN

Population and the Future
Through Science Fiction

Edited by

RALPH S. CLEM
Florida International University

MARTIN HARRY GREENBERG
University of Wisconsin

JOSEPH D. OLANDER
Florida International University

Littlefield, Adams & Company

Copyright © 1979
by
LITTLEFIELD, ADAMS & CO.
81 Adams Drive, Totowa, N.J. 07512

Library of Congress Cataloging in Publication Data
Main entry under title:

No room for man.

(Littlefield Adams quality paperbacks; no. 346)
Bibliography: p.
CONTENTS: Population growth, social consequences of too
many people: Ballard, J. G. Billenium. Aldiss, B. W. Total environment. Silverberg, R. In the beginning.—Feeding the billions,
world food problems: Kornbluth, C. M. Shark ship. Harrison,
H. Roommates.—Population, impact on the environment and
resources: Ehrlich, P. R. Eco-catastrophe. Robinson, F. M. East
wind, west wind.—[etc.]
1. Science fiction, American. 2. Science fiction, English. 3.
Population—Fiction. I. Clem, Ralph S. II. Greenberg, Martin
Harry. III. Olander, Joseph D. PZ1.N74 [PS648.S3]
823'.0876   79-14191 ISBN 0-8226-0346-2

Printed in the United States of America

The editors and publisher gratefully acknowledge the following sources for permission to quote passages from the works indicated.

"Billenium" by J. G. Ballard. Copyright © 1962 by J. G. Ballard. Reprinted by
permission of the author and the author's agents, Scott Meredith Literary Agency,
Inc., 845 Third Avenue, New York, New York 10022.

"Total Environment" by Brian W. Aldiss. Copyright © 1968 by Brian W. Aldiss.
Reprinted by permission of the author.

"In the Beginning" by Robert Silverberg. Copyright © 1970 by Avon Books.
Reprinted by permission of the author and the author's agents, Scott Meredith
Literary Agency, Inc., 845 Third Avenue, New York, New York, 10022.

"Shark Ship" by C. M. Kornbluth. Copyright © 1958 by Mercury Press, Inc.
Reprinted by permission of Robert P. Mills, Ltd., agent for the author's estate.

"Roommates" by Harry Harrison. Copyright © 1971 by Harry Harrison. First
published in *The Ruins of Earth* edited by Thomas M. Disch.

"Eco-Catastrophe" by Paul R. Ehrlich. Copyright © 1969 by Paul R. Ehrlich.
Reprinted by permission of Paul R. Ehrlich.

"East Wind, West Wind" by Frank M. Robinson. Copyright © 1970 by Frank M. Robinson. Reprinted by permission of Curtis Brown, Ltd.

"The Secret" by Maggie Nadler. Copyright © 1971 by Robin Scott Wilson. First appeared in the *Clarion*, edited by Robin Scott Wilson. Reprinted by permission of the author.

"The Census Takers" by Frederik Pohl. Copyright © 1955 by Fantasy House, Inc. Reprinted by permission of the author.

"Statistician's Day" by James Blish. Copyright © 1970 by Avon Books. Reprinted by permission of Robert P. Mills, Ltd., agent for the author's estate.

"Triage" by William Walling. Copyright © 1976 by Condé Nast Publications, Inc. Reprinted by permission of the author.

"Probability Zero! The Population Implosion" by Theodore R. Cogswell. Copyright © 1973 by Random House, Inc. Reprinted by permission of the author and his agent, Kirby McCauley.

"Dolls' Demise" by George Guthridge. Copyright © 1976 with Condé Nast Publications, Inc. Reprinted by permission of the author.

CONTENTS

Part I

Introduction: The Population Problem

It is probably true that most people today have at least some awareness of the world population problem, since the situation is gaining increasing media exposure. The nature of the population problem is simple: *too many people*, a fact usually popularized by terms such as "population explosion." To deal with the problem, groups have been formed advocating no-growth societies, governments spend huge sums of money on population research and birth control programs, and international organizations convene world conferences at which the political rhetoric usually precludes taking substantive action to limit the increase of population; indeed, the desirability of limiting population growth cannot always be agreed upon. Despite the greater publicity being given to the population problem, it is also probably true that those who have some awareness of it lack any real knowledge of the incredible magnitude of the problem, its root causes, or its implications for future society, economic and political systems, and the environment.

The world is currently witnessing a rapid growth of population which is unprecedented in human history. Illustrative of this tremendous increase in population in the contemporary world is the fact that it took almost the entire span of man's existence on this planet, or some 50,000 years, to accumulate a total population of 2 billion persons (a figure reached somewhere around 1930); yet, because of the unparalleled growth which has been taking place in recent decades, it took only about 45 years to add the next 2 billion (it is estimated that the earth's population reached 4 billion persons in 1975). Viewed another way, each year over 80 million persons (or a number equal to the combined populations of Portugal, Spain, Hungary, Austria, Czechoslovakia, and Norway) are added to the world's population. The United Nations has projected population growth to the year 2000, and has predicted a world total of between 5½ billion and 7 billion by that date, depending upon what specific trends actually occur. Although such projections are necessarily only approximate, it is possible that shortly after the turn of the next century, the earth's population could be double what it is now. Given the fact that there are significant difficulties in today's world of 4 billion persons in providing sufficient food and resources, imagine the problems we will face with a population of 8 billion!

To understand the reasons why this alarming increase in population is occurring, one must only appreciate the common sense rule that any group of people (or any living species, for that matter) will grow in accordance with the balance between births and deaths, assuming that no one moves in or out permanently. Thus, if more people are born than die over a given period, then the population will grow; conversely, if more people die than are born, then the size of the group will decline.

Until quite recently in human history, a rough balance existed between births and deaths (referred to as *fertility* and *mortality* by demographers, or those people who study population). This near balance resulted in a very slow growth in the world's population, as is evidenced by the fact that by the birth of Christ there were probably only about 250 million people on earth (a figure just slightly larger than the combined populations of the present-day United States and Canada), and by 1750, only about 750 million (or less than the population of today's Peoples Republic of China). At about the turn of the eighteenth century, there began in Europe a series of social and economic improvements which brought about massive declines in mortality, improvements such as a larger and more reliable food supply, public health and sanitation, and advances in medicine. As these measures took effect, fewer and fewer people died from starvation, epidemics, or unsanitary conditions in hospitals. Eventually, these techniques were spread to virtually all areas of the world, so that by now most countries enjoy considerably lower mortality than ever before.

With the lower mortality levels and continued high fertility, there ensued a period of rapid population growth, because many more people were being born than were dying. In some parts of the world, those areas usually called the "advanced" or "developed" countries, fertility subsequently declined to about the same level as mortality, so that births and deaths were once more in rough balance and population growth slowed considerably. However, in the "developing" areas of the world (Asia, Africa, and Latin America), fertility remains high and mortality is low, so that these regions are now experiencing high rates of population growth. Since over two-thirds of the world's people live in the developing countries, this means that the earth as a whole can expect a continued rapid increase in population until fertility declines (or, unhappily, mortality increases) in Asia, Africa, and Latin America.

In this book it is our intention to stimulate some thought about what this dramatic increase in human numbers might mean for future society. We can already discern that this huge and sudden growth in the world's population is having an impact upon the economy, upon social and political organization, and upon the natural environment; it is more than merely interesting to consider what effects a doubling, or more, in population size might have upon life in the future, because coming generations will possibly have to live some of the scenarios so graphically detailed in the selections to follow. Because *any* discussion of the future is speculative, we have chosen to illustrate possible (probable?) tomorrows through the medium of science fiction, a *genre* whose special interest the future is.

SUGGESTED READINGS:

Ehrlich, Paul R. *The Population Bomb.* New York: Ballantine Books, 1968.

Goldscheider, Calvin. *Population, Modernization, and Social Structure.* Boston: Little, Brown and Company, 1971.

Nam, Charles B., and Gustavus, Susan O. *Population: The Dy-*

namics of Demographic Change. Boston: Houghton Mifflin Company, 1976.

Wrigley, E.A. *Population and History.* New York: McGraw-Hill, 1969.

Part II

Population Growth: Social Consequences of Too Many People

Rapid population growth creates a number of social and economic problems. Most of these problems are related to the fact that most societies cannot expand the number of jobs and schools or raise the standard of living fast enough to keep pace with the tremendous increase in population; indeed, in many areas the government is losing ground in this regard. Population growth rates of three percent per year are not uncommon in Asia, Africa, and Latin America; although three percent may not seem like much, because of compounding such a figure means that a group of people growing at this rate will double in size in only 24 years. Imagine what this means for a country like El Salvador in Central America, which currently is very densely inhabited and is having extreme difficulty in improving the standard of living of its people: if current rates of growth continue, by the year 2000 there will be twice as many people in El Salvador.

In a technical sense, rapid population growth inhibits social and economic advancement because the goods and services which a country produces must be spread over a much larger number of people. The most significant indices of standards of living are what demographers call *per capita* figures, or those which express how much of some commodity or activity each person receives on the average. Thus, although the total national income of a large country like India is greater than a small country like Denmark, each person in Denmark has on the average a much higher income than the average Indian. Furthermore, because the population of India is growing at such a fast rate (2.4 percent as of 1975), the economy must also increase at a fast rate just to maintain the status quo. The same phenomenon applies to such important social services such as education and public health. Think of how many schoolrooms must be built, how many teachers and doctors trained, how many health clinics established in rapidly growing countries in order to keep the standard of living at even current levels!

Beyond these difficulties of providing the material or tangible benefits of life to a large population, some have suggested that an increase in the number of people will have a psychological impact upon the individual. What we are referring to here, obviously, is the condition of crowding, or having of necessity to live in close proximity to others. Recent trends in the spatial organization of society have been towards increasing *density*, or the concentration of more and more people on less and less land. In the United States, for example, almost 60 percent of the population lives on about one percent of the land, resulting in a population density within this area of 3,376 persons per square mile. The socioeconomic process called *urbanization*, which means the increasing concentration of people in cities (which are, of course, much higher density environments than rural areas), is one of the most dramatic of all aspects of human society. By 1965, the United States estimated that about 35 percent of the world's population lived in cities, a figure which continues to grow at an accelerating rate.

Clearly, there are dangers involved in extrapolating from research on the effects of crowding among animals to what conditions might prevail if human society reached higher density levels. Yet, the studies conducted by Calhoun and others with rats, which indicated a rise in antisocial behavior with rising density, may point to serious problems ahead in an increasingly crowded world. Apropos of this, we introduce here three stories relating to life in a future, high density environment. The first, "Billenium" by J. G. Ballard, hypothesizes about the effects of a large population upon the availability of living space. The second, "Total Environment" by Brian Aldiss, presents a view of a planned high density society, a sort of experiment in social engineering which reveals how adaptations might be made in conditions of extreme crowding. Finally, Robert Silverberg's "In the Beginning" postulates an efficiently managed, superficially utopian society in a world of 75 billion people.

SUGGESTED READINGS:

Calhoun, J. B. "Population Density and Social Pathology." *Scientific American*, Vol. 206 (1962).

Davis, Kingsley (ed.). *Cities: Their Origin, Growth and Human Impact.* San Francisco: W.H. Freeman, 1973.

Jones, Gavin W. "The Economic Effect of Declining Fertility in Less Developed Countries." New York: Population Council, 1969.

by J. G. Ballard

Billenium

All day long, and often into the early hours of the morning, the tramp of feet sounded up and down the stairs outside Ward's cubicle. Built into a narrow alcove in a bend of the staircase between the fourth and fifth floors, its plywood walls flexed and creaked with every footstep like the timbers of a rotting windmill. Over a hundred people lived in the top three floors of the old rooming house, and sometimes Ward would lie awake on his narrow bunk until 2 or 3 A.M., mechanically counting the last residents returning from the all-night movies in the stadium half a mile away. Through the window he could hear giant fragments of the amplified dialogue booming among the rooftops. The stadium was never empty. During the day the huge four-sided screen was raised on its davit and athletics meetings or football matches ran continuously. For the people in the houses abutting the stadium the noise must have been unbearable.

Ward, at least, had a certain degree of privacy. Two months earlier, before he came to live on the staircase, he had shared a room with seven others on the ground floor of a house in 755th Street, and the ceaseless press of people jostling past the window had reduced him to a state of chronic exhaustion. The street was always full, an endless clamour of voices and shuffling feet. By 6:30, when he woke, hurrying to take his place in the bathroom queue, the crowds already jammed it from sidewalk to sidewalk, the din punctuated every half minute by the roar of the elevated

8

trains running over the shops on the opposite side of the road. As soon as he saw the advertisement describing the staircase cubicle he had left (like everyone else, he spent most of his spare time scanning the classifieds in the newspapers, moving his lodgings an average of once every two months) despite the higher rental. A cubicle on a staircase would almost certainly be on its own.

However, this had its drawbacks. Most evenings, his friends from the library would call in, eager to rest their elbows after the bruising crush of the public reading room. The cubicle was slightly more than four and a half square metres in floor area, half a square over the statutory maximum for a single person, the carpenters having taken advantage, illegally, of a recess beside a nearby chimney breast. Consequently Ward had been able to fit a small straight-backed chair into the interval between the bed and the door, so that only one person at a time need to sit on the bed—in most single cubicles host and guest had to sit side by side on the bed, conversing over their shoulders and changing places periodically to avoid neckstrain.

"You were lucky to find this place," Rossiter, the most regular visitor, never tired of telling him. He reclined back on the bed, gesturing at the cubicle. "It's enormous, the perspectives really zoom. I'd be surprised if you hadn't got at least five metres here, perhaps even six."

Ward shook his head categorically. Rossiter was his closest friend, but the quest for living space had forged powerful reflexes. "Just over four and a half, I've measured it carefully. There's no doubt about it."

Rossiter lifted one eyebrow. "I'm amazed. It must be the ceiling then."

Manipulating the ceiling was a favourite trick of unscrupulous landlords—most assessments of area were made upon the ceiling, out of convenience, and by tilting back the plywood partitions the rated area of cubicle could be either increased, for the benefit of a prospective tenant (many married couples were thus bamboozled into taking a single cubicle), or decreased temporarily on the visits of the housing inspectors. Ceilings were criss-crossed with pencil marks staking out the rival claims of tenants on opposite sides of a party wall. Someone timid of his rights could be literally squeezed out of existence—in fact, the advertisement "quiet clientele" was usually a tacit invitation to this sort of piracy.

"The wall does tilt a little," Ward admitted. "Actually it's about four degrees out—I used a plumb-line. But there's still plenty of room on the stairs for people to get by."

Rossiter grinned. "Of course, John. I'm just envious, that's all. My room's driving me crazy." Like everyone, he used the term "room" to describe his tiny cubicle, a hangover from the days fifty years earlier when people had indeed lived one to a room, sometimes, unbelievably, one to an apartment or house. The microfilms in the architecture catalogues at the library showed scenes of museums, concert halls and other public buildings in what appeared to be everyday settings, often virtually empty, two or three people wandering down an enormous gallery or staircase. Traffic moved freely along the centre of streets, and in the quieter districts sections of sidewalk would be deserted for fifty yards or more.

Now, of course, the older buildings had been torn down and replaced by housing batteries, or converted into apartment blocks. The great banqueting room in the former City Hall had been split horizontally into four decks, each of these cut up into hundreds of cubicles.

As for the streets, traffic had long since ceased to move about them. Apart from a few hours before dawn when only the sidewalks were crowded, every thoroughfare was always packed with a shuffling mob of pedestrians, perforce ignoring the countless "Keep Left" signs suspended over their heads, wrestling past each other on their way to home and office, their clothes dusty and shapeless. Often "locks" would occur when a huge crowd at a street junction became immovably jammed. Sometimes these locks would last for days. Two years earlier Ward had been caught in one outside the stadium, for over forty-eight hours was trapped in a gigantic pedestrian jam containing over 20,000 people, fed by the crowds leaving the stadium on one side and those approaching it on the other. An entire square mile of the local neighbourhood had been paralysed, and he vividly remembered the nightmare of swaying helplessly on his feet as the jam shifted and heaved, terrified of losing his balance and being trampled underfoot. When the police had finally sealed off the stadium and dispersed the jam he had gone back to his cubicle and slept for a week, his body blue with bruises.

"I hear they may reduce the allocation to three and a half metres," Rossiter remarked.

Ward paused to allow a party of tenants from the sixth floor to pass down the staircase, holding the door to prevent it jumping off its latch. "So they're always saying," he commented. "I can remember that rumour ten years ago."

"It's no rumour," Rossiter warned him. "It may well be necessary soon. Thirty million people packed into this city now, a million increase in just one year. There's been some pretty serious talk at the Housing Department."

Ward shook his head. "A drastic revaluation like that is almost impossible to carry out. Every single partition would have to be dismantled and nailed up again, the administrative job alone is so vast it's difficult to visualise. Millions of cubicles to be redesigned and certified, licences to be issued, plus the complete resettlement of every tenant. Most of the buildings put up since the last revaluation are designed around a four-metre modulus—you can't simply take half a metre off the end of each cubicle and then say that makes so many new cubicles. They may be only six inches wide." He laughed. "Besides, how can you live in just three and a half metres?"

Rossiter smiled. "That's the ultimate argument, isn't it? They used it twenty-five years ago at the last revaluation, when the minimum was cut from five to four. It couldn't be done they all said, no one could stand living in only four square metres, it was enough room for a bed and suitcase, but you couldn't open the door to get in." Rossiter chuckled softly. "They were all wrong. It was merely decided that from then on all doors would open outwards. Four square metres was here to stay."

Ward looked at his watch. It was 7:30. "Time to eat. Let's see if we can get into the food bar across the road."

Grumbling at the prospect, Rossiter pulled himself off the bed. They left the cubicle and made their way down the staircase. This was crammed with luggage and packing cases so that only a narrow interval remained around the bannister. On the floors below the congestion was worse. Corridors were wide enough to be chopped up into single cubicles, and the air was stale and dead, cardboard walls hung with damp laundry and makeshift larders. Each of the five rooms on the floors contained a dozen tenants, their voices reverberating through the partitions.

People were sitting on the steps above the second floor, using the staircase as an informal lounge, although this was against the fire regulations, women chatting with the men queueing in their shirtsleeves outside the washroom, children diving around them. By the time they reached the entrance Ward and Rossiter were having to force their way through the tenants packed together on every landing, loitering around the notice boards or pushing in from the street below.

Taking a breath at the top of the steps, Ward pointed to the food bar on the other side of the road. It was only thirty yards away, but the throng moving down the street swept past like a river at full tide, crossing them from right to left. The first picture show at the stadium started at 9 o'clock, and people were setting off already to make sure of getting in.

"Can't we go somewhere else?" Rossiter asked, screwing his face up at the prospect of the food bar. Not only would it be packed and take them half an hour to be served, but the food was flat and unappetising. The journey from the library four blocks away had given him an appetite.

Ward shrugged. "There's a place on the corner, but I doubt if we can make it." This was two hundred yards upstream; they would be fighting the crowd all the way.

"Maybe you're right." Rossiter put his hand on Ward's shoulder. "You know, John, your trouble is that you never go anywhere, you're too disengaged, you just don't realise how bad everything is getting."

Ward nodded. Rossiter was right. In the morning, when he set off for the library, the pedestrian traffic was moving with him towards the down town offices; in the evening, when he came back, it was flowing in the opposite direction. By and large he never altered his routine. Brought up from the age of ten in a municipal hostel, he had gradually lost touch with his father and mother, who lived on the east side of the city and had been unable, or unwilling, to make the journey to see him. Having surrendered his initiative to the dynamics of the city he was reluctant to try to win it back merely for a better cup of coffee. Fortunately his job at the library brought him into contact with a wide range of young people of similar interests. Sooner or later he would marry, find a double cubicle near the library and settle down. If they had enough children (three was the required minimum) they might even one day own a small room of their own.

They stepped out into the pedestrian stream, carried along by it for ten or twenty yards, then quickened their pace and side-stepped through the crowd, slowly tacking across to the other side of the road. There they found the shelter of the shop-fronts, slowly worked their way back to the food bar, shoulders braced against the countless minor collisions.

"What are the latest population estimates?" Ward asked as they circled a cigarette kiosk, stepping forward whenever a gap presented itself.

Rossiter smiled. "Sorry, John, I'd like to tell you but you might start a stampede. Besides, you wouldn't believe me."

Rossiter worked in the Insurance Department at the City Hall, had informal access to the census statistics. For the last ten years these had been classified information, partly because they were felt to be inaccurate, but chiefly because it was feared they might set off a mass attack of claustrophobia. Minor outbreaks had taken place already, and the official line was that world population had reached a plateau, levelling off at 20,000 million. No one believed this for a moment, and Ward assumed that the 3 percent annual increase maintained since the 1960's was continuing.

How long it could continue was impossible to estimate. Despite the gloomiest prophecies of the Neo-Malthusians, world agriculture had managed to keep pace with the population growth, although intensive cultivation meant that 95 percent of the population was permanently trapped in vast urban conurbations. The outward growth of cities had at last been checked; in fact, all over the world former surburban areas were being reclaimed for agriculture and population additions were confined within the existing urban ghettos. The countryside, as such, no longer existed. Every single square foot of ground sprouted a crop of one type or other. The one-time fields and meadows of the world were now, in effect, factory floors, as highly mechanised and closed to the public as any industrial area. Economic and ideological rivalries had long since faded before one overriding quest—the internal colonisation of the city.

Reaching the food bar, they pushed themselves into the entrance and joined the scrum of customers pressing six deep against the counter.

"What is really wrong with the population problem," Ward confided to Rossiter, "is that no one has ever tried to tackle it. Fifty years ago short-sighted nationalism and industrial expansion put a premium on a rising population curve, and even now the hidden incentive is to have a large family so that you can gain a little privacy. Single people are penalised simply because there are more of them and they don't fit conveniently into double or triple cubicles. But it's the large family with its compact, space-saving logistic that is the real villain."

Rossiter nodded, edging nearer the counter, ready to shout his order. "Too true. We all look forward to getting married just so that we can have our six metres."

Directly in front of them, two girls turned around and smiled, "Six square metres," one of them, a dark-haired girl with a pretty oval face, repeated. "You sound like the sort of young man I ought to get to know. Going into the real-estate business, Henry?"

Rossiter grinned and squeezed her arm. "Hello, Judith. I'm thinking about it actively. Like to join me in a private venture?"

The girl leaned against him as they reached the counter. "Well, I might. It would have to be legal, though."

The other girl, Helen Waring, an assistant at the library, pulled Ward's sleeve. "Have you heard the latest, John? Judith and I have been kicked out of our room. We're on the street right at this minute."

"What?" Rossiter cried. They collected their soups and coffee and edged back to the rear of the bar. "What on earth happened?"

Helen explained: "You know that little broom cupboard outside our cubicle? Judith and I have been using it as a sort of study hole, going in there to read. It's quiet and restful, if you can get used to not breathing. Well, the old girl found out and kicked up a big fuss, said we were breaking the law and so on. In short, out." Helen paused. "Now we've heard she's going to let it as a single."

Rossiter pounded the counter ledge. "A broom cupboard? Someone's going to live there? But she'll never get a licence."

Judith shook her head. "She's got it already. Her brother works in the Housing Department."

Ward laughed into his soup. "But how can she let it? No one will live in a broom cupboard."

Judith stared at him sombrely. "You really believe that, John?"

Ward dropped his spoon. "No, I guess you're right. People will live anywhere. God, I don't know who I feel more sorry for—you two, or the poor devil who'll be living in that cupboard. What are you going to do?"

"A couple in a place two blocks west are subletting half their cubicle to us. They've hung a sheet down the middle and Helen and I'll take turns sleeping on a camp bed. I'm not joking, our room's about two feet wide. I said to Helen that we ought to split up again and sublet one half at twice our rent."

They had a good laugh over all this and Ward said goodnight to the others and went back to his rooming house.

There he found himself with similar problems.

The manager leaned against the flimsy door, a damp cigar butt revolving around his mouth, an expression of morose boredom on his unshaven face.

"You got four point seven two metres," he told Ward, who was standing out on the staircase, unable to get into his room. Other tenants milled, passed onto the landing, where two women in curlers and dressing gowns were arguing with each other, tugging angrily at the wall of trunks and cases. Occasionally the manager glanced at them irritably. "Four seven two. I worked it out twice." He said this as if it ended all possibility of argument.

"Ceiling or floor?" Ward asked.

"Ceiling, whaddya think? How can I measure the floor with all this junk?" He kicked at a crate of books protruding from under the bed.

Ward let this pass. "There's quite a tilt on the wall," he pointed out. "As much as three or four degrees."

The manager nodded vaguely. "You're definitely over the four. Way over." He turned to Ward, who had moved down several steps to allow a man and woman to get past. "I can rent this as a double."

"What, only four and a half?" Ward said incredulously. "How?"

The man who had just passed him leaned over the manager's shoulder and sniffed at the room, taking in every detail in a one-second glance. "You renting a double here, Louie?"

The manager waved him away and then beckoned Ward into the room, closing the door after him.

"It's a nominal five," he told Ward. "New regulation, just came out. Anything over four five is a double now." He eyed Ward shrewdly. "Well, whaddya want? It's a good room, there's a lot of space here, feels more like a triple. You got access to the staircase, window slit—" He broke off as Ward slumped down on the bed and started to laugh. "Whatsa matter? Look, if you want a big room like this you gotta pay for it. I want an extra half rental or you get out."

Ward wiped his eyes, then stood up wearily and reached for the shelves. "Relax, I'm on my way. I'm going to live in a broom cupboard. 'Access to the staircase—' that's really rich. Tell me, Louis, is there life on Uranus?"

Temporarily, he and Rossiter teamed up to rent a double cubicle in a semi-derelict house a hundred yards from the library. The neighbourhood was seedy and faded, the rooming houses crammed with tenants. Most of them were owned by absentee landlords or by the city corporation, and the managers employed were of the lowest type, mere rent-collectors who cared nothing about the way their tenants divided up the living space, and never ventured beyond the first floors. Bottles and empty cans littered the corridors, and the washrooms looked like sumps. Many of the tenants were old and infirm, sitting about listlessly in their narrow cubicles, wheedling at each other back to back through the thin partitions.

Their double cubicle was on the third floor, at the end of a corridor that ringed the building. Its architecture was impossible to follow, rooms letting off at all angles, and luckily the corridor was a cul-de-sac. The mounds of cases ended four feet from the end wall and a partition divided off the cubicle, just wide enough for two beds. A high window overlooked the area ways of the building opposite.

Possessions loaded on to the shelf above his head, Ward lay back on his bed and moodily surveyed the roof of the library through the afternoon haze.

"It's not bad here," Rossiter told him, unpacking his case. "I know there's no real privacy and we'll drive each other insane within a week, but at least we haven't got six other people breathing into our ears two feet away."

The nearest cubicle, a single, was built into the banks of cases half a dozen steps along the corridor, but the occupant, a man of seventy, was deaf and bedridden.

"It's not bad," Ward echoed reluctantly. "Now tell me what the latest growth figures are. They might console me."

Rossiter paused, lowering his voice. "Four per cent. *Eight hundred million extra people in one year*—just less than half the earth's total population in 1950."

Ward whistled slowly. "So they will revalue. What to? Three and a half?"

"Three. From the first of next year,"

"Three square metres!" Ward sat up and looked around him. "It's unbelievable! The world's going insane, Rossiter. For God's sake, when are they going to do something about it? Do you realize there soon won't be room enough to sit down, let alone lie down?"

Exasperated, he punched the wall beside him, on the second blow knocked in one of the small wooden panels that had been lightly papered over.

"Hey!" Rossiter yelled. "You're breaking the place down." He dived across the bed to retrieve the panel, which hung downwards supported by a strip of paper. Ward slipped his hand into the dark interval, carefully drew the panel back on to the bed.

"Who's on the other side?" Rossiter whispered. "Did they hear?"

Ward peered through the interval, eyes searching the dim light. Suddenly he dropped the panel and seized Rossiter's shoulder, pulled him down on to the bed.

"Henry! Look!"

Rossiter freed himself and pressed his face to the opening, focussed slowly and then gasped.

Directly in front of them, faintly illuminated by a grimy sky-light, was a medium-sized room, some fifteen feet square, empty except for the dust silted up against the skirting boards. The floor was bare, a few strips of frayed linoleum running across it, the walls covered with a drab floral design. Here and there patches of the paper peeled off and segments of the picture rail had rotted away, but otherwise the room was in habitable condition.

Breathing slowly, Ward closed the open door of the cubicle with his foot, then turned to Rossiter.

"Henry, do you realise what we've found? Do you realise it, man?"

"Shut up. For Pete's sake keep your voice down." Rossiter examined the room carefully. "It's fantastic. I'm trying to see whether anyone's used it recently."

"Of course they haven't," Ward pointed out. "It's obvious. There's no door into the room. We're looking through it now. They must have panelled over this door years ago and forgotten about it. Look at that filth everywhere."

Rossiter was staring into the room, his mind staggered by its vastness.

"You're right," he murmured. "Now, when do we move in?"

Panel by panel, they pried away the lower half of the door, nailed it on to a wooden frame so that the dummy section could be replaced instantly.

Then, picking an afternoon when the house was half empty and the manager asleep in his basement office, they made their first foray into the room, Ward going in alone while Rossiter kept guard in the cubicle.

For an hour they exchanged places, wandering silently around the dusty room, stretching their arms out to feel its unconfined emptiness, grasping at the sensation of absolute spatial freedom. Although smaller than many of the subdivided rooms in which they had lived, this room seemed infinitely larger, its walls huge cliffs that soared upward to the skylight.

Finally, two or three days later, they moved in.

For the first week Rossiter slept alone in the room, Ward in the cubicle outside, both there together during the day. Gradually they smuggled in a few items of furniture: two armchairs, a table, a lamp fed from the socket in the cubicle. The furniture was heavy and Victorian; the cheapest available, its size emphasized the emptiness of the room. Pride of place was taken by an enormous mahogany wardrobe, fitted with carved angels and castellated mirrors, which they were forced to dismantle and carry into the house in their suitcases. Towering over them, it reminded Ward of the microfilms of gothic cathedrals, with their massive organ lofts crossing vast naves.

After three weeks they both slept in the room, finding the cubicle unbearably cramped. An imitation Japanese screen divided the room adequately and did nothing to diminish its size. Sitting there in the evenings, surrounded by his books and albums, Ward steadily forgot the city outside. Luckily he reached the library by a back alley and avoided the crowded streets. Rossiter and himself began to seem the only real inhabitants of the world, everyone else a meaningless byproduct of their own existence, a random replication of identity which had run out of control.

It was Rossiter who suggested that they ask the two girls to share the room with them.

"They've been kicked out again and may have to split up," he told Ward, obviously worried that Judith might fall into bad company. "There's always a rent freeze after a revaluation but all the landlords know about it so they're not re-letting. It's getting damned difficult to find anywhere."

Ward nodded, relaxing back around the circular red wood table. He played with a tassel of the arsenic green lamp shade, for a moment felt like a Victorian man of letters, leading a spacious, leisurely life among overstuffed furnishings.

"I'm all for it," he agreed, indicating the empty corners. "There's plenty of room here. But we'll have to make damn sure they don't gossip about it."

After due precautions, they let the two girls into the secret, enjoying their astonishment at finding this private universe.

"We'll put a partition across the middle," Rossiter explained, "then take it down each morning. You'll be able to move in within a couple of days. How do you feel?"

"Wonderful!" They goggled at the wardrobe, squinting at the endless reflections in the mirrors.

There was no difficulty getting them in and out of the house. The turnover of tenants was continuous and bills were placed in the mail rack. No one cared who the girls were or noticed their regular calls at the cubicle.

However, half an hour after they arrived neither of them had unpacked her suitcase.

"What's up, Judith?" Ward asked, edging past the girls' beds into the narrow interval between the table and wardrobe.

Judith hesitated, looking from Ward to Rossiter, who sat on his bed, finishing off the plywood partition. "John, it's just that . . . "

Helen Waring, more matter-of-fact, took over, her fingers straightening the bedspread. "What Judith's trying to say is that our position here is a little embarrassing. The partition is—"

Rossiter stood up. "For heaven's sake, don't worry, Helen," he assured her, speaking in the loud whisper they had all involuntarily cultivated. "No funny business, you can trust us. This partition is as solid as a rock."

The two girls nodded, "It's not that," Helen explained, "but it isn't up all the time. We thought that if an older person were here, say Judith's aunt—she wouldn't take up much room and be no trouble, she's really awfully sweet—we wouldn't need to bother about the partition—except at night," she added quickly.

Ward glanced at Rossiter, who shrugged and began to scan the floor.

"Well, it's an idea," Rossiter said. "John and I know how you feel. Why not?"

"Sure," Ward agreed. He pointed to the space between the girls' beds and the table. "One more won't make any difference."

The girls broke into whoops. Judith went over to Rossiter and kissed him on the cheek. "Sorry to be a nuisance, Henry." She smiled at him. "That's a wonderful partition you've made. You couldn't do another one for Auntie—just a little one? She's very sweet but she is getting on."

"Of course," Rossiter said. "I understand. I've got plenty of wood left over."

Ward looked at his watch. "It's seven-thirty, Judith. You'd better get in touch with your aunt. She may not be able to make it tonight."

Judith buttoned her coat. "Oh, she will," she assured Ward. "I'll be back in a jiffy."

The aunt arrived within five minutes, three heavy suitcases soundly packed.

"It's amazing," Ward remarked to Rossiter three months later. "The size of this room still staggers me. It almost gets larger every day."

Rossiter agreed readily, averting his eyes from one of the girls changing behind the central partition. This they now left in place as dismantling it daily had become tiresome. Besides, the aunt's subsidiary partition was attached to it and she resented the continuous upsets. Insuring she followed the entrance and exit drills through the camouflaged door and cubicle was difficult enough.

Despite this, detection seemed unlikely. The room had obviously been built as an afterthought into the central well of the house and any noise was masked by the luggage stacked in the surrounding corridor. Directly below was a small dormitory occupied by several elderly women, and Judith's aunt, who visited them socially, swore that no sounds came through the heavy ceiling. Above, the fanlight let out through a dormer window, its lights indistinguishable from the hundred other bulbs burning in the windows of the house.

Rossiter finished off the new partition he was building and held it upright, fitting it into the slots nailed to the wall between his bed and Ward's. They had agreed that this would provide a little extra privacy.

"No doubt I'll have to do one for Judith and Helen," he confided to Ward.

Ward adjusted his pillow. They had smuggled the two armchairs back to the furniture shop as they took up too much space. The bed, anyway, was more comfortable. He had never got completely used to the soft upholstery.

"Not a bad idea. What about some shelving around the wall? I've got nowhere to put anything."

The shelving tidied the room considerably, freeing large areas of the floor. Divided by their partitions, the five beds were in line along the rear wall, facing the mahogany wardrobe. In between was an open space of three or four feet, a further six feet on either side of the wardrobe.

The sight of so much space fascinated Ward. When Rossiter mentioned that Helen's mother was ill and badly needed personal care he immediately knew where her cubicle could be placed—at the foot of his bed, between the wardrobe and the side wall.

Helen was overjoyed. "It's awfully good of you, John," she told him, "but would you mind if Mother slept beside me? There's enough space to fit an extra bed in."

So Rossiter dismantled the partitions and moved them closer together, six beds now in line along the wall. This gave each of them an interval two and a half feet wide, just enough room to squeeze down the side of their beds. Lying back on the extreme right, the shelves two feet above his head, Ward could barely see the wardrobe, but the space in front of him, a clear six feet to the wall ahead, was uninterrupted.

Then Helen's father arrived.

Knocking on the door of the cubicle, Ward smiled at Judith's aunt as she let him in. He helped her swing out the made-up bed which guarded the entrance, then rapped on the wooden panel. A moment later Helen's father, a small, grey-haired man in an undershirt, braces tied to his trousers with a string, pulled back the panel.

Ward nodded to him and stepped over the luggage piled around the floor at the foot of the beds. Helen was in her mother's cubicle, helping the old woman to drink her evening broth. Rossiter, perspiring heavily, was on his knees by the mahogany wardrobe, wrenching apart the frame of the central mirror with a jimmy. Pieces of the wardrobe lay on his bed and across the floor.

"We'll have to start taking these out tomorrow," Rossiter told him. Ward waited for Helen's father to shuffle past and enter his cubicle. He had rigged up a small cardboard door, and locked it behind him with a crude hook of bent wire.

Rossiter watched him, frowning irritably. "Some people are happy. This wardrobe's a hell of a job. How did we ever decide to buy it?"

Ward sat down on his bed. The partition pressed against his knees and he could hardly move. He looked up when Rossiter was engaged and saw that the dividing line he had marked in pencil was hidden by the encroaching partition. Leaning against the wall, he tried to ease it back again, but Rossiter had apparently nailed the lower edge to the floor.

There was a sharp tap on the outside cubicle door—Judith returning from her office. Ward started to get up and then sat back. "Mr. Waring," he called softly. It was the old man's duty night.

Waring shuffled to the door of his cubicle and unlocked it fussily, clucking to himself.

"Up and down, up and down," he muttered. He stumbled over Rossiter's tool bag and swore loudly, then added meaningly over his shoulder: "If you ask me there's too many people in here. Down below they've only got six to our seven, and it's the same size room."

Ward nodded vaguely and stretched back on his narrow bed, trying not to bang his head on the shelving. Waring was not the first to hint that he move out. Judith's aunt had made a similar suggestion two days earlier. Since he left his job at the library (the small rental he charged the others paid for the little food he needed) he spent most of his time in the room, seeing rather more of the old man than he wanted to, but he had learned to tolerate him.

Settling himself, he noticed that the right-hand spire of the wardrobe, all he had been able to see for the past two months, was now dismantled.

It had been a beautiful piece of furniture, in a way symbolising this whole private world, and the salesman at the store told him there were few like it left. For a moment Ward felt a sudden pang of regret, as he had done as a child when his father, in a mood of exasperation, had taken something away from him and he knew he would never see it again.

Then he pulled himself together. It was a beautiful wardrobe, without doubt, but when it was gone it would make the room seem even larger.

by Brian W. Aldiss

Total Environment

I

"What's that poem about 'caverns measureless to man'?" Thomas
Dixit asked. His voice echoed away among the caverns, the
question unanswered. Peter Crawley, walking a pace or two
behind him, said nothing, lost in a reverie of his own.

It was over a year since Dixit had been imprisoned here. He
had taken time off from the resettlement area to come and have a
last look round before everything was finally demolished. In these
great concrete workings, men still moved—Indian technicians
mostly, carrying instruments, often with their own headlights.
Cables trailed everywhere; but the desolation was mainly an effect
of the constant abrasion all surfaces had undergone. People had
flowed here like water in a subterranean cave; and their corporate
life had flowed similarly, hidden, forgotten.

Dixit was powerfully moved by the thought of all that life. He,
almost alone, was the man who had plunged into it and survived.

Old angers stirring in him, he turned and spoke directly to his
companion. "What a monument to human suffering! They should
leave this place standing as an everlasting memorial to what
happened."

The white man said, "The Delhi government refuses to enter-
tain any such suggestion. I see their point of view, but I also see
that it would make a great tourist attraction!"

"Tourist attraction, man! Is that all it means to you?"

Crawley laughed. "As ever, you're too touchy, Thomas. I take

24

this whole matter much less lightly than you suppose. Tourism just happens to attract me more than human suffering."

They walked on side by side. They were never able to agree.

The battered faces of flats and houses—now empty, once choked with humanity—stood on either side, doors gaping open like old men's mouths in sleep. The spaces seemed enormous; the shadows and echoes that belonged to those spaces seemed to continue indefinitely. Yet before . . . there had scarcely been room to breathe here.

"I remember what your buddy, Senator Byrnes, said," Crawley remarked. "He showed how both East and West have learned from this experiment. Of course, the social scientists are still working over their findings; some startling formulae for social groups are emerging already. But the people who lived and died here were fighting their way towards control of the universe of the ultra-small, and that's where the biggest advances have come. They were already developing power over their own genetic material. Another generation, and they might have produced the ultimate in automatic human population control: anoestrus, where too close proximity to other members of the species leads to reabsorption of the embryonic material in the female. Our scientists have been able to help them there, and geneticists predict that in another decade—"

"Yes, yes, all that I grant you. Progress is wonderful." He knew he was being impolite. These things were important, of revolutionary importance to a crowded Earth. But he wished he walked these eroded passageways alone.

Undeniably, India had learned too, just as Peter Crawley claimed. For Hinduism had been put to the test here and had shown its terrifying strengths and weaknesses. In these mazes, people had not broken under deadly conditions—nor had they thought to break away from their destiny. *Dharma*—duty—had been stronger than humanity. And this revelation was already changing the thought and fate of one-sixth of the human race.

He said, "Progress is wonderful. But what took place here was essentially a religious experience."

Crawley's brief laugh drifted away into the shadows of a great gaunt stairwell. "I'll bet you didn't feel that way when we sent you in here a year ago!"

What had he felt then? He stopped and gazed up at the gloom

of the stairs. All that came to him was the memory of that
appalling flood of life and of the people who had been a part of it,
whose brief years had evaporated in these caverns, whose feet had
endlessly trodden these warren-ways, these lugubrious decks,
these crumbling flights. . . .

II

The concrete steps climbed up into darkness. The steps were
wide, and countless children sat on them, listless, resting against
each other. This was an hour when activity was low and even
small children hushed their cries for a while. Yet there was no
silence on the steps; silence was never complete there. Always, in
the background, the noise of voices. Voices and more voices.
Never silence.

Shamim was aged, so she preferred to run her errands at this
time of day, when the crowds thronging Total Environment were
less. She dawdled by a sleepy seller of life-objects at the bottom of
the stairs, picking over the little artifacts and exclaiming now and
again. The hawker knew her, knew she was too poor to buy, did
not even press her to buy. Shamim's oldest daughter, Malti,
waited for her mother by the bottom step.

Malti and her mother were watched from the top of the steps.

A light burned at the top of the steps. It had burned there for
twenty-five years, safe from breakage behind a strong mesh. But
dung and mud had recently been thrown at it, covering it almost
entirely and so making the top of the stairway dark. A furtive
man called Narayan Farhad crouched there and watched, a
shadow in the shadows.

A month ago, Shamim had had an illegal operation in one of
the pokey rooms off Grand Balcony on her deck. The effects of
the operation were still with her; under her plain cotton sari, her
thin dark old body was bent. Her share of life stood lower than it
had been.

Malti, her oldest daughter, was a meek girl who had not been
conceived when the Total Environment experiment began. Even
meekness had its limits. Seeing her mother dawdle so needlessly,
Malti muttered impatiently and went on ahead, climbing the
infested steps, anxious to be home.

Extracts from Thomas Dixit's report to Senator Jacob Byrnes, back in America: *To lend variety to the habitat, the Environment has been divided into ten decks, each deck five stories high, which allows for an occasional pocket-sized open space. The architecture has been varied somewhat on each deck. On one deck, a sort of blown-up Indian village is presented; on another, the houses are large and appear separate, although sandwiched between decks—I need not add they are hopelessly overcrowded now. On most decks, the available space is packed solid with flats. Despite this attempt at variety, a general bowdlerization of both Eastern and Western architectural styles, and the fact that everything has been constructed out of concrete or a parastyrene for economy's sake, has led to a dreadful sameness. I cannot imagine anywhere more hostile to the spiritual values of life.*

The shadow in the shadows moved. He glanced anxiously up at the light, which also housed a spy-eye; there would be a warning out, and sprays would soon squirt away the muck he had thrown at the fitting; but for the moment, he could work unobserved.

Narayan bared his old teeth as Malti came up the steps towards him, treading among the sprawling children. She was too old to fetch a really good price on the slave market, but she was still strong; there would be no trouble in getting rid of her at once. Of course he knew something of her history, even though she lived on a different deck from him. Malti! He called her name at the last moment as he jumped out on her. Old though he was, Narayan was quick. He wore only his dhoti, arms flashing, interlocking round hers, one good powerful wrench to get her off her feet—now running fast, fearful, up the rest of the steps, moving even as he clamped one hand over her mouth to cut off her cry of fear. Clever old Narayan!

The stairs mount up and up in the four corners of the Total Environment, linking deck with deck. They are now crude things of concrete and metal, since the plastic covers have long been stripped from them.

These stairways are the weak points of the tiny empires, transient and brutal, that form on every deck. They are always guarded, though guards can be bribed. Sometimes gangs or "unions" take over a stairway, either by agreement or bloodshed.

Shamim screamed, responding to her daughter's cry. She began to hobble up the stairs as fast as she could, tripping over infant feet, drawing a dagger out from under her sari. It was a plastic dagger, shaped out of a piece of the Environment.

She called Malti, called for help as she went. When she reached the landing, she was on the top floor of her deck, the Ninth, where she lived. Many people were here, standing, squatting, thronging together. They looked away from Shamim, people with blind faces. She had so often acted similarly herself when others were in trouble.

Gasping, she stopped and stared up at the roof of the deck, blue-dyed to simulate sky, cracks running irregularly across it. The steps went on up there, up to the Top Deck. She saw legs, yellow soles of feet disappearing, faces staring down at her, hostile. As she ran toward the bottom of the stairs, the watchers above threw things at her. A shard hit Shamim's cheek and cut it open. With blood running down her face, she began to wail. Then she turned and ran through the crowds to her family room.

I've been a month just reading through the microfiles. Sometimes a whole deck becomes unified under a strong leader. On Deck Nine, for instance, unification was achieved under a man called Ullhas. He was a strong man, and a great show-off. That was a while ago, when conditions were not as desperate as they are now. Ullhas could never last the course today. Leaders become more despotic as Environment decays.

The dynamics of unity are such that it is always insufficient for a deck simply to stay unified; the young men always need to have their aggressions directed outwards. So the leader of a strong deck always sets out to tyrannize the deck below or above, whichever seems to be the weaker. It is a miserable state of affairs. The time generally comes when, in the midst of a raid, a counter-raid is launched by one of the other decks. Then the raiders return to carnage and defeat. And another paltry empire tumbles.

It is up to me to stop this continual degradation of human life.

As usual, the family room was crowded. Although none of Shamim's own children were here, there were grandchildren— including the lame granddaughter, Shirin—and six great-grand-children, none of them more than three years old. Shamim's third husband, Gita, was not in. Safe in the homely squalor of the room. Shamim burst into tears, while Shirin comforted her and endeavored to keep the little ones off.

"Gita is getting food. I will go and fetch him," Shirin said.

When UHDRE—Ultra-High Density Research Establishment— became operative, twenty-five years ago, all the couples selected for living in the Total Environment had to be under twenty years of age. Before being sealed in, they were inoculated against all diseases. There was plenty of room for each couple then; they had whole suites to themselves, and the best of food; plus no means of birth control. That's always been the main pivot of the UHDRE experiment. Now that first generation has aged severely. They are old people pushing forty-five. The whole life cycle has speeded up— early puberty, early senescence. The second and third generations have shown remarkable powers of adaptation; a fourth generation is already toddling. Those toddlers will be reproducing before their years attain double figures, if present trends continue. Are allowed to continue.

Gita was younger than Shamim, a small wiry man who knew his way around. No hero, he nevertheless had a certain style about him. His life-object hung boldly round his neck on a chain, instead of being hidden, as were most people's life-objects. He stood in the line for food, chattering with friends. Gita was good at making alliances. With a bunch of his friends, he had formed a little union to see that they got their food back safely to their homes; so they generally met with no incident in the crowded walkways of Deck Nine.

The balance of power on the deck was very complex at the moment. As a result, comparative peace reigned, and might continue for several weeks if the strong man on Top Deck did not interfere.

Food delivery grills are fixed in the walls of every floor of every deck. Two gongs sound before each delivery. After the second one, hatches open and steaming food pours from the grills. Hills of rice tumble forward, flavored with meat and spices. Chappattis fall from a separate slot. As the men run forward with their containers, holy men are generally there to sanctify the food.

Great supply elevators roar up and down in the heart of the vast tower, tumbling out rations at all levels. Alcohol also was supplied in the early years. It was discontinued when it led to trouble; which is not to say that it is not secretly brewed inside the Environment. The UHDRE food ration has been generous from the start and has always been maintained at the same level per head of population although, as you know, the food is now ninety-five percent factory-made. Nobody would ever have starved, had it been shared out equally inside the tower. On some of the decks, some of the time, it is still shared out fairly.

One of Gita's sons, Jamsu, had seen the kidnapper Narayan making off to Top Deck with the struggling Malti. His eyes gleaming with excitement, he sidled his way into the queue where Gita stood and clasped his father's arm. Jamsu had something of his father in him, always lurked where numbers made him safe, rather than run off as his brothers and sisters had run off, to marry and struggle for a room or a space of their own.

He was telling his father what had happened when Shirin limped up and delivered her news.

Nodding grimly, Gita said, "Stay with us, Shirin, while I get the food."

He scooped his share into the family pail. Jamsu grabbed a handful of rice for himself.

"It was a dirty wizened man from Top Deck called Narayan Farhad," Jamsu said, gobbling. "He is one of the crooks who hangs about the shirt tails of . . . " He let his voice die.

"You did not go to Malti's rescue, shame on you!" Shirin said.

"Jamsu might have been killed," Gita said, as they pushed through the crowd and moved towards the family room.

"They're getting so strong on Top Deck," Jamsu said. "I hear all about it! We mustn't provoke them or they may attack. They say a regular army is forming round . . . "

Shirin snorted impatiently. "You great babe! Go ahead and name the man! It's Prahlad Patel whose very name you dare not mention, isn't it? Is he a god or something, for Siva's sake? You're afraid of him even from this distance, eh, aren't you?"

"Don't bully the lad," Gita said. Keeping the peace in his huge mixed family was a great responsibility, almost more than he could manage. As he turned into the family room, he said quietly to Jamsu and Shirin, "Malti was a favorite daughter of Shamim's, and now is gone from her. We will get our revenge against this Narayan Farhad. You and I will go this evening, Jamsu, to the holy man Vazifdar. He will even up matters for us, and then perhaps the great Patel will also be warned."

He looked thoughtfully down at his life-object. Tonight, he told himself, I must venture forth alone, and put my life in jeopardy for Shamim's sake.

Prahlad Patel's union has flourished and grown until now he rules all the Top Deck. His name is known and dreaded, we believe, three or four decks down. He is the strongest—yet in some ways curiously the most moderate—ruler in Total Environment at present.

Although he can be brutal, Patel seems inclined for peace. Of course, the bugging does not reveal everything; he may have plans which he keeps secret, since he is fully aware that the bugging exists. But we believe his interests lie in other directions than conquest. He is only about nineteen, as we reckon years, but already gray-haired, and the sight of him is said to freeze the muscles to silence in the lips of his followers. I have watched him over the bugging for many hours since I agreed to undertake this task.

Patel has one great advantage in Total Environment. He lives on the Tenth Deck, at the top of the building. He can therefore be invaded only from below, and the Ninth Deck offers no strong threats at present, being mainly oriented round an influential body of holy men, of whom the most illustrious is one Vazifdar.

The staircases between decks are always trouble spots. No deck-ruler was ever strong enough to withstand attack from above and below. The staircases are also used by single troublemakers, thieves, political fugitives, prostitutes, escaping slaves, hostages. Guards can always be bribed, or favor their multitudinous relations, or join the enemy for one reason or another. Patel, being on the Top Deck, has only four weak points to watch for, rather than eight.

Vazifdar was amazingly holy and amazingly influential. It was whispered that his life-object was the most intricate in all Environment, but there was nobody who would lay claim to having set eyes upon it. Because of his reputation, many people on Gita's deck—yes, and from farther away—sought Vazifdar's help. A stream of men and women moved always through his room, even when he was locked in private meditation and far away from this world.

The holy man had a flat with a balcony that looked out onto mid-deck. Many relations and disciples lived there with him, so that the rooms had been elaborately and flimsily divided by screens. All day, the youngest disciples twittered like birds upon the balconies as Vazifdar held court, discussing among themselves the immense wisdom of his sayings.

All the disciples, all the relations, loved Vazifdar. There had been relations who did not love Vazifdar, but they had passed away in their sleep. Gita himself was a distant relation of Vazifdar's and came into the holy man's presence now with gifts of fresh water and a long piece of synthetic cloth, enough to make a robe.

Vazifdar's brow and cheeks were painted with white to denote his high caste. He received the gifts of cloth and water graciously, smiling at Gita in such a way that Gita—and, behind him, Jamsu—took heart.

Vazifdar was thirteen years old as the outside measured years. He was sleekly fat, from eating much and moving little. His brown body shone with oils; every morning, young women massaged and manipulated him.

He spoke very softly, husbanding his voice, so that he could scarcely be heard for the noise in the room.

"It is a sorrow to me that this woe has befallen your stepchild Malti," he said. "She was a good woman, although infertile."

"She was raped at a very early age, disrupting her womb, dear Vazifdar. You will know of the event. Her parents feared she would die. She could never bear issue. The evil shadowed her life. Now this second woe befalls her."

"I perceive that Malti's role in the world was merely to be a companion to her mother. Not all can afford to purchase who visit the bazaar."

There are bazaars on every floor, crowding down the corridors and balconies, and a chief one on every deck. The menfolk choose such places to meet and chatter even when they have nothing to trade. Like everywhere else, the bazaars are crowded with human-

ity, down to the smallest who can walk—and sometimes even those carry naked smaller brothers clamped tight to their backs.

The bazaars are great centers for scandal. Here also are our largest screens. They glow behind their safety grills, beaming in special programs from outside; our outside world that must seem to have but faint reality as it dashes against the thick securing walls of Environment and percolates through to the screens. Below, the screens, uncheckable and fecund life goes teeming on, with all its injury.

Humbly, Gita on his knees said, "If you could restore Malti to her mother Shamim, who mourns her, you would reap all our gratitude, dear Vazifdar. Malti is too old for a man's bed, and on Top Deck all sorts of humiliations must await her."

Vazifdar shook his head with great dignity. "You know I cannot restore Malti, my kinsman. How many deeds can be ever undone? As long as we have slavery, so long must we bear to have the ones we love enslaved. You must cultivate a mystical and resigned view of life and beseech Shamim always to do the same."

"Shamim is more mystical in her ways than I, never asking much, always working, working, praying, praying. That is why she deserves better than this misery."

Nodding in approval of Shamim's behavior as thus revealed, Vazifdar said, "That is well. I know she is a good woman. In the future lie other events which may recompense her for this sad event."

Jamsu, who had managed to keep quiet behind his father until now, suddenly burst out, "Uncle Vazifdar, can you not punish Narayan Farhad for his sin in stealing poor Malti on the steps? Is he to be allowed to escape to Patel's deck, there to live with Malti and enjoy?"

"Sssh, son!" Gita looked in agitation to see if Jamsu's outburst had annoyed Vazifdar; but Vazifdar was smiling blandly.

"You must know, Jamsu, that we are all creatures of the Lord Siva, and without power. No, no, do not pout! I also am without power in his hands. To own one room is not to possess the whole mansion. But . . . "

It was a long, and heavy *but*. When Vazifdar's thick eyelids closed over his eyes, Gita trembled, for he recalled how, on previous occasions when he had visited his powerful kinsman,

Vazifdar's eyelids had descended in this fashion while he deigned to think on a problem, as if he shut out all the external world with his own potent flesh.

"Narayan Farhad shall be troubled by more than his conscience." As he spoke, the pupils of his eyes appeared again, violet and black. They were looking beyond Gita, beyond the confines of his immediate surroundings. "Tonight he shall be troubled by evil dreams."

"The night-visions!" Gita and Jamsu exclaimed, in fear and excitement.

Now Vazifdar swiveled his magnificent head and looked directly at Gita, looked deep into his eyes. Gita was a small man; he saw himself as a small man within. He shrank still further under that irresistible scrutiny.

"Yes, the night-visions," the holy man said. "You know what that entails, Gita. You must go up to Top Deck and procure Narayan's life-object. Bring it back to me, and I promise Narayan shall suffer the night-visions tonight. Though he is sick, he shall be cured."

III

The women never cease their chatter as the lines of supplicants come and go before the holy men. Their marvelous resignation in that hateful prison! If they ever complain about more than the small circumstances of their lives, if they ever complain about the monstrous evil that has overtaken them all, I never heard of it. There is always the harmless talk, talk that relieves petty nervous anxieties, talk that relieves the almost noticed pressures on the brain. The women's talk practically drowns the noise of their children. But most of the time it is clear that Total Environment consists mainly of children. That's why I want to see the experiment closed down; the children would adapt to our world.

It is mainly on this fourth generation that the effects of the population glut show. Whoever rules the decks, it is the babes, the endless babes, tottering, laughing, staring, piddling, tumbling, running, the endless babes to whom the Environment really belongs. And their mothers, for the most part, are women who—at the same age and in a more favored part of the globe—would still be virginally at school, many only just entering their teens.

Narayan Farhad wrapped a blanket round himself and huddled in his corner of the crowded room. Since it was almost time to sleep, he had to take up his hired space before one of the loathed Dasguptas stole it. Narayan hated the Dasgupta family, its lick-spittle men, its shrill women, its turbulent children—the endless babes who crawled, the bigger ones with nervous diseases who thieved and ran and jeered at him. It was the vilest family on Top Deck, according to Narayan's oft-repeated claims; he tolerated it only because he felt himself to be vile.

He succeeded at nothing to which he turned his hand. Only an hour ago, pushing through the crowds, he had lost his life-object from his pocket—or else it had been stolen; but he dared not even consider that possibility!

Even his desultory kidnapping business was a failure. This bitch he had caught this morning—Malti. He had intended to rape her before selling her, but had become too nervous once he had dragged her in here, with a pair of young Dasguptas laughing at him. Nor had he sold the woman well. Patel had beaten down his price, and Narayan had not the guts to argue. Maybe he should leave this deck and move down to one of the more chaotic ones. The middle decks were always more chaotic. Six was having a slow three-sided war even now, which should make Five a fruitful place, with hordes of refugees to batten on.

. . . And what a fool to snatch so old a girl—practically an old woman!

Through narrowed eyes, Narayan squatted in his corner, acid flavors burning his mouth. Even if his mind would rest and allow him to sleep, the Dasgupta mob was still too lively for any real relaxation. That old Dasgupta, now—he was like a rat, totally without self-restraint, not a proper Hindu at all, doing the act openly with his own daughters. There were many men like that in Total Environment, men who had nothing else in life. Dirty swine! Lucky dogs! Narayan's daughters had thrown him out many months ago when he tried it!

Over and over, his mind ran on his grievances. But he sat collectedly, prodding off with one bare foot the nasty little brats who crawled at him, and staring at the screen flickering on the wall behind its protective mesh.

He liked the screens, enjoyed viewing the madness of outside. What a world it was out there! All that heat, and the necessity for work, and the complication of life! The sheer bigness of the world—he couldn't stand that, would not want it under any circumstances.

He did not understand half he saw. After all, he was born here. His father might have been born outside, whoever his father was; but no legends from outside had come down to him: only the distortions in the general gossip, and the stuff on the screens. Now that he came to reflect, people didn't pay much attention to the screens any more. Even he didn't.

But he could not sleep. Blearily, he looked at images of cattle ploughing fields, fields cut into dice by the dirty grills before the screens. He had already gathered vaguely that this feature was about changes in the world today.

" . . . are giving way to this . . . " said the commentator above the rumpus in the Dasgupta room. The children lived here like birds. Racks were stacked against the walls, and on these rickety contraptions the many little Dasguptas roosted.

" . . . food factories automated against danger of infection . . . " Yak yak yak, then.

"Beef-tissue culture growing straight into plastic distribution packs . . . " Shots of some great interior place somewhere, with meat growing out of pipes, extruding itself into square packs, dripping with liquid, looking rather ugly. Was that the shape of cows now or something? Outside must be a hell of a scaring place, then! " . . . as new factory food at last spells hope for India's future in the . . . " Yak yak yak from the kids. Once, their sleep racks had been built across the screen; but one night the whole shaky edifice collapsed, and three children were injured. None killed, worse luck!

Patel should have paid more for that girl. Nothing was as good as it had been. Why, once on a time, they used to show sex films on the screens—really filthy stuff that got even Narayan excited. He was younger then. Really filthy stuff, he remembered, and pretty girls doing it. But it must be—oh, a long time since that was stopped. The screens were dull now. People gave up watching. Uneasily, Narayan slept, propped in the corner under his scruffy blanket. Eventually, the whole scruffy room slept.

The documentaries and other features piped into Environment are no longer specially made by UHDRE teams for internal con-

sumption. When the U.N. made a major cut in UHDRE's annual subsidy, eight years ago, the private TV studio was one of the frills that had to be axed. Now we pipe in old programs bought off major networks. The hope is that they will keep the wretched prisoners in Environment in touch with the outside world, but this is clearly not happening. The degree of comprehension, between inside and outside grows markedly less on both sides, on an exponential curve. As I see it, a great gulf of isolation is widening between the two environments, just as if they were sailing away from each other into different space-time continua. I wish I could think that the people in charge here—Crawley especially—not only grasped this fact but understood that it should be rectified immediately.

Shamim could not sleep for grief.

Gita could not sleep for apprehension.

Jamsu could not sleep for excitement.

Vazifdar did not sleep.

Vazifdar shut his sacred self away in a cupboard, brought his lids down over his eyes and began to construct, within the vast spaces of his mind, a thought pattern corresponding to the matrix represented by Narayan Farhad's stolen life-object. When it was fully conceived, Vazifdar began gently to inset a little evil into one edge of the thought-pattern. . . .

Narayan slept. What roused him was the silence. It was the first time total silence had ever come to Total Environment.

At first, he thought he would enjoy total silence. But it took on such weight and substance. . . .

Clutching his blanket, he sat up. The room was empty, the screen dark. Neither thing had ever happened before, could not happen! And the silence! Dear Siva, some terrible monkey god had hammered that silence out in darkness and thrown it out like a shield into the world, rolling over all things! There was a ringing quality in the silence—a gong! No, no, not a gong! Footsteps!

It was footsteps, O Lord Siva, do not let it be footsteps!

Total Environment was empty. The legend was fulfilled that said Total Environment would empty one day. All had departed except for poor Narayan. And this thing of the footsteps was coming to visit him in his defenseless corner. . . .

It was climbing up through the cellars of his existence. Soon it would emerge.

Trembling convulsively, Narayan stood up, clutching the corner of the blanket to his throat. He did not wish to face the thing. Wildly, he thought, could he bear it best if it looked like a man or if it looked nothing like a man? It was Death for sure— but how v ould it look? Only Death—his heart fluttered!—only Death could arrive this way. . . .

His helplessness. . . . Nowhere to hide! He opened his mouth, could not scream, clutched the blanket, felt that he was wetting himself as if he were a child again. Swiftly came the image—the infantile, round-bellied, cringing, puny, his mother black with fury, her great white teeth gritting as she smacked his face with all her might, spitting. . . . It was gone, and he faced the gong-like death again, alone in the great dark tower. In the arid air, vibrations of its presence.

He was shouting to it, demanding that it did not come.

But it came. It came with majestic sloth, like the heartbeats of a foetid slumber, came in the door, pushing darkness before it. It was like a human, but too big to be human.

And it wore Malti's face, that sickening innocent smile with which she had run up the steps. No! No, that was not it—oh, he fell down onto the wet floor: it was nothing like that woman, nothing at all. Cease, impossibilities! It was a man, his ebony skull shining, terrible and magnificent, stretching out, grasping, confident. Narayan struck out of his extremity and fell forward. Death was another indelible smack in the face.

One of the roosting Dasguptas blubbered and moaned as the man kicked him, woke for a moment, saw the screen still flickering meaninglessly and reassuringly, saw Narayan tremble under his blanket, tumbled back into sleep.

It was not till morning that they found it had been Narayan's last tremble.

I know I am supposed to be a detached observer. No emotions, no feelings. But scientific detachment is the attitude that has led to much of the inhumanity inherent in Environment. How do we, for all the bugging devices, hope to know what ghastly secret nightmares they undergo in there? Anyhow, I am relieved to hear you are flying over.

It is tomorrow I am due to go into Environment myself.

IV

The central offices of UHDRE were large and repulsive. At the time when they and the Total Environment tower had been built, the Indian Government would not have stood for anything else. Poured cement and rough edges was what they wanted to see and what they got.

From a window in the office building, Thomas Dixit could see the indeterminate land in one direction, and the gigantic TE tower in the other, together with the shantytown that had grown between the foot of the tower and the other UHDRE buildings.

For a moment, he chose to ignore the Project Organizer behind him and gaze out at what he could see of the table-flat lands of the great Ganges delta.

He thought, it's as good a place as any for a man to project his power fantasies. But you are a fool to get mixed up in all this, Thomas!

Even to himself, he was never just Tom.

I am being paid, well paid, to do a specific job. Now I am letting woolly humanitarian ideas get in the way of action. Essentially, I am a very empty man. No center. Father Bengali, mother English, and live all my life in the States. I have excuses . . . Other people accept them; why can't I?

Sighing, he dwelt on his own unsatisfactoriness. He did not really belong to the West, despite his long years there, and he certainly did not belong to India; in fact, he thought he rather disliked India. Maybe the best place for him was indeed the inside of the Environment tower.

He turned impatiently and said, "I'm ready to get going now, Peter."

Peter Crawley, the Special Project Organizer of UHDRE, was a rather austere Bostonian. He removed the horn-rimmed glasses from his nose and said, "Right! Although we have been through the drill many times, Thomas, I have to tell you this once again before we move. The entire—"

"Yes, yes, I know, Peter! You don't have to cover yourself. This entire organization might be closed down if I make a wrong move. Please take it as read."

Without indignation, Crawley said, "I was going to say that we are all rooting for you. We appreciate the risks you are taking. We shall be checking you everywhere you go in there through the bugging system."

"And whatever you see, you can't do a thing."

"Be fair; we have made arrangements to help!"

"I'm sorry, Peter." He liked Crawley and Crawley's decent reserve.

Crawley folded his spectacles with a snap, inserted them in a leather slipcase and stood up.

"The U.N., not to mention subsidiary organizations like the WHO and the Indian government, have their knife into us, Thomas. They want to close us down and empty Environment. They will do so unless you can provide evidence that forms of extra-sensory perception are developing inside the Environment. Don't get yourself killed in there. The previous men we sent in behaved foolishly and never came out again." He raised an eyebrow and added dryly, "That sort of thing gets us a bad name, you know."

"Just as the blue movies did a while ago."

Crawley put his hands behind his back. "My predecessor here decided that immoral movies piped into Environment would help boost the birth rate there. Whether he was right or wrong, world opinion has changed since then as the specter of world famine has faded. We stopped the movies eight years ago, but they have long memories at the U.N., I fear. They allow emotionalism to impede scientific research."

"Do you never feel any sympathy for the thousands of people doomed to live out their brief lives in the tower?"

They looked speculatively at each other.

"You aren't on our side any more, Thomas, are you? You'd like your findings to be negative, wouldn't you, and have the U.N. close us down?"

Dixit uttered a laugh. "I'm not on anyone's *side*, Peter. I'm neutral. I'm going into Environment to look for the evidence of ESP that only direct contact may turn up. What else direct contact will turn up, neither of us can say as yet."

"But you think it will be misery. And you will emphasize that at the inquiry after your return."

"Peter—let's get on with it, shall we?" Momentarily, Dixit was granted a clear picture of the two of them standing in this room;

he saw how their bodily attitudes contrasted. His attitudes were rather slovenly; he held himself rather slump-shouldered, he gesticulated to some extent (too much?); he was dressed in thread-bare tunic and shorts, ready to pass muster as an inhabitant of Environment. Crawley, on the other hand, was very upright, stiff and smart in his movements, hardly ever gestured as he spoke; his dress was faultless.

And there was no need to be awed by or envious of Crawley. Crawley was encased in inhibition, afraid to feel, signaling his aridity to anyone who cared to look out from his own self-preoccupation. Crawley, moreover, feared for his job.

"Let's get on with it, as you say." He came from behind his desk. "But I'd be grateful if you would remember, Thomas, that the people in the tower are volunteers, or the descendants of volunteers.

"When UHDRE began, a quarter-century ago, back in the mid-nineteen-seventies, only volunteers were admitted to the Total Environment. Five hundred young married Indian couples were admitted, plus whatever children they had. The tower was a refuge then, free from famine, immune from all disease. They were glad, heartily glad, to get in, glad of all that Environment provided and still provides. Those who didn't qualify rioted. We have to remember that.

"India was a different place in 1975. It had lost hope. One crisis after another, one famine after another, crops dying, people starving, and yet the population spiraling up by a million every month.

"But today, thank God, that picture has largely changed. Synthetic foods have licked the problem; we don't need the grudging land any more. And at last the Hindus and Muslims have got the birth control idea into their heads. It's only *now*, when a little humanity is seeping back into this death-bowl of a subcontinent, that the U.N. dares complain about the inhumanity of UHDRE."

Dixit said nothing. He felt that this potted history was simply angled towards Crawley's self-justification; the ideas it represented were real enough, heaven knew, but they had meaning for Crawley only in terms of his own existence. Dixit felt pity and impatience as Crawley went on with his narration.

"Our aim here must be unswervingly the same as it was from the start. We have evidence that nervous disorders of a special kind produce extra-sensory perceptions—telepathy and the rest, and maybe kinds of ESP we do not yet recognize. High-density populations with reasonable nutritional standards develop particular nervous instabilities which may be akin to ESP spectra.

"The Ultra-High Density Research Establishment was set up to intensify the likelihood of ESP developing. Don't forget that. The people in Environment are supposed to have some ESP; that's the whole point of the operation, right? Sure, it is not humanitarian. We know that. But that is not your concern. You have to go in and find evidence of ESP, something that doesn't show over the bugging. Then UHDRE will be able to continue."

Dixit prepared to leave. "If it hasn't shown up in a quarter of a century—"

"It's in there! I know it's in there! The failure's in the bugging system. I feel it coming through the screens at me—some mystery we need to get our hands on! If only I could prove it! If only I could get in there myself!"

Interesting, Dixit thought. You'd have to be some sort of voyeur to hold Crawley's job, forever spying on the wretched people.

"Too bad you have a white skin, eh?" he said lightly. He walked towards the door. It swung open, and he passed into the corridor.

Crawley ran after him and thrust out a hand. "I know how you feel, Thomas. I'm not just a stuffed shirt, you know, not entirely void of sympathy. Sorry if I was needling you. I didn't intend to do so."

Dixit dropped his gaze. "I should be the one to apologize, Peter. If there's anything unusual going on in the tower, I'll find it, never worry!"

They shook hands, without wholly being able to meet each other's eyes.

V

Leaving the office block, Dixit walked alone through the sunshine toward the looming tower that housed Total Environment. The concrete walk was hot and dusty underfoot. The sun was the one good thing that India had, he thought: that burning beautiful sun, the real ruler of India, whatever petty tyrants came and went.

The sun blazed down on the tower; only inside did it not shine.

The uncompromising outlines of the tower were blurred by

pipes, ducts and shafts that ran up and down its exterior. It was a building built for looking into, not out of. Some time ago, in the bad years, the welter of visual records gleaned from Environment used to be edited and beamed out on global networks every evening; but all that had been stopped as conditions inside Environment deteriorated, and public opinion in the democracies, who were subsidizing the grandiose experiment, turned against the exploitation of human material.

A monitoring station stood by the tower walls. From here, a constant survey on the interior was kept. Facing the station were the jumbles of merchants' stalls, springing up to cater for tourists, who persisted even now that the tourist trade was discouraged. Two security guards stepped forward and escorted Dixit to the base of the tower. With ceremony, he entered the shade of the entry elevator. As he closed the door, germicides sprayed him, insuring that he entered Environment without harboring dangerous micro-organisms.

The elevator carried him up to the top deck; this plan had been settled some while ago. The elevator was equipped with double steel doors. As it came to rest, a circuit opened, and a screen showed him what was happening on the other side of the doors. He emerged from a dummy air-conditioning unit, behind a wide pillar. He was in Patel's domain.

The awful weight of human overcrowding hit Dixit with its full stink and noise. He sat down at the base of the pillar and let his senses adjust. And he thought, I was the wrong one to send; I've always had this inner core of pity for the sufferings of humanity; I could never be impartial; I've got to see that this terrible experiment is stopped.

He was at one end of a long balcony onto which many doors opened; a ramp led down at the other end. All the doorways gaped, although some were covered by rugs. Most of the doors had been taken off their hinges to serve as partitions along the balcony itself, partitioning off overspill families. Children ran everywhere, their tinkling voices and cries the dominant note in the hubbub. Glancing over the balcony, Dixit took in a dreadful scene of swarming multitudes, the anonymity of congestion; to sorrow for humanity was not to love its prodigality. Dixit had seen this panorama many times over the bugging system; he knew all the staggering figures—1500 people in here to begin with, and by now some 75,000 people, a large proportion of them under four years of age. But pictures and figures were pale abstracts beside the reality they were intended to represent.

The kids drove him into action at last by playfully hurling dirt at him. Dixit moved slowly along, carrying himself tight and cringing in the manner of the crowd about him, features rigid, elbows tucked in to the ribs. *Mutatis mutandis*, it was Crawley's inhibited attitude. Even the children ran between the legs of their elders in that guarded way. As soon as he had left the shelter of his pillar, he was caught in a stream of chattering people, all jostling between the rooms and the stalls of the balcony. They moved very slowly.

Among the crowd were hawkers, and salesmen pressed their wares from the pitiful balcony hovels. Dixit tried to conceal his curiosity. Over the bugging he had had only distant views of the merchandise offered for sale. Here were the strange models that had caught his attention when he was first appointed to the UHDRE project. A man with orange goat-eyes, in fact probably no more than thirteen years of age, but here a hardened veteran, was at Dixit's elbow. As Dixit stared at him, momentarily suspicious he was being watched, the goat-eyed man merged into the crowd; and, to hide his face, Dixit turned to the nearest salesman.

In only a moment, he was eagerly examining the wares, forgetting how vulnerable was his situation.

All the strange models were extremely small. This Dixit attributed to shortage of materials—wrongly, as it later transpired. The biggest model the salesman possessed stood no more than two inches high. It was made, nevertheless, of a diversity of materials, in which many sorts of plastic featured. Some models were simple, and appeared to be little more than an elaborate *tughra* or monogram, which might have been intended for an elaborate piece of costume jewelry; others, as one peered among their interstices, seemed to afford a glimpse of another dimension; all possessed eye-teasing properties.

The merchant was pressing Dixit to buy. He referred to the elaborate models as "life-objects." Noticing that one in particular attracted his potential customer, he lifted it delicately and held it up, a miracle of craftsmanship, perplexing, *outré*, giving Dixit somehow as much pain as pleasure. He named the price.

Although Dixit was primed with money, he automatically shook his head. "Too expensive."

"See, master, I show you how this life-object works!" The man fished beneath his scrap of loincloth and produced a small perforated silver box. Flipping it open, he produced a live wood-louse and slipped it under a hinged part of the model. The insect, in its struggles, activated a tiny wheel; the interior of the model began to rotate, some sets of minute planes turning in counterpoint to others.

"This life-object belonged to a very religious man, master."

In his fascination, Dixit said, "Are they all powered?"

"No, master, only special ones. This was perfect model from Dalcush Bancholi, last generation master all the way from Third Deck, very very fine and masterful workmanship of first quality. I have also still better one worked by a body louse, if you care to see."

By reflex, Dixit said, "Your prices are too high."

He absolved himself from the argument that brewed, slipping away through the crowd with the merchant calling after him. Other merchants shouted to him, sensing his interest in their wares. He saw some beautiful work, all on the tiniest scale, and not only life-objects but amazing little watches with millisecond hands as well as second hands; in some cases, the millisecond was the largest hand; in some, the hour hand was missing or was supplemented by a day hand; and the watches took many extraordinary shapes, tetrakishexahedrons and other elaborate forms, until their format merged with that of the life-objects.

Dixit thought approvingly: the clock and watch industry fulfills a human need for exercising elaborate skill and accuracy, while at the same time requiring a minimum of materials. These people of Total Environment are the world's greatest craftsmen. Bent over one curious watch that involved a color change, he became suddenly aware of danger. Glancing over his shoulder, he saw the man with the unpleasant orange eyes about to strike him. Dixit dodged without being able to avoid the blow. As it caught him on the side of his neck, he stumbled and fell under the milling feet.

VI

Afterwards, Dixit could hardly say that he had been totally unconscious. He was aware of hands dragging him, of being partly carried, of the sound of many voices, of the name "Patel" repeated. . . . And when he came fully to his senses, he was lying in a cramped room, with a guard in a scruffy turban standing by the door. His first hazy thought was that the room was no more than a small ship's cabin; then he realized that, by indigenous standards, this was a large room for only one person.

He was a prisoner in Total Environment.

A kind of self-mocking fear entered him; he had almost expected the blow, he realized; and he looked eagerly about for the bug-eye that would reassure him his UHDRE friends outside were aware of his predicament. There was no sign of the bug-eye. He was not long in working out why; this room had been partitioned out of a larger one, and the bugging system was evidently shut in the other half—whether deliberately or accidentally, he had no way of knowing.

The guard had bobbed out of sight. Sounds of whispering came from beyond the doorway. Dixit felt the pressure of many people there. Then a woman came in and closed the door. She walked cringingly and carried a brass cup of water.

Although her face was lined, it was possible to see that she had once been beautiful and perhaps proud. Now her whole attitude expressed the defeat of her life. And this woman might be no more than eighteen! One of the terrifying features of Environment was the way, right from the start, confinement had speeded life-processes and abridged life.

Involuntarily, Dixit flinched away from the woman.

She almost smiled. "Do not fear me, sir. I am almost as much a prisoner as you are. Equally, do not think that by knocking me down you can escape. I promise you, there are fifty people outside the door, all eager to impress Prahlad Patel by catching you, should you try to get away."

So I'm in Patel's clutches, he thought. Aloud he said, "I will offer you no harm. I want to see Patel. If you are captive, tell me your name, and perhaps I can help you."

As she offered him the cup and he drank, she said, shyly, "I do not complain, for my fate might have been much worse than it is. Please do not agitate Patel about me, or he may throw me out of his household. My name is Malti."

"Perhaps I may be able to help you, and all your tribe, soon.

You are all in a form of captivity here, the great Patel included, and it is from that I hope to deliver you."

Then he saw fear in her eyes.

"You really are a spy from outside!" she breathed. "But we do not want our poor little world invaded! You have so much—leave us our little!" She shrank away and slipped through the door, leaving Dixit with a melancholy impression of her eyes, so burdened in their shrunken gaze.

The babel continued outside the door. Although he still felt sick, he propped himself up and let his thoughts run on. "You have so much—leave us our little. . . . " All their values had been perverted. Poor things, they could know neither the smallness of their own world nor the magnitude of the world outside. This—this dungheap had become to them all there was of beauty and value.

Two guards came for him, mere boys. He could have knocked their heads together, but compassion moved him. They led him through a room full of excited people; beyond their glaring faces, the screen flickered pallidly behind its mesh; Dixit saw how faint the image of outside was.

He was taken into another partitioned room. Two men were talking.

The scene struck Dixit with peculiar force, and not merely because he was at a disadvantage.

It was an alien scene. The impoverishment of even the richest furnishings, the clipped and bastardized variety of Hindi that was being talked, reinforced the impression of strangeness. And the charge of Patel's character filled the room.

There could be no doubt who was Patel. The plump cringing fellow, wringing his hands and protesting, was not Patel. Patel was the stocky white-haired man with the heavy lower lip and high forehead. Dixit had seen him in this very room over the bugging system. But to stand captive awaiting his attention was an experience of an entirely different order. Dixit tried to analyze the first fresh impact Patel had on him, but it was elusive.

It was difficult to realize that, as the outside measured years, Patel could not be much more than nineteen or twenty years of age. Time was impacted here, jellified under the psychic pressures of Total Environment. Like the hieroglyphics of that new relativity, detailed plans of the Environment hung large on one wall of his room, while figures and names were chalked over the others. The room was the nerve center of Top Deck.

He knew something about Patel from UHDRE records. Patel had come up here from the Seventh Deck. By guile as well as force, he had become ruler of Top Deck at an early age. He had surprised UHDRE observers by abstaining from the usual forays of conquest into other floors.

Patel was saying to the cringing man, "Be silent! You try to obscure the truth with argument. You have heard the witnesses against you. During your period of watch on the stairs, you were bribed by a man from Ninth Deck and you let him through here."

"Only for a mere seventeen minutes, Sir Patel!"

"I am aware that such things happen every day, wretched Raital. But this fellow you let through stole the life-object belonging to Narayan Farhad and, in consequence, Narayan Farhad died in his sleep last night. Narayan was no more important than you are, but he was useful to me, and it is in order that he be revenged."

"Anything that you say, Sir Patel!"

"Be silent, wretched Raital!" Patel watched Raital with interest as he spoke. And he spoke in a firm reflective voice that impressed Dixit more than shouting would have done.

"You shall revenge Narayan, Raital, because you caused his death. You will leave here now. You will not be punished. You will go, and you will steal the life-object belonging to that fellow from whom you accepted the bribe. You will bring that life-object to me. You have one day to do so. Otherwise, my assassins will find you wherever you hide, be it even down on Deck One."

"Oh, yes, indeed, Sir Patel, all men know—" Raital was bent almost double as he uttered some face-saving formula. He turned and scurried away as Patel dismissed him.

Strength, thought Dixit. Strength, and also cunning. That is what Patel radiates. An elaborate and cutting subtlety. The phrase pleased him, seeming to represent something actual that he had detected in Patel's makeup. An elaborate and cutting subtlety.

Clearly, it was part of Patel's design that Dixit should witness this demonstration of his methods.

Patel turned away, folded his arms, and contemplated a blank piece of wall at close range. He stood motionless. The guards held Dixit still, but not so still as Patel held himself.

This tableau was maintained for several minutes. Dixit found himself losing track of the normal passage of time. Patel's habit of turning to stare at the wall—and it did not belong to Patel alone—was an uncanny one that Dixit had watched several times over the bugging system. It was that habit, he thought, which might have given Crawley the notion that ESP was rampant in the tower.

It was curious to think of Crawley here. Although Crawley might at this moment be surveying Dixit's face on a monitor, Crawley was now no more than a hypothesis.

Malti broke the tableau. She entered the room with a damp cloth on a tray, to stand waiting patiently for Patel to notice her. He broke away at last from his motionless survey of the wall, gesturing abruptly to the guards to leave. He took no notice of Dixit, sitting in a chair, letting Malti drape the damp cloth round his neck; the cloth had a fragrant smell to it.

"The towel is not cool enough, Malti, or damp enough. You will attend me properly at my morning session, or you will lose this easy job."

He swung his gaze, which was suddenly black and searching, onto Dixit to say, "Well, spy, you know I am Lord here. Do you wonder why I tolerate old women like this about me when I could have girls young and lovely to fawn on me?"

Dixit said nothing, and the self-styled Lord continued, "Young girls would merely remind me by contrast of my advanced years. But this old bag—whom I bought only yesterday—this old bag is only just my junior and makes me look good in contrast. You see, we are masters of philosophy in here, in this prison-universe; we cannot be masters of material wealth like you people outside!"

Again Dixit said nothing, disgusted by the man's implied attitude to women.

A swinging blow caught him unprepared in the stomach. He cried and dropped suddenly to the floor.

"Get up, spy!" Patel said. He had moved extraordinarily fast. He sat back again in his chair, letting Malti massage his neck muscles.

VII

As Dixit staggered to his feet, Patel said, "You don't deny you are from outside?"

"I did not attempt to deny it. I came from outside to speak to you."

"You say nothing here until you are ordered to speak. Your people—you outsiders—you have sent in several spies to us the last few months. Why?"

Still feeling sick from the blow, Dixit said, "You should realize that we are your friends rather than your enemies, and our men emissaries rather than spies."

"Pah! You are a breed of spies! Don't you sit and spy on us from every room? You live in a funny little dull world out there, don't you? So interested in us that you can think of nothing else! Keep working, Malti! Little spy, you know what happened to all the other spies your spying people sent in?"

"They died," Dixit said.

"Exactly. They died. But you are the first to be sent to Patel's deck. What different thing from death do you expect here?"

"Another death will make my superiors very tired, Patel. You may have the power of life and death over me; they have the same over you, and over all in this world of yours. Do you want a demonstration?"

Rising, flinging the towel off, Patel said, "Give me your demonstration!"

Must do, Dixit thought. Staring in Patel's eyes, he raised his right hand above his head and gestured with his thumb. Pray they are watching—and thank God this bit of partitioned room is the bit with the bugging system!

Tensely, Patel stared, balanced on his toes. Behind his shoulder, Malti also stared. Nothing happened.

Then a sort of shudder ran through Environment. It became slowly audible as a mixture of groan and cry. Its cause became apparent in this less crowded room when the air began to grow hot and foul. So Dixit's signal had got through; Crawley had him under survey, and the air-conditioning plant was pumping in hot carbon-dioxide through the respiratory system.

"You see? We control the very air you breathe!" Dixit said. He dropped his arm, and slowly the air returned to normal, although it was at least an hour before the fright died down in the passages.

Whatever the demonstration had done to Patel, he showed nothing. Instead, he said. "You control the air. Very well. But you do not control the will to turn it off permanently—and so you do not control the air. Your threat is an empty one, spy! For some reason, you need us to live. We have a mystery, don't we?"

"There is no reason why I should be anything but honest with you, Patel. Your special environment must have bred special talents in you. We are interested in those talents; but no more than interested."

Patel came closer and inspected Dixit's face minutely, rather as he had recently inspected the blank wall. Strange angers churned inside him; his neck and throat turned a dark mottled color. Finally he spoke.

"We are the center of your outside world, aren't we? We know that you watch us all the time. We know that you are much more than 'interested'! For you, we here are somehow a matter of life and death, aren't we?"

This was more than Dixit had expected.

"Four generations, Patel, four generations have been incarcerated in Environment." His voice trembled. "Four generations, and, despite our best intentions, you are losing touch with reality. You live in one relatively small building on a sizeable planet. Clearly, you can only be of limited interest to the world at large."

"Malti!" Patel turned to the slave girl. "Which is the greater, the outer world or ours?"

She looked confused, hesitated by the door as if longing to escape. "The outside world was great, master, but then it gave birth to us, and we have grown and are growing and gaining strength. The child now is almost the size of the father. So my step-father's son Jamsu says, and he is a clever one."

Patel turned to stare at Dixit, a haughty expression on his face. He made no comment, as if the words of an ignorant girl were sufficient to prove his point.

"All that you and the girl say only emphasizes to me how much you need help, Patel. The world outside is a great and thriving place; you must allow it to give you assistance through me. We are not your enemies."

Again the choleric anger was there, powering Patel's every word.

"What else are you, spy? Your life is so vile and pointless out there, is it not? You envy us because we are superseding you! Our people—we may be poor, you may think of us as in your power, but we rule our own universe. And that universe is expanding and falling under our control more every day. Why, our explorers have gone into the world of the ultra-small. We discover new environments, new ways of living. By your terms, we are scientific peasants, perhaps, but I fancy we have ways of knowing the trade routes of the blood and the eternities of cell-change that you cannot comprehend. You think of us all as captives, eh? Yet you are captive to the necessity of supplying our air and our food and water; we are free. We are poor, yet you covet our riches. We are spied on all the time, yet we are secret. You need to understand us, yet we have no need to understand you. You are in *our* power, spy!"

"Certainly not in one vital respect, Patel. Both you and we are ruled by historical necessity. This Environment was set up twenty-five of our years ago. Changes have taken place not only in here but outside as well. The nations of the world are no longer prepared to finance this project. It is going to be closed down entirely, and you are going to have to live outside. Or, if you don't want that, you'd better cooperate with us and persuade the leaders of the other decks to cooperate."

Would threats work with Patel? His hooded and oblique gaze bit into Dixit like a hook.

After a deadly pause, he clapped his hands once. Two guards immediately appeared.

"Take the spy away," said Patel. Then he turned his back.

A clever man, Dixit thought. He sat alone in the cell and meditated.

It seemed as if a battle of wits might develop between him and Patel. Well, he was prepared. He trusted to his first impression, that Patel was a man of cutting subtlety. He could not be taken to mean all that he said.

Dixit's mind worked back over their conversation. The mystery of the life-objects had been dangled before him. And Patel had taken care to belittle the outside world: "funny dull little world," he had called it. He had made Malti advance her primitive view that Environment was growing, and that had fitted in very well with his brand of boasting. Which led to the deduction that he had known her views beforehand; yet he had bought her only yesterday. Why should a busy man, a leader, bother to question an ignorant slave about her views of the outside world unless he were starved for information of that world, obsessed with it.

Yes, Dixit nodded to himself. Patel was obsessed with outside and tried to hide that obsession; but several small contradictions in his talk had revealed it.

Of course, it might be that Malti was so generally representative of the thousands in Environment that her misinformed ideas could be taken for granted. It was as well, as yet, not to be too certain that he was beginning to understand Patel.

Part of Patel's speech made sense even superficially. These poor devils were exploring the world of the ultra-small. It was the only landscape left for them to map. They were human, and still burning inside them was that unquenchable human urge to open new frontiers.

So they knew some inward things. Quite possibly, as Crawley anticipated, they possessed a system of ESP upon which some reliance might be placed, unlike the wildly fluctuating telepathic radiations which circulated in the outside world.

He felt confident, fully engaged. There was much to understand here. The bugging system, elaborate and over-used, was shown to be a complete failure; the watchers had stayed external to their problem; it remained their problem, not their life. What was needed was a whole team to come and live here, perhaps a team on every deck, anthropologists and so on. Since that was impossible, then clearly the people of Environment must be released from their captivity; those that were unwilling to go far afield should be settled in new villages on the Ganges plain, under the wide sky. And there, as they adapted to the real world, observers could live among them, learning with humility of the gifts that had been acquired at such cost within the thick walls of the Total Environment tower.

As Dixit sat in meditation, a guard brought a meal in to him.

He ate thankfully and renewed his thinking.

From the little he had already experienced—the ghastly pressures on living space, the slavery, the aberrant modes of thought into which the people were being forced, the harshness of the petty rulers—he was confirmed in his view that this experiment in anything like its present form must be closed down at once. The

U.N. needed the excuse of his adverse report before they moved; they should have it when he got out. And if he worded the report carefully, stressing that these people had many talents to offer, then he might also satisfy Crawley and his like. He had it in his power to satisfy all parties, when he got out. All he had to do was get out.

The guard came back to collect his empty bowl.

"When is Patel going to speak with me again?"

The guard said, "When he sends for you to have you silenced for ever."

Dixit stopped composing his report and thought about that instead.

VIII

Much time elapsed before Dixit was visited again, and then it was only the self-effacing Malti who appeared, bringing him a cup of water.

"I want to talk to you," Dixit said urgently.

"No, no, I cannot talk! He will beat me. It is the time when we sleep, when the old die. You should sleep now, and Patel will see you in the morning."

He tried to touch her hand, but she withdrew.

"You are a kind girl, Malti. You suffer in Patel's household."

"He has many women, many servants. I am not alone."

"Can you not escape back to your family?"

She looked at the floor evasively. "It would bring trouble to my family. Slavery is the lot of many women. It is the way of the world."

"It is not the way of the world I come from!"

Her eyes flashed. "Your world is of no interest to us!"

Dixit thought after she had gone, "She is afraid of our world." Rightly.

He slept little during the night. Even barricaded inside Patel's fortress, he could still hear the noises of Environment: not only the voices, almost never silent, but the gurgle and sob of pipes in the walls. In the morning, he was taken into a larger room where Patel was issuing commands for the day to a succession of subordinates.

Confined to a corner, Dixit followed everything with interest. His interest grew when the unfortunate guard Raital appeared. He bounded in and waited for Patel to strike him. Instead, Patel kicked him.

"You have performed as I ordered yesterday?"

Raital began at once to cry and wring his hands. "Sir Patel, I have performed as well as and better than you demanded, incurring great suffering and having myself beaten downstairs where the people of Ninth Deck discovered me marauding. You must invade them, Sir, and teach them a lesson that in their insolence they so dare to mock your faithful guards who only do those things—"

"Silence, you dog-devourer! Do you bring back that item which I demanded of you yesterday?"

The wretched guard brought from the pocket of his tattered tunic a small object, which he held out to Patel.

"Of course I obey, Sir Patel. To keep this object safe when the people caught me, I swallow it whole, sir, into the stomach for safe keeping, so that they would not know what I am about. Then my wife gives me sharp medicine so that I vomit it safely again to deliver to you."

"Put the filthy thing down on that shelf there! You think I wish to touch it when it has been in your worm-infested belly, slave?"

The guard did as he was bid and abased himself.

"You are sure it is the life-object of the man who stole Narayan Farhad's life-object, and nobody else's?"

"Oh, indeed, Sir Patel! It belongs to a man called Gita, the very same who stole Narayan's life object, and tonight you will see he will die of night-visions!"

"Get out!" Patel managed to catch Raital's buttocks with a swift kick as the guard scampered from the room.

A queue of people stood waiting to speak with him, to supplicate and advise. Patel sat and interviewed them, in the main showing a better humor than he had shown his luckless guard. For Dixit, this scene had a curious interest; he had watched Patel's morning audience more than once, standing by Crawley's side in the UHDRE monitoring station; now he was a prisoner waiting uncomfortably in the corner of the room, and the whole atmosphere was changed. He felt the extraordinary intensity of these people's lives, the emotions compressed, everything vivid. Patel himself wept several times as some tale of hardship was unfolded to him. There was no privacy. Everyone stood round him, listening to everything. Short the lives might be; but those annihilating spaces that stretch through ordinary lives, the spaces through which one glimpses uncomfortable glooms and larger poverties, if not presences more sour and sinister, seemed here to have been eradicated. The Total Environment had brought its peoples total involvement. Whatever befell them, they were united, as were bees in a hive.

Finally, a break was called. The unfortunates who had not gained Patel's ear were turned away; Malti was summoned and administered the damp-towel treatment to Patel. Later, he sent her off and ate a frugal meal. Only when he had finished it, and sat momentarily in meditation, did he turn his brooding attention to Dixit.

He indicated that Dixit was to fetch down the object Raital had placed on a shelf. Dixit did so and put the object before Patel. Staring at it with interest, he saw it was an elaborate little model, similar to the ones for sale on the balcony.

"Observe it well," Patel said. "It is the life-object of a man. You have these"—he gestured vaguely—"outside?"

"No."

"You know what they are?"

"No."

"In this world of ours, Mr. Dixit, we have many holy men. I have a holy man here under my protection. On the deck below is one very famous holy man, Vazifdariji. These men have many powers. Tonight, I shall give my holy man this life-object, and with it he will be able to enter the being of the man to whom it belongs, for good or ill, and in this case for ill, to revenge a death with a death."

Dixit stared at the little object, a three-dimensional maze con-structed of silver and plastic strands, trying to comprehend what Patel was saying.

"This is a sort of key to its owner's mind?"

"No, no, not a key, and not to his mind. It is a—well, we do not have a scientific word for it, and our word would mean nothing to you, so I cannot say what. It is, let us say, a replica, a substitute for the man's being. Not his mind, his being. In this case, a man called Gita. You are very interested, aren't you?"

"Everyone here has one of these?"

"Down to the very poorest, and even the older children. A sage works in conjunction with a smith to produce each individual life-object."

"But they can be stolen and then an ill-intentioned holy man can use them to kill the owner. So why make them? I don't understand."

Smiling, Patel made a small movement of impatience. "What you discover of yourself, you record. That is how these things are made. They are not trinkets; they are a man's record of his discovery of himself."

Dixit shook his head. "If they are so personal, why are so many sold by street traders as trinkets?"

"Men die. Then their life-objects have no value, except as trinkets. They are also popularly believed to bestow . . . well, personality-value. There also exist large numbers of forgeries, which people buy because they like to have them, simply as decorations."

After a moment, Dixit said, "So they are innocent things, but you take them and use them for evil ends."

"I use them to keep a power balance. A man of mine called Narayan was silenced by Gita of Ninth Deck. Never mind why. So tonight I silence Gita to keep the balance."

He stopped and looked closely at Dixit, so that the latter received a blast of that enigmatic personality. He opened his hand and said, still observing Dixit. "Death sits in my palm, Mr. Dixit. Tonight I shall have you silenced also, by what you may consider more ordinary methods."

Clenching his hands tightly together, Dixit said. "You tell me about the life-objects, and yet you claim you are going to kill me."

Patel pointed up to one corner of his room. "There are eyes and ears there, while your ever-hungry spying friends suck up the facts of this world. You see, I can tell them—I can tell them so much and they can never comprehend our life. All the important things can never be said, so they can never learn. But they can see you die tonight, and that they will comprehend. Perhaps then they will cease to send spies in here."

He clapped his hands once for the guards. They came forward and led Dixit away. As he went back to his cell, he heard Patel shouting for Malti.

IX

The hours passed in steady gloom. The U.N., the UHDRE, would not rescue him; the Environment charter permitted intervention by only one outsider at a time. Dixit could hear, feel, the vast throbbing life of the place going on about him and was shaken by it.

He tried to think about the life-object. Presumably Crawley had overheard the last conversation, and would know that the holy men, as Patel called them, had the power to kill at a distance. There was the ESP evidence Crawley sought: telecide, or whatever you called it. And the knowledge helped nobody, as Patel himself observed. It had long been known that African witch doctors possessed similar talents, to lay a spell on a man and kill him at a distance; but how they did it had never been established; nor, indeed, had the fact ever been properly assimilated by the West, eager though the West was for new methods of killing. There were things one civilization could not learn from another; the whole business of life-objects, Dixit perceived, was going to be such a matter: endlessly fascinating, entirely insoluble. . . .

His thoughts returned to his cell, and he told himself: Patel still puzzles me. But it is no use hanging about here being puzzled. Here I sit, waiting for a knife in the guts. It must be night now. I've got to get out of here.

There was no way out of the room. He paced restlessly up and down. They brought him no meal, which was ominous.

A long while later, the door was unlocked and opened.

It was Malti. She lifted one finger as a caution to silence, and closed the door behind her.

"It's time for me . . . ?" Dixit said.

She came quickly over to him, not touching him, staring at him.

Though she was an ugly and despondent woman, beauty lay in her time-haunted eyes.

"I can help you escape, Dixit. Patel sleeps now, and I have an understanding with the guards here. Understandings have been reached to smuggle you down to my own deck, where perhaps

you can get back to the outside where you belong. This place is
full of arrangements. But you must be quick. Are you ready?"

"He'll kill you when he finds out!"

She shrugged. "He may not. I think perhaps he likes me.
Prahlad Patel is not inhuman, whatever you think of him."

"No? But he plans to murder someone else tonight. He has
acquired some poor fellow's life-object and plans to have his holy
man kill him with night-visions, whatever they are."

She said, "People have to die. You are going to be lucky. You
will not die, not this night."

"If you take that fatalistic view, why help me?"

He saw a flash of defiance in her eyes. "Because you must take
a message outside for me."

"Outside? To whom?"

"To everyone there, everyone who greedily spies on us here and
would spoil this world. Tell them to go away and leave us and let
us make our own world. Forget us! That is my message! Take it!
Deliver it with all the strength you have! This is our world—not
yours!"

Her vehemence, her ignorance, silenced him. She led him from
the room. There were guards on the outer door. They stood rigid
with their eyes closed, seeing no evil, and she slid between them,
leading Dixit and opening the door. They hurried outside, onto
the balcony, which was still as crowded as ever, people sprawling
everywhere in the disconsolate gestures of public sleep. With the
noise and chaos and animation of daytime fled, Total Environment stood fully revealed for the echoing prison it was.

As Malti turned to go, Dixit grasped her wrist.

"I must return," she said. "Get quickly to the steps down to
Ninth Deck, the near steps. That's three flights to go down, the
inter-deck flight guarded. They will let you through; they expect
you."

"Malti, I must try to help this other man who is to die. Do you
happen to know someone called Gita?"

She gasped and clung to him. "Gita?"

"Gita of the Ninth Deck. Patel has Gita's life-object, and he is
to die tonight."

"Gita is my step-father, my mother's third husband. A good
man! Oh, he must not die, for my mother's sake!"

"He's to die tonight. Malti, I can help you and Gita. I appreciate how you feel about outside, but you are mistaken. You would
be free in a way you cannot understand! Take me to Gita, we'll all
three get out together."

Conflicting emotions chased all over her face. "You are sure
Gita is to die?"

"Come and check with him to see if his life-object has gone!"

Without waiting for her to make a decision—in fact she looked
as if she were just about to bolt back into Patel's quarters—Dixit
took hold of her and forced her along the balcony, picking his way
through the piles of sleepers.

Ramps ran down from balcony to balcony in long zigzags. For
all its multitudes of people—even the ramps had been taken up as
dosses by whole swarms of urchins—Total Environment seemed
much larger than it had when one looked in from the monitoring
room. He kept peering back to see if they were being followed; it
seemed to him unlikely that he would be able to get away.

But they had now reached the stairs leading down to Deck
Nine. Oh, well, he thought, corruption he could believe in; it was
the universal oriental system whereby the small man contrived to
live under oppression. As soon as the guards saw him and Malti,
they all stood and closed their eyes. Among them was the
wretched Raital, who hurriedly clapped palms over eyes as they
approached.

"I must go back to Patel," Malti gasped.

"Why? You know he will kill you," Dixit said. He kept tight
hold of her thin wrist. "All these witnesses to the way you led me
to safety—you can't believe he will not discover what you are
doing. Let's get to Gita quickly."

He hustled her down the stairs. There were Deck Nine guards
at the bottom. They smiled and saluted Malti and let her by. As if
resigned now to doing what Dixit wished, she led him forward,
and they picked their way down a ramp to a lower floor. The
squalor and confusion were greater here than they had been
above, the slumbers more broken. This was a deck without a
strong leader, and it showed.

He must have seen just such a picture as this over the bugging,
in the air-conditioned comfort of the UHDRE offices, and remained comparatively unmoved. You had to be among it to feel

it. Then you caught also the aroma of Environment. It was pungent in the extreme.

As they moved slowly down among the huddled figures abased by fatigue, he saw that a corpse burned slowly on a wood pile. It was the corpse of a child. Smoke rose from it in a leisurely coil until it was sucked into a wall vent. A mother squatted by the body, her face shielded by one skeletal hand. "It is the time when the old die," Malti had said of the previous night; and the young had to answer that same call.

This was the Indian way of facing the inhumanity of Environment: with their age-old acceptance of suffering. Had one of the white races been shut in here to breed to intolerable numbers, they would have met the situation with a general massacre. Dixit, a half-caste, would not permit himself to judge which response he most respected.

Malti kept her gaze fixed on the worn concrete underfoot as they moved down the ramp past the corpse. At the bottom, she led him forward again without a word.

They pushed through the sleazy ways, arriving at last at a battered doorway. With a glance at Dixit, Malti slipped in and rejoined her family. Her mother, not sleeping, crouched over a washbowl, gave a cry and fell into Malti's arms. Brothers and sister and half-brothers and half-sisters and cousins and nephews woke up, squealing. Dixit was utterly brushed aside. He stood nervously, waiting, hoping, in the corridor.

It was many minutes before Malti came out and led him to the crowded little cabin. She introduced him to Shamim, her mother, who curtsied and rapidly disappeared, and to her step-father, Gita.

The little wiry man shooed everyone out of one corner of the room and moved Dixit into it. A cup of wine was produced and offered politely to the visitor. As he sipped it, he said, "If your step-daughter has explained the situation, Gita, I'd like to get you and Malti out of here, because otherwise your lives are worth very little. I can guarantee you will be extremely kindly treated outside."

With dignity, Gita said, "Sir, all this very unpleasant business has been explained to me by my step-daughter. You are most good to take this trouble, but we cannot help you."

"You, or rather Malti, have helped me. Now it is my turn to help you. I want to take you out of here to a safe place. You realize you are both under the threat of death? You hardly need telling that Prahlad Patel is a ruthless man."

"He is very very ruthless, sir," Gita said unhappily. "But we cannot leave here. I cannot leave here—look at all these little people who are dependent on me! Who would look after them if I left?"

"But if your hours are numbered?"

"If I have only one minute to go before I die, still I cannot desert those who depend on me."

Dixit turned to Malti. "You, Malti—you have less responsibility. Patel will have his revenge on you. Come with me and be safe!"

She shook her head. "If I came, I would sicken with worry for what was happening here and so I would die that way."

He looked about him hopelessly. The blind interdependence bred by this crowded environment had beaten him—almost. He still had one card to play.

"When I go out of here, as go I must, I have to report to my superiors. They are the people who—the people who really order everything that happens here. They supply your light, your food, your air. They are like gods to you, with the power of death over every one on every deck—which perhaps is why you can hardly believe in them. They already feel that Total Environment is wrong, a crime against your humanity. I have to take my verdict to them. My verdict, I can tell you now, is that the lives of all you people are as precious as lives outside these walls. The experiment must be stopped; you all must go free.

"You may not understand entirely what I mean, but perhaps the wall screens have helped you grasp something. You will all be looked after and rehabilitated. Everyone will be released from the decks very soon. So, you can both come with me and save your lives; and then, in perhaps only a week, you will be reunited with your family. Patel will have no power then. Now, think over your decision again, for the good of your dependents, and come with me to life and freedom."

Malti and Gita looked anxiously at each other and went into a huddle. Shamim joined in, and Jamsu, and lame Shirin, and more and more of the tribe, and a great jangle of excited talk swelled up. Dixit fretted nervously.

Finally, silence fell. Gita said, "Sir, your intentions are plainly kind. But you have forgotten that Malti charged you to take a message to outside. Her message was to tell the people there to go away and let us make our own world. Perhaps you do not understand such a message and so cannot deliver it. Then I will give you my message, and you can take it to your superiors."

Dixit bowed his head.

"Tell them, your superiors and everyone outside who insists on watching us and meddling in our affairs, tell them that we are shaping our own lives. We know what is to come, and the many problems of having such a plenty of young people. But we have faith in our next generation. We believe they will have many new talents we do not possess, as we have talents our fathers did not possess.

"We know you will continue to send in food and air, because that is something you cannot escape from. We also know that in your hidden minds you wish to see us all fail and die. You wish to see us break, to see what will happen when we do. You do not have love for us. You have fear and puzzlement and hate. We shall not break. We are building a new sort of world, we are getting clever. We would die if you took us out of here. Go and tell that to your superiors and to everyone who spies on us. Please leave us to our own lives, over which we have our own commands."

There seemed nothing Dixit could say in answer. He looked at Malti, but could see she was unyielding, frail and pale and unyielding. This was what UHDRE had bred: complete lack of understanding. He turned and went.

He had his key. He knew the secret place on each deck where he could slip away into one of the escape elevators. As he pushed through the grimy crowds, he could hardly see his way for tears.

X

It was all very informal. Dixit made his report to a board of six members of the UHDRE administration, including the Special

Project Organizer, Peter Crawley. Two observers were allowed to sit in, a grand lady who represented the Indian Government, and Dixit's old friend, Senator Jacob Byrnes, representing the United Nations.

Dixit delivered his report on what he had found and added a recommendation that a rehabilitation village be set up immediately and the Environment wound down.

Crawley rose to his feet and stood rigid as he said, "By your own words, you admit that these people of Environment cling desperately to what little they have. However terrible, however miserable that little may seem to you. They are acclimated to what they have. They have turned their backs to the outside world and don't *want* to come out."

Dixit said, "We shall rehabilitate them, re-educate them, find them local homes where the intricate family patterns to which they are used can still be maintained, where they can be helped back to normality."

"But by what you say, they would receive a paralyzing shock if confronted with the outside world and its gigantic scale."

"Not if Patel still led them."

A mutter ran along the board; its members clearly thought this an absurd statement. Crawley gestured despairingly, as if his case were made, and sat down saying, "He's the sort of tyrant who causes the misery in Environment."

"The one thing they need when they emerge to freedom is a strong leader they know. Gentlemen, Patel is our good hope. His great asset is that he is oriented towards outside already."

"Just what does that mean?" one of the board asked.

"It means this. Patel is a clever man. My belief is that he arranged that Malti should help me escape from his cell. He never had any intention of killing me; that was a bluff to get me on my way. Little, oppressed Malti was just not the woman to take any initiative. What Patel probably did not bargain for was that I should mention Gita by name to her, or that Gita should be closely related to her. But because of their fatalism, his plan was in no way upset."

"Why should Patel want you to escape?"

"Implicit in much that he did and said, though he tried to hide it, was a burning curiosity about outside. He exhibited facets of his culture to me to ascertain my reactions—testing for approval or disapproval, I'd guess, like a child. Nor does he attempt to attack other decks—the time-honored sport of Environment tyrants; his attention is directed inwardly on us.

"Patel is intelligent enough to know that we have real power. He has never lost the true picture of reality, unlike his minions. So *he wants to get out.*

"He calculated that if I got back to you, seemingly having escaped death, I would report strongly enough to persuade you to start demolishing Total Environment immediately."

"Which you are doing," Crawley said.

"Which I am doing. Not for Patel's reasons, but for human reasons. And for utilitarian reasons also—which will perhaps appeal more to Mr. Crawley. Gentlemen, you were right. There are mental disciplines in Environment the world could use, of which perhaps the least attractive is telecide. UHDRE has cost the public millions on millions of dollars. We have to recoup by these new advances. We can only use these new advances by studying them in an atmosphere not laden with hatred and envy of us—in other words, by opening that black tower."

The meeting broke up. Of course, he could not expect anything more decisive than that for a day or two.

Senator Byrnes came over.

"Not only did you make out a good case, Thomas; history is with you. The world's emerging from a bad period and that dark tower, as you call it, is a symbol of the bad times, and so it has to go."

Inwardly, Dixit had his qualifications to that remark. But they walked together to the window of the boardroom and looked across at the great rough bulk of the Environment building.

"It's more than a symbol. It's as full of suffering and hope as our own world. But it's a manmade monster—it must go."

Byrnes nodded. "Don't worry. It'll go. I feel sure that the historical process, that blind evolutionary thing, has already decided that UHDRE's day is done. Stick around. In a few weeks, you'll be able to help Malti's family rehabilitate. And now I'm off to put in my two cents' worth with the chairman of that board."

He clapped Dixit on the back and walked off. Inside he knew lights would be burning and those thronging feet padding across the only world they knew. Inside there, babies would be born this night and men die of old age and night-visions. . . .

Outside, monsoon rain began to fall on the wide Indian land.

by Robert Silverberg

In The Beginning

The city of Chicago is bounded on the north by Shanghai and on the south by Edinburgh. Chicago currently has 37,402 people, and is undergoing a mild crisis of population that will have to be alleviated in the customary manner. Its dominant profession is engineering. Above, in Shanghai, they are mostly scholars; below, in Edinburgh, computer men cluster.

Aurea Holston was born in Chicago in 2368 and has lived there all of her life. Aurea is now fourteen years old. Her husband Memnon is nearly fifteen. They have been married almost two years. God has not blessed them with children. Memnon has traveled through the entire building but Aurea has scarcely ever been out of Chicago. Once she went to visit a fertility expert, an old midwife down in Prague. Once she went up to Louisville, where her powerful uncle, an urban administrator, lives. Many times she and Memnon have been to their friend Siegmund Kluver's apartment in Shanghai. But Aurea does not really care to travel. She loves her own city very much.

Chicago is the city that occupies the 721st through 760th floors of Urban Monad 116. Memnon and Aurea Holston live in a dormitory for childless young couples on the 735th floor. The dorm is currently shared by 31 couples, eight above optimum.

"There's got to be a thinning soon," Memnon says. "We're starting to bulge at the seams. People will have to go."

"Many?" Aurea asks.

"Three couples here, five there—a slice from each dorm. I suppose Urbmon 116 will lose about two thousand couples. That's how many went the last time they thinned."

Aurea trembles. "Where will they go?"

"They tell me that the new urbmon is almost ready. Number 158."

Her soul floods with pity and terror. "How horrid to be sent somewhere else! Memnon, they *wouldn't* make us leave here!"

"Of course not. God bless, we're valuable here! I have a skill rating of—"

"But we have no children. That kind goes first, doesn't it?"

"God will bless us soon." Memnon takes her in his arms. He is strong and tall and lean, with rippling scarlet hair and a taut, earnest expression. Aurea feels weak and fragile beside him, although she is sturdy and supple. Her crown of golden hair is deepening in tone. Her eyes are pale green. Her breasts are full and her lips are broad. Siegmund Kluver says she looks like a goddess of motherhood. Most men desire her and nightwalkers come frequently to share her sleeping platform. Yet she remains barren. Lately she has become quite sensitive about it. The irony of her wasted voluptuousness is not lost on her.

Memnon releases her and she walks wearily through the dormitory. It is a long, narrow room that makes a right-angle bend around the urbmon's central service core. Its walls glow with changing inlaid patterns of blue and gold and green. Rows of sleeping platforms, some deflated, some in use, cover the floor. The furniture is stark and simple and the lighting, though indirectly suffused from the entire area of the floor and the ceiling, is bright almost to harshness. Several viewscreens and three data terminals are mounted on the eastern wall. There are five excretion areas, three communal recreation areas, two cleanser stations, and two privacy areas.

By unspoken custom the privacy shields are never turned on in this dormitory. What one does, one does before the others. The total accessibility of all persons to all other persons is the only rule by which the civilization of the urbmon can survive, and in a mass residence hall such as this the rule is all the more vital. Aurea is a member of a post-privacy culture. One cannot hold oneself apart from people while simultaneously living among them.

Aurea halts by the majestic window at the dormitory's western end, and stares out. The sunset is beginning. Across the way, the magnificent bulk of Urban Monad 117 seems stained with golden red. Aurea follows the shaft of the great tower with her eyes, down from the landing stage at its thousandth-floor tip, down to the building's broad waist. She cannot see, at this angle, very far below the 400th floor of the adjoining structure.

What is it like, she wonders, to live in Urbmon 117? Or 115, or 110, or 140? She has never left the urbmon of her birth. All about her, to the horizon, sprawl the towers of the Chipitts constellation, fifty mighty piles of superstressed concrete, each three kilometers high, each housing some 800,000 human beings, each a self-contained entity. In Urbmon 117, Aurea tells herself, there are people who look just like us. They walk, talk, dress, think, love, just like ourselves. Urbmon 117 is not another world. It is only the building next door. We are not unique. We are not unique. We are not unique.

Fear engulfs her.

"Memnon," she says raggedly, "When the thinning time comes, they're going to send us to Urbmon 158."

Siegmund Kluver is one of the lucky ones. His fertility has won him an unimpeachable place in Urbmon 116. His status is secure.

Though he is just past 14, Siegmund has fathered two children. His son is called Janus and his newborn daughter has been named Persephone. Siegmund lives in a handsome 50-square-meter home on the 787th floor, slightly more than midway up in Shanghai. His specialty is the theory of urban administration, and despite his youth he already spends much of his time as a consultant to the administrators in Louisville. He is short, finely made, quite strong, with a large head and thick curling hair. In boyhood he lived in Chicago and was one of Memnon's closest friends. They still see each other quite often; the fact that they now live in different cities is no bar to their friendship.

Social encounters between the Holstons and the Kluvers always take place at Siegmund's apartment. The Kluvers never come down to Chicago to visit Aurea and Memnon. Siegmund claims there is no snobbery in this. "Why should the four of us sit around a noisy dorm," he asks, "when we can get together in the privacy of my apartment?" Aurea is suspicious of this attitude. Urbmon people are not supposed to place such a premium on privacy. Is the dorm not a good enough place for Siegmund Kluver?

Siegmund once lived in the same dorm as Aurea and Memnon. That was two years ago, when they all were newly married. Several times, in those long-ago days, Aurea yielded her body to Siegmund; in a dormitory such excursions are common, unremarkable, and socially approved. But very swiftly Siegmund's wife became pregnant, qualifying the Kluvers to apply for an apartment of their own, and the progress he was making in his profession permitted him to find room in the city of Shanghai. Aurea has not shared her sleeping platform with Siegmund since he left the dormitory. She is distressed by this, for she enjoyed Siegmund's embraces, but there is little she can do about it. Sexual relationships between people of different cities are currently considered improper.

Now Siegmund is evidently bound for higher things. Memnon says that by the time he is seventeen he will be, not a specialist in the theory of urban administration, but an actual administrator, and will live in Louisville. Already Siegmund spends much time with the leaders of the urbmon; and with their wives as well, Aurea has heard.

Siegmund is an excellent host. His apartment is warm and agreeable, and two of its walls glisten with panels of one of the new decorative materials, which emits a soft hum keyed to the spectral pattern its owner has chosen. Tonight Siegmund has tuned the panels almost into the ultraviolet and the audio emission is pitched close to the hypersonic. He has exquisite taste in handling the room's scent apertures, too: jasmine and hyacinth flavor the air. "Some tingle?" he asks. "Just in from Venus. Quite blessworthy." Aurea and Memnon smile and nod. Siegmund fills a large fluted silver bowl with the costly scintillant fluid and places it on the pedestal-table. A touch of the floor-pedal and the table rises to a height of 150 centimeters.

"Mamelon?" he says. "Will you join us?"

Siegmund's wife slides her baby into the maintenance slot near the sleeping platform and crosses the room to her guests. Mamelon Kluver is quite tall, dark of complexion and hair, elegantly beautiful in a haggard way. Her forehead is high, her cheekbones prominent, her chin sharp; her eyes, alert and glossy and wide-set, seem almost too big, too dominant, in her pale and tapering face. The delicacy of her beauty makes Aurea feel defensive about her own soft features, her snub nose, her rounded cheeks, her full lips, the light dusting of freckles over tawny skin. Mamelon is the oldest person in the room, almost sixteen. Her breasts are swollen with milk; she is only eleven days up from childbed, and she is nursing. Aurea has never known anyone else who nursed. Mamelon has always been different, though. Aurea is still somewhat frightened of Siegmund's wife, who is so cool, so self-possessed, so mature. So passionate, too. At twelve, a new bride, Aurea's sleep was broken again and again by Mamelon's cries of ecstasy, echoing through the dormitory.

Now Mamelon bends forward and puts her lips to the tingle bowl. The four of them drink at the same moment. Tiny bubbles dance on Aurea's lips. The bouquet dizzies her. She peers into the depths of the bowl and sees abstract patterns forming and sundering. Tingle is faintly intoxicating, faintly hallucinogenic, an enhancer of vision, a suppressant of inner disturbance. It comes from certain musky swamps in the lowlands of Venus; the serving Siegmund has offered contains billions of alien microorganisms, fermenting and fissioning even as they are digested and absorbed.

After the ritual of drinking, they talk. Siegmund and Memnon discuss world events; Mamelon shows Aurea her baby. The little girl lies within the maintenance slot, drooling, gurgling, cooing. Aurea says, "What a relief it must be not to be carrying her any longer!"

"One enjoys being able to see one's feet again," Mamelon says.

"Is it very uncomfortable, being pregnant?"

"There are annoyances. Yet there are positive aspects. The moment of birth itself—"

"Does it hurt?" Aurea asks. "I imagine it would. Something that big, ripping through your body—"

"Gloriously blessful. One's entire nervous system awakens. It's impossible to describe the sensation. You must experience it for yourself."

"I wish I could," says Aurea, downcast. She slips a hand into the maintenance slot to touch the child. A quick burst of ions purifies her skin before she makes contact with little Persephone's downy cheek. Aurea says, "God bless, I want to do my duty! The medics say there's nothing wrong with either of us. But—"

"You must be patient, love." Mamelon embraces Aurea lightly. "Bless god, your moment will come."

Aurea is doubtful. For twenty months she has surveyed her flat belly, waiting for it to begin to bulge. It is blessed to create life, she knows. If everyone were like her, who would fill the urbmons? She has a sudden terrifying vision of the colossal towers nearly empty, whole cities sealed off, power failing, walls cracking, just a few shriveled old women shuffling through halls now thronged with happy multitudes.

Her one obsession has led her to her other one, and she turns to Siegmund, breaking into the conversation of the men to say, "Siegmund, is it true that they'll be opening Urbmon 158 soon?"

"So I hear, yes."

"What will it be like?"

"Very much like 116, I imagine. A thousand floors, the usual services. I suppose seventy families per floor, at first, maybe 250,000 people altogether, but it won't take long to bring it up to par."

Aurea clamps her palms together. "How many people will be sent there from here, Siegmund?"

"I'm sure I don't know that."

"There'll be some, won't there?"

Memnon says mildly, "Aurea, let's talk about something pleasant."

"Some people will be sent there from here," she persists. "Come on, Siegmund. You're up in Louisville with the bosses all the time. *How many?*"

Siegmund laughs. "You've really got an exaggerated idea of my significance in this place, Aurea. Nobody's said a word to me about how Urbmon 158 will be stocked."

"You know the theory of these things, though. You can project."

"Well, yes." Siegmund is quite cool; this subject has a purely impersonal interest for him. He seems unaware of the source of Aurea's agitation. "Naturally, if we're going to do our duty to god by creating life, we've also got to be sure that there's a place for everyone to live," he says. "So we go on building urban monads, and, naturally, whenever a new urbmon is added to the Chipitts constellation, it has to be stocked from the other Chipitts buildings. That makes good genetic sense. Even though each urbmon is big enough to provide an adequate gene-mix, our tendency to stratify into cities and villages within the building leads to a good deal of inbreeding, which they say isn't good for the species on a long-term basis. But if we take 5,000 people from each of 50 urbmons, say, and toss them together into a new urbmon, it gives us a pooled gene-mix of 250,000 individuals that we didn't have before. Actually, though, easing population pressure is the most urgent reason for erecting new buildings."

"Keep it clean, Siegmund," Memnon warns.

Siegmund grins. "No, I mean it. Oh, sure there's a cultural imperative telling us to breed and breed and breed. That's natural, after the agonies of the pre-urbmon days, when everybody went around wondering where we were going to put all the people. But even in a world of urban monads we have to plan in an orderly way. The excess of births and deaths is pretty consistent. Each urbmon is designed to hold 800,000 people comfortably, with room to pack in maybe 100,000 more, but that's the top. At the moment, you know, every urbmon in the Chipitts constellation more than twenty years old is at least 10,000 people above optimum, and a couple are pushing maximum. Things aren't too bad in 116, but you know yourselves that there are trouble spots. Why, Chicago has 38,000—"

"37,402 this morning," Aurea says.

"Whatever. That's close to a thousand people a floor. The programmed optimum density for Chicago is only 32,000, though. That means that the waiting list in your city for a private apartment is getting close to a generation long. The dorms are packed, and people aren't dying fast enough to make room for the new families, which is why Chicago is offloading some of its best people to places like Edinburgh and Boston and—well, Shanghai. Once the new building is open—"

Aurea says, steely-voiced, "How many from 116 will be sent there?"

"The theory is, 5,000 from each monad, at current levels," Siegmund says. "It'll be adjusted slightly to compensate for population variations in different buildings, but figure on 5,000. Now, there'll be about a thousand people in 116 who'll volunteer to go—"

"*Volunteer?*" Aurea gasps. It is inconceivable to her that anyone will want to leave his native urbmon.

Siegmund smiles. "Older people, love. In their twenties and thirties. Bored, maybe stalemated in their careers, tired of their neighbors, who knows? It sounds obscene, yes. But there'll be a thousand volunteers. That means that about 4,000 more will have to be picked from lot."

"I told you so this morning," Memnon says.

"Will these 4,000 be picked at random throughout the whole urbmon?" Aurea asks.

Gentley Siegmund says, "At random, yes. From the newlywed dorms. From the childless."

At last. The truth revealed.

"Why from us?" Aurea wails.

"Kindest and most blessworthy way," says Siegmund. "We can't uproot small children from their urbmon matrix. Dorm couples haven't the same kind of community ties that we—that others—that—" He falters. Aurea starts to sob. He says, "Love, I'm sorry. It's the system, and it's a good system. Ideal, in fact."

"Memnon, we're going to be *expelled!*"

Siegmund tries to reassure her. She and Memnon have only a slim chance of being chosen, he insists. In this urbmon thousands upon thousands of people are eligible for transfer. And so many variable factors exist—but she will not be consoled. Unashamed, she lets raw emotion spew into the room, and then she feels shame. She knows she has spoiled the evening for everyone. But Siegmund and Mamelon are kind about it, and Memnon does not chide her as he hurries her out, into the dropshaft, down 52 floors to their home in Chicago.

That night, although she wants him intensely, she turns her back on Memnon when he reaches for her. She lies awake listening a long time to the gasps and happy groans of the couples lying on the sleeping platforms about her, and then sleep comes. Aurea dreams of being born. She is down in the power plant of Urban Monad 116, 400 meters underground and they are sealing her in a liftshaft capsule. The building throbs. She is close to the heat-sink and the urine-reprocessing plant and the refuse compactors and all the rest of the service gear that keeps the structure alive, all those dark, hidden sectors of the urbmon that she had to tour when she was a schoolgirl. Now the liftshaft carries her up, up through Reykjavik where the maintenance people live, up through brawling Prague where everyone has ten babies, up through Rome, Boston, Edinburgh, Chicago, Shanghai, even through Louisville where the administrators move in unimaginable luxury, and now she is at the summit of the building, at the landing stage where the quickboats fly in from distant towers, and a hatch opens in the landing stage and Aurea is ejected. She soars into the sky, safe within her capsule while the cold winds of the upper atmosphere buffet it. She is six kilometers above the ground, looking down for the first time on the entire urbmon world. So this is how it is, she thinks. So many buildings. And yet so much open space!

She drifts across the constellation of towers. It is early spring, and Chipitts is greening. Below her are the tapered structures that hold the 40,000,000 + people of this urban cluster. She is awed by the neatness of the constellation, the geometrical placement of the buildings to form a series of hexagons within the larger area. Green plazas separate the buildings. No one enters the plazas, ever, but their well-manicured lawns are a delight to behold from the windows of the urbmon. The lower-class people on the lower floors have the best views of the gardens and pools, which is a compensation of sorts. From her vantage point high above, Aurea does not expect to see the plazas well, but her dreaming mind gives her an intense clarity of vision and she discerns small golden floral heads, she smells the tang of floral fragrance.

Her mind whirls as she engorges herself on the complexities of Chipitts. How many cities at forty to an urban monad? Two hundred. How many villages at seven or eight to a city? More than a thousand. How many families? How many nightwalkers now prowling, now slipping into available beds? How many births a day? How many deaths? How many joys? How many sorrows? Within each tower, there are schools, hospitals, sports arenas, houses of worship, theatres, everything urban people require. The urbmons are self-sufficient, closed ecologies that even purify and recycle wastes. Only food, Aurea knows, must come from outside—from the agricultural communes that lie beyond the urban constellation.

She rises effortlessly to a height of ten kilometers. She wishes to behold the agricultural communes.

She sees them now, stretching to the horizon, flat bands of

green bordered in brown. Seven eighths of the land area of the continent, she has been told endlessly, is used for the production of food. Busy little men and women oversee the machines that till the fertile fields. Aurea has heard of the terrible rites of the farming folk, the bizarre and primitive customs of those who must live beyond the urban world. Perhaps that is all fantasy; no one she knows has ever visited the communes. No one she knows has ever set foot outside Urban Monad 116. The courier pods trundle endlessly and without supervision toward the urbmons, carrying produce through subterranean channels. Food in; machinery and manufactured goods out. A balanced economy. Aurea is borne upward on a transport of joy. How miraculous it is that there can be 75,000,000,000 people living harmoniously on one small world! God bless, she thinks. A full room for every family. A meaningful and enriching city life. Friends, lovers, mates, children.

Children. Dismay seizes her and she begins to spin.

In her dizziness she seems to vault to the edge of space, so that she sees the entire planet; all of its urban constellations are jutting toward her like spikes. She sees not only Chipitts but also Sansan and Boswash, and Berpar, Wienbud, Shankong, Bocarac, every gathering of towers. And also she sees the plains teeming with food, the former deserts, the former savannahs, the former forests. It is all quite wonderful, but it is terrifying as well, and she wonders a moment if the way man has reshaped his environment is the best of all possible ways. Yes, she tells herself, yes; we are servants of god this way, we avoid strife and greed and turmoil, we bring new life into the world, we thrive, we multiply. We multiply. And doubt smites her and she begins to fall, and the capsule splits and releases her, leaving her bare body unprotected. And she sees the spiky tips of Chipitts' fifty towers below her, but now there is a new tower, fifty-first, and she falls toward it, toward a gleaming bronzed needle-sharp summit, and she cries out as it penetrates her and she is impaled. And she wakes, sweating and shaking, her tongue dry, her mind dazed by a vision beyond her grasp, and she clutches Memnon, who murmurs sleepily and sleepily enters her.

They are beginning now to tell the people of Urban Monad 116 about the new building. Aurea hears it from the wallscreen as she does her morning chores in the dormitory. Out of the patterns of light and color on the wall there congeals a view of an unfinished tower. Construction machines swarm over it, metal arms moving frenziedly, welding arcs glimmering off octagonal steel-paneled torsos. The familiar voice of the screen says, "Friends, what you see is Urbmon 158, one month eleven days from completion. God willing, it'll shortly be the home of a great many happy Chipittsians who will have the honor of establishing first-generation status there. The news from Louisville is that 802 residents of your own Urbmon 116 have already signed up for transfer to the new building, as soon as—"

Next, a day later, comes an interview with Mr. and Mrs. Dismas Cullinan of Boston, who, with their nine littles, were the very first people in 116 to request transfer. Mr. Cullinan, a meaty, red-faced man, is a specialist in sanitary engineering. He explains, "I see a real opportunity to move up to the planning level over in 158. I figure I can jump eighty, ninety floors in status in a hell of a hurry." Mrs. Cullinan pats her middle. Number ten is on the way. She purrs over the immense social advantages the move will confer on her children. Her eyes are too bright; her upper lip is thicker than the lower one and her nose is sharp. "She looks like a bird of prey," someone in the dorm comments. Someone else says, "She's obviously miserable here. Hoping to grab rungs fast over there." The Cullinan children range from two to thirteen years of age. Unfortunately, they resemble their parents. One of them claws at her brother while on screen. Aurea says, "The building's better off without the lot of them."

Interviews with other transferees follow. On the fourth day of the campaign, the screen offers an extensive tour of the interior of 158, showing the ultra-modern conveniences it will offer. Thermal irrigation for everybody, super-speed liftshafts and dropshafts, three-wall screens, a novel programming system for delivery of meals from the central kitchens, and other wonders, representing the finest in urban progress. The number of volunteers for transfer is now up to 914.

Perhaps, Aurea thinks, they will fill the entire quota with volunteers.

Memnon says, "The figure is fake. Siegmund tells me they've got only 91 volunteers so far."

"Then why—"

"To encourage the others."

In the second week, the transmissions dealing with the new building now indicate that the number of volunteers has leveled off at 1,060. Siegmund admits privately that this is close to the actual figure, and that few additional volunteers are expected. The screen begins gently to introduce the possibility that conscription of transferees will be necessary. Two management men from Louisville and a pair of helix adjusters from Chicago are shown discussing the need for a proper genetic mix at the new building. A moral engineer from Shanghai speaks about the importance of being blessworthy. It is blessworthy to obey the divine plan and its representatives on Earth, he says. The quality of life in Urbmon 158 will be diminished if its initial population does not reach planned levels. This would be a crime against those who do go to 158. Therefore it is each man's duty to society to accept transfer if transfer is offered.

Next there is an interview with Kimon and Freya Kurtz, ages 14 and 13, from a dorm in Bombay. They are not about to volunteer, they admit, but they wouldn't mind being conscripted. "The way we look at it," Kimon Kurtz declares, "it could be a great opportunity. I mean, once we had some children, we'd be able to find top status for them right away. It's a brand new world over there—no limits on how fast you can rise. The readjustment of going over would be a little nudgy at first, but we'd be jumping soon enough. And we'd know that our littles wouldn't have to enter a dorm when they were old enough to marry. They could get rooms of their own right away, even before they had littles too. So even though we're not eager to leave our friends and all, we're ready to go if the wheel points to us." Freya Kurtz, ecstatic, breathless, says, "Yes. That's right."

The softening-up process continues with an account of how the conscriptees will be chosen: 3,878 in all, no more than 100 from any one city or 30 from any one dorm. The pool of eligibles consists of married men and women between the ages of twelve and seventeen who have no children, a current pregnancy not being counted as a child. Selection will be by random lot.

At last the names of the conscripts are released.

The screen's cheerful voice announces, "From Chicago's 735th floor dormitory the following blessworthy ones have been chosen, and may god give them fertility in their new life:

"Brock, Aylward and Alison.

"Feuermann, Sterling and Natasha.

"Holston, Memnon and Aurea—"

She will be wrenched from her matrix. She will be torn from the pattern of memories and affections that defines her identity. She is terrified of going.

She will fight the order.

"Memnon, file an appeal! Do something fast!" She kneads the gleaming wall of the dormitory. He looks at her blankly; he is about to leave for work. He has already said there is nothing they can do. He goes out.

Aurea follows him into the corridor. The morning rush has begun; the citizens of 735th-floor Chicago stream past. Aurea sobs. The eyes of others are averted from her. She knows nearly all of these people. She has spent her life among them. She tugs at Memnon's hand. "Don't just walk out on me!" she whispers harshly. "How can we let them throw us out of 116?"

"It's the law, Aurea. People who don't obey the law go down the chute and contribute combustion mass to the generators. Is that what you want?"

"I won't go! Memnon, I've always lived here! I—"

"You're talking like a flippo," he says, keeping his voice low. He pulls her back inside the dormitory. "Pop a pill, Aurea. See the floor consoler, why don't you? Stay calm and let's adjust."

"I want you to file an appeal."

"There is no appeal."

"I refuse to go."

He seizes her shoulders. "Look at it rationally, Aurea. One building isn't that different from another. We'll have some of our friends there. We'll make new friends. We—"

"No."

"There's no alternative," he says. "Except down the chute."

"I'd rather go down the chute, then!"

For the first time since they were married, he looks at her with contempt. He cannot abide irrationality. "Don't spew nonsense," he tells her. "See the consoler, pop a pill, think it through. I've got to leave, now."

He goes again, and this time she does not go after him. She slumps on the floor, feeling cold plastic against her bare skin. The others in the dorm tactfully ignore her. She sees images: her schoolroom, her first lover, her parents, her sisters and brothers, all melting, flowing across the floor. She presses her thumbs to her eyes. She will not be cast out. Gradually she calms. I have influence, she tells herself. If Memnon will not act, I will act for us. She wonders if she can ever forgive Memnon for his cowardice, for his opportunism. She will visit her uncle.

She strips off her morning robe and dons a chaste gray girlish cloak. From the hormone chest she selects a capsule that will cause her to emanate the odor that inspires men to act protectively toward her. She looks sweet, demure, virginal; she could pass for ten or eleven years of age.

The liftshaft takes her to the 975th floor, the heart of Louisville. All is steel and spongeglass here. The corridors are spacious and lofty. Few people rush through the halls, though silent machines glide on unfathomable errands. This is the abode of those who administer the plans. Aurea is scanned by hidden sensors, asked to name her business, evaluated, shunted into a waiting room. At length her mother's brother consents to see her.

His office is nearly as large as a private suite. He sits behind a broad polygonal desk from which protrudes a bank of shimmering monitor dials. He wears formal top-level clothes, a sleek tunic tipped with epaulets in the infrared. Aurea feels the blast of heat from where she stands. He is cool, distant, polite. His handsome face appears to be fashioned from burnished copper.

"It's been many months, hasn't it, Aurea?" he says. A patronizing smile escapes him. "How have you been?"

"Fine, Uncle Lewis."

"Your husband—"

"Fine."

"Any littles yet?"

"Uncle Lewis, we've been picked to go to 158!"

His smile does not waver. "How fortunate! God bless, you can start a new life right at the top!"

"I don't want to go. Get me out of it." She rushes toward him, a frightened child, tears flowing. A forcefield captures her when she is two meters from his desk. Her breasts feel it first, and as they flatten painfully against the invisible barrier she averts her head and injures her cheek. She drops to her knees and sobs.

He comes to her. He lifts her. He tells her to be brave, to do her duty to god. He is kind and calm at first, but as she goes on protesting, his voice turns cold, and abruptly Aurea begins to feel unworthy of his attention. He reminds her of her obligations to society. He hints delicately that the chute awaits those who persist in abrading the smooth texture of community life. Then he smiles again, and his icy blue eyes meet hers, and he tells her to be brave and go. She creeps away. She feels disgraced by her weakness.

As she plunges downward from Louisville, her uncle's spell ebbs and her indignation revives. Perhaps she can get help elsewhere. She returns to the dorm and changes her clothing and her hormone balance. Now she is clad in iridescent mesh through which her breasts, thighs, and buttocks are intermittently visible, and she exudes an odor of distilled lust. She notifies the data terminal that she requests a private meeting with Siegmund Kluver of Shanghai. Eight minutes later word comes that he has consented to meet with her in one of the rendezvous cubicles on the 790th floor. She goes up.

He seems cross and impatient. "Why did you pull me away from my work?" he asks.

"You know Memnon and I have been—"

"Yes, of course, Mamelon and I will be sorry to lose your friendship."

Aurea attempts a provocative stance. She knows she cannot win Siegmund's aid merely by making herself available; he is hardly that easily swayed. But perhaps she can lead him to feel regret at her departure. She whispers, "Help us get out of going, Siegmund."

"How can I—"

"You have connections. Amend the program somehow. Support our appeal. You're a rising man in the building. You can do it."

"No one can do such a thing."

"Please, Siegmund." She approaches him, pulls her shoulders

back, lets her nipples come thrusting through her garment of mesh. She moistens her lips, narrows her eyes to slits. Huskily she says, "Don't you want me to stay? Wouldn't you like to take a turn or two with me? You know I'd do anything if you'd help us get off that list. *Anything.*"

She sees him smile and knows she has oversold herself; he is amused not tempted, by her offer. Her face crumples. She turns away.

"You don't want me," she mutters.

"Aurea, please! You're asking the impossible!" He catches her shoulders and pulls her toward him. His hands slip within the mesh and caress her. She knows that he is merely consoling her with a counterfeit of desire. He says, "If there was any way I could fix things, I would. But we'd all get tossed down the chute." His fingers find her body's core. She does not want him now, not this way. She tries to free herself. His embrace is mere kindness; he will take her out of pity. She stiffens.

"No," she says, and then she realizes how hopeless everything is, and she yields to him only because she knows that there will never be another chance.

Memnon says, "I've heard from Siegmund about what happened today. And from your uncle. You've got to stop this, Aurea."

"Let's go down the chute, Memnon."

"Come with me to the consoler. I've never seen you act this way."

"I've never felt so threatened."

"Why can't you adjust to it?" He asks. "It's really a grand chance for us."

"I can't. I can't." She slumps forward, defeated, broken.

"Stop it," he tells her. "Brooding sterilizes. Won't you cheer up a bit?"

She will not be consoled. He summons the machines; they take her to the consoler. In his office she is examined and her metabolism is probed. The consoler draws the story from her. He is an elderly man, kind, gentle, somehow bored. At the end he tells her, "Conflict sterilizes. You must learn to comply with the demands of society." He recommends treatment.

"I don't want treatment," she says, but Memnon authorizes it, and they take her away. "Where am I going?" she asks. "For how long?"

"To the 780th floor, for about a week."

"To the moral engineers?"

"Yes," they tell her.

For a week she lives in a sealed chamber filled with warm sparkling fluids. She floats idly on a pulsing tide. They speak to her over audio channels. Occasionally she glimpses an eye peering through an optical fiber dangling above her. They drain the tensions and resistances from her. On the eighth day Memnon comes for her. They open the chamber and she is lifted forth, nude, dripping, her skin puckered. Machines towel her dry and clothe her. Memnon leads her by the hand. Aurea smiles quite often. "I love you," she tells Memnon.

"God bless," he says. "I've missed you so much."

The day is at hand, and she has paid her farewells. She has had two months to say goodbye, first to her blood kin, then to her friends in her village, then to others whom she has known within Chicago, and at last to Siegmund and Mamelon Kluver, her only acquaintances outside her native city. Aurea has revisited the home of her parents and her old schoolroom, and she has taken a tour of the urbmon, like a visitor from outbuilding, so that she may see the power plant and the service core and the conversion stations one final time.

Meanwhile Memnon has been busy too; each night he reports on what he has accomplished. The 5,202 citizens of Urban Monad 116 who are destined to transfer to the new structure have elected twelve delegates to the steering committee of Urbmon 158, and Memnon is one of the twelve. It is a great honor. Night after night the delegates take part in a multiscreen linkage embracing all of Chipitts, so that they can plan the social framework of the building they will share. It has been decided, Memnon reports, to have fifty cities of twenty floors apiece, and to name the cities not after the vanished cities of old Earth, as has been the general custom, but after distinguished men of the past: Newton, Einstein, Plato, Galileo, and so forth. Memnon will be given responsibility for an entire sector of heat-diffusion engineers. It will be administrative rather than technical work, and so he and Aurea will live in Newton, the highest city.

Memnon expands and throbs with increased importance. He cannot wait for the hour of transfer. "We'll be really important people," he tells Aurea exultantly. "And in ten or fifteen years we'll be legendary figures in 158. The first settlers. The founders, the pioneers. They'll be making ballads about us in another century."

"And I was unwilling to go," Aurea says mildly. "How strange to think of myself acting like that!"

"It's an error to react with fear until you know the real shape of things," Memnon replies. "The ancients thought it would be a calamity to have 5,000,000,000 people in the world. Yet we have fifteen times that many and look how happy we are!"

"Yes. We are very happy. And we'll always be happy, Memnon."

The signal comes. The machines are at the door to fetch them. Memnon indicates the box that contains their few possessions. Aurea glows. She glances about the dorm. We will have our own room in 158, she tells herself.

Those members of the dorm who are not leaving form a line, and offer Memnon and Aurea one last embrace.

Memnon follows the machines out, and Aurea follows Memnon. They go up to the landing stage on the thousandth floor. It is an hour past dawn and summer sunlight gleams on the tips of Chipitts' towers. The transfer operation has already begun; quickboats capable of carrying 100 passengers each will be moving back and forth between Urbmons 116 and 158 all day.

"And so we leave this place," Memnon says. "We begin a new life. Bless god!"

"God bless!" cries Aurea.

They enter the quickboat and it soars aloft. The pioneers bound for Urbmon 158 gasp as they see, for the first time, how their world really looks from above. The towers are beautiful, Aurea tells herself. They glisten. On and on they stretch, fifty-one of them, like a ring of spears in a broad green carpet. She is very happy. Memnon folds his hand over hers. She wonders how she could ever have feared this day. She wishes she could apologize to the universe for her foolishness.

She lets her free hand rest lightly on the curve of her belly. New life now sprouts within her. Each moment the cells divide and the little one grows. They have dated the hour of conception to the evening of the day when she was discharged by the consoler's office. Conflict indeed sterilizes, Aurea has realized. Now the poison of resistance has been drained from her; she is able to fulfill a woman's proper destiny.

"It'll be strange," she says to Memnon, "living in such an empty building. Only 250,000! How long will it take for us to fill it?"

"Twelve or thirteen years," he answers. "We'll have few deaths, because we're all young. And lots of births."

She laughs. "Good. I hate an empty house."

The quickboat's voice says, "We now will turn to the southeast, and on the left to the rear you can catch a last glimpse of Urbmon 116."

Her fellow passengers strain to see. Aurea does not make the effort. Urbmon 116 has ceased to concern her.

Part III

Feeding The Billions: World Food Problems

There are, as we have indicated earlier, a whole host of social, economic, and political problems stemming from rapid population growth. Some of these problems are of major importance, others of only abstract interest. Yet, there is one aspect of the population crisis in which we now find ourselves which is literally a life or death situation: how will the world manage to feed this rapidly increasing number of people?

For most of mankind's existence on this planet, the availability of food has been directly related to the size of population. Simply put, there were at any given period in history as many people as there was food to support them. Indeed, historically famine and malnutrition have been principal contributors to high mortality. This precarious balance between food and people was most clearly articulated by an English economist, Thomas Robert Malthus, who, in 1798 in his well-known "An Essay on the Principle of Population," formulated the famous "Malthusian Principle;" that is, population tends to grow at a much faster rate than does food production, so that every so often a famine is required to bring the number of people back into line with food supply.

For some time after Malthus published his ideas on population and food, the basic relationship that he stipulated (people increase faster than food) was not in evidence. Coincidentally, at about Malthus' time there began a series of innovations in agriculture, sometimes referred to as the "Agricultural Revolution," which resulted in tremendous increases in food production. Whereas, as Malthus correctly noted, food production has increased historically only very slowly, the Agricultural Revolution, through new farming practices, mechanization and improved implements, and the introduction of new crops (such as corn and potatoes from the Western Hemisphere), brought about hitherto unprecedented growth in the means of subsistence. Further, the opening up of new lands for cultivation, such as the American Midwest, the Pampas in Argentina, the steppe region in what is now the Soviet Union, and Australia and New Zealand, added huge increments to world food supplies. What these trends meant was that, contrary to what Malthus had postulated, food production increased at a faster rate than population.

Lately, however, there has been substantial evidence to suggest that the Malthusian view may, over the long term, prove to be correct. First, since the Second World War food production on the world scale has virtually levelled off or declined to much slower growth rates than before. Secondly, as we have detailed earlier, population growth has accelerated to a rate never before seen in history. Thus, at some time during the past two decades, the rate of population growth once again overtook and surpassed the rate at which food production increased. With the rapid growth of population, the world's surplus of food has been decreased to the bare minimum, raising the possibility that unforeseen crop failures could lead to massive starvation.

Compounding the food problem on the world scale are sharp regional differentials in food production and consumption. Generally speaking, the more developed regions (Europe, North America, Australia and New Zealand) produce and consume vastly greater quantities of food per person than do the developing regions (Asia, Africa, and Latin America). On the average, each person in the more affluent countries consumes about 2,000 pounds of grain (or the equivalent in other foods) per year, while yearly per capita consumption in the developing areas is only approximately 500 pounds. These widely divergent figures represent explosive international implications. Some statesmen have already declared that food will be a "weapon" in international relations, much as oil became a powerful lever in diplomacy and economics. Indeed, some have already proposed that agricultural surplus countries such as the United States should have a contingency plan worked out for allotting scarce food to those countries where it will do the most good, and leave those nations with little hope of making it through the crisis to fend for themselves; this proposal is usually called "triage" after a system of battlefield medicine developed by the French army. The moral implications of and potential for international (or internal) violence related to the increasingly more critical people and food balance are obvious.

It is by no means an absolute certainty that the world will be unable to feed its future, much larger population; many new programs and agricultural production strategies are being proposed to increase the amount of food produced on the world scale: (1) expand the area of cultivation; or (2) increase production, or *yields*, on existing acreage. Until recent times, mankind has relied mostly upon the expansion of agricultural land as the principal method of raising more food; as more food was required, new lands were brought under cultivation. Unfortunately, land which is suitable for cultivation without expensive modifications (such as irrigation) is finite, and there are few areas in the world where surplus land exists today on any appreciable scale. Indeed, agricultural development schemes within recent years which have focused on increasing acreage have met, at best, with only limited success, because the new lands brought into cultivation were marginal in terms of farming potential. In the Soviet Union, for example, a program of increasing acreage beginning in the early 1950's resulted in the planting of over 100 million acres of new farm land (an amount greater than all the farmland in Canada), the greatest such expansion in history. Yet, because these new lands were not well-suited for agriculture, the returns in terms of food production have not been nearly as great as the Soviet government would have liked.

If there is an answer to the food problem, it must be, therefore, in increasing the yields on land already cultivated, particularly in the developing countries where production per unit of land is almost universally low. There have been some notable successes in this regard, mainly those associated with the programs usually referred to as the "Green Revolution." The Green Revolution is an agricultural development plan which, through the breeding of new, higher-yielding crop varieties, the use of fertilizers, and the adoption of modern farming methods, hopes to raise food production. In Mexico, the Green Revolution has brought about a three-fold increase in wheat yields over a period of twenty years, and in Taiwan rice yields doubled over about the same length of time. Yet, the Green Revolution is not without its drawbacks. Because the Green Revolution package is expensive, richer farmers can take advantage of the program while in most cases the poor farmers continue with the traditional practices. In India, such a situation has been politically and socially disjunctive, with many small landowners losing their farms and joining the ranks of the urban unemployed. Further, relying on one strain of crop (*monoculture*) can have serious consequences if that variety is attacked by a pest (a circumstance which has already occurred in the United States with corn and in the Philippines with rice).

Perhaps the greatest danger of all those associated with the Green Revolution, and the most subtle, is that the existence of the program has instilled in many people what is very probably a false sense of security. The notion that "something is being done" to raise food production disguises the fact that the root cause of our present dilemma is not that we don't have enough food, but rather that there are too many people. On this point, Dr. Norman Borlaug, an American scientist known widely as the "father" of the Green Revolution (for which he won the Nobel Peace Prize), has stated many times that increasing food production through higher yields is a stopgap measure, a program which is only buying us some precious time in which to lower the rates of population growth.

Thus, we are confronted once again with the spectre of famine. Each year, at present rates of growth, over eighty million persons are added to the world's population; the question which becomes increasingly more important with each passing year is: can we feed them?

Very frequently one hears that in order to solve the world's food problems it is required only to utilize more intensively the oceans and their vast resources, a sort of "farming of the seas." The facts indicate, however, that although the oceans can (or do) provide significant amounts of food, particularly much-needed protein, the potential for increasing production above current levels by any significant amount is not promising. The most obvious use of ocean resources for food is fishing, an activity in which some countries (notably Japan and the Soviet Union) have grown increasingly proficient. About 70 million tons of fish are "harvested" annually, or approximately 40 pounds per person average on the world scale. The Japanese alone, however, account for over 10 million tons, and the average Japanese consumes 70 pounds of fish per year. Faced with limited agricultural resources on their densely-populated islands, the Japanese have taken to the sea with technologically sophisticated fishing fleets, including ships designed to locate schools of fish, and others which serve as seagoing factories of processing plants.

The use of the oceans is not without its problems, though, and in recent years the world's catch of fish has been declining. Overfishing probably has contributed to this decline, but also of importance is the fact that the oceans remain a mystery in many respects, and clearly considerably more research is required to attain an understanding of how much food can be expected from the sea. International efforts are essential in this regard, including laws of the sea to regulate catches and establish territorial waters; the necessity for international cooperation has been illustrated recently by the "Cod War" between Iceland and Britain, where two countries dependent on fishing have clashed over territorial rights.

SUGGESTED READINGS:

Brown, Lester R. *Seeds of Change: The Green Revolution and Development in the 1970's.* New York: Praeger, 1970.

Brown, Lester R. *By Bread Alone.* New York: Praeger, 1974.

Malthus, Thomas Robert. *An Essay on the Principle of Population* (and related writings with commentary), edited by Philip Appleman. New York: Norton, 1976.

Paddock, William, and Paddock, Paul. *Famine 1975! America's Decision: Who Will Survive?* Boston: Little, Brown and Co., 1976.

In the following story, the noted author C.M. Kornbluth hypothesizes a sea-borne society whose very existence depends upon a successful catch. Incidentally, the reliance of this future society upon the smaller creatures of the sea is not far-fetched; some marine biologists have predicted that the food potential from tiny shrimp-like krill approaches that of the larger marine species.

by C. M. Kornbluth

Shark Ship

It was the spring swarming of the plankton; every man and woman and most of the children aboard Grenville's Convoy had a job to do. As the seventy-five gigantic sailing ships ploughed their two degrees of the South Atlantic, the fluid that foamed beneath their cutwaters seethed also with life. In the few weeks of the swarming, in the few meters of surface water where sunlight penetrated in sufficient strength to trigger photosynthesis, microscopic spores burst into microscopic plants, were devoured by minute animals which in turn were swept into the maws of barely visible sea monsters almost a tenth of an inch from head to tail; these in turn were fiercely pursued and gobbled in shoals by the fierce little brit, the tiny herring and shrimp that could turn a hundred miles of green water to molten silver before your eyes.

Through the silver ocean of the swarming the Convoy scudded and tacked in great controlled zigs and zags, reaping the silver of the sea in the endlessly reeling bronze nets each ship payed out behind.

The Commodore in *Grenville* did not sleep during the swarming; he and his staff dispatched cutters to scout the swarms, hung on the meteorologists' words, digested the endless reports from the scout vessels, and toiled through the night to prepare the dawn signal. The mainmast flags might tell the captains "Convoy course five degrees right," or "Two degrees left," or only "Convoy course; no change." On those dawn signals depended the life for the next six months of the million and a quarter souls of the Convoy. It had not happened often, but it had happened that a succession of blunders reduced a convoy's harvest below the minimum necessary to sustain life. Derelicts were sometimes sighted and salvaged from such convoys; strong-stomached men and women were needed for the first boarding and clearing away of human debris. Cannibalism occurred, an obscene thing one had nightmares about.

The seventy-five captains had their own particular purgatory to endure throughout the harvest, the Sail-Seine Equation. It was their job to balance the push on the sails and the drag of the ballooning seines so that push exceeded drag by just the number of pounds that would keep the ship on course and in station, given every conceivable variation of wind force and direction, temperature of water, consistency of brit, and smoothness of hull. Once the catch was salted down it was customary for the captains to converge on *Grenville* for a roaring feast by way of letdown.

Rank had its privileges. There was no such relief for the captains' Net Officers or their underlings in Operations and Maintenance, or for their Food Officers under whom served the Processing and Stowage people. They merely worked, streaming the nets twenty-four hours a day, keeping them bellied out with lines from mast and outriding gigs, keeping them spooling over the great drum amidships, tending the blades that had to scrape the brit from the nets, without damaging the nets, repairing the damage when it did occur; and without interruption of the harvest, flash-cooking the part of the harvest to be cooked, drying the part to be dried, pressing oil from the harvest as required, and stowing what was cooked and dried and pressed where it would not spoil, where it would not alter the trim of the ship, where it would not be pilfered by children. This went on for weeks after the silver had gone thin and patchy against the green, and after the silver had altogether vanished.

The routines of many were not changed at all by the swarming season. The blacksmiths, the sailmakers, the carpenters, the watertenders, to a degree the storekeepers, functioned as before, tending to the fabric of the ship, renewing, replacing, reworking. The ships were things of brass, bronze, and unrusting steel. Phosphor-bronze strands were woven into net, lines, and cables; cordage, masts and hull were metal; all were inspected daily by the First Officer and his men and women for the smallest pinhead of corrosion. The smallest pinhead of corrosion could spread; it could send a ship to the bottom before it had done spreading, as the chaplains were fond of reminding worshipers when the ships rigged for church on Sundays. To keep the hellish red of iron rust and the sinister blue of copper rust from invading, the squads of oilers were always on the move, with oil distilled from the catch. The sails and the clothes alone could not be preserved; they wore out. It was for this that the felting machines down below chopped wornout sails and clothing into new fibers and twisted and rolled them with kelp and glue from the catch into new felt for new sails and clothing.

While the plankton continued to swarm twice a year, Grenville's Convoy could continue to sail the South Atlantic, from ten-mile limit to ten-mile limit. Not one of the seventy-five ships in the Convoy had an anchor.

The Captains' Party that followed the end of Swarming 283 was slow getting under way. McBee, whose ship was Port Squadron 19, said to Salter of Starboard Squadron 30: "To be frank, I'm too damned exhausted to care whether I ever go to another party, but I didn't want to disappoint the Old Man."

The Commodore, trim and bronzed, not showing his eighty years, was across the great cabin from them greeting new arrivals.

Salter said: "You'll feel differently after a good sleep. It was a great harvest, wasn't it? Enough weather to make it tricky and interesting. Remember 276? *That* was the one that wore me out. A grind, going by the book. But this time, on the fifteenth day my foretopsail was going to go about noon, big rip in her, but I needed her for my S-S balance. What to do? I broke out a balloon spinnaker—now wait a minute, let me tell it first before you throw the book at me—and pumped my fore trim tank out. Presto! No trouble; foretopsail replaced in fifteen minutes."

McBee was horrified. "You could have lost your net!"

"My weatherman absolutely ruled out any sudden squalls."

"Weatherman. You could have lost your net!"

Salter studied him. "Saying that once was thoughtless, McBee. Saying it twice is insulting. Do you think I'd gamble with twenty thousand lives?"

McBee passed his hands over his tired face. "I'm sorry," he said. "I told you I was exhausted. Of course under special circumstances it can be a safe maneuver." He walked to a porthole for a glance at his own ship, the nineteenth in the long echelon behind *Grenville*. Salter stared after him. "Losing one's net" was a phrase that occurred in several proverbs; it stood for abysmal folly. In actuality a ship that lost its phosphor-bronze wire mesh was doomed, and quickly. One could improvise with sails or try to jury-rig a net out of the remaining rigging, but not well enough to feed twenty thousand hands, and no fewer than that were needed for maintenance. Grenville's Convoy had met a derelict which lost its net back before 240; children still told horror stories about it, how the remnants of port and starboard watches, mad to a man, were at war, a war of vicious night forays with knives and clubs.

Salter went to the bar and accepted from the Commodore's steward his first drink of the evening, a steel tumbler of colorless fluid distilled from a fermented mash of sargassum weed. It was about forty percent alcohol and tasted pleasantly of iodides.

He looked up from his sip and his eyes widened. There was a man in captain's uniform talking with the Commodore and he did not recognize his face. But there had been no promotions lately!

The Commodore saw him looking and beckoned him over. He saluted and then accepted the old man's handclasp. "Captain Salter," the Commodore said, "my youngest and rashest, and my best harvester; Salter, this is Captain Degerand of the White Fleet."

Salter frankly gawked. He knew perfectly well that Grenville's Convoy was far from sailing alone upon the seas. On watch he had beheld distant sails from time to time. He was aware that cruising the two-degree belt north of theirs was another convoy and that in the belt south of theirs was still another, in fact that the seaborne population of the world was a constant one billion, eighty million. But never had he expected to meet face to face any of them except the one and a quarter million who sailed under Grenville's flag.

Degerand was younger than he, all deeply tanned skin and flashing pointed teeth. His uniform was perfectly ordinary and very queer. He understood Salter's puzzled look. "It's woven cloth," he said. "The White Fleet was launched several decades after Grenville's. By then they had machinery to reconstitute fibers suitable for spinning and they equipped us with it. It's six of one and half a dozen of the other. I think our sails may last longer than yours, but the looms require a lot of skilled labor when they break down."

The Commodore had left them.

"Are we very different from you?" Salter asked

Degerand said: "Our differences are nothing. Against the dirt men we are brothers—blood brothers."

The term "dirt men" was discomforting; the juxtaposition with "blood" more so. Apparently he was referring to whoever it was that lived on the continents and islands—a shocking breach of manners, of honor, of faith. The words of the Charter circled through Salter's head: " . . . return for the sea and its bounty . . . renounce and abjure the land from which we. . . . " Salter had been ten years old before he knew that there *were* continents and islands. His dismay must have shown on his face.

"They have doomed us," the foreign captain said. "We cannot refit. They have sent us out, each upon our two degrees of ocean in larger or smaller convoys as the richness of the brit dictated, and they have cut us off. To each of us will come the catastrophic storm, the bad harvest, the lost net, and death."

It was Salter's impression that Degerand had said the same words many times before, usually to large audiences.

The Commodore's talker boomed out: "Now hear this!" His huge voice filled the stateroom easily; his usual job was to roar through a megaphone across a league of ocean, supplementing flag and lamp signals. "Now hear this!" he boomed. "There's tuna on the table—big fish for big sailors!"

A grinning steward whisked a felt from the sideboard, and there by Heaven it lay! A great baked fish as long as your leg, smoking hot and trimmed with kelp! A hungry roar greeted it; the captains made for the stack of trays and began to file past the steward, busy with knife and steel.

Salter marveled to Degerand: "I didn't dream there were any left that size. When you think of the tons of brit that old-timer must have gobbled!"

The foreigner said darkly: "We slew the whales, the sharks, the perch, the cod, the herring—everything that used the sea but us. They fed on brit and one another and concentrated it in firm savory flesh like that, but we were jealous of the energy squandered in the long food chain; we decreed that the chain would stop with the link brit-to-man."

Salter by then had filled a tray. "Brit's more reliable," he said. "A convoy can't take chances on fisherman's luck." He happily bolted a steaming mouthful.

"Safety is not everything," Degerand said. He ate, more slowly than Salter. "Your Commodore said you were a rash seaman."

"He was joking. If he believed that, he would have to remove me from command."

The Commodore walked up to them, patting his mouth with a handkerchief and beaming. "Surprised, eh?" he demanded. "Glasgow's lookout spotted that big fellow yesterday half a kilometer away. He signaled me and I told him to lower and row for him. The boat crew sneaked up while he was browsing and gaffed him clean. Very virtuous of us. By killing him we economize on brit and provide a fitting celebration for my captains. Eat hearty! It may be the last we'll ever see."

Degerand rudely contradicted his senior officer. "They can't be wiped out clean, Commodore, not exterminated. The sea is deep. Its genetic potential cannot be destroyed. We merely make temporary alterations of the feeding balance."

"Seen any sperm whale lately?" the Commodore asked, raising his white eyebrows. "Go get yourself another helping, captain, before it's gone." It was a dismissal; the foreigner bowed and went to the buffet.

The Commodore asked: "What do you think of him?"

"He has some extreme ideas," Salter said.

"The White Fleet appears to have gone bad," the old man said. "That fellow showed up on a cutter last week in the middle of harvest wanting my immediate, personal attention. He's on the staff of the White Fleet Commodore. I gather they're all like him. They've got slack; maybe rust has got ahead of them, maybe they're overbreeding. A ship lost its net and they didn't let it go. They cannibalized rigging from the whole fleet to make a net for it."

"But—"

"But—but—but. Of course it was the wrong thing and now they're all suffering. Now they haven't the stomach to draw lots and cut their losses." He lowered his voice. "Their idea is some sort of raid on the Western Continent, that America thing, for steel and bronze and whatever else they find not welded to the deck. It's nonsense, of course, spawned by a few silly-clever people on the staff. The crews will never go along with it. Degerand was sent to invite us in!"

Salter said nothing for a while and then: "I certainly hope we'll have nothing to do with it."

"I'm sending him back at dawn with my compliments, and a negative, and my sincere advice to his Commodore that he drop the whole thing before his own crew hears of it and has him bowspritted." The Commodore gave him a wintry smile. "Such a reply is easy to make, of course, just after concluding an excellent harvest. It might be more difficult to signal a negative if we had a couple of ships unnetted and only enough catch in salt to feed sixty per cent of the hands. Do you think you could give the hard answer under those circumstances?"

"I think so, sir."

The Commodore walked away, his face enigmatic. Salter thought he knew what was going on. He had been given one small foretaste of top command. Perhaps he was being groomed for Commodore—not to succeed the old man, surely, but his successor.

McBee approached, full of big fish and drink. "Foolish thing I said," he stammered. "Let's have drink, forget about it, eh?"

He was glad to.

"Damn fine seaman!" McBee yelled after a couple more drinks. "Best little captain in the Convoy! Not a scared old crock like poor old McBee, 'fraid of every puff of wind!"

And then he had to cheer up McBee until the party began to thin out. McBee fell asleep at last and Salter saw him to his gig before boarding his own for the long row to the bobbing masthead lights of his ship.

Starboard Squadron 30 was at rest in the night. Only the slowly moving oil lamps of the women on their ceaseless rust patrol were alive. The brit catch, dried, came to some seven thousand tons. It was a comfortable margin over the 5670 tons needed for six months' full rations before the autumnal swarming and harvest. The trim tanks along the keel had been pumped almost dry by the ship's current prison population as the cooked and dried and salted cubes were stored in the glass-lined warehouse tier; the gigantic vessel rode easily on a swelling sea before a Force One westerly breeze.

Salter was exhausted. He thought briefly of having his cox'n whistle for a bosun's chair so that he might be hauled at his ease up the fifty-yard cliff that was the hull before them, and dismissed the idea with regret. Rank hath its privileges and also its obligations. He stood up in the gig, jumped for the ladder, and began the long climb. As he passed the portholes of the cabin tiers he virtuously kept eyes front, on the bronze plates of the hull inches from his nose. Many couples in the privacy of their double cabins would be celebrating the end of the backbreaking, night-and-day toil. One valued privacy aboard the ship; one's own 648 cubic feet of cabin, one's own porthole, acquired an almost religious meaning, particularly after the weeks of swarming cooperative labor.

Taking care not to pant, he finished the climb with a flourish, springing onto the flush deck. There was no audience. Feeling a little ridiculous and forsaken, he walked aft in the dark with only the wind and the creak of the rigging in his ears. The five great basket masts strained silently behind their breeze-filled sails; he paused a moment beside Wednesday mast, huge as a redwood, and put his hands on it to feel the power that vibrated in its steel latticework.

Six intent women went past, their hand lamps sweeping the deck; he jumped, though they never noticed him. They were in something like a trance state while on their tour of duty. Normal courtesies were suspended for them; with their work began the job of survival. One thousand women, five percent of the ship's company, inspected night and day for corrosion. Sea water is a vicious solvent and the ship had to live in it; fanaticism was the answer.

His stateroom above the rudder waited; the hatchway to it glowed a hundred feet down the deck with the light of a wasteful lantern. After harvest, when the tanks brimmed with oil, one type acted as though the tanks would brim forever. The captain wearily walked around and over a dozen stay ropes to the hatchway and blew out the lamp. Before descending he took a mechanical look around the deck; all was well—

Except for a patch of paleness at the fantail.

"Will this day never end?" he asked the darkened lantern and went to the fantail. The patch was a little girl in a nightdress wandering aimlessly over the deck, her thumb in her mouth. She

seemed to be about two years old and was more than half asleep.
She could have gone over the railing in a moment; a small wail, a
small splash—

He picked her up like a feather. "Who's your daddy, princess?"
he asked.

"Dunno," she grinned. The devil she didn't! It was too dark to
read her ID necklace and he was too tired to light the lantern. He
trudged down the deck to the crew of inspectors. He said to their
chief: "One of you get this child back to her parents' cabin," and
held her out.

The chief was indignant. "Sir, we are on watch!"

"File a grievance with the Commodore if you wish. Take the
child."

One of the rounder women did, and made cooing noises while
her chief glared. "Bye-bye, princess," the captain said. "You
ought to be keel-hauled for this, but I'll give you another chance."

"Bye-bye," the little girl said, waving, and the captain went
yawning down the hatchway to bed.

His stateroom was luxurious by the austere standards of the
ship. It was equal to six of the standard nine-by-nine cabins in
volume, or to three of the double cabins for couples. These
however had something he did not. Officers above the rank of
lieutenant were celibate. Experience had shown that this was the
only answer to nepotism, and nepotism was a luxury which no
convoy could afford. It meant, sooner or later, inefficient command. Inefficient command meant, sooner or later, death.

Because he thought he would not sleep, he did not.

Marriage. Parenthood. What a strange business it must be! To
share a bed with a wife, a cabin with two children decently behind
their screen for sixteen years . . . what did one talk about in bed?
His last mistress had hardly talked at all, except with her eyes.
When these showed signs that she was falling in love with him,
Heaven knew why, he broke with her as quietly as possible and
since then irritably rejected the thought of acquiring a successor.
That had been two years ago when he was thirty-eight and
already beginning to feel like a cabin-crawler fit only to be
dropped over the fantail into the wake. An old lecher, a roué, a
user of women. Of course she had talked a little; what did they
have in common to talk about? With a wife ripening beside him,

with children to share, it would have been different. That pale, tall, quiet girl deserved better than he could give; he hoped she was decently married now in a double cabin, perhaps already heavy with the first of her two children.

A whistle squeaked above his head; somebody was blowing into one of the dozen speaking tubes clustered against the bulkhead. Then a push-wire popped open the steel lid of Tube Seven, Signals. He resignedly picked up the flexible reply tube and said into it: "This is the captain. Go ahead."

"*Grenville* signals Force Three squall approaching from astern, sir."

"Force Three squall from astern. Turn out the fore-starboard watch. Have them reef sail to Condition Charlie."

"Fore-starboard watch, reef sail to Condition Charlie, aye-aye."

"Execute."

"Aye-aye, sir." The lid of Tube Seven, Signals, popped shut. At once he heard the distant, penetrating shrill of the pipe, the faint vibration as one-sixth of the deck crew began to stir in their cabins, awaken, hit the deck bleary-eyed, begin to trample through the corridors and up the hatchways to the deck. He got up himself and pulled on clothes, yawning. Reefing from Condition Fox to Condition Charlie was no serious matter, not even in the dark, and Walters on watch was a good officer. But he'd better have a look.

Being flush-decked, the ship offered him no bridge. He conned her from the "first top" of Friday mast, the rear-most of her five. The "first top" was a glorified crow's nest fifty feet up the steel basketwork of that great tower; it afforded him a view of all masts and spars in one glance.

He climbed to his command post too far gone for fatigue. A full moon now lit the scene, good. That much less chance of a green topman stepping on a ratline that would prove to be a shadow and hurtling two hundred feet to the deck. That much more snap in the reefing; that much sooner it would be over. Suddenly he was sure he would be able to sleep if he ever got back to bed again.

He turned for a look at the bronze, moonlit heaps of the great net on the fantail. Within a week it would be cleaned and oiled, within two weeks stowed below in the cable tier, safe from wind and weather.

The regiments of the fore-starboard watch swarmed up the masts from Monday to Friday, swarmed out along the spars as bosun's whistles squealed out the drill—

The squall struck.

Wind screamed and tore at him; the captain flung his arms around a stanchion. Rain pounded down upon his head and the ship reeled in a vast, slow curtsey, port to starboard. Behind him there was a metal sound as the bronze net shifted inches sideways, back.

The sudden clouds had blotted out the moon; he could not see the men who swarmed along the yards but with sudden terrible clarity he felt through the soles of his feet what they were doing. They were clawing their way through the sail-reefing drill, blinded and deafened by sleety rain and wind. They were out of phase by now; they were no longer trying to shorten sail equally on each mast; they were trying to get the thing done and descend. The wind screamed in his face as he turned and clung. Now they were ahead of the job on Monday and Tuesday masts, behind the job on Thursday and Friday masts.

So the ship was going to pitch. The wind would catch it unequally and it would kneel in prayer, the cutwater plunging with a great, deep stately obeisance down into the fathoms of ocean, the stern soaring slowly, ponderously, into the air until the topmost rudder-trunnion streamed a hundred-foot cascade into the boiling froth of the wake.

That was half the pitch. It happened, and the captain clung, groaning aloud. He heard above the screaming wind loose gear rattling on the deck, clashing forward in an avalanche. He heard a heavy clink at the stern and bit his lower lip until it ran with blood that the tearing cold rain flooded from his chin.

The pitch reached its maximum and the second half began, after interminable moments when she seemed frozen at a five-degree angle forever. The cutwater rose, rose, rose, the bowsprit blocked out horizon stars, the loose gear countercharged astern in a crushing tide of bales, windlass cranks, water-breakers, stilling coils, steel sun reflectors, lashing tails of bronze rigging—

Into the heaped piles of the net, straining at its retainers on the two great bollards that took root in the keel itself four hundred feet below. The energy of the pitch hurled the belly of the net open crashing, into the sea. The bollards held for a moment.

A retainer cable screamed and snapped like a man's back, and then the second cable broke. The roaring slither of the bronze links thundering over the fantail shook the ship.

The squall ended as it had come; the clouds scudded on and the moon bared itself, to shine on a deck scrubbed clean. The net was lost.

Captain Salter looked down the fifty feet from the rim of the crow's nest and thought: I should jump. It would be quicker that way.

But he did not. He slowly began to climb down the ladder to the bare deck.

Having no electrical equipment, the ship was necessarily a representative republic rather than a democracy. Twenty thousand people can discuss and decide only with the aid of microphones, loudspeakers, and rapid calculators to balance the ayes and noes. With lungpower the only means of communication and an abacus in a clerk's hands the only tallying device, certainly no more than fifty people can talk together and make sense, and there are pessimists who say the number is closer to five than fifty. The Ship's Council that met at dawn on the fantail numbered fifty.

It was a beautiful dawn; it lifted the heart to see salmon sky, iridescent sea, spread white sail of the Convoy ranged in a great slanting line across sixty miles of oceanic blue.

It was the kind of dawn for which one lived—a full catch salted down, the water-butts filled, the evaporators trickling from their thousand tubes nine gallons each sunrise to sunset, wind enough for easy steerageway, and a pretty spread of sail. These were the rewards. One hundred and forty-one years ago Grenville's Convoy had been launched at Newport News, Virginia, to claim them.

Oh, the high adventure of the launching! The men and women who had gone aboard thought themselves heroes, conquerors of nature, self-sacrificers for the glory of NEMET! But NEMET meant only Northeastern Metropolitan Area, one dense warren that stretched from Boston to Newport, built up and dug down, sprawling westward, gulping Pittsburgh without a pause, beginning to peter out past Cincinnati.

The first generation asea clung and sighed for the culture of NEMET, consoled itself with its patriotic sacrifice; any relief was better than none at all, and Grenville's Convoy had drained one and a quarter million population from the huddle. They were immigrants into the sea; like all immigrants they longed for the Old Country. Then the second generation. Like all second generations they had no patience with the old people or their tales. *This* was real, this sea, this gale, this rope! Then the third generation. Like all third generations it felt a sudden desperate hollowness and lack of identity. What was real: Who are we? What is NEMET which we have lost? But by then grandfather and grandmother could only mumble vaguely; the culture heritage was gone, squandered in three generations, spent forever. As always, the fourth generation did not care.

And those who sat in counsel on the fantail were members of the fifth and sixth generations. They knew all there was to know about life. Life was the hull and masts, the sail and rigging, the net and the evaporators. Nothing more. *Nothing less.* Without masts there was no life. Nor was there life without the net.

The Ship's Council did not command; command was reserved to the captain and his officers. The Council governed, and on occasion tried criminal cases. During the black Winter Without Harvest eighty years before it had decreed euthanasia for all persons over sixty-three years of age and for one out of twenty of the other adults aboard. It had rendered bloody judgment on the ringleaders of Peale's Mutiny. It had sent them into the wake and Peale himself had been bowspritted, given the maritime equivalent of crucifixion. Since then no megalomaniacs had decided to make life interesting for their shipmates, so Peale's long agony had served its purpose.

The fifty of them represented every department of the ship and every age group. If there was wisdom aboard, it was concentrated there on the fantail. But there was little to say.

The eldest of them, Retired Sailmaker Hodgins, presided. Venerably bearded, still strong of voice, he told them:

"Shipmates, our accident has come. We are dead men. Decency demands that we do not spin out the struggle and sink into— unlawful eatings. Reason tells us that we cannot survive. What I propose is an honorable voluntary death for us all, and the legacy of our ship's fabric to be divided among the remainder of the Convoy at the discretion of the Commodore."

He had little hope of his old man's viewpoint prevailing. The

Chief Inspector rose at once. She had only three words to say: *"Not my children."*

Women's heads nodded grimly and men's with resignation. Decency and duty and common sense were all very well until you ran up against the steel bulkhead. *Not my children.*

A brilliant young chaplain asked: "Has the question ever been raised as to whether a collection among the fleet might not provide cordage enough to improvise a net?"

Captain Salter should have answered that, but he, murderer of the twenty thousand souls in his care, could not speak. He nodded jerkily at his signals officer.

Lieutenant Zwingli temporized by taking out his signals slate and pretending to refresh his memory. He said: "At 0035 today a lamp signal was made to *Grenville* advising that our net was lost. *Grenville* replied as follows: 'Effective now, your ship no longer part of Convoy. Have no recommendations. Personal sympathy and regrets. Signed, Commodore.' "

Captain Salter found his voice. "I've sent a couple of other messages to *Grenville* and to our neighboring vessels. They do not reply. This is as it should be. We are no longer part of the Convoy. Through our own—lapse—we have become a drag on the Convoy. We cannot look to it for help. I have no word of condemnation for anybody. This is how life is."

And then a council member spoke whom Captain Salter knew in another role. It was Jewel Flyte, the tall, pale girl who had been his mistress two years ago. She must be serving as an alternate, he thought, looking at her with new eyes. He did not know she was even that; he had avoided her since then. And no, she was not married; she wore no ring. And neither was her hair drawn back in the semiofficial style of the semiofficial voluntary celibates, the superpatriots (or simply sex-shy people, or dislikers of children) who surrendered their right to reproduce for the good of the ship (or their own convenience). She was simply a girl in the uniform of a—a what? He had to think hard before he could match the badge over her breast to a department. She was Ship's Archivist with her crossed key and quill, an obscure clerk and shelf-duster under—far under!—the Chief of Yeomen Writers. She must have been elected alternate by the Yeomen in a spasm of sympathy for her blind-alley career.

"My job," she said in her calm, steady voice, "is chiefly to search for precedents in the Log when unusual events must be recorded and nobody recollects offhand the form in which they should be recorded. It is one of those provoking jobs which must be done by someone but which cannot absorb the full time of a person. I have therefore had many free hours of actual working time. I have also remained unmarried and am not inclined to sports or games. I tell you this so you may believe me when I say that during the past two years I have read the Ship's Log in its entirety."

There was a little buzz. Truly an astonishing, and an astonishingly pointless, thing to do! Wind and weather, storms and calms, messages and meetings and censuses, crimes, trials, and punishments of a hundred and forty-one years; what a bore!

"Something I read," she went on, "may have some bearing on our dilemma." She took a slate from her pocket and read: "Extract from the Log dated June 30, Convoy Year 72. 'The Shakespeare-Joyce-Melville Party returned after dark in the gig. They had not accomplished any part of their mission. Six were dead of wounds; all bodies were recovered. The remaining six were mentally shaken but responded to our last ataractics. They spoke of a new religion ashore and its consequences on population. I am persuaded that we seabornes can no longer relate to the continentals. The clandestine shore trips will cease.' The entry is signed 'Scolley, Captain.'"

A man named Scolley smiled for a brief proud moment. His ancestor! And then like the others he waited for the extract to make sense. Like the others he found that it would not do so.

Captain Salter wanted to speak and wondered how to address her. She had been "Jewel" and they all knew it; could he call her "Yeoman Flyte" without looking like, being, a fool? Well, if he was fool enough to lose his net he was fool enough to be formal with an ex-mistress. "Yeoman Flyte," he said, "where does the extract leave us?"

In her calm voice she told them all: "Penetrating the few obscure words, it appears to mean that until Convoy Year 72 the Charter was regularly violated, with the connivance of successive captains. I suggest that we consider violating it once more, to survive."

The Charter. It was a sort of ground swell of their ethical life, learned early, paid homage every Sunday when they were rigged for church. It was inscribed in phosphor-bronze plates on Monday mast of every ship at sea, and the wording was always the same.

IN RETURN FOR THE SEA AND ITS BOUNTY WE RENOUNCE AND ABJURE FOR OURSELVES AND OUR DESCENDANTS THE LAND FROM WHICH WE SPRUNG: FOR THE COMMON GOOD OF MAN WE SET SAIL FOREVER.

At least half of them were unconsciously murmuring the words.

Retired Sailmaker Hodgins rose, shaking. "Blasphemy!" he said. "The woman should be bowspritted!"

The chaplain said thoughtfully: "I know a little more about what constitutes blasphemy than Sailmaker Hodgins, I believe, and assure you that he is mistaken. It is a superstitious error to believe that there is any religious sanction for the Charter. It is no ordinance of God but a contract between men."

"It is a Revelation!" Hodgins shouted. "A Revelation! It is the newest testament! It is God's finger pointing the way to the clean hard life at sea, away from the grubbing and filth, from the overbreeding and the sickness!"

That was a common view.

"What about my children?" demanded the Chief Inspector. "Does God want them to starve or be—be—" She could not finish the question, but the last unspoken word of it rang in all their minds.

Eaten.

Aboard some ships with an accidental preponderance of the elderly, aboard other ships where some blazing personality generations back had raised the Charter to a powerful cult, suicide might have been voted. Aboard other ships where nothing extraordinary had happened in six generations, where things had been easy and the knack and tradition of hard decision making had been lost, there might have been confusion and inaction and the inevitable degeneration into savagery. Aboard Salter's ship the Council voted to send a small party ashore to investigate. They used every imaginable euphemism to describe the action, took six hours to make up their minds, and sat at last on the fantail cringing a little, as if waiting for a thunderbolt.

The shore party would consist of Salter, Captain; Flyte, Archivist; Pemberton, Junior Chaplain; Graves, Chief Inspector.

Salter climbed to his conning top on Friday mast, consulted a chart from the archives, and gave the order through speaking tube to the tiller gang: "Change course red four degrees."

The repeat came back incredulously.

"Execute," he said. The ship creaked as eighty men heaved the tiller; imperceptibly at first the wake began to curve behind them.

Ship Starboard 30 departed from its ancient station; across a mile of sea the bosun's whistles could be heard from Starboard 31 as she put on sail to close the gap.

"They might have signaled something." Salter thought, dropping his glasses at last on his chest. But the masthead of Starboard 31 remained bare of all but its commission pennant.

He whistled up his signals officer and pointed to their own pennant. "Take that thing down," he said hoarsely, and went below to his cabin.

The new course would find them at last riding off a place the map described as New York City.

Salter issued what he expected would be his last commands to Lieutenant Zwingli; the whaleboat was waiting in its davits; the other three were in it.

"You'll keep your station here as well as you're able," said the captain. "If we live, we'll be back in a couple of months. Should we not return, that would be a potent argument against beaching the ship and attempting to live off the continent—but it will be your problem then and not mine."

They exchanged salutes. Salter sprang into the whaleboat, signaled the deck hands standing by at the ropes, and the long creaking descent began.

Salter, Captain, age forty; unmarried *ex officio;* parents Clayton Salter, master instrument maintenanceman, and Eva Romano, chief dietician; selected from dame school age ten for A Track training; seamanship school certificate at age sixteen, navigation certificate at age twenty, First Lieutenants School age twenty-four, commissioned ensign age twenty-four, lieutenant at thirty, commander at thirty-two, commissioned captain and succeeded to command of Ship Starboard 30 the same year.

Flyte, Archivist, age twenty-five; unmarried; parents Joseph Flyte, entertainer, and Jessie Waggoner, entertainer; completed dame school age fourteen, B Track training; Yeoman's School certificate at age sixteen, Advanced Yeoman's School certificate at age eighteen; efficiency rating, 3.5.

Pemberton, Chaplain, age thirty; married to Riva Shields, nurse; no children by choice; parents Will Pemberton, master distiller-watertender, and Agnes Hunt, felter-machinist's mate; completed dame school age twelve, B Track training; Divinity School Certificate at age twenty; midstarboard watch curate, later fore-starboard chaplain.

Graves, Chief Inspector, age thirty-four; married to George Omany, blacksmith third class; two children; completed dame school age fifteen; Inspectors School Certificate at age sixteen; inspector third class, second class, first class, master inspector, then chief; efficiency rating, 4.0; three commendations.

Versus the Continent of North America.

They all rowed for an hour; then a shoreward breeze came up and Salter stepped the mast. "Ship your oars," he said and then wished he dared countermand the order. Now they would have time to think of what they were doing.

The very water they sailed was different in color from the deep water they knew, and different in its way of moving. The life in it—

"Great God!" Mrs. Graves cried, pointing astern.

It was a huge fish, half the size of their boat. It surfaced lazily and slipped beneath the water in an uninterrupted arc. They had seen steel-gray skin, not scales, and a great slit of a mouth.

Salter said, shaken: "Unbelievable. Still, I suppose in the unfished offshore waters a few of the large forms survive. And the intermediate sizes to feed them—" And footlong smaller sizes to feed *them*, and—

Was it mere arrogant presumption that Man had permanently changed the life of the sea?

The afternoon sun slanted down and the tip of Monday mast sank below the horizon's curve astern; the breeze that filled their sail bowled them toward a mist which wrapped vague concretions they feared to study too closely. A shadowed figure huge as a mast with one arm upraised; behind it blocks and blocks of something solid.

"This is the end of the sea," said the captain.

Mrs. Graves said what she would have said if a silly

underinspector had reported to her blue rust on steel: "Nonsense!" Then, stammering: "I beg your pardon, captain. Of course you are correct."

"But it sounded strange," Chaplain Pemberton said helpfully. "I wonder where they all are?"

Jewel Flyte said in her quiet way: "We should have passed over the discharge from waste tubes before now. They used to pump their waste through tubes under the sea and discharge it several miles out. It colored the water and it stank. During the first voyaging years the captains knew it was time to tack away from land by the color and the bad smell."

"They must have improved their disposal system by now," Salter said. "It's been centuries."

His last word hung in the air.

The chaplain studied the mist from the bow. It was impossible to deny it; the huge thing was an Idol. Rising from the bay of a great city, an Idol, and a female one—the worst kind! "I thought they had them only in High Places," he muttered, discouraged.

Jewel Flyte understood. "I think it has no religious significance," she said. "It's a sort of—huge piece of scrimshaw."

Mrs. Graves studied the vast thing and saw in her mind the glyphic arts as practiced at sea: compacted kelp shaved and whittled into little heirloom boxes, miniature portrait busts of children. She decided that Yeoman Flyte had a dangerously wild imagination. Scrimshaw! Tall as a mast!

There should be some commerce, thought the captain. Boats going to and fro. The Place ahead was plainly an island, plainly inhabited; goods and people should be going to it and coming from it. Gigs and cutters and whaleboats should be plying this bay and those two rivers; at that narrow bit they should be lined up impatiently waiting, tacking and riding under sea anchors and furled sails. There was nothing but a few white birds that shrilled nervously at their solitary boat.

The blocky concretions were emerging from the haze; they were sunset-red cubes with regular black eyes dotting them; they were huge dice laid down side by side by side, each as large as a ship, each therefore capable of holding twenty thousand persons.

Where were they all?

The breeze and the tide drove them swiftly through the neck of water where a hundred boats should be waiting. "Furl the sail," said Salter. "Out oars."

With no sounds but the whisper of the oarlocks, the cries of the white birds, and the slapping of the wavelets, they rowed under the shadow of the great red dice to a dock, one of a hundred teeth projecting from the island's rim.

"Easy the starboard oars," said Salter; "handsomely the port oars. Up oars. Chaplain, the boat hook." He had brought them to a steel ladder; Mrs. Graves gasped at the red rust thick on it. Salter tied the painter to a corroded brass ring. "Come along," he said, and began to climb.

When the four of them stood on the iron-plated dock Pemberton, naturally, prayed. Mrs. Graves followed the prayer with half her attention or less; the rest she could not divert from the shocking slovenliness of the prospect—rust, dust, litter, neglect. What went on in the mind of Jewel Flyte her calm face did not betray. And the captain scanned those black windows a hundred yards inboard—no; inland!—and waited and wondered.

They began to walk to them at last, Salter leading. The sensation under foot was strange and dead, tiring to the arches and the thighs.

The huge red dice were not as insane close-up as they had appeared from the distance. They were thousand-foot cubes of brick, the stuff that lined ovens. They were set back within squares of green, cracked surfacing which Jewel Flyte named "cement" or "concrete" from some queer corner of her erudition.

There was an entrance, and written over it: THE HERBERT BROWNELL JR. MEMORIAL HOUSES. A bronze plaque shot a pang of guilt through them all as they thought of The Compact, but its words were different and ignoble.

NOTICE TO ALL TENANTS

A project Apartment is a Privilege and not a Right. Daily Inspection is the Cornerstone of the Project. Attendance at Least Once a Week at the Church or Synagogue of your Choice is Required for Families wishing to remain in Good Standing; Proof of Attendance must be presented on Demand. Possession of Tobacco or Alcohol will be considered Prima Facie Evidence of Undesirability. Excessive Water

Use, Excessive Energy Use and Food Waste will be Grounds for Desirability Review. The speaking of Languages other than American by persons over the Age of Six will be considered Prima Facie Evidence of Nonassimilability, though this shall not be construed to prohibit Religious Ritual in Languages other than American.

Below it stood another plaque in paler bronze, an afterthought:

None of the foregoing shall be construed to condone the Practice of Depravity under the Guise of Religion by Whatever Name, and all Tenants are warned that any Failure to report the Practice of Depravity will result in summary Eviction and Denunciation.

Around this later plaque some hand had painted with crude strokes of a tar brush a sort of anatomical frame at which they stared in wondering disgust.

At last Pemberton said: "They were a devout people." Nobody noticed the past tense, it sounded so right.

"Very sensible," said Mrs. Graves. "No nonsense about them."

Captain Salter privately disagreed. A ship run with such dour coercion would founder in a month; could land people be that much different?

Jewel Flyte said nothing, but her eyes were wet. Perhaps she was thinking of scared little human rats dodging and twisting through the inhuman maze of great fears and minute rewards.

"After all," said Mrs. Graves, "it's nothing but a Cabin Tier. We have cabins and so had they. Captain, might we have a look?"

"This *is* a reconnaissance," Salter shrugged. They went into a littered lobby and easily recognized an elevator which had long ago ceased to operate; there were many hand-run dumbwaiters at sea.

A gust of air flapped a sheet of printed paper across the chaplain's ankles; he stooped to pick it up with a kind of instinctive outrage—leaving paper unsecured, perhaps to blow overboard and be lost forever to the ship's economy! Then he flushed at his silliness. "So much to unlearn," he said, and spread the paper to look at it. A moment later he crumpled it in a ball and hurled it from him as hard and as far as he could and wiped his hands with loathing on his jacket. His face was utterly shocked.

The others stared. It was Mrs. Graves who went for the paper.

"Don't look at it," said the chaplain.

"I think she'd better," Salter said.

The maintenancewoman spread the paper, studied it, and said: "Just some nonsense. Captain, what do you make of it?"

It was a large page torn from a book, and on it were simply polychrome drawings and some lines of verse in the style of a child's first reader. Salter repressed a shocked guffaw. The picture was of a little boy and a little girl quaintly dressed, locked in murderous combat, using teeth and nails. "*Jack and Jill went up the hill,*" said the text, "*to fetch a pail of water. She threw Jack down and broke his crown; it was a lovely slaughter.*"

Jewel Flyte took the page from his hands. All she said was, after a long pause: "I suppose they couldn't start them too young." She dropped the page and she too wiped her hands.

"Come along," the captain said. "We'll try the stairs."

The stairs were dust, rat dung, cobwebs, and two human skeletons. Murderous knuckledusters fitted loosely the bones of the two right hands. Salter hardened himself to pick up one of the weapons but could not bring himself to try it on. Jewel Flyte said apologetically: "Please be careful, captain. It might be poisoned. That seems to be the way they were."

Salter froze. By God, but the girl was right! Delicately, handling the spiked steel thing by its edges, he held it up. Yes; stains—it *would* be stained, and perhaps with poison also. He dropped it into the thoracic cage of one skeleton and said: "Come on." They climbed in quest of a dusty light from above; it was a doorway onto a corridor of many doors. There was evidence of fire and violence. A barricade of queer pudgy chairs and divans had been built to block the corridor and had been breached. Behind it were sprawled three more heaps of bones.

"They have no heads," the chaplain said hoarsely. "Captain Salter, this is not a place for human beings. We must go back to the ship, even if it means honorable death. This is not a place for human beings."

"Thank you, chaplain," said Salter. "You've cast your vote. Is anybody with you?"

"Kill your own children, chaplain," said Mrs. Graves. "Not mine."

Jewel Flyte gave the chaplain a sympathetic shrug and said: "No."

One door stood open, its lock shattered by blows of a fire axe. Salter said: "We'll try that one." They entered into the home of an ordinary middle-class death-worshiping family as it had been a century ago, in the one hundred and thirty-first year of Merdeka the Chosen.

Merdeka the Chosen, the All-Foreigner, the Ur-Alien, had never intended any of it. He began as a retail mail-order vendor of movie and television stills, eight-by-ten glossies for the fan trade. It was a hard dollar; you had to keep an immense stock to cater to a tottery Mae Bush admirer, to the pony-tailed screamer over Rip Torn, and to everybody in between. He would have no truck with pinups. "Dirty, lascivious pictures!" he snarled when broadly hinting letters arrived. "Filth! Men and women kissing, ogling, pawing each other! Orgies! Bah!" Merdeka kept a neutered dog, a spayed cat, and a crumpled, uncomplaining housekeeper who was technically his wife. He was poor; he was very poor. Yet he never neglected his charitable duties, contributing every year to the Planned Parenthood Federation and the Midtown Hysterectomy Clinic.

They knew him in the Third Avenue saloons where he talked every night, arguing with Irishmen, sometimes getting asked outside to be knocked down. He let them knock him down and sneered from the pavement. Was *this* their argument? *He* could argue. He spewed facts and figures and clichés in unanswerable profusion. Hell, man, the Russians'll have a bomb base on the moon in two years and in two years the army and the air force will still be beating each other over the head with pigs' bladders. Just a minute, let me tell you; the goddammycin's making idiots of us all; do you know of any children born in the past two years that're healthy? And: 'flu be go to hell; it's our own germ warfare from Camp Crowder right outside Baltimore that got out of hand, and it happened the week of the twenty-fourth. And: the human animal's obsolete; they've proved at M.I.T., Steinwitz and Kohlmann *proved* that the human animal cannot survive the current radiation levels. And: enjoy your lung cancer, friend; for every automobile and its stinking exhaust there will be two-point-seven-oh-three cases of lung cancer, and we've got to have our automobiles, don't we? And: delinquency my foot; they're insane and it's got to the point where the economy cannot support mass insanity; they've got to be castrated; it's the only way. And: they should dig up the body of Metchnikoff and throw it to the dogs; he's the degenerate who invented venereal prophylaxis and since then vice without punishment has run hogwild through the world; what we need on the streets is a few of those old-time locomotor ataxia cases limping and drooling to show the kids where vice leads.

He didn't know where he came from. The delicate New York way of establishing origins is to ask: "Merdeka, hah? What kind of a name is that now?" And to this he would reply that he wasn't a lying Englishman or a loudmouthed Irishman or a perverted Frenchman or a chiseling Jew or a barbarian Russian or a toadying German or a thick-headed Scandihoovian, and if his listener didn't like it, what did he have to say in reply?

He was from an orphanage, and the legend at the orphanage was that a policeman had found him, two hours old, in a garbage can coincident with the death by hemorrhage on a trolley car of a luetic young woman whose name appeared to be Merdeka and who had certainly been recently delivered of a child. No other facts were established, but for generation after generation of orphanage inmates there was great solace in having one of their number who indisputably had got off to a worse start then they.

A watershed of his career occurred when he noticed that he was, for the seventh time that year, reordering prints of scenes from Mr. Howard Hughes' production *The Outlaw*. These were not the off-the-bust stills of Miss Jane Russell, surprisingly, but were group scenes of Miss Russell suspended by her wrists and about to be whipped. Merdeka studied the scene, growled "Give it to the bitch!" and doubled the order. It sold out. He canvassed his files for other whipping and torture stills from *Dessert Song*-type movies, made up a special assortment, and it sold out within a week. Then he knew.

The man and the opportunity had come together, for perhaps the fiftieth time in history. He hired a model and took the first specially posed pictures himself. They showed her cringing from a whip, tied to a chair with a clothes-line, and herself brandishing the whip.

Within two months Merdeka had cleared six thousand dollars and he put every cent of it back into more photographs and direct-mail advertising. Within a year he was big enough to attract the postoffice obscenity people. He went to Washington and screamed in their faces: "My stuff isn't obscene and I'll sue you if you bother me, you stinking bureaucrats! You show me one breast, you show me one behind, you show me one human being touching another in my pictures! You can't and you know you can't! I don't believe in sex and I don't push sex, so you leave me the hell alone! Life is pain and suffering and being scared so people like to look at my pictures; my pictures are about *them*, the scared little jerks! You're just a bunch of goddam perverts if you think there's anything dirty about my pictures!"

He had them there; Merdeka's girls always wore at least full panties, bras, and stockings; he had them there. The postoffice obscenity people were vaguely positive that there was *something* wrong with pictures of beautiful women tied down to be whipped or burned with hot irons, but what?

The next year they tried to get him on his income tax; those deductions for the Planned Parenthood Federation and the Midtown Hysterectomy Clinic were preposterous, but he proved them with canceled checks to the last nickel. "In fact," he indignantly told them, "I spend a lot of time at the Clinic and sometimes they let me watch the operations. *That's* how highly they think of me at the Clinic."

The next year he started *DEATH: the Weekly Picture Magazine* with the aid of a half-dozen bright young grads from the new Harvard School of Communicationeering. As *DEATH*'s Communicator in Chief (only yesterday he would have been its Publisher, and only fifty years before he would have been its Editor) he slumped biliously in a pigskin-paneled office, peering suspiciously at the closed-circuit TV screen which had a hundred wired eyes through-out *DEATH*'s offices, sometimes growling over the voice circuit:

"You! What's your name? Boland? You're through, Boland. Pick up your time at the paymaster." For any reason; for no reason. He was a living legend in his narrow-lapel charcoal flannel suit and stringy bullfighter neckties; the bright young men in their Victorian Revival frock coats and pearl-pinned cravats wondered at his—not "obstinacy"; not when there might be a mike even in the corner saloon; say, his "timelessness."

The bright young men became bright young-old men, and the magazine which had been conceived as a vehicle for deadheading house ads of the mail order picture business went into the black. On the cover of every issue of *DEATH* was a pictured execution-of-the-week, and no price for one was ever too high. A fifty-thousand-dollar donation to a mosque had purchased the right to secretely snap the Bread Ordeal by which perished a Yemenite suspected of tapping an oil pipeline. An interminable illustrated "History of Flagellation" was a staple of the reading matter, and the "Medical Section" (in color) was tremendously popular. So too was the weekly "Traffic Report."

When the last of the Compact Ships was launched into the Pacific the event made *DEATH* because of the several fatal accidents which accompanied the launching; otherwise Merdeka ignored the ships. It was strange that he who had unorthodoxies about everything had no opinion at all about the Compact Ships and their crews. Perhaps it was that he really knew he was the greatest manslayer who ever lived, and even so could not face commanding total extinction, including that of the sea-borne leaven. The more articulate Sokei-an, who in the name of Rinzei Zen Buddhism was at that time depopulating the immense area dominated by China, made no bones about it: "Even I in my Hate may err; let the celestial vessels be." The opinions of Dr. Spät, European member of the trio, are forever beyond recovery due to his advocacy of the "one-generation" plan.

With advancing years Merdeka's wits cooled and gelled. There came a time when he needed a theory and was forced to stab the button of the intercom for his young-old Managing Communicator and growl at him: "Give me a theory!" And the M.C. reeled out: "The structural intermesh of *DEATH: The Weekly Picture Magazine* with Western culture is no random point-event but a rising world-line. Predecessor attitudes such as the Hollywood dogma 'No breasts—blood!' and the tabloid press's exploitation of violence were floundering and empirical. It was Merdeka who sigma-ized the convergent traits of our times and asymptotically congruentizes with them publicationwise. Wrestling and the roller derby as blood sports, the routinization of femicide in the detective tale, the standardization at one million per year of traffic fatalities, the wholesome interest of our youth in gang rumbles, all point toward the Age of Hate and Death. The ethic of Love and Life is obsolescent, and who is to say that Man is the loser thereby? Life and Death compete in the marketplace of ideas for the Mind of Man—"

Merdeka growled something and snapped off the set. Merdeka leaned back. Two billion circulation this week, and the auto ads were beginning to Tip. Last year only the suggestion of a dropped shopping basket as the Dynajetic 16 roared across the page, this year a hand, limp on the pictured pavement. Next year, blood. In February the Sylphella Salon chain ads had Tipped, with a crash: "—and the free optional judo course for slenderized Madame or Mademoiselle: learn how to kill a man with your lovely bare hands, with or without mess as desired." Applications had risen twenty-eight percent. By *God* there was a structural intermesh for you!

It was too slow; it was still too slow. He picked up a direct-line phone and screamed into it: "Too slow! What am I paying you people for? The world is wallowing in filth! Movies are dirtier than ever! Kissing! Pawing! Ogling! Men and women together— obscene! Clean up the magazine covers! Clean up the ads!"

The person at the other end of the direct line was Executive Secretary of the Society for Purity in Communications; Merdeka had no need to announce himself to him, for Merdeka was S.P.C.'s principal underwriter. He began to rattle off at once: "We've got the Mothers' March on Washington this week, sir, and a mass dummy pornographic mailing addressed to every Middle Atlantic State female between the ages of six and twelve next week, sir; I believe this one-two punch will put the Federal Censorship Commission over the goal line before recess—"

Merdeka hung up. "Lewd communications," he snarled. "Breeding, breeding, breeding, like maggots in a garbage can. Burning and breeding. But we will make them clean."

He did not need a Theory to tell him that he could not take away Love without providing a substitute.

He walked down Sixth Avenue that night, for the first time in years. In this saloon he had argued; outside that saloon he had been punched in the nose. Well, he was winning the argument, all the arguments. A mother and daughter walked past uneasily, eyes on the shadows. The mother was dressed Square; she wore a sheath dress that showed her neck and clavicles at the top and her legs from mid-shin at the bottom. In some parts of town she'd be spat on, but the daughter, never. The girl was Hip; she was covered from neck to ankles by a loose, unbelted sack-culotte. Her mother's hair floated; hers was hidden by a cloche. Nevertheless the both of them were abruptly yanked into one of those shadows they prudently had eyed, for they had not watched the well-lit sidewalk for waiting nooses.

The familiar sounds of a Working Over came from the shadows as Merdeka strolled on. "I mean cool!" an ecstatic young voice—boy's, girl's what did it matter?—breathed between crunching blows.

That year the Federal Censorship Commission was created, and the next year the old Internment Camps in the southwest were filled to capacity by violators, and the next year the First Church of Merdeka was founded in Chicago. Merdeka died of an aortal aneurism five years after that, but his soul went marching on.

"The Family That Prays Together Slays Together," was the wall motto in the apartment, but there was no evidence that the implied injunction had been observed. The bedroom of the mother and the father was secured by steel doors and terrific locks, but Junior had got them all the same; somehow he had burned through the steel.

"Thermite?" Jewel Flyte asked herself softly, trying to remember. First he had got the father, quickly and quietly with a wire garotte as he lay sleeping, so as not to alarm his mother. To her he had taken her own spiked knobkerry and got in a mortal stroke, but not before she reached under her pillow for a pistol. Junior's teenage bones testified by their arrangement to the violence of that leaden blow.

Incredulously they looked at the family library of comic books, published in a series called "The Merdekan Five-Foot Shelf of Classics." Jewel Flyte leafed slowly through one called *Moby Dick* and found that it consisted of a near-braining in a bedroom, agonizingly depicted deaths at sea, and for a climax the eating alive of one Ahab by a monster. "Surely there must have been more," she whispered.

Chaplain Pendleton put down *Hamlet* quickly and held onto a wall. He was quite sure that he felt his sanity slipping palpably away, that he would gibber in a moment. He prayed and after a while felt better; he rigorously kept his eyes away from the Classics after that.

Mrs. Graves snorted at the waste of it all, at the picture of the ugly, pop-eyed, busted-nose man labeled MERDEKA THE CHOSEN, THE PURE, THE PURIFER. There were *two* tables, which was a folly. Who needed two tables? Then she looked closer, saw that one of them was really a blood-stained flogging bench and felt slightly ill. Its name-plate said *Correctional Furniture Corp. Size 6, Ages 10-14.* She had, God knew, slapped her children more than once when they deviated from her standard of perfection, but when she saw those stains she felt a stirring of warmth for the parricidal bones in the next room.

Captain Salter said: "Let's get organized. Does anybody think there are any of them left?"

"I think not," said Mrs. Graves. "People like that can't survive. The world must have been swept clean. They, ah, killed one another but that's not the important point. This couple had one child, age ten to fourteen. This cabin of theirs seems to be built for one child. We should look at a few more cabins to learn whether a one-child family is—was—normal. If we find out that it was, we can suspect that they are—gone. Or nearly so." She coined a happy phrase: "By race suicide."

"The arithmetic of it is quite plausible," Salter said. "If no factors work except the single-child factor, in one century of five generations a population of two billion will have bred itself down to 125 million. In another century, the population is just under four million. In another, 122 thousand . . . by the thirty-second generation the last couple descended from the original two billion will breed one child, and that's the end. And there are the other factors. Besides those who do not breed by choice"—his eyes avoided Jewel Flyte—"there are the things we have seen on the stairs, and in the corridor, and in these compartments."

"Then there's our answer." said Mrs. Graves. She smacked the obscene table with her hand, forgetting what it was. "We beach the ship and march the ship's company onto dry land. We clean up, we learn what we have to do to get along—" Her words trailed off. She shook her head. "Sorry," she said gloomily. "I'm talking nonsense."

The chaplain understood her, but he said: "The land is merely another of the many mansions. Surely they could learn!"

"It's not politically feasible," Salter said. "Not in its present form." He thought of presenting the proposal to the Ship's Council in the shadow of the mast that bore the Compact, and twitched his head in an involuntary negative.

"There is a formula possible," Jewel Flyte said.

The Brownells burst in on them then, all eighteen of the Brownells. They had been stalking the shore party since its landing. Nine sack-culotted women in clothes and nine men in penitential black, they streamed through the gaping door and surrounded the sea people with a ring of spears. Other factors had indeed operated, but this was not yet the thirty-second generation of extinction.

The leader of the Brownells, a male, said with satisfaction: "Just when we needed—new blood." Salter understood that he was not speaking in genetic terms.

The females, more verbal types, said critically: "Evil-doers, obviously. Displaying their limbs without shame, brazenly flaunting the rotted pillars of the temple of lust. Come from the accursed sea itself, abode of infamy, to seduce us from our decent and regular lives."

"We know what to do with the women," said the male leader. The rest took up the antiphon.

"We'll knock them down."

"And roll them on their backs."

"And pull one arm out and tie it fast."

"And pull the other arm out and tie it fast."

"And pull one limb out and tie it fast."

"And pull the other limb out and tie it fast."

"And then—"

"We'll beat them to death and Merdeka will smile."

Chaplain Pemberton stared incredulously. "You must look into your hearts," he told them in a reasonable voice. "You must look deeper than you have, and you will find that you have been deluded. This is not the way for human beings to act. Somebody has misled you dreadfully. Let me explain—"

"Blasphemy," the leader of the females said, and put her spear expertly into the chaplain's intestines. The shock of the broad, cold blade pulsed through him and felled him. Jewel Flyte knelt beside him instantly, checking heartbeat and breathing. He was alive.

"Get up," the male leader said. "Displaying and offering yourself to such as we is useless. We are pure in heart."

A male child ran to the door. "Wagners!" he screamed. "Twenty Wagners coming up the stairs!" His father roared at him: "Stand straight and don't mumble!" and slashed out with the butt of his spear, catching him hard in the ribs. The child grinned, but only after the pure-hearted eighteen had run to the stairs.

Then he blasted a whistle down the corridor while the sea-people stared with what attention they could divert from the bleeding chaplain. Six doors popped open at the whistle and men and women emerged from them to launch spears into the backs of the Brownells clustered to defend the stairs. "Thanks, pop!" the boy kept screaming while the pure-hearted Wagners swarmed over the remnants of the pure-hearted Brownells; at last his screaming bothered one of the Wagners and the boy was himself speared.

Jewel Flyte said: "I've had enough of this. Captain, please pick the chaplain up and come along."

"They'll kill us."

"You'll have the chaplain," said Mrs. Graves. "One moment." She darted into a bedroom and came back hefting the spiked knobkerry.

"Well, perhaps," the girl said. She began undoing the long row of buttons down the front of her coveralls and shrugged out of the garment, then unfastened and stepped out of her underwear. With the clothes over her arm she walked into the corridor and to the stairs, the stupefied captain and inspector following.

To the pure-hearted Merdekans she was not Phryne winning her case; she was Evil incarnate. They screamed, broke, and ran wildly, dropping their weapons. That a human being could do such a thing was beyond their comprehension; Merdeka alone knew what kind of monster this was that drew them strangely and horribly, in violation of all sanity. They ran as she had hoped they would; the other side of the coin was spearing even more swift and thorough than would have been accorded to her fully clothed. But they ran, gibbering with fright and covering their eyes, into apartments and corners of the corridor, their backs turned on the awful thing.

The sea-people picked their way over the shambles at the stairway and went unopposed down the stairs and to the dock. It was a troublesome piece of work for Salter to pass the chaplain down to Mrs. Graves in the boat, but in ten minutes they had cast off, rowed out a little, and set sail to catch the land breeze generated by the differential twilight cooling of water and brick. After playing her part in stepping the mast, Jewel Flyte dressed.

"It won't always be that easy," she said when the last button was fastened. Mrs. Graves had been thinking the same thing, but had not said it to avoid the appearance of envying that superb young body.

Salter was checking the chaplain as well as he knew how. "I think he'll be all right," she said. "Surgical repair and a long rest. He hasn't lost much blood. This is a strange story we'll have to tell the Ship's Council."

Mrs. Graves said: "They've no choice. We've lost our net and the land is there waiting for us. A few maniacs oppose us—what of it?"

Again a huge fish lazily surfaced; Salter regarded it thoughtfully. He said: "They'll propose scavenging bronze ashore and fashioning another net and going on just as if nothing had happened. And really, we could do that, you know."

Jewel Flyte said: "No. Not forever. This time it was the net, at the end of harvest. What if it were three masts in midwinter, in mid-Atlantic?"

"Or," said the captain, "the rudder—anytime. Anywhere. But can you imagine telling the Council they've got to walk off the ship onto land, take up quarters in those brick cabins, change *everything*? And fight maniacs, and learn to *farm*?"

"There must be a way," said Jewel Flyte. "Just as Merdeka, whatever it was, was a way. There were too many people, and Merdeka was the answer to too many people. There's always an answer. Man is a land mammal in spite of brief excursions at sea. We are seed stock put aside, waiting for the land to be cleared so we could return. Just as these offshore fish are waiting very patiently for us to stop harvesting twice a year so they can return to deep water and multiply. What's the way, captain?"

He thought hard. "We could," he said slowly, "begin by simply sailing in close and fishing the offshore waters for big stuff. Then tie up and build a sort of bridge from the ship to the shore. We'd continue to live aboard the ship but we'd go out during daylight to try farming."

"It sounds right."

"And keep improving the bridge, making it more and more solid, until before they notice it it's really a solid part of the ship and a solid part of the shore. It might take . . . mmm . . . ten years?"

"Time enough for the old shellbacks to make up their minds," Mrs. Graves unexpectedly snorted.

"And we'd relax the one-to-one reproduction rule, and some young adults will simply be crowded over the bridge to live on the land—" His face suddenly fell. "And then the whole damned farce starts all over again, I suppose. I pointed out that it takes thirty-two generations bearing one child apiece to run a population of two billion into zero. Well, I should have mentioned that it takes thirty-two generations bearing four children apiece to run a population of two into two billion. Oh, what's the use, Jewel?"

She chuckled. "There was an answer last time," she said. "There will be an answer the next time."

"It won't be the same answer as Merdeka," he vowed. "We grew up a little at sea. This time we can do it with brains and not with nightmares and superstition."

"I don't know," she said. "Our ship will be the first, and then the other ships will have their accidents one by one and come and tie up and build their bridges hating every minute of it for the first two generations and then not hating it, just living it . . . and who will be the greatest man who ever lived?"

The captain looked horrified.

"Yes, you! Salter, the Builder of the Bridge; Tommy, do you know an old word for 'bridge-builder'? *Pontifex.*"

Oh, my God!" Tommy Salter said in despair.

A flicker of consciousness was passing through the wounded chaplain; he heard the words and was pleased that somebody aboard was praying.

Roommates

Americans, perhaps more than any other group in the world, have an inherent belief in the ability of technology to overcome social and economic problems. Thus, it comes as no surprise to hear or read about programs aimed at producing food by non-conventional means. Just such a program currently being brought into production involves the utilization of yeast to convert petroleum derivatives into protein. Most innovations such as this have inevitably encountered resistance from consumers because of price, taste, or suitability for cooking in traditional dishes. Yet, if there were no alternatives...

Some readers will recognize this story as the basis of the popular film "Soylent Green."

by Harry Harrison

Roommates

SUMMER

The August sun struck in through the open window and burned on Andrew Rusch's bare legs until discomfort dragged him awake from the depths of heavy sleep. Only slowly did he become aware of the heat and the damp and gritty sheet beneath his body. He rubbed at his gummed-shut eyelids, then lay there, staring up at the cracked and stained plaster of the ceiling, only half awake and experiencing a feeling of dislocation, not knowing in those first waking moments just where he was, although he had lived in this room for over seven years. He yawned and the odd sensation slipped away while he groped for the watch that he always put on the chair next to the bed, then he yawned again as he blinked at the hands mistily seen behind the scratched crystal. Seven . . . seven o'clock in the morning, and there was a little number 9 in the middle of the square window. Monday the ninth of August, 1999—and hot as a furnace already, with the city still imbedded in the heat wave that had baked and suffocated New York for the past ten days. Andy scratched at a trickle of perspiration on his side, then moved his legs out of the patch of sunlight and bunched the pillow up under his neck. From the other side of the thin partition that divided the room in half there came a clanking whir that quickly rose to a high-pitched drone.

"Morning . . . " he shouted over the sound, then began coughing. Still coughing he reluctantly stood and crossed the room to
draw a glass of water from the wall tank; it came out in a thin,
brownish trickle. He swallowed it, then rapped the dial on the
tank with his knuckles and the needle bobbed up and down close
to the *Empty* mark. It needed filling, he would have to see to that
before he signed in at four o'clock at the precinct. The day had
begun.

A full-length mirror with a crack running down it was fixed to
the front of the hulking wardrobe and he poked his face close to
it, rubbing at his bristly jaw. He would have to shave before he
went in. No one should ever look at himself in the morning, naked
and revealed, he decided with distaste, frowning at the dead white
of his skin and the slight bow to his legs that was usually
concealed by his pants. And how did he manage to have ribs that
stuck out like those of a starved horse, as well as a growing
potbelly—both at the same time? He kneaded the soft flesh and
thought that it must be the starchy diet, that and sitting around
on his chunk most of the time. But at least the fat wasn't showing
on his face. His forehead was a little higher each year, but wasn't
too obvious as long as his hair was cropped short. You have just
turned 30, he thought to himself, and the wrinkles are already
starting around your eyes. And your nose is too big—wasn't it
Uncle Brian who always said that was because there was Welsh
blood in the family? And your canine teeth are a little too obvious
so when you smile you look a bit like a hyena. You're a handsome
devil, Andy Rusch, and it's a wonder a girl like Shirl will even
look at you, much less kiss you. He scowled at himself, then went
to look for a handkerchief to blow his impressive Welsh nose.

There was just a single pair of clean undershorts in the drawer
and he pulled them on; that was another thing he had to remember today, to get some washing done. The squealing whine was
still coming from the other side of the partition as he pushed
through the connecting door.

"You're going to give yourself a coronary, Sol," he told the
gray-bearded man who was perched on the wheelless bicycle,
pedaling so industriously that perspiration ran down his chest and
soaked into the bath towel that he wore tied around his waist.

"Never a coronary," Solomon Kahn gasped out, pumping
steadily. "I been doing this every day for so long that my ticker

would miss it if I stopped. And no cholesterol in my arteries either since a regular flushing with alcohol takes care of that. And no lung cancer since I couldn't afford to smoke even if I wanted to, which I don't. And at the age of 75 no prostatitis because. . . . "

"Sol, please—spare me the horrible details on an empty stomach. Do you have an ice cube to spare?"

"Take two—it's a hot day. And don't leave the door open too long."

Andy opened the small refrigerator that squatted against the wall and quickly took out the plastic container of margarine, then squeezed two ice cubes from the tray into a glass and slammed the door. He filled the glass with water from the wall tank and put it on the table next to the margarine. "Have you eaten yet?" he asked.

"I'll join you, these things should be charged by now."

Sol stopped pedaling and the whine died away to a moan, then vanished. He disconnected the wires from the electrical generator that was geared to the rear axle of the bike, and carefully coiled them up next to the four black automobile storage batteries that were racked on top of the refrigerator. Then, after wiping his hands on his soiled towel sarong, he pulled out one of the bucket seats, salvaged from an ancient 1975 Ford, and sat down across the table from Andy.

"I heard the six o'clock news," he said. "The Eldsters are organizing another protest march today on relief headquarters. *That's* where you'll see coronaries!"

"I won't, thank God, I'm not on until four and Union Square isn't in our precinct." He opened the breadbox and took out one of the six-inch-square red crackers, then pushed the box over to Sol. He spread margarine thinly on it and took a bite, wrinkling his nose as he chewed. "I think this margarine has turned."

"How can you tell?" Sol grunted, biting into one of the dry crackers. "Anything made from motor oil and whale blubber is turned to begin with."

"Now you begin to sound like a naturist," Andy said, washing his cracker down with cold water. "There's hardly any flavor at all to the fats made from petrochemicals and you know there aren't any whales left so they can't use blubber—it's just good chlorella oil."

"Whales, plankton, herring oil, it's all the same. Tastes fishy.

I'll take mine dry so I don't grow no fins." There was a sudden staccato rapping on the door and he groaned. "Not yet eight o'clock and already they are after you."

"It could be anything," Andy said, starting for the door.

"It could be but it's not, that's the callboy's knock and you know it as well as I do and I bet you dollars to doughnuts that's just who it is. See?" He nodded with gloomy satisfaction when Andy unlocked the door and they saw the skinny, bare-legged messenger standing in the dark hall.

"What do you want, Woody?" Andy asked.

"I don' wan' no-fin," Wood lisped over his bare gums. Though he was in his early twenties he didn't have a tooth in his head. "Lieutenan' says bring, I bring." He handed Andy the message board with his name written on the outside.

Andy turned toward the light and opened it, reading the lieutenant's spiky scrawl on the slate, then took the chalk and scribbled his initials after it and returned it to the messenger. He closed the door behind him and went back to finish his breakfast, frowning in thought.

"Don't look at me that way," Sol said, "I didn't send the message. Am I wrong in guessing it's not the most pleasant of news?"

"It's the Eldsters, they're jamming the Square already and the precinct needs reinforcements."

"But why you? This sounds like a job for the harness bulls."

"Harness bulls! Where do you get that medieval slang? Of course they need patrolmen for the crowd, but there have to be detectives there to spot known agitators, pickpockets, purse-grabbers and the rest. It'll be murder in the park today. I have to check in by nine, so I have enough time to bring up some water first."

Andy dressed slowly in slacks and a loose sport shirt, then put a pan of water on the windowsill to warm in the sun. He took the two five-gallon plastic jerry cans, and when he went out Sol looked up from the TV set, glancing over the top of his old-fashioned glasses.

"When you bring back the water I'll fix you a drink—or do you think it is too early?"

"Not the way I feel today, it's not."

The hall was ink black once the door had closed behind him

and he felt his way carefully along the wall to the stairs, cursing and almost falling when he stumbled over a heap of refuse someone had thrown there. Two flights down a window had been knocked through the wall and enough light came in to show him the way down the last two flights to the street. After the damp hallway the heat of Twenty-fifth Street hit him in a musty wave, a stifling miasma compounded of decay, dirt and unwashed humanity. He had to make his way through the women who already filled the steps of the building, walking carefully so that he didn't step on the children who were playing below. The sidewalk was still in shadow but so jammed with people that he walked in the street, well away from the curb to avoid the rubbish and litter banked high there. Days of heat had softened the tar so that it gave underfoot, then clutched at the soles of his shoes. There was the usual line leading to the columnar red water point on the corner of Seventh Avenue, but it broke up with angry shouts and some waved fists just as he reached it. Still muttering, the crowd dispersed and Andy saw that the duty patrolman was locking the steel door.

"What's going on?" Andy asked. "I thought this point was open until noon?"

The policeman turned, his hand automatically staying close to his gun until he recognized the detective from his own precinct. He tilted back his uniform cap and wiped the sweat from his forehead with the back of his hand.

"Just had the orders from the sergeant, all points closed for 24 hours. The reservoir level is low because of the drought, they gotta save water."

"That's a hell of a note," Andy said, looking at the key still in the lock. "I'm going on duty now and this means I'm not going to be drinking for a couple of days. . . . "

After a careful look around, the policeman unlocked the door and took one of the jerry cans from Andy. "One of these ought to hold you." He held it under the faucet while it filled, then lowered his voice. "Don't let it out, but the word is that there was another dynamiting job on the aqueduct upstate."

"Those farmers again?"

"It must be. I was on guard duty up there before I came to this precinct and it's rough, they just as soon blow you up with the aqueduct at the same time. Claim the city's stealing their water."

"They've got enough," Andy said, taking the full container. "More than they need. And there are 35 million people here in the city who get damn thirsty."

"Who's arguing?" the cop asked, slamming the door shut again and locking it tight.

Andy pushed his way back through the crowd around the steps and went through to the backyard first. All of the toilets were in use and he had to wait, and when he finally got into one of the cubicles he took the jerry cans with him; one of the kids playing in the pile of rubbish against the fence would be sure to steal them if he left them unguarded.

When he had climbed the dark flights once more and opened the door to the room he heard the clear sound of ice cubes rattling against glass.

"That's Beethoven's Fifth Symphony that you're playing," he said, dropping the containers and falling into a chair.

"It's my favorite tune," Sol said, taking two chilled glasses from the refrigerator and, with the solemnity of a religious ritual, dropped a tiny pearl onion into each. He passed one to Andy, who sipped carefully at the chilled liquid.

"It's when I taste one of these. Sol, that I almost believe you're not crazy after all. Why do they call them Gibsons?"

"A secret lost behind the mists of time. Why is a Stinger a Stinger or a Pink Lady a Pink Lady?"

"I don't know—why? I never tasted any of them."

"I don't know either, but that's the name. Like those green things they serve in the knockjoints, Panamas. Doesn't mean anything, just a name."

"Thanks," Andy said, draining his glass. "The day looks better already."

He went into his room and took his gun and holster from the drawer and clipped it inside the waistband of his pants. His shield was on his key ring where he always kept it and he slipped his notepad in on top of it, then hesitated a moment. It was going to be a long and rough day and anything might happen. He dug his nippers out from under his shirts, then the soft plastic tube filled with shot. It might be needed in the crowd, safer than a gun with all those old people milling about. Not only that, but with the new austerity regulations you had to have a damn good reason for using up any ammunition. He washed as well as he could with the pint of water that had been warming in the sun on the windowsill, then scrubbed his face with the small shard of gray and gritty soap until his whiskers softened a bit. His razor blade was beginning to show obvious nicks along both edges and, as he honed it against the inside of his drinking glass, he thought that it was time to think about getting a new one. Maybe in the fall.

Sol was watering his window box when Andy came out, carefully irrigating the rose of herbs and tiny onions. "Don't take any wooden nickels," he said without looking up from his work. Sol had a million of them, all old. What in the world was a wooden nickel?

The sun was higher now and the heat was mounting in the sealed tar and concrete valley of the street. The band of shade was smaller and the steps were so packed with humanity that he couldn't leave the doorway. He carefully pushed by a tiny, runny-nosed girl dressed only in ragged gray underwear and descended a step. The gaunt women moved aside reluctantly, ignoring him, but the men stared at him with a cold look of hatred stamped across their features that gave them a strangely alike appearance, as though they were all members of the same angry family. Andy threaded his way through the last of them and when he reached the sidewalk he had to step over the outstretched leg of an old man who sprawled there. He looked dead, not asleep, and he might be for all that anyone cared. His foot was bare and filthy and a string tied about his ankle led to a naked baby that was sitting vacantly on the sidewalk chewing on a bent plastic dish. The baby was as dirty as the man and the string was tied about its chest under the pipestem arms because its stomach was swollen and heavy. Was the old man dead? Not that it mattered, the only work he had to do in the world was to act as an anchor for the baby and he could do that job just as well alive or dead.

Out of the room now, well away and unable to talk to Sol until he returned, he realized that once again he had not managed to mention Shirl. It would have been a simple enough thing to do, but he kept forgetting it, avoiding it. Sol was always talking about how horny he always was and how often he used to get laid when he was in the army. He would understand.

Th ey were roommates, that was all. There was nothing else between them. Friends, sure. But bringing a girl in to live wouldn't change that.

So why hadn't he told him?

FALL

"Everybody says this is the coldest October ever, I never seen a colder one. And the rain too, never hard enough to fill the reservoir or anything, but just enough to make you wet so you feel colder. Ain't that right?"

Shirl nodded, hardly listening to the words, but aware by the rising intonation of the woman's voice that a question had been asked. The line moved forward and she shuffled a few steps behind the woman who had been speaking—a shapeless bundle of heavy clothing covered with a torn plastic raincoat, with a cord tied about her middle so that she resembled a lumpy sack. Not that I look much better, Shirl thought, tugging the fold of blanket farther over her head to keep out the persistent drizzle. It wouldn't be much longer now, there were only a few dozen people ahead, but it had taken a lot more time than she thought it would; it was almost dark. A light came on over the tank car, glinting off its black sides and lighting up the slowly falling curtain of rain. The line moved again and the woman ahead of Shirl waddled forward, pulling the child after her, a bundle as wrapped and shapeless as its mother, its face hidden by a knotted scarf, that produced an almost constant whimpering.

"Stop that," the woman said. She turned to Shirl, her puffy face a red lumpiness around the dark opening of her almost toothless mouth. "He's crying because he's been to see the doc, thinks he's sick but it's only the kwash." She held up the child's swollen, ballooning hand. "You can tell when they swell up and get the black spots on the knees. Had to sit two weeks in the Bellevue clinic to see a doc who told me what I knew already. But that's the only way you get him to sign the slip. Got a peanut-butter ration that way. My old man loves the stuff. You live on my block, don't you? I think I seen you there?"

"Twenty-sixth Street," Shirl said, taking the cap off the jerry can and putting it into her coat pocket. She felt chilled through and was sure she was catching a cold.

"That's right, I knew it was you. Stick around and wait for me, we'll walk back together. It's getting late and plenty of punks would like to grab the water, they can always sell it. Mrs. Ramirez in my building, she's a spic but she's all right, you know, her family been in the building since the World War Two, she got a black eye so swole up she can't see through it and two teeth knocked out. Some punk got her with a club and took her water away."

"Yes, I'll wait for you, that's a good idea," Shirl said, suddenly feeling very alone.

"Cards," the policeman said and she handed him the three Welfare cards, hers, Andy's and Sol's. He held them to the light, then handed them back to her. "Six quarts," he called out to the valve man.

"That's not right," Shirl said.

"Reduced ration today, lady, keep moving, there's a lot of people waiting."

She held out the jerry can and the valve man slipped the end of a large funnel into it and ran in the water. "Next," he called out.

The jerry can gurgled when she walked and was tragically light. She went and stood near the policeman until the woman came up, pulling the child with one hand and in the other carrying a five-gallon kerosene can that seemed almost full. She must have a big family.

"Let's go," the woman said and the child trailed, mewling faintly, at the end of her arm.

As they left the Twelfth Avenue railroad siding it grew darker, the rain soaking up all the failing light. The buildings here were mostly old warehouses and factories with blank solid walls concealing the tenants hidden away inside, the sidewalks wet and empty. The nearest streetlight was a block away. "My husband will give me hell coming home this late," the woman said as they turned the corner. Two figures blocked the sidewalk in front of them.

"Let's have the water," the nearest one said, and the distant light reflected from the knife he held before him.

"No, don't! Please don't!" the woman begged and swung her can of water out behind her, away from them. Shirl huddled against the wall and saw, when they walked forward, that they were just young boys, teen-agers. But they still had a knife.

"The water!" the first one said, jabbing his knife at the woman.

"Take it," she screeched, swinging the can like a weight on the end of her arm. Before the boy could dodge it caught him full in the side of the head, knocking him howling to the ground, the knife flying from his fingers. "You want some too?" she shouted, advancing on the second boy. He was unarmed.

"No, I don't want no trouble," he begged, pulling at the first one's arm, then retreating when she approached. When she bent to pick up the fallen knife, he managed to drag the other boy to his feet and half carry him around the corner. It had only taken a few seconds and all the time Shirl had stood with her back to the wall, trembling with fear.

"They got some surprise," the woman crowed, holding the worn carving knife up to admire it. "I can use this better than they can. Just punks, kids." She was excited and happy. During the entire time she had never released her grip on the child's hand; it was sobbing louder.

There was no more trouble and the woman went with Shirl as far as her door. "Thank you very much," Shirl said. "I don't know what I would have done. . . . "

"That's no trouble," the woman beamed. "You saw what I did to him—and who got the knife now!" She stamped away, hauling the heavy can in one hand, the child in the other. Shirl went in.

"Where have you been?" Andy asked when she pushed open the door. "I was beginning to wonder what had happened to you." It was warm in the room, with a faint odor of fishy smoke, and he and Sol were sitting at the table with drinks in their hands.

"It was the water, the line must have been a block long. They only gave me six quarts, the ration has been cut again." She saw his black look and decided not to tell him about the trouble on the way back. He would be twice as angry then and she didn't want his meal to be spoiled.

"That's really wonderful," Andy said sarcastically. "The ration was already too small—so now they lower it even more. Better get out of those wet things, Shirl, and Sol will pour you a Gibson. His homemade vermouth has ripened and I bought some vodka."

"Drink up," Sol said, handing her the chilled glass. "I made some soup with that ener-G junk, it's the only way it's edible, and it should be just about ready. We'll have that for the first course, before—" He finished the sentence by jerking his head in the direction of the refrigerator.

"What's up?" Andy asked. "A secret?"

"No secret," Shirl said, opening the refrigerator, "just a surprise. I got these today in the market, one for each of us." She took out a plate with three small soylent burgers on it. "They're the new ones, they had them on TV, with the smoky-barbecue flavor."

"They must have cost a fortune," Andy said. "We won't eat for the rest of the month."

"They're not as expensive as all that. Anyway, it was my own money, not the budget money, I used."

"It doesn't make any difference, money is money. We could probably live for a week on what these things cost."

"Soup's on," Sol said, sliding the plates onto the table. Shirl had a lump in her throat so she couldn't say anything; she sat and looked at her plate and tried not to cry.

"I'm sorry," Andy said. "But you know how prices are going up—we have to look ahead. City income tax is higher, 80 percent now, because of the raised Welfare payment, so it's going to be rough going this winter. Don't think I don't appreciate it. . . . "

"If you do, so why don't you shut up right there and eat your soup?" Sol said.

"Keep out of this, Sol," Andy said.

"I'll keep out of it when you keep the fight out of my room. Now come on, a nice meal like this, it shouldn't be spoiled."

Andy started to answer him, then changed his mind. He reached over and took Shirl's hand. "It is going to be a good dinner," he said. "Let's all enjoy it."

"Not that good," Sol said, puckering his mouth over a spoonful of soup. "Wait until you try this stuff. But the burgers will take the taste out of our mouths."

There was silence after that while they spooned up the soup, until Sol started on one of his army stories about New Orleans and it was so impossible they had to laugh, and after that things were better. Sol shared out the rest of the Gibsons while Shirl served the burgers.

"If I was drunk enough this would almost taste like meat," Sol announced, chewing happily.

"They are good," Shirl said. Andy nodded agreement. She finished the burger quickly and soaked up the juice with a scrap of weedcracker, then sipped at her drink. The trouble on the way home with the water already seemed far distant. What was it the woman had said was wrong with the child?

"Do you know what 'kwash' is?" she asked.

Andy shrugged. "Some kind of disease, that's all I know. Why do you ask?"

"There was a woman next to me in line for the water, I was talking to her. She had a little boy with her who was sick with this kwash. I don't think she should have had him out in the rain, sick like that. And I was wondering if was catching."

"That you can forget about," Sol said. " 'Kwash' is short for 'kwashiorkor.' If, in the interest of good health, you watched the medical programs like I do, or opened a book, you would know all about it. You can't catch it because it's a deficiency disease like beriberi."

"I never heard of that either," Shirl said.

"There's not so much of that, but there's plenty of kwash. It comes from not eating enough protein. They used to have it only in Africa but now they got it right across the whole U.S. Isn't that great? There's no meat around, lentils and soybeans cost too much, so the mamas stuff the kids with weedcrackers and candy, whatever is cheap. . . . "

The light bulb flickered, then went out. Sol felt his way across the room and found a switch in the maze of wiring on top of the refrigerator. A dim bulb lit up, connected to his batteries. "Needs a charge," he said, "but it can wait until morning. You shouldn't exercise after eating, bad for the circulation and digestion."

"I'm sure glad you're here, doctor," Andy said. "I need some medical advice. I've got this trouble. You see—everything I eat goes to my stomach . . . ."

"Very funny, Mr. Wiseguy. Shirl, I don't see how you put up with this joker."

They all felt better after the meal and they talked for a while, until Sol announced he was turning off the light to save the juice in the batteries. The small bricks of sea coal had burned to ash and the room was growing cold. They said good night and Andy went in first to get his flashlight; their room was even colder than the other.

"I'm going to bed," Shirl said. "I'm not really tired, but it's the only way to keep warm."

Andy flicked the overhead light switch uselessly. "The current is still off and there are some things I have to do. What is it—a week now since we had any electricity in the evening?"

"Let me get into bed and I'll work the flash for you—will that be all right?"

"It'll have to do."

He opened his notepad on top of the dresser, lay one of the reusable forms next to it, then began copying information into the report. With his left hand he kept a slow and regular squeezing on the flashlight that produced steady illumination. The city was quiet tonight with the people driven from the streets by the cold and the rain; the whir of the tiny generator and the occasional squeak of the stylo on plastic sounded unnaturally loud. There was enough light from the flash for Shirl to get undressed by. She shivered when she took off her outer clothes and quickly pulled on heavy winter pajamas, a much-darned pair of socks she used for sleeping in, then put her heavy sweater on top. The sheets were cold and damp, they hadn't been changed since the water shortage, though she did try to air them out as often as she could. Her cheeks were damp, as damp as the sheets were when she put her fingertips up to touch them, and she realized that she was crying. She tried not to sniffle and bother Andy. He was doing his best, wasn't he? Everything that it was possible to do. Yes, it had been a lot different before she came here, an easy life, good food and a warm room, and her own bodyguard, Tab, when she went out. And all she had to do was sleep with him a couple of times a week. She had hated it, even the touch of his hands, but at least it had been quick. Having Andy in bed was different and good and she wished that he were there right now. She shivered again and wished she could stop crying.

WINTER

New York City trembled on the brink of disaster. Every locked warehouse was a nucleus of dissent, surrounded by crowds who were hungry and afraid and searching for someone to blame. Their anger incited them to riot, and the food riots turned to water riots and then to looting, wherever this was possible. The police fought back, only the thinnest of barriers between angry protest and bloody chaos.

At first nightsticks and weighted clubs stopped the trouble, and when this failed gas dispersed the crowds. The tension grew, since the people who fled only reassembled again in a different place. The solid jets of water from the riot trucks stopped them easily when they tried to break into the welfare stations, but there were not enough trucks, nor was there more water to be had once they had pumped dry their tanks. The Health Department had forbid the use of river water: it would have been like spraying poison. The little water that was available was badly needed for the fires that were springing up throughout the city. With the streets blocked in many places the fire-fighting equipment could not get through and the trucks were forced to make long detours. Some of the fires were spreading and by noon all of the equipment had been committed and was in use.

The first gun was fired a few minutes past 12 on the morning of December 21st, by a Welfare Department guard who killed a man who had broken open a window of the Tompkins Square food depot and had tried to climb in. This was the first but not the last shot fired—nor was it the last person to be killed.

Flying wire sealed off some of the trouble areas, but there was only a limited supply of it. When it ran out the copters fluttered helplessly over the surging streets and acted as aerial observation posts for the police, finding the places where reserves were sorely needed. It was a fruitless labor because there were no reserves, everyone was in the front line.

After the first conflict nothing else made a strong impression on Andy. For the rest of the day and most of the night, he along with every other policeman in the city was braving violence and giving violence to restore law and order to a city torn by battle. The only rest he had was after he had fallen victim to his own gas and had managed to make his way to the Department of Hospitals ambulance for treatment. An orderly washed out his eyes and gave him a tablet to counteract the gut-tearing nausea. He lay on one of the stretchers inside, clutching his helmet, bombs and club to his chest, while he recovered. The ambulance driver sat on another stretcher by the door, armed with a .30-caliber carbine, to discourage anyone from too great an interest in the ambulance or its valuable surgical contents. Andy would like to have lain there longer, but the cold mist was rolling through the open doorway, and he began to shiver so hard that his teeth shook together. It was difficult to drag to his feet and climb to the ground, yet once he was moving he felt a little better—and warmer. The attack had been broken up and he moved slowly to join the nearest cluster of blue-coated figures, wrinkling his nose at the foul odor of his clothes.

From this point on, the fatigue never left him and he had memories only of shouting faces, running feet, the sound of shots, screams, the thud of gas grenades, of something unseen that had been thrown at him and hit the back of his hand and raised an immense bruise.

By nightfall it was raining, a cold downpour mixed with sleet, and it was this and exhaustion that drove the people from the streets, not the police. Yet when the crowds were gone the police found that their work was just beginning. Gaping windows and broken doorways had to be guarded until they could be repaired, the injured had to be found and brought in for treatment, while the Fire Department needed aid in halting the countless fires. This went on through the night and at dawn Andy found himself slumped on a bench in the precinct, hearing his name being called off from a list by Lieutenant Grassioli.

"And that's all that can be spared," the lieutenant added. "You men draw rations before you leave and turn in your riot equipment. I want you all back here at eighteen-hundred and I don't want excuses. Our troubles aren't over yet."

Sometime during the night the rain had stopped. The rising sun cast long shadows down the crosstown streets, putting a golden sheen on the wet, black pavement. A burned-out brownstone was still smoking and Andy picked his way through the charred wreckage that littered the street in front of it. On the corner of Seventh Avenue were the crushed wrecks of two pedicabs, already stripped of any usable parts, and a few feet farther on, the huddled body of a man. He might be asleep, but when Andy passed, the upturned face gave violent evidence that the man was dead. He walked on, ignoring it. The Department of Sanitation would be collecting only corpses today.

The first cavemen were coming out of the subway entrance,

blinking at the light. During the summer everyone laughed at the cavemen—the people whom Welfare had assigned to living quarters in the stations of the now-silent subways—but as the cold weather approached, the laughter was replaced by envy. Perhaps it was filthy down there, dusty, dark, but there were always a few electric heaters turned on. They weren't living in luxury, but at least Welfare didn't let them freeze. Andy turned into his own block.

Going up the stairs in his building, he trod heavily on some of the sleepers but was too fatigued to care—or even notice. He had trouble fumbling his key into the lock and Sol heard him and came to open it.

"I just made some soup," Sol said. "You timed it perfectly."

Andy pulled the broken remains of some weedcrackers from his coat pocket and spilled them onto the table.

"Been stealing food?" Sol asked, picking up a piece and nibbling on it. "I thought no grub was being given out for two more days?"

"Police ration."

"Only fair. You can't beat up the citizenry on an empty stomach. I'll throw some of these into the soup, give it some body. I guess you didn't see TV yesterday so you wouldn't know about all the fun and games in Congress. Things are really jumping. . . . "

"Is Shirl awake yet?" Andy asked, shucking out of his coat and dropping heavily into a chair.

Sol was silent a moment, then he said slowly, "She's not here."

Andy yawned. "It's pretty early to go out. Why?"

"Not today, Andy." Sol stirred the soup with his back turned. "She went out yesterday, a couple of hours after you did. She's not back yet—"

"You mean she was out all the time during the riots—and last night too? What did you do?" He sat upright, his bone-weariness forgotten.

"What could I do? Go out and get myself trampled to death like the rest of the old fogies? I bet she's all right, she probably saw all the trouble and decided to stay with friends instead of coming back here."

"What friends? What are you talking about? I have to go find her."

"Sit!" Sol ordered. "What can you do out there? Have some soup and get some sleep, that's the best thing you can do. She'll be okay. I know it," he added reluctantly.

"What do you know, Sol?" Andy took him by the shoulders, half turning him from the stove.

"Don't handle the merchandise!" Sol shouted, pushing the hand away. Then, in a quieter voice: "All I know is she just didn't go out of here for nothing, she had a reason. She had her old coat on, but I could see what looked like a real nifty dress underneath. And nylon stockings. A fortune on her legs. And when she said so long I saw she had lots of makeup on."

"Sol—what are you trying to say?"

"I'm not trying—I'm saying. She was dressed for visiting, not for shopping, like she was on the way out to see someone. Her old man, maybe, she could be visiting him."

"Why should she want to see him?"

"You tell me? You two had a fight, didn't you? Maybe she went away for a while to cool off."

"A fight . . . I guess so." Andy dropped back into the chair, squeezing his forehead with his palms. Had it only been last night? No, the night before last. It seemed 100 years since they had had that stupid argument. But they were bickering so much these days. One more fight shouldn't make any difference. He looked up with sudden fear. "She didn't take her things—anything with her?" he asked.

"Just a little bag," Sol said, and put a steaming bowl on the table in front of Andy. "Eat up. I'll pour one for myself." Then, "She'll be back."

Andy was almost too tired to argue—and what could be said? He spooned the soup automatically, then realized as he tasted it that he was very hungry. He ate with his elbow on the table, his free hand supporting his head.

"You should have heard the speeches in the Senate yesterday," Sol said. "Funniest show on earth. They're trying to push this Emergency Bill through—some emergency, it's only been 100 years in the making—and you should hear them talking all around the little points and not mentioning the big ones." His voice settled into a rich Southern accent. "Faced by dire straits, we propose a survey of all the ee-mense riches of this the greatest ee-luvial basin, the delta, suh, of the mightiest of rivers, the

Mississippi. Dikes and drains, suh, science, suh, and you will have here the richest farmlands in the Western World!" Sol blew on his soup angrily. " 'Dikes' is right—another finger in the dike. They've been over this ground a thousand times before. But does anyone mention out loud the sole and only reason for the Emergency Bill? They do not. After all these years they're too chicken to come right out and tell the truth, so they got it hidden away in one of the little riders tacked onto the bottom."

"What are you talking about?" Andy asked, only half listening, still worrying about Shirl.

"Birth control, that's what. They are finally getting around to legalizing clinics that will be open to anyone—married or not— and making it a law that all mothers *must* be supplied with birth-control information. Boy, are we going to hear some howling when the bluenoses find out about that—and the Pope will really plotz!"

"Not now, Sol, I'm tired. Did Shirl say anything about when she would be back?"

"Just what I told you. . . . " He stopped and listened to the sound of footsteps coming down the hall. They stopped—and there was a light knocking on the door.

Andy was there first, twisting at the knob, tearing the door open.

'Shirl!" he said. "Are you all right?"

"Yes, sure—I'm fine."

He held her to him, tightly, almost cutting off her breath. "With the riots—I didn't know what to think," he said. "I just came in a little while ago myself. Where have you been? What happened?"

"I just wanted to get out for a while, that's all. She wrinkled her nose. "What's that funny smell?"

He stepped away from her, anger welling up through the fatigue. "I caught some of my own puke gas and heaved up. It's hard to get off. What do you mean that you wanted to get out for a while?"

"Let me get my coat off."

Andy followed her into the other room and closed the door behind them. She was taking a pair of high-heeled shoes out of the bag she carried and putting them into the closet. "Well?" he said.

"Just that, it's not complicated. I was feeling trapped in here, with the shortages and the cold and everything, and never seeing you, and I felt bad about the fight we had. Nothing seemed to be going right. So I thought if I dressed up and went to one of the restuarants where I used to go, just have a cup of kofee or something, I might feel better. A morale booster, you know." She looked up at his cold face, then glanced quickly away.

"Then what happened?" he asked.

"I'm not in the witness box, Andy. Why the accusing tone?"

He turned his back and looked out the window. "I'm not accusing you of anything, but—you were out all night. How do you expect me to feel?"

"Well, you know how bad it was yesterday, I was afraid to come back. I was up at Curley's—"

"The meateasy?"

"Yes, but if you don't eat anything it's not expensive. It's just the food that costs. I met some people I knew and we talked, they were going to a party and invited me and I went along. We were watching the news about the riots on TV and no one wanted to go out, so the party just went on and on." She paused. "That's all."

"All?" An angry question, a dark suspicion.

"That's all," she said, and her voice was now as cold as his.

She turned her back to him and began to pull off her dress, and their words lay like a cold barrier between them. Andy dropped onto the bed and turned his back on her as well so that they were like strangers, even in the tiny room.

SPRING

The funeral drew them together as nothing else had during the cold depths of the winter. It was a raw day, gusting wind and rain, but there was still a feeling that winter was on the way out. But it had been too long a winter for Sol and his cough had turned into a cold, the cold into pneumonia, and what can an old man do in a cold room without drugs in a winter that does not seem to end? Die, that was all, so he had died. They had forgotten their differences during his illness and Shirl had nursed him as best she could, but careful nursing does not cure pneumonia. The funeral had been as brief and cold as the day and in the early darkness they went to the room. They had not been back a half an hour before there was a quick rapping on the door. Shirl gasped.

"The callboy. They can't. You don't have to work today."

"Don't worry. Even Grassy wouldn't go back on his word about a thing like this. And besides, that's not the callboy's knock."

"Maybe a friend of Sol's who couldn't get to the funeral."

She went to unlock the door and had to blink into the darkness of the hall for a moment before she recognized the man standing there.

"Tab! It is you, isn't it? Come in, don't stand there. Andy, I told you about Tab my bodyguard. . . . "

"Afternoon, Miss Shirl," Tab said stolidly, staying in the hall. "I'm sorry, but this is no social call. I'm on the job now."

"What is it?" Andy asked, walking over next to Shirl.

"You have to realize I take the work that is offered to me," Tab said. He was unsmiling and gloomy. "I've been in the bodyguard pool since September, just the odd jobs, no regular assignment, we take whatever work we can get. A man turns down a job he goes right back to the end of the list. I have a family to feed. . . . "

"What are you trying to say?" Andy asked. He was aware that someone was standing in the darkness behind Tab and he could tell by the shuffle of feet that there were others out of sight down the hall.

"Don't take no stuff," the man in back of Tab said in an unpleasant nasal voice. He stayed behind the bodyguard where he could not be seen. "I got the law on my side. I paid you. Show him the order!"

"I think I understand now," Andy said. "Get away from the door, Shirl. Come inside, Tab, so we can talk to you."

Tab started forward and the man in the hall tried to follow him. "You don't go in there without me—" he shrilled. His voice was cut off as Andy slammed the door in his face.

"I wish you hadn't done that," Tab said. He was wearing his spike-studded iron knucks, his fist clenched tight around them.

"Relax," Andy said. "I just wanted to talk to you alone first, find out what was going on. He has a squat-order, doesn't he?"

Tab nodded, looking unhappily down at the floor.

"What on earth are you two talking about?" Shirl asked, worriedly glancing back and forth at their set expressions.

Andy didn't answer and Tab turned to her. "A squat-order is issued by the court to anyone who can prove they are really in need of a place to live. They only give so many out, and usually just to people with big families that have had to get out of some other place. With a squat-order you can look around and find a vacant apartment or room or anything like that, and the order is a sort of search warrant. There can be trouble, people don't want to have strangers walking in on them, that kind of thing, so anyone with a squat-order takes along a bodyguard. That's where I come in, the party out there in the hall, name of Belicher, hired me."

"But what are you doing here?" Shirl asked, still not understanding.

"Because Belicher is a ghoul, that's why," Andy said bitterly. "He hangs around the morgue looking for bodies."

"That's one way of saying it," Tab answered, holding on to his temper. "He's also a guy with a wife and kids and no place to live, that's another way of looking at it."

There was a sudden hammering on the door and Belicher's complaining voice could be heard outside. Shirl finally realized the significance of Tab's presence, and she gasped. "You're here because you're helping them," she said. "They found out that Sol is dead and they want this room."

Tab could only nod mutely.

"There's still a way out," Andy said. "If we had one of the men here from my precinct, living in here, then these people couldn't get in."

The knocking was louder and Tab took a half step backward toward the door. "If there was somebody here now, that would be okay, but Belicher could probably take the thing to the squat court and get occupancy anyway because he has a family. I'll do what I can to help you—but Belicher, he's still my employer."

"Don't open that door," Andy said sharply. "Not until we have this straightened out."

"I have to—what else can I do?" He straightened up and closed his fist with the knucks on it. "Don't try to stop me, Andy. You're a policeman, you know the law about this."

"Tab, must you?" Shirl asked in a low voice.

He turned to her, eyes filled with unhappiness. "We were good friends once, Shirl, and that's the way I'm going to remember it.

But you're not going to think much of me after this because I have
to do my job. I have to let them in."

"Go ahead—open the damn door," Andy said bitterly, turning
his back and walking over to the window.

The Belichers swarmed in. Mr. Belicher was thin, with a
strangely shaped head, almost no chin and just enough intelligence to sign his name to the Welfare application. Mrs. Belicher
was the support of the family; from the flabby fat over her body
came the children, all seven of them, to swell the Relief allotment
on which they survived. Number eight was pushing an extra bulge
out of the dough of her flesh; it was really number 11 since three
of the younger Belichers had perished through indifference or
accident. The largest girl, she must have been all of 12, was
carrying the sore-covered infant which stank abominably and
cried continuously. The other children shouted at each other now,
released from the silence and tension of the dark hall.

"Oh, looka the nice fridge," Mrs. Belicher said, waddling over
and opening the door.

"Don't touch that," Andy said, and Belicher pulled him by the
arm.

"I like this room—it's not big, you know, but nice. What's in
here?" He started toward the open door in the partition.

"That's my room," Andy said, slamming it shut in his face.
"Just keep out of there."

"No need to act like that," Belicher said, sidling away quickly
like a dog that has been kicked too often. "I got my rights. The
law says I can look wherever I want with a squat-order." He
moved farther away as Andy took a step toward him. "Not that
I'm doubting your word, mister, I believe you. This room here is
fine, got a good table, chairs, bed. . . . "

"Those things belong to me. This is an empty room, and a small
one at that. It's not big enough for you and all your family."

"It's big enough, all right. We lived in smaller. . . . "

"Andy—stop them! Look—" Shirl's unhappy cry spun Andy
around and he saw that two of the boys had found the packets of
herbs that Sol had grown so carefully in his window box, and
were tearing them open, thinking that it was food of some kind.

"Put these things down," he shouted, but before he could reach
them they had tasted the herbs, then spat them out.

"Burn my mouth!" the bigger boy screamed and sprayed the contents of the packet on the floor. The other boy bounced up and down with excitement and began to do the same thing with the rest of the herbs. They twisted away from Andy and before he could stop them the packets were empty.

As soon as Andy turned away, the younger boy, still excited, climbed on the table—his mud-stained foot wrappings leaving filthy smears—and turned up the TV. Blaring music crashed over the screams of the children and the ineffectual calls of their mother. Tab pulled Belicher away as he opened the wardrobe to see what was inside.

"Get these kids out of here," Andy said, white-faced with rage.

"I got a squat-order, I got rights," Belicher shouted, backing away and waving an imprinted square of plastic.

"I don't care what rights you have," Andy told him, opening the hall door. "We'll talk about that when these brats are outside."

Tab settled it by grabbing the nearest child by the scruff of the neck and pushing it out through the door. "Mr. Rusch is right," he said. "The kids can wait outside while we settle this."

Mrs. Belicher sat down heavily on the bed and closed her eyes, as though all this had nothing to do with her. Mr. Belicher retreated against the wall saying something that no one heard or bothered to listen to. There were some shrill cries and angry sobbing from the hall as the last child was expelled.

Andy looked around and realized that Shirl had gone into their room; he heard the key turn in the lock. "I suppose this is it?" he said, looking steadily at Tab.

The bodyguard shrugged helplessly. "I'm sorry, Andy, honest to God I am. What else can I do? It's the law, and if they want to stay here you can't get them out."

"It's the law, it's the law," Belicher echoed tonelessly.

There was nothing Andy could do with his clenched fists and he had to force himself to open them. "Help me carry these things into the other room, will you, Tab?"

"Sure," Tab said, and took the other end of the table. "Try and explain to Shirl about my part in this, will you? I don't think she understands that it's just a job I have to do."

Their footsteps crackled on the dried herbs and seeds that littered the floor and Andy did not answer him.

Part IV

Population: Impact on the Environment and Resources

Some people may be shocked to hear that in New York it has, on occasion, rained sulphuric acid, or that by the year 2000 (at current rates of consumption) many economically vital natural resources will be depleted. We probably tend not to view such unhappily factual trends as being related to population problems, but indeed they are. One of the most critical implications of rapid population growth derives from the impact of too many people upon the earth's environment. This impact is essentially two-fold: (1) the effects of increasing demands upon resources; and (2) the effects of a larger and larger population upon environmental quality.

The tremendous increase in population size has obviously placed a heavy burden upon the earth's ability to provide resources for food, industry, transportation and other economic activities. Between 1850 and 1970, for example, world consumption of iron ore rose from about 50 million tons annually to almost 600 million tons. This twelve-fold increase in the use of iron ore, compared to an increase in population size by about four times over the same period, points to another factor in addition to population growth which contributed to the meteoric rise in rates of resource utilization: not only did the size of the world's population grow, but the per capita consumption rate likewise increased dramatically. Thus, we have *compounded* the direct implications of population growth with the indirect impact of rising individual consumption; there are many more people and each new person consumes on the average more resources than his predecessor.

The combined impact of rising population and consumption results in an ever-increasing rate of resource utilization and, therefore, we are being forced closer and closer to the limits of our reserves of many important minerals. There are too many unknowns and variables involved to forecast with any accuracy just how long the earth's resources will hold out—economic conditions, exploration for new deposits, advances in manufacturing technology, substitution of one resource for another—all are effectively unpredictable; yet, we can agree that at some point these resources are finite and will be exhausted. Again, how much faith should we place upon science and technology to bail us out of the resource dilemma? The answer to that question must remain subjective and individual, but clearly the crunch is coming.

Beyond the question of resource consumption is that of who is doing the consuming. There is in the contemporary world an incredible dichotomy between the advanced countries on the one hand, which use massive quantities of raw materials, and the underdeveloped areas on the other, which utilize very little. The United States alone, for instance, with only about five percent of the world's population, consumes approximately a half of the natural gas produced, a third of the petroleum and aluminum, and a fifth of steel production. How long the developing countries will tolerate such a lop-sided situation remains to be seen, but such events as the oil crisis of 1973 and the formation of producer cartels in most resource fields indicates a rising discontent on the part of the disadvantaged and an increasing desire to participate in the benefits of an advanced economy.

Perhaps more evident to most people is the other impact of population growth upon the ecosystem: the deterioration of environmental quality. Such direct hazards as air, water, and noise pollution, and the introduction of harmful substances into the ecosystem as by-products of industry and farming, as well as less tangible, aesthetic factors are well known symptoms of the decay in our natural surroundings which we have allowed to proceed virtually unchecked. Population growth is related directly to many of these problems. More people equals more automobiles, a greater demand on sewer and waste treatment facilities, an increasing need for food which means using more fertilizer, pesticides, and herbicides to boost yields (substances which eventually find their way into the ecosystem), and so on. Just to cite one concrete example of how population growth impeded improvement in environmental quality, Paul Ehrlich noted that despite advances in air pollution controls in Los Angeles (with its famous "smog"), the tremendous increase in the number of people in the Los Angeles metropolitan area cancelled out per capita gains; even with less-polluting cars, a huge increase in the number of automobiles keeps pollution at high levels.

It is, unfortunately, wishful thinking to consign the most damaging aspects of pollution to the future. In 1952, an estimated 4,000 persons died during an air pollution crisis in London. Even a cursory glance at newspapers and television will reveal such current stories as lead poisoning in Newark, the contamination of dairy cattle in Michigan by a powerful toxic substance, mercury poisoning and related birth defects in Japan, a company in Virginia indicted for allowing a harmful chemical into a river which served as a commercial fishery, the list could go on and on. The solutions to problems such as these are complicated by economic and political interrelationships which seemingly inevitably force us to choose between the lesser of two (or more) evils. Thus, to close down a factory because it generates air pollution means a loss of jobs; to substitute a relatively less-polluting fuel may mean increased costs; improvements in sewage treatment facilities could bring about higher taxes. Perhaps in the future we will simply be forced to make more and more of these difficult choices.

SUGGESTED READINGS:

Ehrlich, Paul R., and Ehrlich, Anne H. *Population Resources, Environment: Issues in Human Ecology.* San Francisco: W. H. Freeman, 1970.

Meadows, D. H., (*et al*). *The Limits to Growth.* Washington, D. C.: Potomac Associates, 1972.

Park, Charles F., Jr. *Earthbound: Minerals, Energy, and Man's Future.* San Francisco: Freeman, Cooper and Company, 1975.

by Paul R. Ehrlich

Eco-Catastrophe!

The end of the ocean came late in the summer of 1979, and it came even more rapidly than the biologists had expected. There had been signs for more than a decade, commencing with the discovery in 1968 that DDT slows down photosynthesis in marine plant life. It was announced in a short paper in the technical journal *Science*, but to ecologists it smacked of doomsday. They knew that all life in the sea depends on photosynthesis, the chemical process by which green plants bind the sun's energy and make it available to living things. And they knew that DDT and similar chlorinated hydrocarbons had polluted the entire surface of the earth, including the sea.

But that was only the first of many signs. There had been the final gasp of the whaling industry in 1973, and the end of the Peruvian anchovy fishery in 1975. Indeed, a score of other fisheries had disappeared quietly from overexploitation and various eco-catastrophes by 1977. The term "eco-catastrophe" was coined by a California ecologist in 1969 to describe the most spectacular of man's attacks on the systems which sustain his life. He drew his inspiration from the Santa Barbara offshore oil disaster of that year, and from the news which spread among naturalists that virtually all of the Golden State's seashore bird life was doomed because of chlorinated hydrocarbon interference with its reproduction. Eco-catastrophes in the sea became increasingly common in the early 1970's. Mysterious "blooms" of previously rare microorganisms began to appear in offshore waters. Red tides—killer outbreaks of a minute single-celled plant—returned to the Florida Gulf coast and were sometimes accompanied by tides of other exotic hues.

It was clear by 1975 that the entire ecology of the ocean was changing. A few types of phytoplankton were becoming resistant to chlorinated hydrocarbons and were gaining the upper hand. Changes in the phytoplankton community led inevitably to changes in the community of zooplankton, the tiny animals which eat the phytoplankton. These changes were passed on up the chains of life in the ocean to the herring, plaice, cod, and tuna. As the diversity of life in the ocean diminished, its stability also decreased.

Other changes had taken place by 1975. Most ocean fishes that returned to freshwater to breed, like the salmon, had become extinct, their breeding streams so dammed up and polluted that their powerful homing instinct only resulted in suicide. Many fishes and shellfishes that bred in restricted areas along the coasts followed them as onshore pollution escalated.

By 1977 the annual yield of fish from the sea was down to 30 million metric tons, less than one-half the per capita catch of a decade earlier. This helped malnutrition to escalate sharply in a world where an estimated 50 million people per year were already dying of starvation. The United Nations attempted to get all chlorinated hydrocarbon insecticides banned on a worldwide basis, but the move was defeated by the United States. This opposition was generated primarily by the American petrochemical industry, operating hand in glove with its subsidiary, the United States Department of Agriculture. Together they persuaded the government to oppose the U.N. move—which was not difficult since most Americans believed that Russia and China were more in need of fish products than was the United States. The United Nations also attempted to get fishing nations to adopt strict and enforced catch limits to preserve dwindling stocks. This move was blocked by Russia who, with the most modern electronic equipment, was in the best position to glean what was left in the sea. It was, curiously, on the very day in 1977 when the Soviet Union announced its refusal that another ominous article appeared in

Science. It announced that incident solar radiation had been so reduced by worldwide air pollution that serious effects on the world's vegetation could be expected.

Apparently it was a combination of ecosystem destabilization, sunlight reduction, and a rapid escalation in chlorinated hydrocarbon pollution from massive Thanodrin applications which triggered the ultimate catastrophe. Seventeen huge Soviet-financed Thanodrin plants were operating in underdeveloped countries by 1978. They had been part of a massive Russian "aid offensive" designed to fill the gap caused by the collapse of America's ballyhooed "Green Revolution."

It became apparent in the early '70s that the "Green Revolution" was more talk than substance. Distribution of high yield "miracle" grain seeds had caused temporary local spurts in agricultural production. Simultaneously, excellent weather had produced record harvests. The combination permitted bureaucrats, especially in the United States Department of Agriculture and the Agency for International Development (AID), to reverse their previous pessimism and indulge in an outburst of optimistic propaganda about staving off famine. They raved about the approaching transformation of agriculture in the underdeveloped countries (UDCs). The reason for the propaganda reversal was never made clear. Most historians agree that a combination of utter ignorance of ecology, a desire to justify past errors, and pressure from agro-industry (which was eager to sell pesticides, fertilizers, and farm machinery to the UDCs and agencies helping the UDCs) was behind the campaign. Whatever the motivation, the results were clear. Many concerned people, lacking the expertise to see through the Green Revolution drivel, relaxed. The population-food crisis was "solved."

But reality was not long in showing itself. Local famine persisted in northern India even after good weather brought an end to the ghastly Bihar famine of the mid-'60s. East Pakistan was next, followed by a resurgence of general famine in northern India. Other foci of famine rapidly developed in Indonesia, the Philippines, Malawi, the Congo, Egypt, Colombia, Ecuador, Hondurus, the Dominican Republic, and Mexico.

Everywhere hard realities destroyed the illusion of the Green Revolution. Yields dropped as the progressive farmers who had first accepted the new seeds found that their higher yields brought lower prices—effective demand (hunger plus cash) was not sufficient in poor countries to keep prices up. Less progressive farmers, observing this, refused to make the extra effort required to cultivate the "miracle" grains. Transport systems proved inadequate to bring the necessary fertilizer to the fields where the new and extremely fertilizer-sensitive grains were being grown. The same systems were also inadequate to move produce to markets. Fertilizer plants were not built fast enough, and most of the underdeveloped countries could not scrape together funds to purchase supplies, even on concessional terms. Finally, the inevitable happened, and pests began to reduce yields in even the most carefully cultivated fields. Among the first were the famous "miracle rats" which invaded Philippine "miracle rice" fields early in 1969. They were quickly followed by many insects and viruses, thriving on the relatively pest-susceptible new grains, encouraged by the vast and dense plantings, and rapidly acquiring resistance to the chemicals used against them. As chaos spread until even the most obtuse agriculturists and economists realized that the Green Revolution had turned brown, the Russians stepped in.

In retrospect it seems incredible that the Russians, with the American mistakes known to them, could launch an even more incompetent program of aid to the underdeveloped world. Indeed, in the early 1970's there were cynics in the United States who claimed that outdoing the stupidity of American foreign aid would be physically impossible. Those critics were, however, obviously unaware that the Russians had been busily destroying their own environment for many years. The virtual disappearance of sturgeon from Russian rivers caused a great shortage of caviar by 1970. A standard joke among Russian scientists at that time was that they had created an artificial caviar which was indistinguishable from the real thing—except by taste. At any rate the Soviet Union, observing with interest the progressive deterioration of relations between the UDCs and the United States, came up with a solution. It had recently developed what it claimed was the ideal insecticide, a highly lethal chlorinated hydrocarbon complexed with a special agent for penetrating the external skeletal armor of insects. Announcing that the new pesticide, called Thanodrin, would truly produce a Green Revolution, the Soviets entered into negotiations with various UDCs for the construction of massive Thanodrin factories. The USSR would bear all the costs; all it wanted in return were certain trade and military concessions.

It is interesting now, with the perspective of years, to examine in some detail the reasons why the UDCs welcomed the Thanodrin plan with such open arms. Government officials in these countries ignored the protests of their own scientists that Thanodrin would not solve the problems which plagued them. The governments now knew that the basic cause of their problems was over-population, and that these problems had been exacerbated by the dullness, daydreaming, and cupidity endemic to all governments. They knew that only population control and limited development aimed primarily at agriculture could have spared them the horrors they now faced. They knew it, but they were not about to admit it. How much easier it was simply to accuse the Americans of failing to give them proper aid; how much simpler to accept the Russian panacea.

And then there was the general worsening of relations between the United States and the UDCs. Many things had contributed to this. The situation in America in the first half of the 1970s deserves our close scrutiny. Being more dependent on imports of raw materials than the Soviet Union, the United States had, in the early 1970s, adopted more and more heavy-handed policies in order to insure continuing supplies. Military adventures in Asia and Latin America had further lessened the international credibility of the United States as a great defender of freedom—an image which had begun to deteriorate rapidly during the pointless and fruitless Viet Nam conflict. At home, acceptance of the carefully manufactured image lessened dramatically, as even the more romantic and chauvinistic citizens began to understand the role of the military and the industrial system in what John Kenneth Galbraith had aptly named "The New Industrial State."

At home in the USA the early '70s were traumatic times. Racial violence grew and the habitability of the cities diminished, as nothing substantial was done to ameliorate either racial inequities or urban blight. Welfare rolls grew as automation and general technological progress forced more and more people into the category of "unemployable." Simultaneously a taxpayers' revolt occurred. Although there was not enough money to build the schools, roads, water systems, sewage systems, jails, hospitals, urban transit lines, and all the other amenities needed to support a burgeoning population, Americans refused to tax themselves more heavily. Starting in Youngstown, Ohio, in 1969 and followed closely by Richmond, California, community after community was forced to close its schools or curtail educational operations for lack of funds. Water supplies, already marginal in quality and quantity in many places by 1970, deteriorated quickly. Water rationing occurred in 1,723 municipalities in the summer of 1974, and hepatitis and epidemic dysentery rates climbed about 500 percent between 1970 and 1974.

Air pollution continued to be the most obvious manifestation of environmental deterioration. It was, by 1972, quite literally in the eyes of all Americans. The year 1973 saw not only the New York and Los Angeles smog disasters, but also the publication of the surgeon general's massive report on air pollution and health. The public had been partially prepared for the worst by the publicity given to the U.N. pollution conference held in 1972. Deaths in the late '60s caused by smog were well known to scientists, but the public had ignored them because they mostly involved the early demise of the old and sick rather than people dropping dead on the freeways. But suddenly our citizens were faced with nearly 200,000 corpses and massive documentation that they could be the next to die from respiratory disease. They were not ready for that scale of disaster. After all, the U.N. conference had not predicted that accumulated air pollution would make the planet uninhabitable until almost 1990. The population was terrorized as TV screens became filled with scenes of horror from the disaster areas. Especially vivid was NBC's coverage of hundreds of unattended people choking out their lives outside of New York's hospitals. Terms like nitrogen oxide, acute bronchitis and cardiac arrest began to have real meaning for most Americans.

The ultimate horror was the announcement that chlorinated hydrocarbons were now a major constituent of air pollution in all American cities. Autopsies of smog disaster victims revealed an average chlorinated hydrocarbon load in fatty tissue equivalent to 26 parts per million of DDT. In October, 1973, the Department of Health, Education and Welfare announced studies which showed unequivocally that increasing death rates from hypertension, cirrhosis of the liver, liver cancer, and a series of other diseases had resulted from the chlorinated hydrocarbon load. They estimated that Americans born since 1964 (when DDT usage began) now had a life expectancy of only 49 years, and predicted that if current patterns continued, this expectancy would reach 42 years by 1980, when it might level out. Plunging insurance stocks triggered a stock market panic. The president of a major pesticide went on television to "publicly eat a teaspoonful of DDT" (it was really powdered milk) and announce that HEW had been infiltrated by Communists. Other giants of the petro-chemical industry, attempting to dispute the indisputable evidence, launched a massive pressure campaign on Congress to force HEW to "get out of agriculture's business." They were aided by the agro-chemical journals, which had decades of experience in misleading the public about the benefits and dangers of pesticides. But by now the public realized that it had been duped. The Nobel Prize for medicine and physiology was given to Drs. J. L. Radomski and W. B. Diechmann, who in the late 1960's had pioneered in the documentation of the long-term lethal effects of chlorinated hydrocarbons. A presidential commission with unimpeachable credentials directly accused the agro-chemical complex of "condemning many millions of Americans to an early death." The year 1973 was the year in which Americans finally came to understand the direct threat to their existence posed by environmental deterioration.

And 1973 was also the year in which most people finally comprehended the indirect threat. Even the president of Union Oil Company and several other industrialists publicly stated their concern over the reduction of bird populations which had resulted from pollution by DDT and other chlorinated hydrocarbons. Insect populations boomed because they were resistant to most pesticides and had been freed, by the incompetent use of those pesticides, from most of their natural enemies. Rodents swarmed over crops, multiplying rapidly in the absence of predatory birds. The effect of pests on the wheat crop was especially disastrous in the summer of 1973, since that was also the year of the great drought. Most of us can remember the shock which greeted the announcement by atmospheric physicists that the shift of the jet stream which had caused the drought was probably permanent. It signalled the birth of the Midwestern desert. Man's air-polluting activities had by then caused gross changes in climatic patterns. The news, of course, played hell with commodity and stock markets. Food prices skyrocketed, as savings were poured into hoarded canned goods. Official assurances that food supplies would remain ample fell on deaf ears, and even the government showed signs of nervousness when California migrant field workers went out on strike again in protest against the continued use of pesticides by growers. The strike burgeoned into farm burning and riots. The workers, calling themselves "The Walking Dead," demanded immediate compensation for their shortened lives, and crash research programs to attempt to lengthen them.

It was in the same speech in which President Edward Kennedy, after much delay, finally declared a national emergency and called out the National Guard to harvest California's crops that the first mention of population control was made. Kennedy pointed out that the United States would no longer be able to offer any food aid to other nations and was likely to suffer food shortages herself. He suggested that, in view of the manifest failure of the Green Revolution, the only hope of the UDCs lay in population control. His statement, you will recall, created an uproar in the underdeveloped countries. Newspaper editorials accused the United States of wishing to prevent small countries from becoming large nations and thus threatening American hegemony. Politicians asserted that President Kennedy was a "creature of the giant drug combine" that wished to shove its pills down every woman's throat.

Among Americans, religious opposition to population control was very slight. Industry in general also backed the idea. Increasing poverty in the UDCs was both destroying markets and threatening supplies of raw materials. The seriousness of the raw material situation had been brought home during the congressional hard resources hearings in 1971. The exposure of the ignorance of the cornucopian economists had been quite a spectacle—a spectacle brought into virtually every American's home in living color. Few would forget the distinguished geologist from the University of California who suggested that economists be legally required to learn at least the most elementary facts of geology. Fewer still would forget that an equally distinguished Harvard economist added that they might be required to learn some economics too. The overall message was clear: America's resource situation was bad and bound to get worse. The hearings had led to a bill requiring the Departments of State, Interior, and Commerce to set up a joint resource procurement council with the express purpose of "insuring that proper consideration of American resource needs be an integral part of American foreign policy."

Suddenly the United States discovered that it had a national consensus: population control was the only possible salvation of the underdeveloped world. But that same consensus led to heated debate. How could the UDCs be persuaded to limit their populations, and should not the United States lead the way by limiting its own? Members of the intellectual community wanted America to set an example. They pointed out that the United States was in the midst of a new baby boom: her birth rate, well over 20 per thousand per year, and her growth rate of over one percent per annum were among the very highest of the developed countries. They detailed the deterioration of the American physical and psychic environments, the growing health threats, the impending food shortages, and the insufficiency of funds for desperately needed public works. They contended that the nation was clearly unable or unwilling to properly care for the people it already had. What possible reason could there be, they queried, for adding any more? Besides, who would listen to requests by the United States for population control when that nation did not control her own profligate reproduction?

Those who opposed population controls for the U.S. were equally vociferous. The military-industrial complex, with its all-too-human mixture of ignorance and avarice, still saw strength and prosperity in numbers. Baby food magnates, already worried by the growing nitrate pollution of their products, saw their market disappearing. Steel manufacturers saw a decrease in aggregate demand and slippage for that holy of holies, the Gross National Product. And military men saw, in the growing population-food-environment crisis, a serious threat to their carefully nurtured cold war. In the end, of course, economic arguments held sway, and the "inalienable right of every American couple to determine the size of its family," a freedom invented for the occasion in the early '70s, was not compromised.

The population control bill, which was passed by Congress early in 1974 was quite a document, nevertheless. On the domestic front, it authorized an increase from 100 to 150 million dollars in funds for "family planning" activities. This was made possible by a general feeling in the country that the growing army on welfare needed family planning. But the gist of the bill was a series of measures designed to impress the need for population control on the UDCs. All American aid to countries with overpopulation problems was required by law to consist in part of population control assistance. In order to receive any assistance each nation was required not only to accept the population control aid, but also to match it according to a complex formula. "Overpopulation" itself was defined by a formula based on U.N. statistics, and the UDCs were required not only to accept aid, but also to show progress in reducing birth rates. Every five years the status of the aid program for each nation was to be re-evaluated.

The reaction to the announcement of this program dwarfed the response to President Kennedy's speech. A coalition of UDCs attempted to get the U.N. General Assembly to condemn the United States as a "genetic aggressor." Most damaging of all to the American cause was the famous "25 Indians and a dog" speech by Mr. Shankarnarayan, Indian Ambassador to the U.N. Shankarnarayan pointed out that for several decades the United States, with less than six percent of the people of the world, had consumed roughly 50 percent of the raw materials used every year. He described vividly America's contribution to worldwide environmental deterioration, and he scathingly denounced the miserly record of United States foreign aid as "unworthy of a fourth-rate power, let alone the most powerful nation on earth."

It was the climax of his speech, however, which most historians claim once and for all destroyed the image of the United States. Shankarnarayan informed the assembly that the average American family dog was fed more animal protein per week than the average Indian got in a month. "How do you justify taking fish from protein-starved Peruvians and feeding them to your animals?" he asked. "I contend," he concluded, "that the birth of an American baby is a greater disaster for the world than that of 25 Indian babies." When the applause had died away, Mr. Sorensen, the American representative, made a speech which said essentially that "other countries look after their own self-interest, too." When the vote came, the United States was condemned.

This condemnation set the tone of U.S.-UDC relations at the time the Russian Thanodrin proposal was made. The proposal seemed to offer the masses in the UDCs an opportunity to save themselves and humiliate the United States at the same time; and in human affairs, as we all know, biological realities could never interfere with such an opportunity. The scientists were silenced, the politicians said yes; the Thanodrin plants were built, and the results were what any beginning ecology student could have predicted. At first Thanodrin seemed to offer excellent control of many pests. True, there was a rash of human fatalities from improper use of the lethal chemical, but, as Russian technical advisors were prone to note, these were more than compensated for by increased yields. Thanodrin use skyrocketed throughout the underdeveloped world. The Mikoyan design group developed a dependable, cheap agricultural aircraft which the Soviets donated to the effort in large numbers. MIG sprayers became even more common in UDCs than MIG interceptors.

Then the troubles began. Insect strains with cuticles resistant to Thanodrin penetration began to appear. And as streams, rivers, fish culture ponds and onshore waters became rich in Thanodrin, more fisheries began to disappear. Bird populations were decimated. The sequence of events was standard for broadcast use of a synthetic pesticide: great success at first, followed by removal of natural enemies and development of resistance by the pest. Populations of crop-eating insects in areas treated with Thanodrin made steady comebacks and soon became more abundant than ever. Yields plunged, while farmers in their desperation increased the Thanodrin dose and shortened the time between treatments. Death from Thanodrin poisoning became common. The first violent incident occurred in the Canete Vally of Peru, where farmers had suffered a similar chlorinated hydrocarbon disaster in the mid-'50s. A Russian advisor serving as an agricultural pilot was assaulted and killed by a mob of enraged farmers in January, 1978. Trouble spread rapidly during 1978, especially after the word got out that two years earlier Russia herself had banned the use of Thanodrin at home because of its serious effects on ecological systems. Suddenly Russia, and not the United States, was the *bête noir* in the UDCs. "Thanodrin parties" became epidemic, with farmers, in their ignorance, dumping carloads of Thanodrin concentrate into the sea. Russian advisors fled, and four of the Thanodrin plants were leveled to the ground. Destruction of the plants in Rio and Calcutta led to hundreds of thousands of gallons of Thanodrin concentrate being dumped directly into the sea.

Mr. Shankarnarayan again rose to address the U.N., but this time it was Mr. Potemkin, representative of the Soviet Union, who was on the hot seat. Mr. Potemkin heard his nation described as the greatest mass killer of all time as Shankarnarayan predicted at least 30 million deaths from crop failures due to overdependence on Thanodrin. Russia was accused of "chemical aggression," and the General Assembly, after a weak reply by Potemkin, passed a vote of censure.

It was in January, 1979, that huge blooms of a previously unknown variety of diatom were reported off the coast of Peru. The blooms were accompanied by a massive die-off of sea life and of the pathetic remainder of the birds which had once feasted on the anchovies of the area. Almost immediately, another huge bloom was reported in the Indian Ocean, centering around the Seychelles, and then a third in the South Atlantic off the African coast. Both of these were accompanied by spectacular die-offs of marine animals. Even more ominous were growing reports of fish and bird kills at oceanic points where there were no spectacular blooms. Biologists were soon able to explain the phenomenon: the diatom had evolved an enzyme which broke down Thanodrin; that enzyme also produced a breakdown product which interfered with the transmission of nerve impulses, and was therefore lethal to animals. Unfortunately, the biologists could suggest no way of repressing the poisonous diatom bloom in time. By September, 1979, all important animal life in the sea was extinct. Large areas of coastline had to be evacuated, as windrows of dead fish created a monumental stench.

But stench was the least of man's problems. Japan and China were faced with almost instant starvation from a total loss of the seafood on which they were so dependent. Both blamed Russia for their situation and demanded immediate mass shipments of food. Russia had none to send. On October 13, Chinese armies attacked Russia on a broad front. . . .

A pretty grim scenario. Unfortunately, we're a long way into it already. Everything mentioned as happening before 1970 has actually occurred; much of the rest is based on projections of trends already appearing. Evidence that pesticides have long-term lethal effects on human beings has started to accumulate, and recently Robert Finch, Secretary of the Department of Health, Education and Welfare, expressed his extreme apprehension about the pesticide situation. Simultaneously the petro-chemical industry continues its unconscionable poison-peddling. For instance, Shell Chemical has been carrying on a high-pressure campaign to sell the insecticide Azodrin to farmers as a killer of cotton pests. They continue their program even though they know that Azodrin is not only ineffective, but often *increases* the pest density. They've covered themselves nicely in an advertisement which states, "Even if an overpowering migration [*sic*] develops, the flexibility of Azodrin lets you regain control fast. Just increase the dosage according to label recommendations." It's a great game—get people to apply the poison and kill the natural enemies of the pests. Then blame the increased pests on "migration" and sell even more pesticide!

Right now fisheries are being wiped out by overexploitation, made easy by modern electronic equipment. The companies producing the equipment know this. They even boast in advertising that only their equipment will keep fishermen in business until the final kill. Profits must obviously be maximized in the short run. Indeed, Western society is in the process of completing the rape and murder of the planet for economic gain. And, sadly, most of the rest of the world is eager for the opportunity to emulate our behavior. But the underdeveloped peoples will be denied that opportunity—the days of plunder are drawing inexorably to a close.

Most of the people who are going to die in the greatest cataclysm in the history of man have already been born. More than three and a half billion people already populate our moribund globe, and about half of them are hungry. Some 10 to 20 million will starve to death *this year.* In spite of this, the population of the earth will have increased by 70 million in 1969. For mankind has artificially lowered the death rate of the human population, while in general, birth rates have remained high. With the input side of the population system in high gear and the output side slowed down, our fragile planet has filled with people at an incredible rate. It took several million years for the population to reach a total of two billion people in 1930, while a *second two billion will have been added by 1975!* By that time some experts feel that food shortages will have escalated the present level of world hunger and starvation in famines of unbelievable proportions. Other experts, more optimistic, think the ultimate food-population collision will not occur until the decade of the 1980's. Of course more massive famine may be avoided if other events cause a prior rise in the human death rate.

Both worldwide plague and thermonuclear war are made more probable as population growth continues. These, along with famine, make up the trio of potential "death rate solutions" to the population problem—solutions in which the birth rate-death rate imbalance is redressed by a rise in the death rate rather than by a lowering of the birth rate. Make no mistake about it, *the imbalance will be redressed.* The shape of the population-growth curve is one familiar to the biologist. It is the outbreak part of an outbreak-crash sequence. A population grows rapidly in the presence of abundant resources, finally runs out of food or some other necessity and crashes to a low level or extinction. Man is not only running out of food, he is also destroying the life support systems of the Spaceship Earth. The situation was recently summarized very succinctly: "It is the top of the ninth inning. Man, always a threat at the plate, has been hitting Nature hard. It is important to remember, however, that NATURE BATS LAST."

If Paul Ehrlich's scenario is somehow averted and we manage to stop all the *known* destruction that the human race is carrying on, are we safe for all time? Not exactly. Not as long as a clerk's blunder drops one chunk of plutonium into our atmosphere and a blown oxygen tank and an aborted Apollo 13 mission drops another. Not as long as thalidomide can come on the market as it did in Europe, or the SST can destroy our eardrums here. We will always have the unexpected. Sometimes the unexpected may take trivial forms (those walking catfish aren't all *that* bad). But once in a while it will be serious, and very likely now and then it may be catastrophic. That's the price we pay for an occasional—

by Frank M. Robinson

"East Wind, West Wind"

It wasn't going to be just another bad day, it was going to be a terrible one. The inversion layer had slipped over the city four days before and it had been like putting a lid on a kettle; the air was building up to a real Donora, turning into a chemical soup so foul I wouldn't have believed it if I hadn't been trying to breathe the stuff. Besides sticking in my throat, it made my eyes feel like they were being bathed in acid. You could hardly see the sun—it was a pale, sickly disc floating in a mustard-colored sky—but even so, the streets were an oven and the humidity was so high you could have wrung the water out of the air with your bare hands . . . dirty water, naturally.

On the bus a red-faced salesman with denture breath recognized my Air Central badge and got pushy. I growled that we didn't *make* the air—not yet, at any rate—and finally I took off the badge and put it in my pocket and tried to shut out the coughing and the complaints around me by concentrating on the faint, cheery sound of the "corn poppers" laundering the bus's exhaust. Five would have gotten you ten, of course, that their effect was strictly psychological, that they had seen more than twenty thousand miles of service and were now absolutely worthless. . . .

At work I hung up my plastic sportscoat, slipped off the white surgeon's mask (black where my nose and mouth had been) and filled my lungs with good machine-pure air that smelled only faintly of oil and electric motors; one of the advantages of working for Air Central was that our office air was the best in the city. I dropped a quarter in the coffee vendor, dialed it black, and inhaled the fumes for a second while I shook the sleep from my eyes and speculated about what Wanda would have for me at the Investigator's Desk. There were thirty-nine other Investigators besides myself but I was junior and my daily assignment card was usually just a listing of minor complaints and violations that had to be checked out.

Wanda was young and pretty and redhaired and easy to spot even in a secretarial pool full of pretty girls. I offered her some of my coffee and looked over her shoulder while she flipped through the assignment cards. "That stuff out there is easier to swim through than to breathe," I said. "What's the index?"

"Eighty-four point five," she said quietly. "And rising."

I just stared at her. I had thought it was bad, but hardly that bad, and for the first time that day I felt a sudden flash of panic. "And no alert? When it hits seventy-five this city's supposed to close up like a clam!"

She nodded down the hall to the Director's office. "Lawyers from Sanitary Pick-Up, Oberhausen Steel, and City Light and Power got an injunction—they were here to break the news to Monte at eight sharp. Impractical, unnecessary, money-wasting, and fifteen thousand employees would be thrown out of work if they had to shut down the furnaces and incinerators. They got an okay right from the top of Air Shed Number Three."

My jaw dropped. "How could they? Monte's supposed to have the last word!"

"So go argue with the politicians—if you can stand the hot air." She suddenly looked very fragile and I wanted to run out and slay a dragon or two for her. "The chicken-hearts took the easy way out, Jim. Independent Weather's predicting a cold front for early this evening and rising winds and rain for tomorrow."

The rain would clean up the air, I thought. But Independent Weather could be bought and as a result it had a habit of turning in cheery predictions that frequently didn't come true. Air Central had tried for years to get IW outlawed but money talks and their lobbyist in the capital was quite a talker. Unfortunately, if they were wrong this time, it would be as if they had pulled a plastic bag over the city's head.

I started to say something, then shut up. If you let it get to you, you wouldn't last long on the job. "Where's my list of small-fry?"

She gave me an assignment card. It was blank except for *See Me* written across its face. "Humor him, Jim, he's not feeling well."

This worried me a little because Monte was the father of us all—a really sweet old guy, which hardly covers it all because he could be hard as nails when he had to. There wasn't anyone who knew more about air control than he.

I took the card and started up the hall and then Wanda called after me. She had stretched out her long legs and hiked up her skirt. I looked startled and she grinned. "Something new—sulfur-proof nylons." Which meant they wouldn't dissolve on a day like today when a measurable fraction of the air we were trying to breathe was actually dilute sulfuric acid. . . .

When I walked into his office, old Monte was leaning out the window, the fly ash clinging to his busy gray eyebrows like cinnamon to toast, trying to taste the air and predict how it would go today. We had eighty Sniffers scattered throughout the city, all computerized and delivering their data in neat, graphlike form, but Monte still insisted on breaking internal air security and seeing for himself how his city was doing.

I closed the door. Monte pulled back inside, then suddenly broke into one of his coughing fits.

"Sit down, Jim," he wheezed, his voice sounding as if it were being wrung out of him, "be with you in a minute." I pretended not to notice while his coughing shuddered to a halt and he rummaged through the desk for his little bottle of pills. It was a plain office, as executive offices went, except for Monte's own paintings on the wall—the type I like to call Twentieth Century Romantic. A mountain scene with a crystal clear lake in the foreground and anglers battling huge trout, a city scene with palm trees lining the boulevards, and finally, one of a man standing by an old automobile on a winding mountain road while he looked off at a valley in the distance.

Occasionally Monte would talk to me about his boyhood around the Great Lakes and how he actually used to go swimming in them. Once he tried to tell me that orange trees used to grow within the city limits of Santalosdiego and that the oranges were as big as tennis balls. It irritated me and I think he knew it; I was the youngest Investigator for Air Central but that didn't necessarily make me naive.

When Monte stopped coughing I said hopefully, "IW claims a cold front is coming in."

He huddled in his chair and dabbed at his mouth with a handkerchief, his thin chest working desperately trying to pump his lungs full of air. "IW's a liar," he finally rasped. "There's no cold front coming in, it's going to be a scorcher for three more days."

I felt uneasy again. "Wanda told me what happened," I said.

He fought a moment longer for his breath, caught it, then gave a resigned shrug. "The bastards are right, to an extent. Stop garbage pick-ups in a city this size and within hours the rats will be fighting us in the streets. Shut down the power plants and you knock out all the air conditioners and purifiers—right during the hottest spell of the year. Then try telling the yokels that the air on the outside will be a whole lot cleaner if only they let the air on the inside get a whole lot dirtier."

He hunched behind his desk and drummed his fingers on the top while his face slowly turned to concrete. "But if they don't let me announce an alert by tomorrow morning," he said quietly, "I'll call in the newspapers and. . . . " The coughing started again and he stood up, a gnomelike little man slightly less alive with every passing day. He leaned against the windowsill while he fought the spasm. "And we think this is bad," he choked, half to himself. "What happens when the air coming in is as dirty as the air already here? When the Chinese and the Indonesians and the Hottentots get toasters and ice-boxes and all the other goodies?"

"Asia's not that industrialized yet," I said uncomfortably.

"Isn't it?" He turned and sagged back into his chair, hardly making a dent in the cushion. I was bleeding for the old man but I couldn't let him know it. I said in a low voice, "You wanted to see me," and handed him the assignment card.

He stared at it for a moment, his mind still on the Chinese, then came out of it and croaked, "That's right, give you something to chew on." He pressed a button on his desk and the wall opposite faded into a map of the city and the surrounding area, from the ocean on the west to the low-lying mountains on the east. He waved at the section of the city that straggled off into the canyons of the foothills. "Internal combustion engine—someplace back there." His voice was stronger now, his eyes more alert. "It isn't a donkey engine for a still or for electricity, it's a private automobile."

I could feel the hairs stiffen on the back of my neck. Usually I drew minor offenses, like trash burning or secret cigarette smoking, but owning or operating a gasoline-powered automobile was a felony, one that was sometimes worth your life.

"The Sniffer in the area confirms it," Monte continued in a tired voice, "but can't pinpoint it."

"Any other leads?"

"No, just this one report. But—we haven't had an internal combustion engine in more than three years." He paused. "Have fun with it, you'll probably have a new boss in the morning." *That* was something I didn't even want to think about. I had my hand on the doorknob when he said quietly. "The trouble with being boss is that you have to play Caesar and his Legions all the time."

It was as close as he came to saying good-bye and good luck. I didn't know what to say in return, or how to say it, and found myself staring at one of his canvases and babbling, "You sure used a helluva lot of blue."

"It was a fairly common color back then," he growled. "The sky was full of it."

And then he started coughing again and I closed the door in a hurry; in five minutes I had gotten so I couldn't stand the sound.

I had to stop in at the lab to pick up some gear from my locker and ran into Dave Ice, the researcher in charge of the Sniffers. He was a chubby, middle-aged little man with small, almost feminine hands; it was a pleasure to watch him work around delicate machinery. He was our top-rated man, after Monte, and I think if there was anybody whose shoes I wanted to step into someday, it would have been Dave Ice. He knew it, liked me for it, and usually went out of his way to help.

When I walked in he was changing a sheet of paper in one of the smoke shade detectors that hung just outside the lab windows. The sheet he was taking out looked as it it had been coated with lampblack.

"How long an exposure?"

He looked up, squinting over his bifocals. "Hi, Jim—a little more than four hours. It looks like it's getting pretty fierce out there."

"You haven't been out?"

"No, Monte and I stayed here all night. We were going to call an alert at nine this morning but I guess you know what happened."

I opened my locker and took out half a dozen new masks and a small canister of oxygen; if you were going to be out in traffic for any great length of time, you had to go prepared. Allowable vehicles were buses, trucks, delivery vans, police electrics and the like. Not all exhaust control devices worked very well and even the electrics gave off a few acid fumes. And if you were stalled in a tunnel, the carbon monoxide ratings really zoomed. I hesitated at the bottom of the locker and then took out my small Mark II gyrojet and shoulder holster. It was pretty deadly stuff: no recoil and the tiny rocket pellet had twice the punch of a .45.

Dave heard the clink of metal and without looking up asked quietly, "Trouble?"

"Maybe," I said. "Somebody's got a private automobile—gasoline—and I don't suppose they'll want to turn it in."

"You're right," he said, sounding concerned, "they won't." And then: "I heard something about it; if it's the same report, it's three days old."

"Monte's got his mind on other things," I said. I slipped the masks into my pocket and belted on the holster. "Did you know he's still on his marching Chinese kick?"

Dave was concentrating on one of the Sniffer drums slowly rolling beneath its scribing pens, logging a minute-by-minute record of the hydrocarbons and the oxides of nitrogen and sulfur that were sickening the atmosphere. "I don't blame him," he said, absently running a hand over his glistening scalp. "They've started tagging chimney exhausts in Shanghai, Djakarta and Mukden with radioactives—we should get the first results in another day or so."

The dragon's breath, I thought. When it finally circled the globe it would mean earth's air sink had lost the ability to cleanse itself and all of us would start strangling a little faster.

I got the rest of my gear and just before I hit the door, Dave said: "Jim?" I turned. He was wiping his hands on a paper towel and frowning at me over his glasses. "Look, take care of yourself, huh, kid?"

"Sure thing," I said. If Monte was my professional father, then Dave was my uncle. Sometimes it was embarrassing but right then it felt good. I nodded good-bye, adjusted my mask, and left.

Outside it seemed like dusk; trucks and buses had turned on their lights and almost all pedestrians were wearing masks. In a lot across the street some kids were playing tag and the thought suddenly struck me that nowadays most kids seemed small for their age; but I envied them . . . the air never seemed to bother kids. I watched for a moment, then started up the walk. A few doors down I passed an apartment building, half hidden in the growing darkness, that had received a "political influence" exemption a month before. Its incinerator was going full blast now, only instead of floating upward over the city the small charred bits of paper and garbage were falling straight down the front of the building like a kind of oily black snow.

I suddenly felt I was suffocating and stepped out into the street and hailed a passing electricab. Forest Hills, the part of the city that Monte had pointed out, was wealthy and the homes were large, though not so large that some of them couldn't be hidden away in the canyons and gullies of the foothills. If you lived on a side road or at the end of one of the canyons it might even be possible to hide a car out there and drive it only at night. And if any of your neighbors found out . . . well, the people who lived up in the relatively pure air of the highlands had a different view of things than those who lived down in the atmosphere sewage of the flats. *But where would a man get a gasoline automobile in the first place?*

And did it all really matter? I thought, looking out the window of the cab at the deepening dusk and feeling depressed. Then I shook my head and leaned forward to give the driver instructions. Some places could be checked out relatively easily.

The Carriage Museum was elegant—and crowded, considering that it was a weekday. The main hall was a vast cave of black marble housing a parade of ancient internal combustion vehicles shining under the subdued lights; most of them were painted a lustrous black though there was an occasional gray and burst of red and a few sparkles of old gold from polished brass head lamps and fittings.

I felt like I was in St. Peter's, walking on a vast seal of marble while all about me the crowds shuffled along in respectful silence. I kept my eyes to the floor, reading off the names on the small bronze plaques: *Rolls Royce Silver Ghost, Mercer Raceabout, Isotta-Fraschini, Packard Runabout, Hispano-Suiza, Model J Duesenberg, Flying Cloud Reo, Cadillac Imperial V16, Pierce Arrow,* the first of the *Ford V8s, Lincoln Zephyr, Chrysler Windsor Club Coup.* . . . And in small halls off to the side, the lesser breeds: *Hudson Terraplane, Henry J., Willys Knight,* something called a *Jeepster,* the *Mustang, Knudsen,* the 1986 *Volkswagen,* the last *Chevrolet.* . . .

The other visitors to the museum were all middle-aged or older; the look on their faces was something I had never seen before— something that was not quite love and not quite lust. It flowed across their features like ripples of water whenever they brushed a fender or stopped at a hood that had been opened so they could stare at the engine, all neatly chromed or painted. They were like my father, I thought. They had owned cars when they were young, before Turn-In Day and the same date a year later when even most private steam and electrics were banned because of congestion. For a moment I wondered what it had been like to own one, then canceled the thought. The old man had tried to tell me often enough, before I had stormed out of the house for good, shouting how could he love the damned things so much when he was coughing his lungs out. . . .

The main hall was nothing but bad memories. I left it and looked up the office of the curator. His secretary was on a coffee break so I rapped sharply and entered without waiting for an answer. On the door it had said "C. Pearson," who turned out to be a thin, overdressed type, all regal nose and pencil moustache, in his mid-forties. "Air Central," I said politely, flashing my wallet ID at him.

He wasn't impressed. "May I?" I gave it to him and he reached for the phone. When he hung up he didn't bother apologizing for the double check, which I figured made us even. "I have nothing to do with the heating system or the air-conditioning," he said easily, "but if you'll wait a minute I'll—"

"I only want information," I said.

He made a small tent of his hands and stared at me over his fingertips. He looked bored. "Oh?"

I sat down and he leaned toward me briefly, then thought better of it and settled back in his chair. "How easy would it be," I asked casually, "to steal one of your displays?"

His moustache quivered slightly. "It wouldn't be easy at all—they're bolted down, there's no gasoline in their tanks, and the batteries are dummies."

"Then none ever have been?"

A flicker of annoyance. "No, of course not."

I flashed my best hat-in-hand smile and stood up. "Well, I guess that's it, then, I won't trouble you any further." But before I turned away I said, "I'm really not much on automobiles but I'm curious. How did the museum get started?"

He warmed up a little. "On Turn-In Day a number of museums like this one were started up all over the country. Some by former dealers, some just by automobile lovers. A number of models were donated for public display and. . . . "

When he had finished I said casually, "Donating a vehicle to a museum must have been a great ploy for hiding private ownership."

"Certainly the people in your bureau would be aware of how strict the government was," he said sharply.

"A lot of people must have tried to hide their vehicles," I persisted.

Dryly. "It would have been difficult . . . like trying to hide an elephant in a playpen."

But still, a number would have tried, I thought. They might even have stockpiled drums of fuel and some spare parts. In the city, of course, it would have been next to impossible. But in remote sections of the country, in the mountain regions out west or in the hills of the Ozarks or in the forests of northern Michigan or Minnesota or in the badlands of the Dakotas. . . . A few could have succeeded, certainly, and perhaps late at night a few weed-grown stretches of highway would have been briefly lit by the headlights of automobiles flashing past with muffled exhausts, tires singing against the pavement. . . .

I sat back down. "Are there many automobile fans around?"

" I suppose so, if attendance records here are any indication."

"Then a smart man with a place in the country and a few

automobiles could make quite a bit of money renting them out, couldn't he?"

He permitted himself a slight smile. "It would be risky. I really don't think anybody would try it. And from everything I've read, I rather think the passion was for actual ownership—I doubt that rental would satisfy that."

I thought about it for a moment while Pearson fidgeted with a letter opener and then, of course, I had it. "All those people who were fond of automobiles, there used to be clubs of them, right?"

His eyes lidded over and it grew very quiet in his office. But it was too late and he knew it. "I believe so," he said after a long pause, his voice tight, "but. . . ."

"But the government ordered them disbanded," I said coldly. "Air Control regulations thirty-nine and forty, sections three through seven, 'concerning the dissolution of all organizations which in whole or in part, intentionally or unintentionally, oppose clean air.' " I knew the regulations by heart. "But there still are clubs, aren't there? Unregistered clubs? Clubs with secret membership files?" A light sheen of perspiration had started to gather on his forehead. "You would probably make a very good membership secretary, Pearson. You're in the perfect spot for recruiting new members—"

He made a motion behind his desk and I dove over it and pinned his arms behind his back. A small address book had fallen to the floor and I scooped it up. Pearson looked as if he might faint. I ran my hands over his chest and under his arms and then let him go. He leaned against the desk, gasping for air.

"I'll have to take you in," I said.

A little color was returning to his cheeks and he nervously smoothed down his damp black hair. His voice was on the squeaky side. "What for? You have some interesting theories but. . . ."

"My theories will keep for court," I said shortly. "You're under arrest for smoking—section eleven thirty point five of the health and safety code." I grabbed his right hand and spread the fingers so the tell-tale stains showed. "You almost offered me a cigarette when I came in, then caught yourself. I would guess that ordinarily you're pretty relaxed and sociable, you probably smoke a lot—and you're generous with your tobacco. Bottom right hand drawer for the stash, right?" I jerked it open and they were there, all right. "One cigarette's a misdemeanor, a carton's a felony, Pearson. We can accuse you of dealing and make it stick." I smiled grimly. "But we're perfectly willing to trade, of course."

I put in calls to the police and Air Central and sat down to wait for the cops to show. They'd sweat Pearson for all the information he had but I couldn't wait around a couple of hours. The word would spread that Pearson was being held, and Pearson himself would probably start remembering various lawyers and civil rights that he had momentarily forgotten. My only real windfall had been the address book. . . .

I thumbed through it curiously, wondering exactly how I could use it. The names were scattered all over the city, and there were a lot of them. I could weed it down to those in the area where the Sniffer had picked up the automobile, but that would take time and nobody was going to admit that he had a contraband vehicle hidden away anyway. The idea of paying a visit to the club I was certain must exist kept recurring to me and finally I decided to pick a name, twist Pearson's arm for anything he might know about him, then arrange to meet at the club and work out from there.

Later, when I was leaving the museum, I stopped for a moment just inside the door to readjust my mask. While I was doing it the janitor showed up with a roll of weatherstripping and started attaching it to the edge of the doorway where what looked like thin black smoke was seeping in from the outside. I was suddenly afraid to go back out there. . . .

The wind was whistling past my ears and a curve was coming up. I feathered the throttle, downshifted, and the needle on the tach started to drop. The wheel seemed to have a life of its own and twitched slightly to the right. I rode high on the outside of the track, the leafy limbs of trees that lined the asphalt dancing just outside my field of vision. The rear started to come around in a skid and I touched the throttle again and then the wheel twitched back to center and I was away. My eyes were riveted on Number Nine, just in front of me. It was the last lap and if I could catch him there would be nothing between me and the checkered flag. . . .

I felt relaxed and supremely confident, one with the throbbing power of the car. I red-lined it and through my dirt-streaked goggles I could see I was crawling up on the red splash that was Number Nine and next I was breathing the fumes from his twin exhausts. I took him on the final curve and suddenly I was alone in the world of the straightaway with the countryside peeling away on both sides of me, placid cows and ancient barns flowing past and then the rails lined with people. I couldn't hear their shouting above the scream of my car. Then I was flashing under banners stretched across the track and thundering toward the finish. There was the smell of burning rubber and spent oil and my own perspiration, the heat from the sun, the shimmering asphalt, and out of the corner of my eye a blur of grandstands and cars and a flag swooping down. . . .

And then it was over and the house lights had come up and I was hunched over a toy wheel in front of me, gripping it with both hands, the sweat pouring down my face and my stomach burning because I could still smell exhaust fumes and I wanted desperately to put on my face mask. It had been far more real than I had thought it would be—the curved screen gave the illusion of depth and each chair had been set up like a driver's seat. They had even pumped in odors. . . .

The others in the small theatre were stretching and getting ready to leave and I gradually unwound and got to my feet, still feeling shaky. "Lucky you could make it, Jim," a voice graveled in my ear. "You missed Joe Moore and the lecture but the documentary was just great, really great. Next week we've got *Meadowdale '73* which has its moments but you don't feel like you're really there and getting an eyeful of cinders, if you know what I mean."

"Who's Joe Moore?" I mumbled.

"Old time race track manager—full of anecdotes, knew all the great drivers. Hey! You okay?"

I was finding it difficult to come out of it. The noise and the action and the smell, but especially the feeling of actually driving. . . . It was more than just a visceral response. You had to be raised down in the flats where you struggled for your breath every day to get the same feeling of revulsion, the same feeling of having done something dirty. . . .

"Yeah, I'm okay," I said. "I'm feeling fine."

"Where'd you say you were from, anyway?"

"Bosnywash," I lied. He nodded and I took a breath and time

out to size him up. Jack Ellis was bigger and heavier than Pearson and not nearly as smooth or as polished—Pearson perspired, my bulky friend sweated. He was in his early fifties, thinning brown hair carefully waved, the beginning of a small paunch well hidden by a lot of expensive tailoring, and a hulking set of shoulders that were much more than just padding. A business bird, I thought. The hairy-chested genial backslapper. . . .

"You seen the clubrooms yet?"

"I just got in," I said. "First time here."

"Hey, great! I'll show you around!" He talked like he was programmed. "A little fuel and a couple of stiff belts first, though—dining room's out of this world. . . . "

And it almost was. We were on the eighty-seventh floor of the new Trans-America building and Ellis had secured a window seat. Above, the sky was almost as bright a blue as Monte had used in his paintings. I couldn't see the street below.

"Have a card," Ellis said, shoving the pasteboard at me. It read *Warshawsky & Warshawsky, Automotive Antiques,* with an address in the Avenues. He waved a hand at the room. "We decorated all of this—pretty classy, huh?"

I had to give him that. The walls were covered with murals of old road races, while from some hidden sound system came a faint, subdued purring—the roaring of cars drifting through the esses of some long-ago race. In the center of the room was a pedestal holding a highly-chromed engine block that slowly revolved under a baby spot. While I was admiring the setting a waitress came up and set down a lazy Susan; it took a minute to recognize it as an old-fashioned wooden steering wheel, fitted with sterling silver hors d'oeuvre dishes between the spokes.

Ellis ran a thick thumb down the menu. "Try a Barney Oldfield," he suggested. "Roast beef and American cheese on pumpernickel."

While I was eating I got the uncomfortable feeling that he was looking me over and that somehow I didn't measure up. "You're pretty young," he said at last. "We don't get many young members—or visitors, for that matter."

"Grandfather was a dealer," I said easily. "Had a Ford agency in Milwaukee—I guess it rubbed off."

He nodded around a mouthful of sandwich and looked mournful for a moment. "It used to be a young man's game, kids worked on engines in their backyards all the time. Just about everybody owned a car. . . . "

"You, too?"

"Oh sure—hell, the old man ran a gas station until Turn-In Day." He was lost in his memories for a moment, then said, "You got a club in Bosnywash?"

"A few, nothing like this," I said cautiously. "And the law's pretty stiff." I nodded at the window. "They get pretty uptight about the air back east. . . . " I let my voice trail off.

He frowned. "You don't *believe* all that guff, do you? Biggest goddamn pack of lies there ever was, but I guess you got to be older to know it. Power plants and incinerators, they're the ones to blame, always have been. Hell, people, too—every time you exhale you're polluting the atmosphere, ever think of that? And Christ, man, think of every time you work up a sweat. . . . "

"Sure," I nodded, "sure, it's always been blown up." I made a mental note that someday I'd throw the book at Ellis.

He finished his sandwich and started wiping his fat face like he was erasing a blackboard. "What's your interest? Mine's family sedans, the old family workhorse. Fords, Chevys, Plymouths—got a case of all the models from '50 on up, one-eighteenth scale. How about you?"

I didn't answer him, just stared out the window and worked with a toothpick for a long time until he began to get a little nervous. Then I let it drop. "I'm out here to buy a car," I said.

His face went blank, as if somebody had just pulled down a shade. "Damned expensive hobby," he said, ignoring it. "Should've taken up photography instead."

"It's for a friend of mine," I said. "Money's no object."

The waitress came around with the check and Ellis initialed it. "Damned expensive," he repeated vaguely.

"I couldn't make a connection back home," I said. "Friends suggested I try out here."

He was watching me now. "How would you get it back east?"

"Break it down," I said. "Ship it east as crates of machine parts."

"What makes you think there's anything for sale out here?"

I shrugged. "Lots of mountains, lots of forests, lots of empty space, lots of hiding places. Cars were big out here, there must have been a number that were never turned in."

"You're a stalking horse for somebody big, aren't you?"

"What do you think?" I said. "And what difference does it make anyway? Money's money."

If it's true that the pupil of the eye expands when it sees something that it likes, it's also true that it contracts when it doesn't—and right then his were in the cold buckshot stage.

"All right," he finally said. "Cash on the barrelhead and remember, when you have that much money changing hands, it can get dangerous." He deliberately leaned across the table so that his coat flapped open slightly. The small gun and holster were almost lost against the big man's girth. He sat back and spun the lazy Susan with a fat forefinger, spearing an olive as it slid past. "You guys run true to form," he continued quietly. "Most guys from back east come out to buy—I guess we've got a reputation." He hesitated. "We also try and take all the danger out of it."

He stood up and slapped me on the back as I pushed to my feet. It was the old Jack Ellis again, he of the instant smile and the sparkling teeth.

"That is, we try and take the danger out of it for *us,*" he added pleasantly.

It was late afternoon and the rush hour had started. It wasn't as heavy as usual—business had been letting out all day—but it was bad enough. I slipped on a mask and started walking toward the warehouse section of town, just outside the business district. The buses were too crowded and it would be impossible to get an electricab that time of day. Besides, traffic was practically standing still in the steamy murk. Headlights were vague yellow dots in the gathering darkness and occasionally I had to shine my pocket flash on a street sign to determine my location.

I had checked in with Monte who said the hospitals were filling up fast with bronchitis victims; I didn't ask about the city morgue. The venal bastards at Air Shed Number Three were even getting worried; they had promised Monte that if it didn't clear by morning, he could issue his alert and close down the city. I told him I had uncovered what looked like a car ring but he sounded only faintly interested. He had bigger things on his mind; the ball was in my court and what I was going to do with it was strictly up to me.

A few more blocks and the crowds thinned. Then I was alone on the street with the warehouses hulking up in the gloom around me, ancient monsters of discolored brick and concrete layered with years of soot and grime. I found the address I wanted, leaned against the buzzer by the loading dock door, and waited. There was a long pause, then faint steps echoed inside and the door slid open. Ellis stood in the yellow dock light, the smile stretching across his thick face like a rubber band. "Right on time," he whispered. "Come on in, Jim, meet the boys."

I followed him down a short passageway, trying not to brush up against the filthy whitewashed walls. Then we were up against a steel door with a peephole. Ellis knocked three times, the peephole opened, and he said, "Joe sent me." I started to panic. *For God's sake, why the act?* Then the door opened and it was as if somebody had kicked me in the stomach. What lay beyond was a huge garage with at least half a dozen ancient cars on the tool-strewn floor. Three mechanics in coveralls were working under the overhead lights; two more were waiting inside the door. They were bigger than Ellis and I was suddenly very glad I had brought along the Mark II.

"Jeff, Ray, meet Mr. Morrison." I held out my hand. They nodded at me, no smiles. "C'mon," Ellis said, "I'll show you the set-up." I tagged after him and he started pointing out the wonders of his domain. "Completely equipped garage—my old man would've been proud of me. Overhead hoist for pulling motors, complete lathe set-up . . . a lot of parts we have to machine ourselves, can't get the originals anymore and of course the last of the junkers was melted down a long time ago." He stopped by a workbench with a large rack full of tools gleaming behind it. "One of the great things about being in the antique business—you hit all the country auctions and you'd be surprised at what you can pick up. Complete sets of torque wrenches, metric socket sets, spanner wrenches, feeler gauges, you name it."

I looked over the bench—he was obviously proud of the assortment of tools—then suddenly felt the small of my back grow cold. It was phony, I thought, the whole thing was phony. But I couldn't put my finger on just why.

Ellis walked over to one of the automobiles on the floor and patted a fender affectionately. Then he unbuttoned his coat so that the pistol showed, hooked his thumbs in his vest, leaned against the car behind him and smiled. Someplace he had even found a broomstraw to chew on.

"So what can we do for you, Jim? Limited stock, sky-high prices, but never a dissatisfied customer!" He poked an elbow against the car behind him. "Take a look at this '73 Chevy Biscayne, probably the only one of its kind in this condition in the whole damned country. Ten thou and you can have it—and that's only because I like you." He sauntered over to a monster in blue and silver with grillwork that looked like a set of kitchen knives. "Or maybe you'd like a '76 Caddy convertible, all genuine simulated-leather upholstery, one of the last of the breed." He didn't add why but I already knew—in heavy traffic the high levels of monoxide could be fatal to a driver in an open car.

"Yours," Ellis was saying about another model, "for a flat fifteen"—he paused and shot me a friendly glance—"oh hell, for you, Jim, make it twelve and a half and take it from me, it's a bargain. Comes with the original upholstery and tires and there's less than ten thousand miles on it—the former owner was a little old lady in Pasadena who only drove it to weddings."

He chuckled at that, looking at me expectantly. I didn't get it. "Maybe you'd just like to look around. Be my guest, go right ahead." His eyes were bright and he looked very pleased with himself; it bothered me.

"Yeah," I said absently, "I think that's what I'd like to do." There was a wall phone by an older model and I drifted over to it.

"That's an early Knudsen two-seater," Ellis said. "Popular make for the psychedelic set, that paint job is the way they really came. . . . "

I ran my hand lightly down the windshield, then turned to face the cheerful Ellis. "You're under arrest," I said. "You and everybody else here."

His face suddenly looked like shrimp in molded gelatin. One of the mechanics behind him moved and I had the Mark II out winging a rocket past his shoulder. No noise, no recoil, just a sudden shower of sparks by the barrel and in the far end of the garage a fifty-gallon oil drum went *karrump* and there was a hole in it you could have stuck your head through.

The mechanic went white. "*Jesus Christ, Jack, you brought in some kind of nut!"* Ellis himself was pale and shaking, which surprised me; I thought he'd be tougher than that.

"Against the bench," I said coldly, waving the pistol. "Hands in front of your crotch and don't move them." The mechanics were obviously scared stiff and Ellis was having difficulty keeping control. I took down the phone and called in.

After I hung up, Ellis mumbled, "What's the charge?"

"Charges," I corrected. "Sections three, four and five of the Air Control laws. Maintenance, sale and use of internal combustion engines."

Ellis stared at me blankly. "You don't know?" he said faintly.

"Know what?"

"I don't handle internal combustion engines." He licked his lips. "I really don't, it's too risky, it's . . . it's against the law."

The workbench, I suddenly thought. The goddamned workbench. I knew something was wrong then, I should have cooled it.

"You can check me," Ellis offered weakly. "Lift a hood, look for yourself."

He talked like his face was made of panes of glass sliding against one another. I waved him forward. "*You* check it, Ellis, you open one up." Ellis nodded like a dipping duck, waddled over to one of the cars, jiggled something inside, then raised the hood and stepped back.

I took one glance and my stomach slowly started to knot up. I was no motor buff but I damned well knew the difference between a gasoline engine and water boiler. Which explained the workbench—the tools had been window dressing. Most of them were brand new because most of them had obviously never been used. There had been nothing to use them on.

"The engines are steam," Ellis said, almost apologetically. "I've got a license to do restoration work and drop in steam engines. They don't allow them in cities but it's different on farms and country estates and in some small towns." He looked at me. "The license cost me a goddamned fortune."

It was a real handicap being a city boy, I thought. "Then why the act? Why the gun?"

"This?" he asked stupidly. He reached inside his coat and dropped the pistol on the floor; it made a light thudding sound and bounced, a pot metal toy. "The danger, it's the sense of danger, it's part of the sales pitch." He wanted to be angry now but he had been frightened too badly and couldn't quite make it. "The customers pay a lot of dough, they want a little drama. That's why—you know—the peephole and everything." He took a deep breath and when he exhaled it came out as a giggle, an incongruous sound from the big man. I found myself hoping he didn't have a heart condition. "I'm well known," he said defensively. "I take ads. . . . "

"The club," I said. "It's illegal."

Even if it was weak, his smile was genuine and then the score became crystal clear. The club was like a speakeasy during the Depression, with half the judges and politicians in town belonging to it. Why not? Somebody older wouldn't have my bias. . . . Pearson's address book had been all last names and initials but I had never connected any of them to anybody prominent; I handn't been around enough to know what connection to make.

I waved Ellis back to the workbench and stared glumly at the group. The mechanic I had frightened with the Mark II had a spreading stain across the front of his pants and I felt sorry for him momentarily.

Then I started to feel sorry for myself. Monte should have given me a longer briefing, or maybe assigned another Investigator to go with me, but he had been too sick and too wrapped up with the politics of it all. So I had gone off half-cocked and come up with nothing but a potential lawsuit for Air Central that would probably amount to a million dollars by the time Ellis got through with me.

It was a black day inside as well as out.

I holed up in a bar during the middle of the evening, which was probably the smartest thing I could have done. Despite their masks, people on the street had started to retch and vomit and I could feel my own nausea grow with every step. I saw one man try and strike a match to read a street sign; it wouldn't stay lit, there simply wasn't enough oxygen in the air. The ambulance sirens were a steady wail now and I knew it ws going to be a tough night for heart cases. They'd be going like flies before morning, I thought. . . .

Another customer slammed through the door, wheezing and coughing and taking huge gulps of the machine-pure air of the bar. I ordered another drink and tried to shut out the sound; it was too reminiscent of Monte hacking and coughing behind his desk at work.

And come morning, Monte might be out of a job, I thought. I for certain would be; I had loused up in a way that would cost the department money—the unforgivable sin in the eyes of the politicians.

I downed half my drink and started mentally reviewing the events of the day, giving myself a passing score only on figuring out that Pearson had had a stash. I hadn't known about Ellis' operation, which in one sense wasn't surprising. Nobody was going to drive something that looked like an old gasoline-burner around a city—the flatlanders would stone him to death.

But somebody still had a car, I thought. Somebody who was rich and immune from prosecution and a real nut about cars in the first place. . . . But it kept sliding away from me. Really rich men were too much in the public eye, ditto politicians. They'd be washed up politically if anybody ever found out. If nothing else, some poor bastard like the one at the end of the bar trying to flush out his lungs would assassinate him.

Somebody with money, but not too much. Somebody who was a car nut—they'd have to be to take the risks. And somebody for whom those risks were absolutely minimal. . . .

And then the lightbulb flashed on above my head, just like in the old cartoons. I wasn't dead certain I was right but I was willing to stake my life on it—and it was possible I might end up doing just that.

I slipped on a mask and almost ran out of the bar. Once outside, I sympathized with the guy who had just come in and who had given me a horrified look as I plunged out into the darkness.

It was smothering now, though the temperature had dropped a little so my shirt didn't cling to me in dirty, damp folds. Buses were being led through the streets; headlights died out completely within a few feet. The worst thing was that they left tracks in what looked like a damp, grayish ash that covered the street. Most of the people I bumped into—mere shadows in the night—had soaked their masks in water, trying to make them more effective. There were lights still on in the lower floors of most of the office buildings and I figured some people hadn't tried to make it home at all; the air was probably purer among the filing cabinets than in their own apartments. Two floors up, the buildings were completely hidden in the smoky darkness.

It took a good hour of walking before the sidewalks started to slant up and I knew I was getting out toward the foothills . . . I thanked God the business district was closer to the mountains than the ocean. My legs ached and my chest hurt and I was tired and depressed but at least I wasn't coughing anymore.

The buildings started to thin out and the streets finally became completely deserted. Usually the cops would pick you up if they caught you walking on the streets of Forest Hills late at night, but that night I doubted they were even around. They were probably too busy ferrying cases of cardiac arrest to St. Francis. . . .

The Sniffer was located on the top of a small, ancient building off on a side street. When I saw it I suddenly found my breath hard to catch again—a block down, the street abruptly turned into a canyon and wound up and out of sight. I glanced back at the building, just faintly visible through the grayed-down moonlight. The windows were boarded up and there was a For Rent sign on them. I walked over and flashed my light on the sign. It was old and peeling and had obviously been there for years; apparently nobody had ever wanted to rent the first floor. Ever? Maybe somebody had, I thought, but had decided to leave it boarded up. I ran my hand down the boards and suddenly paused at a knothole; I could feel heavy plate glass through it. I knelt and flashed my light at the hole and looked at a dim reflection of myself staring back. The glass had been painted black on the inside so it acted like a black marble mirror.

I stepped back and something about the building struck me. The boarded-up windows, I thought, the huge, oversized windows. . . . And the oversized, boarded-up doors. I flashed the light again at the concrete facing just above the doors. The words were there all right, blackened by time but still readable, cut into the concrete itself by order of the proud owner a handful of decades before. But you could still noodle them out: *RICHARD SIEBEN LINCOLN-MERCURY.*

Jackpot, I thought triumphantly. I glanced around—there was nobody else on the street—and listened. Not a sound, except for the faint murmur of traffic still moving in the city far away. A hot muggy night in the core city, I thought, but this night the parks and the fire escapes would be empty and five million people would be tossing and turning in their cramped little bedrooms; it'd be suicide to try and sleep outdoors.

In Forest Hills it was cooler—and quieter. I glued my ear to the boards over the window and thought I could hear the faint shuffle of somebody walking around and, once, the faint clink of metal against metal. I waited a moment, then slipped down to the side door that had "Air Central" on it in neat black lettering. All Investigators had master keys and I went inside. Nobody was upstairs; the lights were out and the only sound was the soft swish of the Sniffer's scribing pens against the paper roll. There was a stairway in the back and I walked silently down it. The door at the bottom was open and I stepped through it into a short hallway. Something, maybe the smell of the air, told me it had been used recently. I closed the door after me and stood for a second in the darkness. There was no sound from the door beyond. I tried the knob and it moved silently in my grasp.

I cracked the door open and peered throught the slit—nothing—then eased it open all the way and stepped out onto the showroom floor. There was a green-shaded lightbulb hanging from the ceiling, swaying slightly in some minor breeze so the shadows chased each other around the far corners of the room. Walled off at the end were two small offices where salesmen had probably wheeled and dealed long ago. There wasn't much else, other than a few tools scattered around the floor in the circle of light.

And directly in the center, of course, the car.

I caught my breath. There was no connection between it and Jack Ellis' renovated family sedans. It crouched there on the floor, a mechanical beast that was almost alive. Sleek curving fenders that blended into a louvered hood with a chromed steel bumper curving flat around the front to give it an oddly sharklike appearance. The headlamps were set deep into the fenders, the lamp wells outlined with chrome. The hood flowed into a windshield and that into a top which sloped smoothly down in back and tucked in neatly just after the rear wheels. The wheels themselves had wire spokes that gleamed wickedly in the light, and through a side window I could make out a neat array of meters and rocker switches, and finally bucket seats covered with what I instinctively knew was genuine black leather.

Sleek beast, powerful beast, I thought. I was unaware of walking up to it and running my hand lightly over a fender until a voice behind me said, "It's beautiful, isn't it?"

I turned like an actor in a slow-motion film. "Yeah, Dave," I said, "it's beautiful." Dave Ice of Air Central. In charge of all the Sniffers.

He must have been standing in one of the salesman's offices; it was the only way I could have missed him. He walked up and stood on the other side of the car and ran his left hand over the hood with the same affectionate motion a woman might use in stroking her cat. In his right hand he held a small Mark II pointed directly at my chest.

"How'd you figure it was me?" he asked casually.

"I thought at first it might be Monte," I said. "Then I figured you were the real nut about machinery."

His eyes were bright, too bright. "Tell me," he asked curiously, "would you have turned in Monte?"

"Of course," I said simply. I didn't add that it would have been damned difficult; that I hadn't even been able to think about that part of it.

So might've I, so might've I," he murmured. "When I was your age."

"For a while the money angle threw me," I said.

He smiled faintly. "It's a family heirloom. My father bought it when he was young, he couldn't bring himself to turn it in." He cocked his head. "Could you?" I looked at him uneasily and didn't answer and he said casually, "Go ahead, Jimmy, you were telling me how you cracked the case."

I flushed. "It had to be somebody who knew—who was absolutely sure—that he wasn't going to get caught. The Sniffers are pretty efficient, it would have been impossible to prevent their detecting the car—the best thing would be to censor the data from them. And Monte and you were the only ones who could have done that."

Another faint smile. "You're right."

"You slipped up a few nights ago," I said.

He shrugged. "Anybody could've. I was sick, I didn't get to the office in time to doctor the record."

"It gave the game away," I said. "Why only once? The Sniffer should have detected it far more often than just once."

He didn't say anything and for a long moment both of us were lost in admiration of the car.

Then finally, proudly: "It's the real McCoy, Jim. Six cylinder in-line engine, 4.2 liters displacement, nine-to-one compression ratio, twin overhead cams and twin Zenith-Stromberg carbs. . . . " He broke off. "You don't know what I'm talking about, do you?"

"No," I confessed, "I'm afraid not."

"Want to see the motor?"

I nodded and he stepped forward, waved me back with the Mark II, and opened the hood. To really appreciate it, of course, you had to have a thing for machinery. It was clean and polished and squatted there under the hood like a beautiful mechanical pet—so huge I wondered how the hood could close at all.

And then I realized with a shock that I hadn't been reacting like I should have, that I hadn't reacted like I should have ever since the movie at the club. . . .

"You can sit in it if you want to," Dave said softly. "Just don't touch anything." His voice was soft. "Everything works on it, Jim, everything works just dandy. It's oiled and greased and the tank is full and the battery is charged and if you wanted to, you could drive it right off the showroom floor."

I hesistated. "People in the neighborhood—"

—mind their own business," he said. "They have a different attitude, and besides, it's usually late at night and I'm out in the hills in seconds. Go ahead, get in." Then his voice hardened into command: "Get in!"

I stalled a second longer, then opened the door and slid into the seat. The movie was real now, I was holding the wheel and could sense the gearshift at my right and in my mind's eye I could feel the wind and hear the scream of the motor. . . .

There was something hard pressing against the side of my head. I froze. Dave was holding the pistol just behind my ear and in the side mirror I could see his finger tense on the trigger and pull back a millimeter. *Dear God. . . .*

He relaxed. "You'll have to get out," he said apologetically. "It would be appropriate, but a mess just the same."

I got out. My legs were shaking and I had to lean against the car. "It's a risky thing to own a car," I chattered. "Feeling runs pretty high against cars. . . . "

He nodded. "It's too bad."

"You worked for Air Central for years," I said. "How could you do it, and own this, too?"

"You're thinking about the air," he said carefully. "But Jim"— his voice was patient—"machines don't foul the air, men do. They foul the air, the lakes, and the land itself. And there's no way to stop it." I started to protest and he held up a hand. "Oh sure, there's always a time when you care—like you do now. But time . . . you know, time wears you down, it really does, no matter how eager you are. You devote your life to a cause and then you find yourself suddenly growing fat and bald and you discover nobody gives a damn about your cause. They're paying you your cushy salary to buy off their own consciences. So long as there's a buck to be made, things won't change much. It's enough to drive you—" He broke off. "You don't *really* think that anybody gives a damn about anybody else, do you?" He stood there looking faintly amused, a pudgy little man whom I should've been able to take with one arm tied behind my back. But he was ten times as dangerous as Ellis had ever imagined himself to be. "Only suckers care, Jim. I. . . . "

I dropped to the floor then, rolling fast to hit the shadows beyond the circle of light. His Mark II sprayed sparks and something burned past my shirt collar and squealed along the concrete floor. I sprawled flat and jerked my own pistol out. The first shot went low and there was the sharp sound of scored metal and I cursed briefly to myself—I must have brushed the car. Then there was silence and I scrabbled further back into the darkness. I wanted to pot the light but the bulb was still swaying back and forth and chances were I'd miss and waste the shot. Then there was the sound of running and I jumped to my feet and saw Dave heading for the door I had come in by. He seemed oddly defenseless—he was chubby and slow and knock-kneed and ran like a woman.

"Dave!" I screamed. "Dave! STOP!"

It was an accident, there was no way to help it. I aimed low and to the side, to knock him off his feet, and at the same time he decided to do what I had done and sprawl flat in the shadows. If he had stayed on his feet, the small rocket would have brushed him at knee level. As it was, it smashed his chest.

He crumpled and I ran up and caught him before he could hit the floor. He twisted slightly in my arms so he was staring at the car as he died. I broke into tears. I couldn't help that, either. I would remember the things Dave had done for me long after I had forgotten that one night he had tried to kill me. A threat to kill is unreal—actual blood and shredded flesh has its own reality.

I let him down gently and walked slowly over to the phone in the corner. Monte should still be in his office, I thought. I dialed and said, "The Director, please," and waited for the voice-actuated relay to connect me. "Monte, Jim Morrison here. I'm over at—" I paused. "I'm sorry, I thought it was Monte—" And then I shut up and let the voice at the other end of the line tell me that Monte had died with the window open and the night air filling his lungs with urban vomit. "I'm sorry," I said faintly, "I'm sorry, I'm very sorry," but the voice went on and I suddenly realized that I was listening to a recording and that there was nobody in the office at all. Then, as the voice continued, I knew why.

I let the receiver fall to the floor and the record started in again, as if expecting condolences from the concrete.

I should call the cops, I thought. I should—

But I didn't. Instead, I called Wanda. It would take an hour or more for her to collect the foodstuffs in the apartment and to catch an electricab but we could be out of the city before morning came.

And that was pretty funny because morning was never coming. The recording had said dryly that the tagged radioactive chimney exhausts had arrived, that the dragon's breath had circled the globe and the winds blowing in were as dirty as the air already over the city. Oh, it wouldn't happen right away, but it wouldn't be very long, either. . . .

Nobody had given a damn, I thought; not here nor any other place. Dave had been right, dead right. They had finally turned it all into a sewer and the last of those who cared had coughed his lungs out trying for a breath of fresh air that had never come, too weak to close a window.

I walked back to the car sitting in the circle of light and ran a finger down the scored fender where the small rocket had scraped the paint. Dave would never have forgiven me, I thought. Then I opened the door and got in and settled slowly back into the seat. I fondled the shift and ran my eyes over the instrument panel, the speedometer and the tach and the fuel and the oil gauges and the small clock. . . . The keys dangled from the button at the end of the hand brake. It was a beautiful piece of machinery, I thought again. I had never really loved a piece of machinery . . . until now.

I ran my hands around the wheel, then located the starter switch on the steering column. I jabbed in the key and closed my eyes and listened to the scream of the motor and felt its power shake the car and wash over me and thunder through the room. The movie at the club had been my only lesson but in its own way it had been thorough and it would be enough. I switched off the motor and waited.

When Wanda got there we would take off for the high ground. For the mountains and the pines and that last clear lake and that final glimpse of blue sky before it all turned brown and we gave up in final surrender to this climate of which we're so obviously proud. . . .

Part V

Solutions?

It is clear to most observers that the world's population is growing much too quickly, and that this rapid increase in the numbers of people is having, and will continue to have, serious consequences for society across a number of dimensions. Given the desirability of limiting population size, the key question becomes: how? Remember that the basis of the current population explosion is the imbalance between fertility and mortality; that is, the number of deaths has been reduced substantially, but the number of births remains relatively high, resulting in a dramatic growth in the earth's population.

In order to "solve" the population problem, it is essential that the centuries-old balance between births and deaths be restored. Hypothetically, there are two approaches to this "solution": (1) lower fertility, or (2) raise mortality. When such concepts are discussed, we touch on the broader subject of *population policy*, or, what attitudes and programs governments take with regard to the problems engendered by population growth.

Certainly, no government (at least under present circumstances) could in any way advocate openly a population policy based on higher mortality. No politician or bureaucrat can be expected to come out in favor of death! This obvious fact means that in the contemporary world government policies directed at the population problem have focused upon the lowering of fertility as the mechanism to slow the growth of population. The principal means by which it is intended to lower the number of births is *family planning*; family planning is largely a euphemism for the provision of contraceptive knowledge and devices to high fertility societies.

Sadly, family planning has not provided the solution to population growth, although it is clearly a desirable service to offer to couples who wish to use contraception. Demographers are increasingly inclined to view fertility as an extremely complex phenomenon which is influenced by a whole range of social, psychological, and economic forces, and which cannot be controlled by merely providing people with contraceptive devices. Apparently, such factors as the status of women in society (particularly the employment of women in non-agricultural pursuits), raising the income and educational levels of people, the change from an agricultural to an industrial-service economy (which reduces the economic role of children) and old-age insurance (in most societies parents must eventually count on their children for support, and the more children, the less risk that one will not have anybody to depend on) all have contributed to the decline of fertility in the advanced countries, and may do the same in the developing world where the number of births remains high. It is obvious, however, that such policies require massive investment funds, which most of the developing countries by definition are sorely lacking in, and at the present time there is little indication that a sufficient commitment exists in the advanced countries to provide such funds on an adequate scale.

Beyond policies such as those discussed above, which attempt to indirectly lower fertility by manipulating what seem to be causal factors involved, it is not unlikely that some governments may choose to attack the population problem by directly limiting fertility through, for example, mandatory sterilization programs. Indeed, at this writing there are reliable reports that such a program is in the planning stages in India, a country which has perhaps the world's most critical population problem (it is estimated that each year some 13 million persons, or a number about equal to the population of Australia, is added to India). According to these reports, each couple would be allowed two children (in some cases three), after which sterilization of one parent would be required. In the not-too-distant past even the contemplation of such a policy would have seemed an outrageous intrusion by government into the lives of individual families, but similar programs may be just around the corner in some countries.

SUGGESTED READINGS:
Blake, Judith. "Population Policy for Americans: Is the Government Being Misled?" *Science*, Vol. 164 (May 2, 1969).
Davis, Kingsley. "Population Policy: Will Current Programs Succeed?" *Science*, Vo. 158 (November 10, 1967).
Harkavy, Oscar (*et al*). "Family Planning and Public Policy: Who is Misleading Whom?" *Science*, Vol. 165 (July 25, 1969).

In this selection, the author describes the trials and tribulations of a woman determined to circumvent a government policy against having more than two children, a policy which is enforced with terrible finality.

by Maggie Nadler

The Secret

Sixteen-year-old Sally Morgan nods in response to her mother's words. She will not go to school today; tomorrow she will bring a note stating that she was sick. She knows what this means: her mother has been asked to take over the day shift again temporarily and she, Sally, will be needed at home during those crucial hours between nine and five. She brushes a stray lock of brown hair back from her forehead and tries to concentrate on her breakfast, although she is not hungry. It doesn't work. She pushes away the toast and eggs in disgust. Her stomach is churning. The fear is always there. Her eyes meet her mother's, remain locked for a moment in perfect understanding, and drop to the table again. On a nearby shelf, the radio is blaring away—a noisy early-morning news program. She turns it up a bit louder. The baby may wake up at any minute and start crying. Better to risk the anger of that old biddy in the next apartment than to let the sound of crying get out. It is always this way. Her fair, pretty face, sobered with the weight of early responsibility, breaks into a frown.

Across from her, her younger sister Jill is dawdling over her breakfast as usual, picking at it bite by dainty bite, studying it, worrying at it. She will finish it all, eventually; she always does. But why won't she hurry? Her fastidiousness, accompanied by that exasperating sullenness, annoys Sally, although she tries hard to be patient.

THE SECRET

At the stove, their mother is preparing the baby's formula. Sally's mind returns to the problem at hand, the same problem always at hand: the baby. A little modern-day Moses swaddled in blankets instead of bulrushes. It would all be rather pleasantly exciting if it were not so terrifying. The little baby brother, blond, beautiful, ten months old, in constant danger . . . how she loves him! So here she will be today, stuck in the tiny three-room apartment, the dingy, cramped apartment with walls like pasteboard, when she could be at school with her friends. She sighs. David has been attentive lately; she's almost certain he really likes her. Now she won't see him for a whole day, maybe longer. But she is needed here. She turns her attention back to her sister; as soon as Jill has finished eating, Sally will clear the table and do the dishes. Why won't the kid hurry?

Sitting stubbornly hunched over her breakfast, picking at it, slowly but surely making it disappear, thirteen-year-old Jill— thin-faced, sullen—glowers up at her sister. Darn Sally anyway, putting on airs, acting just like a grownup, and all on account of the brat. She used to be fun, but not any more. Now, do this, do that, yak, yak, yak. And why? We had to be different, have one more baby than everybody else. Privileged character. Mom says it's because of Daddy just dying and all, she wanted his last baby, but I know different. She wanted a *son*. Yeah. Sally and me were always a big disappointment to her even if Sally's too dumb to see it. *Take good care of your brother, now.* Brother, brother, brother this, brother that. Big deal. Just a stupid baby, and we have to have a big fuss. Nobody visits us; I can't even have my friends over. Darn Mom and Sally. I hope somebody finds out. . . .

Jill has finished her breakfast now, flings down her napkin defiantly, and gets up. As she does so, Sally catches a look on her face that she has never seen before. Or rather, has seen many times but failed to interpret correctly. *My God! She hates the baby!* Just like that: suddenly she knows. The thought is hideous. *God! What if—no, that couldn't ever happen—but then again, what if—*Slowly, her mind in a turmoil, she begins to clear away.

And then there is the mother, moving about the kitchen with an energy which masks the quiet desperation of the doomed or nearly doomed. Days like this one are the worst. She cannot bear to be away from home during the daylight hours. If only she could call in sick, but she doesn't dare. At forty, she is partially handicapped; arthritis has worked its calciumed way into the fine joints of her fingers, making excessive hand motion an agony, disqualifying her for most kinds of work. With jobs so scarce, she must hang on to the one she has, and therefore her work record must be perfect in all respects. She is fortunate to have a job at all. The one she holds now—radio dispatcher for a taxi company—was obtained for her through the influence of the foreman at Richard's plant, out of pity or perhaps even a sense of guilt. Richard. Richard. Richard, unable even to get insurance on account of the heart condition. But it wasn't his heart that killed him, finally, but a great chunk of metallic debris, loosed prematurely by an incautious crane operator, striking him, crushing him out of all semblance to humanity. Richard. Richie. Dick. Dickie. Rick. The name in all its variations and inflections rolls around in her mind for a while like pinballs in a machine. The names are charged with emotion: father and son coalesced. Richard, the father, her husband, and Dickie, his son.

Suddenly she stiffens. What is that scraping noise beyond the thin wall? Miss Hadley on the other side, moving her chair a bit closer, the better to hear you, my dears? She often does that. So far she hasn't heard much of interest; from long habit, her next-apartment neighbors keep their voices down when in the kitchen. But that doesn't stop her from trying. In all the years they've lived next to her, they have never been in her apartment nor she in theirs, yet they know her well enough from seeing her around the building, from the pounding on the walls and the querulous voice raised in protest against the noise they make. Malicious old bitch, always spying on the neighbors in as many ways as she can dream up. She has had a one-way glass panel installed in her door and often sits behind it keeping an eye out to see who calls on blond Miss Coombs across the hall, plus whatever other interesting tidbits of information she can manage to pick up. Once she was even observed, binoculars in hand, peering into a window of a building across the way. And so on. At least she hasn't complained about the radio yet today. With luck, maybe she won't at all.

Miss Hadley would dearly love to cause trouble for her neighbors, but she's stalemated there; they have an advantage which they may press at any moment. Cats. Miss Hadley has cats: four of them, two more than the zoning rules permit. The Morgans know this because they have often seen the animals make the perilous leap from Miss Hadley's window sill to their own and back again. She knows that they know. However much she may hate everything else in the world, she loves those cats. And so, the uneasy truce: don't bother us and we won't report you.

The mother stands very still, listening intently, but there is no further sound. Perhaps she has only imagined it. She has become hypersensitive (and why not?) and her mind sometimes plays tricks on her. She feels ill now, and very tired. If only Richard were still here. He would know what to do. Richard. Richard. Richard—

"Mother! What's wrong?" It is Sally's voice, from far away.

She realizes that she has been standing rigid, trembling, with her teeth tightly clenched against a scream.

Miss Priscilla Hadley, gaunt, white-haired, and prim, never loved by man or cherished by family, sits alone in her apartment. She is not listening through the walls now, nor is she observing the world from any one of her customary vantage points. She scarcely notices the radio blasting away next door. She is weeping. Great sobs wrack her as she twists on the sofa-bed. Her beloved cats have been poisoned. One of them, old Tom, companion of a dozen years, has just died; another, Scruffy, is in great pain and is obviously not going to live. The other two will probably recover. For a long time she remains on the bed, her head buried in her hands. If she ever catches up with whoever did this . . . It has to have been deliberate. Somebody fed them something. *Please let me find out who it was.* But she knows it's hopeless. The world is full of dirty, vicious cat haters. It could have been anybody.

After a while she gets up and goes to the phone to call the Animal Protective Society. She will have Scruffy put to sleep and both cats cremated; she cannot bear to think of them ending on a trash heap. While dialing, she first becomes aware of the noise. It's that family on the right again, the woman and those two teen-agers. Once she had hoped for children of her own; now the very thought appalls her. She wonders which of the three is responsible for the constant racket: all of them, probably, acting in perfect accord. It would be just like them; tight-mouthed, antisocial bunch, won't give you the time of day but, when it comes to annoyances . . . At this moment, her thoughts are interrupted by the sound of a voice at the other end. She makes arrangements. A man will come to pick up Scruffy and Tom; the ashes will be returned to her later in the week. As she hangs up, she is aware of the sound of a nearby door slamming; mechanically, she goes over to her own door and looks out. Yes, it's them; that mousy nobody and the younger girl. Strange, the mother doesn't usually go out mornings. Despite her distracting grief, impressions click in her mind with computer like precision. And where's the older one? Brats, both of them. Her lip curls slightly in disgust as tears well up in her eyes again. They had better not annoy her today.

The baby awakens and begins to wail fretfully. Sally hurries to give him his bottle. Jill and mother, barely on time, leave the apartment together. Downstairs, on the sidewalk, they separate. Jill walks in one direction, toward school, her mother in another, toward the monorail stop.

Mrs. Morgan boards the mono at the station. Her arthritic hand fumbles with the token while the conductor looks on in irritation and people jostle behind her. She gets it in the slot, finally, and moves forward. She is lucky; there is one seat left in the rapidly filling car. She sinks into it gratefully. At first she tries to distract herself by reading the advertisements posted in neat rows above her head. But the signs—BUY LIFE INSURANCE . . . SUPPORT OUR BOYS IN BOLIVIA . . . FIGHT CRIME: REPORT INFRACTIONS—are disquieting and eventually she turns her attention inward while allowing her gaze to wander. At once her thoughts crowd tumultuously in upon each other, filling her head, pounding out against the optic nerve in a steady, relentless rhythm: Baby. Danger. Please God. Baby. Danger. Please God. Danger. Please . . . She is so alone, so frighteningly alone in the world. If only there were some relatives or close trustworthy friends to take in one of the children! Something might be worked out. But there is no one. How long can luck hold out? Surely there are other women, perhaps many, perhaps nearby, doing the same thing she is doing, but she will never know who they are, or how numerous, or how they manage. Yet they must exist, each one living her own personal twenty-four-hour nightmare, a far-flung secret sisterhood united in guilt and terror. It is necessary for her to believe in their existence; otherwise, she would not be able to go on. Her mind grasps frantically at straws of reassurance. There have been many cases—haven't there?—of people hidden successfully for long periods of time, for years, even. Slaves, during the Civil War (she remembers this from fifth-grade history). Or even (dimly recalling another textbook) during World War II in Europe, enemies of the—what were they called—Nazi? Of course it's possible. She's read it. It will only be for two years more. Sally finishes school then, and pretty as she is, she'll have no trouble finding a husband right away. *And after that we can move somewhere else and pass ourselves off as a two-child family. Jill will be old enough to take on more responsibility by then, not that she'll be able to replace Sally, of course, but at least we'll be safe.*

Moving. The thought presents new worries. With housing so scarce, it may take a while. But she will not allow herself to think about that so far in advance. They'll find something when the time comes. For the time being, they are very fortunate to live in a building where, with the exception of the inquisitive Miss Hadley, people mind their own business. Only Miss Hadley takes an interest in their doings, and with care, she can be circumvented. It could be worse, much worse. Thank God Dickie is a relatively quiet baby. His occasional crying can easily be covered up by the sound of the radio. If he were the type to cry all night, it would have been hopeless. *But we've survived for ten months; the worst is past.* Of course, it's a lonely life. No one has visited the apartment in well over a year. It must be awfully hard on the girls not to be able to have their school friends over.

The car lurches suddenly at a sharp curve and a stab of searing pain shoots through her abdomen, souvenir of that night ten months ago when, with only Sally to assist her, she gave birth, twisting on the rock-hard mattress of Jill's bed and muffling her screams in a pillow. Tears well up in her eyes and she turns her head to stare out the window. It's an unfortunate moment to choose. To her right, only feet away, the massive white hulk of the Public Abortion Clinic sails by. PAC, focus of all her troubles and guilts. Only two children to a mother, in this society. But you want more? Sorry, madam. That's the law.

And she has dared to defy the law, she, a gray-haired, poorly educated, careworn widow of forty, one woman alone against the world. When she felt the forbidden life within her, she did not destroy it but rejoiced, and she wore loose clothes and thanked

God that she was large-boned and Dickie a small baby who scarcely showed. Now she must deal with the consequences.

Suddenly she snaps out of her reverie. It's her stop, and she nearly missed it. She jumps up and gets off just in time. This is fortunate. The stops are far apart, and had she ridden to the next one, she would have had to walk a long way and would undoubtedly have been late. She hurries across the platform and down the stairs past the three lower tiers of monorail tracks. She wishes they had a phone so she could call Sally around noon to check up on the baby.

Sally has fed the baby and crooned to him and rocked him to sleep in her arms. Now she carries him back to his "bed"—an old hamper lodged deep within the recess of the large bedroom closet, hidden from view by hanging clothes. What a place for a kid . . . but it has to be, she reminds herself. As she tucks him in, her attention is attracted by a slight rustling noise in one corner. Kneeling, she peers into the gloom, and sees a small hole where the wall meets the floor. Oh, no! Mice? Or rats? Surely not rats. Mice, more likely. The building in which they live is theoretically not a tenement, just as their neighborhood is theoretically not a slum, but they've had trouble with rodents before, although not recently. Sally does not like rodents; she has heard that they sometimes attack sleeping children. What should she do? She heads for the kitchen, hastily searches the cabinet above the sink. Yes, there it is: the nearly empty box of rat poison left over from some long-forgotten time. Hastening back to the closet, she sprinkles blue crystals liberally around the hole. There. That's better. The box is now empty. She throws it in the trash bag, which she notes is almost filled. She may as well empty it now. There is nobody in the hall. Little Dickie is safely asleep. Violating her mother's rule that he must never be left alone, even for an instant, she slips out, for just one moment, to the trash closet.

Miss Hadley sits in her kitchen eating the one sausage a day she permits herself. The sausage is long and plump, liberally sprinkled with sauerkraut and sheathed in a stiff bun; Miss Hadley chews it with the brisk short jawstrokes of one to whom ingestion is a distasteful chore to be completed as quickly as possible. Since she eats only to keep up her strength, she is taking her noonday meal today exactly as usual. After finishing, as usual, she disposes of all her garbage (wrapping paper and a few crumbs) in the trash closet down the hall.

Miss Hadley enjoys going through other people's trash and garbage: it is one of her dearest pleasures. In adddition to obtaining valuable insights into her neighbors' lives, she occasionally finds some very good scraps for her cats. Now she spots a new waste bag that hadn't been there the day before and, from force of habit, examines it avidly. Her hawk-eyes are drawn at once to a small cardboard container, a cylindrical box with a bright red label bearing a skull and crossbones: DANGER.

Danger

Danger. Poison. The cats. Immediately, everything falls into place. The blood drains from her face; her hands tremble. Feverishly she flings herself upon the pile, digging, tearing, clawing, through apple cores and orange rinds and potato peels and used tissue, all the way to the bottom, where she finds some papers. One of them is a crumpled envelope. She smooths it out and reads the name of the addressee: Mrs. Mildred Morgan. Morgan! It's them! Of course, who else, dirty scum, filthy rotten swine! They have the apartment next to the fire-escape platform. It would have been easy for them to put something out there. The fact that the Morgans have never shown the slightest animosity toward her pets is disregarded in the voluptuous wave of fury that possesses her. She sways, wringing her hands. She'll get them for this. She'll get them, she'll get them, she'll get them.

But how? A feeling of helplessness overtakes her. She won't be able to prove anything against them. The most she can do is complain to the landlord about their radio and maybe he will force them to keep it down. And that's not enough, oh, no, not nearly enough. No punishment is really great enough for them. But she'll think of something. She'll think of something if it takes the rest of her life.

Tears of rage and grief well up in her eyes and her whole body begins to tremble violently.

Jill gets home at four o'clock. She is in a vile mood, sulky and defiant. One of her friends has just asked her, for the nth time, why they can't play at *her* house for a change. She is sick of the story of an alcoholic mother who prevents her from bringing friends home. As her friends have pointed out often enough, Roz's mother is alcoholic and Roz has people over all the time. It's nothing to be ashamed of. So Jill has to say that her own mother is not only alcoholic, but violent. She stomps into the bedroom, flings herself down on her bed, and immerses herself in a teen-love comic book. Oh, she's so tired of it all.

Mrs. Morgan is home by five-thirty, weary but full of questions about Sally's day. She doesn't have to fix supper; Sally has already prepared it, as a surprise. The three of them sit down to casserole and canned soup. The radio is going. Sally and Jill exchange sharp words across the table; their mother referees tiredly. Jill is whining now about how she never has any fun and how she wishes they didn't have to live this way. The mother's abstracted replies show that she is only half listening. She doesn't suspect, Sally thinks, she really doesn't notice. Maybe it's better that way—or is it? But nothing will happen. Everything will be all right.

At six, the sky suddenly darkens. There's going to be a storm. Yes, there it is, the first crashing peal of thunder. Mrs. Morgan rushes to Dickie's bed. He is awake, and frightened. He can hear the thunder and he is afraid of storms. He's going to start crying any second. She carries him into the living room. Sally quickly turns the radio louder, then goes to sit beside her mother on the couch. Jill takes a chair. The four sit locked in a private world of sound: heavy rain-patter punctuated by bursts of thunder, baby's crying, and above it all, the sensual pounding of the radio music. Thump. Thump. Thump. Thump, goes the heavy beat. Rain. Thunder. Baby. Music. Rain. Thunder. Baby. Music. Rain. Thunder. Baby—

Baby.

The music has stopped.

The radio has gone dead. The lights are out.

And suddenly the shrill, plaintive wailing of the baby can be clearly heard against the counterpoint of storm sounds. Quickly. Mrs. Morgan claps a hand over Dickie's mouth, causing him to sputter and gasp. For a timeless moment she holds it there and then, mercifully, the music starts up again. Huddled together, she and Sally exchange frightened whispers. Has anyone heard? Noticed? No, of course not. It was only for a second. Nobody would notice, not even that old bat next door, unless she happened to be listening for it right at that particular instant. We've got to stop being so paranoid. Other people aren't keeping track of every single move we make.

Seated in a hard-backed chair in her tiny antiseptic kitchen, Miss Hadley presses her ear against the wall. She has been in this position for hours, ever since the younger daughter got home. She is waiting for them to say something about her cats. They will, eventually. She knows they will. Miss Hadley's ears are sharp, but not sharp enough to hear over the din of the radio. Still she perseveres, fascinated, obsessed. The guilty always reveal themselves. She will catch them eventually. A storm has come up, but she hardly notices, even when cold rain blows in her open window. All her attention is rivited upon that one tiny fragment of space, that microcosm where her ear meets the wall. Her head is filled with infernal music, throbbing, pounding. . . .

Then suddenly, without warning, the lights go and the music dies out, giving way to another sound. It's only for an instant, but in that instant she knows. A shrill sound. A wailing sound.

Of course! Casual observations, snips of information collected over the past months and mentally filed away for future reference now click with deadly accuracy in her computer-mind. So that's what they've been up to all this time! A baby; how very perfect! She'd had babies too. Her cats were her babies, and now they're gone. The images of Tom and Scruffy float lazily in the black void behind her eyeballs as, shaking with excitement, she reaches for the telephone.

The mother sits sobbing wildly, face buried in her hands, flanked by those two scared-looking daughters of hers, while the policeman talks to her in a gentle but firm voice. Why did she do it? She knows the provisions of the law. No, he's not allowed to divulge who reported them. And so on. He feels sorry for them all: when will people learn?

He and his discreetly invisible plainclothes partner turn to go. The woman flings herself upon them, kicking, scratching, biting, screaming. They are prepared for that. The officer pulls an in-haler-sedative cartridge from his pocket and clamps it over her nose and mouth while his partner holds her. Within seconds she is unconscious. Before leaving, the cop feels called upon to administer some words of comfort, which he addresses to the older girl.

The infant won't suffer, he assures her. It's entirely painless.

He'll just be sleeping and he'll never wake up. That's all there is to it. Now it is her turn to burst into hysterical sobbing. White-faced, the younger one approaches her sister and awkwardly tries to put her arms around her. The older girl jerks away. She screams a profanity. She slaps the younger girl again and again, with all her strength. The child stumbles backward into a corner and cowers there in terrified incomprehension. The officers wonder what it is all about: just hysteria, probably.

The two turn to leave once more. The uniformed one goes back into the bedroom and gently picks up the sleeping baby. Absently, he runs a hand through the downy hair. He loves children but he also knows about the evils of overpopulation he has been to the Police Academy. He is a good citizen. He has two small boys of his own and his wife has been sterilized. He displays the flag on Flag Day.

Tenderly bearing their sleeping burden, the two men leave the apartment behind them and disappear into the night.

The Census Takers

To demographers, a census, which is a count of a population and its characteristics, is the basis for most studies of population trends. In the United States, for instance, a census is taken every ten years (officially for purposes of allotting representation in Congress), and the wealth of information contained in the census tabulations provides grist for the demographers' mills for years. In the following story, however, the census is utilized to systematically eliminate "surplus" people, a policy of population control through the mechanism of mortality.

by Frederik Pohl

The Census Takers

It gets to be a madhouse around here along about the end of the first week. Thank heaven we only do this once a year, that's what I say! Six weeks on, and forty-six weeks off—that's pretty good hours, most people think. But they don't know what those six weeks are like.

It's bad enough for the field crews, but when you get to be an Area Boss like me it's frantic. You work your way up through the ranks, and then they give you a whole C.A. of your own; and you think you've got it made. Fifty three-man crews go out, covering the whole Census Area; a hundred and fifty men in the field, and twenty or thirty more in Area Command—and you boss them all. And everything looks great, until Census Period starts and you've got to work those hundred and fifty men; and six weeks is too unbearably long to live through, and too impossibly short to get the work done; and you begin living on black coffee and thiamin shots and dreaming about the vacation hostel in Point Loma.

Anybody can panic, when the pressure is on like that. Your best field men begin to crack up. But you can't afford to, because you're the Area Boss. . . .

Take Witeck. We were Enumerators together, and he was as good a man as you ever saw, absolutely nerveless when it came to processing the Overs. I counted on that man the way I counted on my own right arm; I always bracketed him with the greenest, shakiest new cadet Enumerators, and he never gave me a moment's trouble for years. Maybe it was too good to last; maybe I should have figured he would crack.

I set up my Area Command in a plush penthouse apartment. The people who lived there were pretty well off, you know, and they naturally raised the dickens about being shoved out. "Blow it," I told them. "Get out of here in five minutes, and we'll count you first." Well, that took care of *that*; they were practically kissing my feet on the way out. Of course, it wasn't strictly by the book, but you have to be a little flexible; that's why some men become Area Bosses, and others stay Enumerators.

Like Witeck.

Along about Day Eight things were really hotting up. I was up to my neck in hurry-ups from Regional Control—we were running a little slow—when Witeck called up. "Chief," he said, "I've got an In."

I grabbed the rotary file with one hand and a pencil with the other. "Blue-card number?" I asked.

Witeck sounded funny over the phone. "Well, Chief," he said, "he doesn't have a blue card. He says—"

"No blue card?" I couldn't believe it. Come in to a strange C.A. without a card from your own Area Boss, and you're one In that's a cinch to be an Over. "What kind of a crazy C.A. does he come from, without a blue card?"

Witeck said, "He don't come from any C.A., Chief. He says—"

"You mean he isn't from this country?"

"That's right, Chief. He—"

"Hold it!" I pushed away the rotary file and grabbed the immigration roster. There were only a couple of dozen names on it, of course—we have enough trouble with our own Overs, without taking on a lot of foreigners, but still there were a handful every year who managed to get on the quotas. "I.D number?" I demanded.

"Well, Chief," Witeck began, "he doesn't have an I.D. number. The way it looks to me—"

Well, you can fool around with these irregulars for a month, if you want to, but it's no way to get the work done. I said, "Over him!" and hung up. I was a little surprised, though; Witeck knew the ropes, and it wasn't like him to buck an irregular onto me. In the old days, when we were both starting out, I'd seen him Over a whole family just because the spelling of their names on their registry cards was different from the spelling on the checklist.

But we get older. I made a note to talk to Witeck as soon as the rush was past. We were old friends; I wouldn't have to threaten him with being Overed himself, or anything like that. He'd know, and maybe that would be all he would need to snap him back. I certainly would talk to him, I promised myself, as soon as the rush was over, or anyway as soon as I got back from Point Loma.

I had to run up to Regional Control to take a little talking-to myself just then, but I proved to them that we were catching up and they were only medium nasty. When I got back Witeck was on the phone again. "Chief," he said, real unhappy, "this In is giving me a headache. I—"

"Witeck," I snapped at him, "are you bothering me with another In? Can't you handle anything by yourself?"

He said, "It's the same one, Chief. He says he's a kind of ambassador, and—"

"Oh," I said. "Well, why the devil don't you get your facts straight in the first place? Give me his name and I'll check his legation."

"Well, Chief," he began again, "he, uh, doesn't have any legation. He says he's from the"—he swallowed—"from the middle of the earth."

"You're crazy," I'd seen it happen before, good men breaking under the strain of census taking. They say in cadets that by the time you process your first five hundred Overs you've had it; either you take a voluntary Over yourself, or you split wide open and they carry you off to a giggle farm. And Witeck was past the five hundred mark, way past.

There was a lot of yelling and crying from the filter center, which I'd put out by the elevators, and it looked like Jumpers. I stabbed the transfer button on the phone and called to Carias, my number-two man: "Witeck's flipped or something. Handle it!"

And then I forgot about it, while Carias talked to Witeck on the phone; because it was Jumpers, all right, a whole family of them.

There was a father and a mother and five kids—*five* of them. Aren't some people disgusting? The field Enumerator turned them over to the guards—they were moaning and crying—and came up and gave me the story. It was bad.

"You're the head of the household?" I demanded of the man.

He nodded, looking at me like a sick dog. "We—we weren't Jumping," he whined. "Honest to heaven, mister—you've got to believe me. We were—"

I cut in, "You were packed and on the doorstep when the field crew came by. Right?" He started to say something, but I had him dead to rights. "That's plenty friend," I told him. "That's Jumping, under the law: Packing, with intent to move, while a census Enumeration crew is operating in your locale. Got anything to say?"

Well, he had plenty to say, but none of it made any sense. He turned my stomach, listening to him. I tried to keep my temper—you're not supposed to think of individuals, no matter how worthless and useless and generally unfit they are; that's against the whole principle of the Census—but I couldn't help telling him: "I've met your kind before, mister. Five kids! If it wasn't for people like you we wouldn't *have* any Overs, did you ever think of that? Sure you didn't—you people never think of anything but yourself! Five kids, and then when Census comes around you think you can get smart and Jump." I tell you, I was shaking. "You keep your little beady eyes peeled, sneaking around, watching the Enumerators, trying to count how many it takes to make an Over; and then you wait until they get close to you, so you can Jump. Ever stop to think what trouble that makes for us?" I demanded. "Census is supposed to be fair and square, everybody an even chance—and how can we make it that way unless everybody stands still to be counted?" I patted Old Betsy, on my hip. "I haven't Overed anybody myself in five years," I told him, "but I swear, I'd like to handle you personally!"

He didn't say a word once I got started on him. He just stood there, taking it. I had to force myself to stop, finally; I could have gone on for a long time, because if there's one thing I hate it's these lousy, stinking breeders who try to Jump when they think one of them is going to be an Over in the count-off. Regular Jumpers are bad enough, but when it's the people who make the mess in the first place—

Anyway, time was wasting. I took a deep breath and thought things over. Actually, we weren't too badly off; we'd started off Overing every two-hundred-and-fiftieth person, and it was beginning to look as though our preliminary estimate was high; we'd just cut back to Overing every three-hundredth. So we had a little margin to play with.

I told the man, dead serious; "You know I could Over the lot of you on charges, don't you?" He nodded sickly. "All right, I'll give you a chance. I don't want to bother with the red tape; if you'll take a voluntary Over for yourself, we'll start the new count with your wife."

Call me soft, if you want to; but I still say that it was a lot better than fussing around with charges and a hearing. You get into a hearing like that and it can drag on for half an hour or more; and then Regional Control is on your tail because you're falling behind.

It never hurts to give a man a break, even a Jumper, I always say—as long as it doesn't slow down your Census.

Carias was waiting at my desk when I got back; he looked worried about something, but I brushed him off while I initialed the Overage report on the man we'd just processed. He'd been an In, I found out when I canceled his blue card. I can't say I was surprised. He'd come from Denver, and you know how they keep exceeding their Census figures; no doubt he thought he'd have a better chance in my C.A. than anywhere else. And no doubt he was right, because we certainly don't encourage breeders like him—actually, if he hadn't tried to Jump it was odds-on that the whole damned family would get by without an Over for years.

Carias was hovering right behind me as I finished. "I hate these voluntaries," I told him, basketing the canceled card. "I'm going to talk to Regional Control about it; there's no reason why they can't be processed like any other Over, instead of making me okay each one individually. Now, what's the matter?"

He rubbed his jaw. "Chief," he said, "it's Witeck."

"Now what? Another In?"

Carias glanced at me, then away. "Uh, no, Chief. It's the same one. He claims he comes from, uh, the center of the earth."

I swore out loud. "So he has to turn up in my C.A.!" I complained bitterly. "He gets out of the nuthouse, and right away—"

"Carias said, "Chief, he might not be crazy. He makes it sound pretty real."

I said: "Hold it, Carias. Nobody can live in the center of the earth. It's solid, like a potato."

"Sure, Chief," Carias nodded earnestly. "But he says it isn't. He says there's a what he calls neutronium shell, whatever that is, with dirt and rocks on both sides of it. We live on the outside. He lives on the inside. His people—"

"Carias!" I yelled. "You're as bad as Witeck. This guy turns up, no blue card, no I.D. number, no credentials of any kind. What's he going to say, 'Please sir, I'm an Over, please process me'? Naturally not! So he makes up a crazy story, and you fall for it!"

"I know, Chief," Carias said humbly.

"Neutronium shell!" I would have laughed out loud, if I'd had the time. "Neutronium my foot! Don't you know it's *hot* down there?"

"He says it's hot neutronium," Carias said eagerly. "I asked him that myself, Chief. He said it's just the shell that—"

"Get back to work!" I yelled at him. I picked up the phone and got Witeck on his wristphone. I tell you, I was boiling. As soon as Witeck answered I lit into him; I didn't give him a chance to get a word in. I gave it to him up and down and sidewise; and I finished off by giving him a direct order. "You Over that man," I told him, "or I'll personally Over you! You hear me?"

There was a pause. Then Witeck said, "Jerry? Will you listen to me?"

That stopped me. It was the first time in ten years, since I'd been promoted above him, that Witeck had dared call me by my first name. He said, "Jerry, listen. This is something big. This guy is really from the center of the earth, no kidding. He—"

"Witeck," I said, "You've cracked."

"No, Jerry, honest! And it worries me. He's right there in the next room, waiting for me. He says he had no idea things were like this on the surface; he's talking wild about cleaning us off and starting all over again; he says—"

"*I* say he's an Over!" I yelled. "No more talk, Witeck. You've got a direct order—now carry it out!"

So that was that.

We got through the Census Period after all, but we had to do it shorthanded; and Witeck was hard to replace. I'm a sentimentalist, I guess, but I couldn't help remembering old times. We started even; he might have risen as far as I—but of course he made his choice when he got married and had a kid; you can't be a breeder and an officer of the Census both. If it hadn't been for his record he couldn't even have stayed on as an Enumerator.

I never said a word to anyone about his crackup. Carias might have talked, but after we found Witeck's body I took him aside. "Carias," I said reasonably, "we don't want any scandal, do we? Here's Witeck, with an honorable record; he cracks, and kills himself, and that's bad enough. We won't let loose talk make it worse, will we?"

Carias said uneasily, "Chief, where's the gun he killed himself with? His own processor wasn't even fired."

You can let a helper go just so far. I said sharply, "Carias, we still have at least a hundred Overs to process. You can be on one end of the processing—or you can be on the other. You understand me?"

He coughed. "Sure, Chief. I understand. We don't want any loose talk."

And that's how it is when you're an Area Boss. But I didn't ever get my vacation at Point Loma; the tsunami there washed out the whole town the last week of the Census. And when I tried Baja California, they were having that crazy volcanic business; and the Yellowstone Park bureau wouldn't even accept my reservation because of some trouble with the geysers, so I just stayed home. But the best vacation of all was just knowing that the Census was done for another year.

Carias was all for looking for this In that Witeck was talking about, but I turned him down. "Waste of time," I told him. "By now he's a dozen C.A.'s away. We'll never see him again, him or anybody like him—I'll bet my life on that."

Statistician's Day

If the various countries of the world do indeed manage to control population growth (hopefully through lower fertility), the implications will be far-reaching. One consequence of slower rates of growth is an "older" population, that is, statistically the average age of slower growing populations is older than rapidly growing societies. Put another way, more slowly growing populations have a higher percentage of the people in the older age groups, and societies which are experiencing rapid growth have a relatively high percentage of children and young adults. The United Nations has estimated that in the developed regions of the world (Europe, Northern America, the U.S.S.R., Japan, Australia) about 28 percent of the population is under 15 years old, whereas in the developing countries of Asia, Africa, and Latin America, over 40 percent of the total population is less than 15 years of age.

As a society undergoes the change from rapid to slower growth, the percentage of young people declines, creating a number of effects which are usually not foreseen. In the United States, for example, the end of the "baby boom" eventually translated into declining enrollments in schools and universities (contributing, among other reasons, to smaller enrollments and a general retreat in higher education). Some have even noted that manufacturers of baby products have shifted their advertising campaign to the adult market to help offset the reduction in the population of infants.

As the next story recounts, there may even be problems beyond school enrollments and baby products in a future no-growth society.

by James Blish

Statistician's Day

Wiberg had been a foreign correspondent for the *New York Times* for fourteen years, ten of them devoted also to his peculiar speciality, and had at one time or another spent a total of eighteen weeks in England. (He was, as one would expect, precise about such matters.) As a result, he was considerably surprised by the home of Edmund Gerrard Darling.

Population Control had been instituted just ten years ago, after the fearful world famine of 1980, and since that time England had not changed much. Driving along the M.4 motorway from London, he saw again the high-rise "developments" which had obliterated the Green Belt which once had surrounded the city, just as they had taken over Westchester County in New York, Arlington in Virginia, Evanston in Illinois, Berkeley in California. Few new ones had been built since—after all, with population static, there was no need—though the hurried construction of many of them was going to force replacement before long.

Similarly, the town of Maidenhead, stabilized at 20,000 souls, looked just as it had when he had passed through it last time on the way to Oxford. (Then, he had been paying this kind of call on the coastal erosion expert Charles Charleston Shackleton, who had also been something of a writer.) This time, however, he had to turn off the motorway at Maidenhead Thicket, and suddenly found himself in a kind of countryside he had not dreamed existed any more, at least certainly not anywhere between London and Reading.

A road exactly one car wide, completely overhung with trees, led him nearly five miles to a roundabout the mall of which a child could have spat across, were it not for the moss-grown, ten-foot World War I memorial pillar in the middle. On the other side of this was Shurlock Row, his destination—a village which seemed to consist of nothing but a church, a pub and five or six shops. There must have been a duckpond somewhere nearby, too, for he could hear a faint quacking.

"The Phygtle," the novelist's home, was also on the High Street—there seemed to be no other. It was a large, two-storey thatched cottage, with white walls and oak timbers which had been painted black. Over the thatching, which was necessarily very recent, there was chicken-wire to discourage birds; the rest of the house looked as though it had been started about the Sixteenth Century, and probably had.

Wiberg parked the Morris and felt in his inside jacket pocket for the canned Associated Press obituary, which rewarded him with a faint but reassuring crackle. He did not need to take it out; he knew it by heart by now. It had been the arrival by mail, a week ago, of that galley proof which had started him on this journey. The obit was not due to be published for nearly a year, but Darling had been reported ill, and that always made a good pretext—indeed, the usual one.

He got out of the car and walked to the stable-type front door, which at his knock was opened by a plump, ruddy, well-scrubbed young girl in a housemaid's uniform. He gave all his name.

"Ah, yes, Mr. Wiberg, Sir Edmund's expectin' ye," she said in a strong Irish accent. "Perhaps ye'd care to be waitin' in the garden?"

"I'd like that," he said. The girl was evidently brand new, for the novelist was not a knight but an O. M., an honor a good deal higher; but Darling reputedly cared little for such gauds and probably did not even bother to correct her.

He was led through a large dining room with a low beamed ceiling and a fireplace built of hand-made briquettes, and out a glazed door at the back. The gardens covered about half an acre, and consisted chiefly of flowering shrubs and rose bushes through which gravel paths wound; there were also several old apple and pear trees, and even a fig tree. Part of the area had been hedged off as a vegetable garden, which included a small potting shed, and the whole was screened from the road and from the neighbors by a willow-withe fence and close-set evergreens.

What interested Wiberg most, however, was a brick guest house or staff annex at the back of the gardens. This, he knew from the obit, had its own bathroom (or wardrobe, as middle-class British-ers still delicately called it); and it was in this building that Darling had done his writing in the days when his family had still been living at home. It had originally had a peaked, tiled roof, but much of this had been cut away to accommodate the famous little astronomical observatory.

The seeing around here, Wiberg reflected, must have been terrible even before Darling had been born, but again, that wouldn't have mattered much to Darling. He was an amateur of the sciences ("the world's finest spectactor sport," he had called them), and had built the observatory not for research, but only because he liked to look at the heavens.

Wiberg peered in a window, but there was no remaining trace of the novelist's occupancy; evidently only the maid used the outbuilding now. Wiberg sighed. He was not a particularly sensi-tive man—he could not afford to be—but there were times when his occupation depressed even him.

He resumed prowling around the garden, sniffing at roses and at stands of wallflowers. He had never encountered the latter in the States and they had a spicy, exotic odor, rather like that of flowering tobacco, or what he imagined as the smell of the herbs used by ancient Egyptian embalmers.

Then the maid called him. He was led back through the dining room, and then around the L of an immense, book-lined lounge with a polished-stone fireplace to the main staircase. At the head of these was the master bedroom. As he approached the door, the maid called out, "Mind your head, sir," but she was a moment too late; he cracked the crown of it on the lintel.

A chuckle came from inside. "You're far from the first," a male voice said. "One had to be bloody careful carrying a kid through that door."

The impact had been minor and Wiberg forgot it instantly. Edmund Gerrard Darling, in a plaid robe, was propped up amid pillows in an immense bed—a feather bed, judging by the way even his slight frame sank into it. He still had quite a lot of his hair, although it began farther back from his forehead than it had even in his most recent jacket photograph, and he wore the same rimless glasses with the gold bows. His face, though still patrician, had become a little heavier in its contours despite his illness, giving it a rather avuncular expression hard to reconcile with that of a man who, as a critic, had for nearly sixty years mercilessly flayed his colleagues for their ignorance of elementary English, let alone any other literature.

"I'm honored and pleased to see you, sir," Wiberg said, producing his notebook.

"I wish I could say as much," Darling said, waving him to a wing chair. "However, I've expected you for a long time. There's really only one question remaining in my mind, and I'd appreciate your answering it straight off—always providing, of course, that you're allowed to".

"Anything at all, sir. After all, I came to ask questions, too. What is it?"

"Are you," the novelist said, "only the advance man for the executioner, or are you the executioner himself?"

Wilberg manged an uncertain laugh. "I'm afraid I don't understand the question, sir."

In point of fact, he understood it perfectly. What he did not understand was how Darling had come by enough information to have been able to frame it. For ten whole years, the chief secret of PopCon had been extremely well kept.

"If you won't answer my question, I need hardly feel obligated to answer yours," Darling said. "You won't deny, I trust, that you've got my obituary in your pocket?"

This was so common a suspicion in Wiberg's experience that he had no trouble responding to it with every appearance of complete candor.

"Of course I do," he said. "As I'm sure you know, both large newspapers like the *Times* and the big press associations keep obituaries of eminent or newsworthy living people standing in their files, in case of accident. Every so often they have to be updated as a matter of course; and every reporter who's sent out on an interview briefs himself first from those files, also as a matter of course.

"I began as a newspaperman," Darling said. "Hence I also

know that it is not the custom of large journals to send one of their chief foreign correspondents on such cubs' assignments."

"Not everyone to be interviewed is a Nobel Prize winner," Wiberg said. "And when such a figure is eighty years of age, and is reliably reported to be ill, getting from him what may be a final interview is not assigned to a cub. If you choose to regard this simply as updating an obituary, sir, there's nothing I can do to prevent you. No doubt there is something a little ghoulish about it, but as I know you're also aware, a lot of newspaper work is amenable to the same description."

"I know, I know," Darling said testily. "And under the circumstances, without your for a minute wishing to exalt yourself in any way, the fact that you were given the assignment might also be taken as a gesture of respect. Eh?"

"Well," Wiberg said, "yes, sir, I might put it that way." In fact, he had been just about to put it exactly that way.

"Bosh."

Wiberg shrugged. "As I say, sir, I can't prevent you from seeing it in any light you choose. But I do regret it."

"I didn't say I saw it in a different light. What I said was, 'Bosh.' What you have told me is largely true, but also so irrelevant as to be actively misleading. I had hoped you would tell me the facts, to which I think I am entitled. Instead, you have answered my question with what obviously is a standard line of chatter for difficult customers."

Wiberg leaned back in the chair, his apprehension growing. "Then perhaps you'll tell me what you see as the relevant facts, sir?"

"You don't deserve it, but there would be no sense in my keeping from you what you already know—which was precisely what I wanted you to see in my case," Darling said. "Very well, let's stay with the newspapers a while."

He fingered in the breast pocket of his jacket and produced a cigarette, and then pressed a torpedo switch on his nightstand. The maid came in at once.

"Matches," he said.

"Sir, the doctor—'

"Bother the doctor, I now know when I'm going to die almost to the day. Never mind, don't look so distressed, just bring me some matches, and light the fire with them on your way past."

The day was still warm, but for some reason Wilberg too was glad to see the little grate begin to catch. Darling drew on the cigarette and then regarded it appreciatively.

"Damn nonsense anyhow, those statistics," he said. "Which in fact has a direct bearing on the subject. When you get to be in your sixties, Mr. Wiberg, you begin to become rather a fan of the obituary notices. Your boyhood heroes begin to die, your friends begin to die, and insensibly you become interested in the deaths of people you neither knew nor cared about, and then of people you never even heard of.

"It's perhaps rather a mean pastime, with no little amount of self-congratulation in it: 'Well, *he's* gone, but *I'm* still here.' Of course, if you're of at all an introspective turn of mind, it can also begin to make you increasingly aware of your own growing isolation in the world. And if your inner resources are few, it can also increase your fear of your own death.

"Luckily, one of my interests for many years has been in the sciences, with particular emphasis upon mathematics. And after a lot of reading of death notices in the *New York Times,* the *Times* of London, and some other large newspapers I keep up with, at first casually, then assiduously, I began to become conscious of a run of coincidences. Do you follow me so far?"

"I think so," Wiberg said guardedly. "What kind of coincidences?"

"I could produce you specific examples, but I think a general description will suffice. To find such coincidences, one must read the minor death notices, as well as the deaths that produce the headlines and the formal obituaries. Then, you will find, say, a day in which what seems to be an abnormally large number of doctors have died. On another day, an abnormally large number of lawyers. And so on.

"I first noticed this on a day when almost all the chief executives of a large American engineering firm had been killed in the same airplane disaster. This struck me as peculiar, because by that time it had become standard practice among American firms *never* to allow more than two executives to travel on the same flight. On a hunch, I ran down the minor notices, and I found that it had been a very bad day for engineers in general. And also I found something quite unexpected: that almost all of them had died in some sort of travel accident. The plane crash had been the unlucky coincidence that drew my attention to what seemed to be a real pattern.

"I began to keep tallies. I discovered a good many other correlations. For one, in deaths-by-travel, whole families often die—and in such instances, it most often turns out that the wife may be related to the husband by profession, as well as simply by matrimony."

"Interesting . . . and a little eerie," Wiberg agreed. "But as you say, obviously only coincidence. In so small a sample—"

"It's not a small sample after you watch it for twenty years," Darling said. "And I no longer believe that any part of it is coincidence except the initial plane crash that started me looking for it. It isn't, in fact, a question of belief at all any more. I kept exact records, and periodically I phone my figures in to the computation center at London University, without, of course, telling the programmers what the figures stand for. I had the last such computation run when I got your cable asking to visit me, with a chi-square test. I got a significance of point zero zero zero one at the five per cent level of confidence. That's better than anything the anti-cigarette forces have ever been able to come up with, and we've had regiments of medical asses, and even whole governments, behaving as if those figures stood for a real phenomenon, ever since about 1950.

"And while I'm at it, I run counter-checks. It occurred to me that the *age* at death might be the really significant factor. The chi-square test shows that it is not; there is no correlation with age at all. But it is *perfectly* clear that these deaths are being selected for upon the basis of business, trade or profession."

"Hmm. Suppose—for the sake of argument—that this is really happening. Can you suggest how?"

"*How* is not the problem," Darling said. "It cannot be a natural phenomenon, because natural forces like biological selection do not show that high a degree of specificity, or act over so brief a secular period. The real question, therefore, is: Why? And there can be only one answer to that."

"Which is?"

"Excuse me, sir," Wiberg said, "but with all due respect, the idea seems to me to be, well, faintly paranoid."

"It is massively paranoid, but it is happening; I notice that you don't dispute that. And it is the policy-makers who are paranoid, not I."

"What would be the use of such a policy—or what would someone imagine its use to be?"

The novelist looked steadily into Wiberg's eyes through the rimless glasses.

"Universal Population Control," he said, "has been officially in force for ten years, and unofficially, it seems, for twenty. And it works; the population is now static. Most people believe, and are told, that it consists entirely of enforced birth control. They do not stop to think that to maintain a genuinely static population, you also need an absolutely predictable economy. Second, they do not stop to think—and are *not* told, indeed the facts they would need to deduce it are now suppressed even on the grammar-school level—that at our present state of knowledge we can control only *numbers* of births; we cannot control *who* gets born. Oh, of course we can now control the sex of the child, that's easy; but we cannot control whether he will turn out to be an architect, a navvy or just a plain ordinary clot.

"Yet in a completely controlled economy, one must take care to have only a fixed number of architects, navvies and clots extant at any given era. Since you can't do that by birth control, *you must do it by death control.* Hence, when you find yourself with an uneconomic surplus of, say, novelists, you skim off the surplus. Of course, you try to confine the skimming to the oldest, but since the period in which such a surplus is going to appear is inherently unpredictable, how old the oldest are when the skimming takes place varies too widely to attain statistical significance. It is probably further masked by such tactical considerations as making all the deaths look accidental and unconnected, which must often mean killing off a few younger members of a given class and leaving a few oldsters behind for Nature to deal with.

"Also, of course, it simplifies record-keeping for the historian. If one knows as a matter of policy that a given novelist is scheduled to die on or about a given date, one need never lack for a final interview and an up-dated obituary. And the same excuse, or a similar one—such as a routine visit by the victim's physician—can become the agency of his actual death.

"Which brings me back, Mr. Wiberg, to my original question. Which are you—the Angel of Death himself, or just his harbinger?"

In the ensuing silence, the fire popped loudly in the grate. At last Wiberg said:

"I cannot tell you whether or not your hypothesis is valid. As you suggested yourself at the beginning of this interview, if it were true, I wouldn't be allowed to tell you so, as a simple logical consequence. All I can say is that I enormously admire your ingenuity—and I'm not entirely surprised by it.

"But again for the sake of the argument, let's push the logic one step further. Assume that the situation is just as you postulate it to be. Assume further that you have been selected to be . . . 'skimmed off' . . . say, about a year from now. And assume, finally, that I was originally only to be your final interviewer, not your executioner. Wouldn't your revealing to me your conclusions *force* me to become your executioner instead?"

"It might," Darling said, with astonishing cheerfulness. "It is a consequence I had not overlooked. My life has been very rich, and my present illness is so annoying that being shut of a year of it—since I know very well that it's incurable—would not strike me as a terrible deprivation. On the other hand, the risk does not seem to me to be very real anyhow. Killing me a year early would produce a slight mathematical discontinuity in the system. It would not be a significant discontinuity, but bureaucrats hate any deviation from established procedure, whether it matters or not. Either way, *I* wouldn't care. But I wonder about you, Mr. Wiberg. I really do."

"About me?" Wiberg said uneasily. "Why about me?"

There was no doubt, now, but that the old malicious glitter was back in Darling's eyes, in full vitality.

"You are a statistician. I can tell by the way in which you received, and followed, my statistical terms. I, on the other hand, am an amateur mathematician, not limited in my interests to stochastic procedures; and one of my interests is projective geometry. I have been watching population statistics, and death figures, and so on, but I have also been constructing curves. I therefore know that next April fourteenth will be the day of my death. Let us call it, for the sake of commemoration, Novelists' Day.

"Well then, Mr. Wiberg. I also know that this coming November third is what we might call Statisticians' Day. And I do not think you are very safely under age, Mr. Wiberg.

"Tell me: *How will you face it?* Eh? How will *you* face it? Speak up, Mr. Wiberg, speak up. Your time, too, is running out."

Triage

Historically, one of the most important checks on population growth has been mankind's age-old propensity for war. In Europe alone, for instance, there were an estimated 23.5 million military deaths between 1600 and 1918, and the Second World War accounted for between 30 and 35 million dead (both military and civilian). In addition to deaths due directly to combat, warfare takes an additional toll through the devastation of agriculture and the economy, through the spreading of disease, and, perhaps most importantly, in terms of "non-births," or the people who would have been born had not their prospective parents been killed. Unhappily, advances in technology have resulted in ever-increasing casualties, particularly with the extension of military action to civilian areas through aerial bombing.

In the absence of large scale military conflict, it may become necessary to control population growth by other, more subtle means. The moral and political implications of such a necessity are illustrated graphically in the following story.

by William Walling

Triage

(Tre-áhzh) [Fr. "sorting"]. Classification of casualties of war, or other disaster, to determine priority of treatment: Class 1—those who will die regardless of treatment; Class 2—those who will live regardless of treatment; Class 3—those who can be saved only by prompt treatment.

We have met the enemy, and he is us. From Walt Kelly's cartoon strip, Pogo.

The man waited with outward patience, standing stiff-backed, knees together, opposite the desk where a nervous male secretary feigned work under his punishing scrutiny. Seemingly quite at ease, the man was tall, forceful in appearance, with a proud aquiline nose, sleek dirty-blond hair, and chill hazel eyes. The wraparound collar of his pearl-gray jacket was buttoned even though a power brownout had once again paralyzed Greater New York during the night and early morning hours, leaving the anteroom overwarm and stuffy.

The secretary darted occasional furtive looks toward the tall man. At last, their glances crossed. The secretary squirmed. "Sorry . . . for the delay, Mr. Rook. I can't imagine what's keeping her."

"Madame Duiño is busy, Harold." The man folded his arms. "Don't trouble yourself; pretend that I'm not here."

"Yes, sir." The secretary plunged back into his paperwork. When the intercom buzzed, moments later, he said hastily. "You

223

can go right in now, sir." The inner door eased shut; the secretary looked immensely relieved.

The office of Dr. Victoria Maria-Luisa Ortega de Duiño, Chairperson of the Traigé Committee, UN Department of Environment and Population, was as severe and desiccated as the woman herself. A blue-and-white United Nations ensign hung behind her desk on the left; on the right, atop a travertine pedestal, the diorite bas-relief presented to her by Emilio Quintana, Mexico's preeminent sculptor, depicted a stylized version of UNDEP's logo: the globe of Earth, with a set of balanced scales and the motto TERRA STABILITA superimposed across it. A pair of guest chairs hand-crafted of clear Honduras mahogany were adrift upon a sea of wall-to-wall shag the color of oatmeal. Save for an old-fashioned French pendulum clock, and the floor-to-ceiling video panels—now dark—Sra. Duiño's sanctum was enclosed by barren, oyster-white walls. Lined damask draperies shrouded a picture window overlooking the East River ninety floors below.

Rook did not take a seat. He chose a spot just inside the door, studying the old woman with an indolent expression.

If aware of the man's presence, Dr. Duniño gave no sign, occupying herself with the sheaf of papers before her on the desktop. Her hair, as short and brittle as her temper, was roached stiffly backward to form a platinum aura; her features were wrinkled, sagging, though her eyes retained the dark and shining luster of youth. Around her frail neck, pendant against the lace *mantilla* thrown over her shoulders, was a large silver crucifix. In six months and eleven days, Victoria Duiño would celebrate her eighty-eighth birthday. She was the most reviled and detested human on Earth.

"My apologies, Bennett." The old woman looked up at last. "Please sit down. I had not intended to keep you away from your desk so long."

"Quite all right, Victoria." The tall man made it a point to remain standing. "I take it the matter is pressing?"

"No. Not really." She touched a button; a hologram condensed in the largest video tank across the office, allowing them to eavesdrop on a courtroom scene. Now in its penultimate stages, the trial was taking place half a continent away. "I merely wished to assure myself that we were obtaining full PR value from the Sennich Trial," she said. "Have you been following it?"

Bennett Rook turned with leisurely grace. He listened briefly to the defense attorney's final plea. "Alas, no," he said. "Actually, I've been too busy. It is the gluttony action you mentioned in your memo?"

The old woman made no rejoinder. Her interest in the trial was exclusively political. In her mind, the guilty verdict soon to be handed down was a foregone conclusion. One Nathan Sennich, and a pair of miserable codefendants, had resurrected the ancient sin of gluttony, which reflected but one symptom of an ailing society in her opinion. But, for UNDEP, the trial carried important propaganda overtones; widespread public indignation, fanned by tabloid journalism, had begun to create a welcome avalanche of letters and calls. If UNDEP press releases were to add fuel to the fire, were to milk the sordid affair for all it was worth . . .

"The gall of those swine!" she said. "In a starving world, they dared slaughter and gorge themselves on the roasted flesh of a fawn stolen from Denver's zoo."

Rook's lip curled. His voice was resonant, unruffled. "Grotesque, Victoria. But I can't imagine what's in it for us. In forty-eight hours, or less, the remains of our mischievous gourmands will be fertilizing crops in Denver's greenbelts; or perhaps those of the Denver Zoo itself. Poetic justice, eh?"

"Don't make light of it." A throaty burr crept into Sra. Duiño's voice. "I asked you to get PR cracking on this action. You have ignored my request. We stand to reap a certain amount of public sympathy if trial coverage is properly handled, Bennett."

"We?" The man's brows lifted. "Triage Committee? Nothing could improve our image Victoria. Day before yesterday *L'Oservatore Romano* once again referred to you as the 'Matriarch of Death'. PR abandoned all attempts to 'sell' the committee years ago."

"You know perfectly well what I meant," said the old woman tautly. "Bennett, must we always fence? Can't you ever sit down and converse with me sociably?"

Rook smiled an arctic smile. He rocked on his heels, returning her stare with steadfast calm. "There are several matters we shall never see in the same light, Victoria. Nothing personal, you understand; if you want the truth, I rather like you. If I did not, I would tell you so. I am no hypocrite."

"No," she agreed, "you are not a hypocrite. Blunt perhaps; but not a hypocrite."

He made a slight gesture, turning over the flats of his hands. "Blunt then, if you will."

Dr. Duiño watched him with unwinking concentration," she said, "not your enmity."

Rook sighed. "I'd rather not discuss it."

"Why not? Are you afraid?"

Rook tensed the least bit. "I'm afraid of nothing. Pardon me; of almost nothing."

"Your use of a qualifier makes me curious."

"My only fear," he said slowly, "is for the continuation of our species."

"And mine, Bennett. But that is what we are laboring so earnestly to ensure."

"To little avail," he said.

"That is not a fair and reasonable statement."

"Oh?" Rook stood firm under her withering gaze, his eyes aglow with patriotic fervor. "You are familiar with this week's global delta, of course."

Victoria Duiño hesitated. "I am. It is most encouraging—less than one-quarter of one percent."

"Bravo!" Rook clapped his hands in genteel emphasis. "Despite our sanctions, proscriptions, lawful executions and extensive triage judgments; despite floods, earthquakes, plagues and the further encroachment of desertlands upon our remaining arable soil, there are now some twenty-five thousand *more* human beings on Earth than the nine and three-quarter billions we could not feed last week. And you tell me all's right with the world."

Sra. Duiño looked taken aback. After a moment, she said quietly. "Zero population growth will be a reality in one and one-half to three years."

"Too damned little, Victoria—too damned *late*. With sterner measures, we would be on the down-slope instead of approaching the crest."

"I am familiar with your views," said the woman. " 'Sterner measures', as you call them, would have made us less than human. I refuse to subscribe to inhumanity as a cure-all for the world's ills."

"Humane philosophy is a luxury we cannot afford."

"Bennett, Bennett! You are intelligent, industrious, thoroughly dedicated; that is why I selected you from the crowd these many years past. But have you no compassion, no slight twinge of conscience for the dreadful judgments we must pass day after day, month after month, year after year?"

"None," said Rook. "It's an interesting facet of human nature; mortal danger to a single individual—the victim of a mine disaster, or someone trapped in a fire—never fails to stimulate a tidal wave of public sympathy, while similar disasters affecting gross numbers are mere statistics, hardly worth a shrug. We do what must be done. We do it analytically, dispassionately, dutifully. Were it otherwise, there would be no sane committee members."

"I . . . see. And you think me a senile, idealistic old fool who should step aside and allow a younger individual, such as yourself, to chair the committee?"

Bennett Rook stood perfectly still. "Senile? Hardly. Your mind is clear and sharp as ever; you are one of very few who can best me in debate. Idealism I will not answer; I am not qualified. But you are less of a fool than anyone I have ever met. I admire you vastly, respect you enormously, even love you in my own manner, perhaps. Yet, given the opportunity, I would replace you tomorrow."

"Because I am too soft?"

"Because you are too soft," he said.

"Thank you for stopping by, Bennett. May I remind you once again to prod PR on the Sennich Trial coverage?"

"I'll take care of it immediately." Rook tipped his head; there was nothing sarcastic about his deference. "Good day, Victoria." His eyes were veiled as he left the office.

In silent reflection, Victoria Duiño gazed at the closed door for quite some time before resuming her labors.

And the Egyptians will I give over into the hand of a cruel lord; and a fierce king shall rule over them, saith the Lord, the Lord of hosts.

And the waters shall fail from the sea, and the river shall be wasted and dried up. (Isaiah 19:4,5)

In midafternoon, the intercom's buzz interrupted Victoria Duiño's train of thought. "Yes, Harold?"

"Cardinal Freneaux is in the anteroom, madame. And your grand-daughter is calling—channel sixteen."

She glanced at the clock. "If I am not mistaken, His Eminence made an appointment for three. It is now but two fifty-eight. Surely he will allow me two minutes to indulge my only grand-child."

"Surely he will, madame. I will tell him."

"Thank you, Harold." Keeping one eye and a portion of her attention on a flashing digital readout, Dr. Duiño switched on the vidicom. "Monique, I can't talk very long just now. I trust that you and Stewart are well?"

"Hello, Grandma." The image that formed in the small tube was of a petite, attractive young woman whose dark hair was in disarray. Her eyes were red-rimmed, desperate.

Victoria Duiño straightened in her chair. "What is it, child? What has happened?"

"I've got . . . big troubles, Grandma."

"What sort of troubles? Can I help?"

"Oh, God. I hope so! I . . . doubt it. I just got back from the doctor. I'm . . . in the family way, if you know what I mean."

"Monique!" Sra. Duiño clutched the arms of her chair. "How did it happen? Were you careless?"

"No. I don't know. I . . . took my pills. I never missed. I just don't know, Grandma. Fate, I guess—or bad luck."

After the first flush of emotion had washed through her. Victoria relaxed and began to think. She seized a yellow legal pad and a stylus. "I want to know where you buy your birth-control tablets."

"What? But, Grandma, what does that have to do with—?"

"Never mind, child. Just tell me. I assume you buy them regularly in one specific place?"

"Uh, yes. At Gilbert's Pharmacy here in the arcology complex. But I—"

"Have you any left?"

"A few," said the younger woman. "I think. Yes; a few."

"Send them to me. Mail them this afternoon—special delivery and insure the package. Address it to Harold Strabough, United Nations Tower, and beneath the address write the initials V.M.L.

That will assure prompt attention. I should receive it tomorrow."

"I . . . all right, Grandma. I will. Oh, Stew's so broken up; we would have been approved for parenthood within the year. What can we do?"

"Leave that to me."

"Can you . . . ? Do you think you can do something?"

"I think so, Monique. I want you to be as calm as you can about this. Follow the doctor's instructions verbatim, and let me know at once if any complications arise."

"Grandma, wh . . . what will they do to me—to my baby?"

"Nothing, for the time being," said Dr. Duiño with assurance. "Unauthorized birth is a crime; unauthorized pregnancy is not. We have many months to effect a solution. Don't be afraid."

"Stew's talking kind of wild," said her granddaughter. "He's been raving about running off to Brazil."

"Hum-m-mph! To live in the jungle with the other outcasts, I suppose. Think about that, Monique. Would the Amazon Basin be a fit place for Stewart and yourself to raise an infant? It is a jungle, just now, in more ways than one. You wouldn't last long enough to give birth, let alone build anything more than an animal existence for yourselves."

"Are you sure, Grandma?"

"Absolutely certain," said the old woman. "I am in a position to know. Do exactly as I have advised. I'll call you later in the week when we have more time to chat. Above all, don't despair, my dear. Until later, then."

"God bless you, Grandma. And . . . thank you. I love you."

Seething inside, Victoria switched off the vidicom. She permitted herself the use of an expletive not in keeping with the dignity of her high office, then seized her bamboo cane and rose stifly to stand upright, her mind whirling. Monique's call had come at a most inopportune moment; she had only seconds to contemplate its ramifications before receiving the Cardinal.

Diminutive and birdlike, she hunched beside the desk, squinting down at the carpet. It was an attack, of course. But from what quarter? She had been the victim of numberless attacks, both political and physical, during her long career. She had survived eleven attempts on her life, attempts ranging from clumsy bunglings like the homemade bomb thrown by that theology student in Buenos Aires which had permanently impaired the hearing in her right ear, to the ingenious poisoned croissants, four years ago, which had resulted in the death of a loved and trusted friend.

The old woman heaved a sigh, feeling something wither and die inside her. Damn them! There was no time to think about it now. No time. She closed her eyes tightly, washing the residue of Monique's call from her mind, and pressed the intercom button. She hobbled to mid-office, leaning on her cane.

His Eminence, Louis Cardinal Freneaux stood framed in the doorway, a wasted figure whose rich robe hung loosely about him. Victoria knew that he made it a point of honor to limit his caloric intake to something commensurate with that of the most deprived member of his vast flock. She respected him for it, and considered him one of the more intelligent churchmen in her acquaintance. Beneath the red skullcap, the Cardinal's eyes were lackluster and sad.

"You are looking very well, my dear," he said.

"Thank you, Louis. At my age, I can't imagine a nicer compliment."

She bent stiffly as if to kiss the prelate's ring.

"That . . . is not necessary," he said, withdrawing. "My visit is official, I'm afraid."

Sra. Duiño straightened slowly. "Is it to be like that?"

"Please don't be offended, Victoria."

"I take it the Holy Father is even more displeased with me than usual!" she said. "I am truly sorry to have caused him further pain. What is it this time?"

"Egypt."

The old woman nodded once. She turned slowly and stumped toward her desk, motioning the Cardinal to a chair. "Four million inhabitants of the Nile Delta, formerly Class Three, were declared Class One last week. I fear there was little choice; the vote was unanimous."

"Deplorable!" said the Cardinal.

"No one deplored its necessity more than I. Damanhûr, El Mansûra and Tanta, Zagazig, El Faiyûm and El Minya share the fate of numberless villages scattered along the dry gulch that was once a mighty river."

"There are many Coptic Christians in Egypt," said Cardinal Freneaux. "They have petitioned the Holy See for redress."

"Oh?" Victoria's dark eyes flashed. "And why, pray, have they not petitioned the Father and Teacher in Moscow who refuses to allow them to help themselves? More than a decade ago, UNDEP warned of what the Aswan Dam was doing to the Nile. The weight of Lake Nasser upon the land, swollen by spring floods in East Africa, helped create a severe seismic disturbance; the upper Rift Valley developed a subsidiary fracture, and the river found a new path through Nubia to the Red Sea. Today, Cairo is a dusty ruin, as dead and forgotten as the pyramids to the west."

"Rationalization is useless, Victoria." The Cardinal frowned. "We must be practical."

"*Practical,* is it? In modern Egypt, more than three thousand *fellahin* crowd every remaining square mile of arable land. *Something* had to give, Louis."

The Cardinal coughed apologetically. "Four million . . . somethings," he said in a low voice.

Victoria Duiño reacted as if the Cardinal had slapped her. "That was unkind of you. They are four million helpless human beings; they work and love and have aspirations and laugh together on rare occasions, even as you or I. Unfortunately, they also have appetites. Do you—does the Holy Father—suppose that we *enjoy* our work?"

"Of course not, Victoria."

"Then why does he refrain from exercising whatever influence he has over Eastern Orthodox churchmen inside the Soviet Union? Why can't they aid in making the Kremlin realize that its insensate drive for world domination is literally starving millions? With Soviet help instead of hindrance our triage activities would dwindle significantly."

Cardinal Freneaux made a small sound of disgruntlement. "You know how little public opinion is worth in Russia."

Sra. Duiño silently recited a Hail Mary, allowing her temper to subside. She tapped a stylus on the desktop. "Louis, the impoverished portion of the Third World sprawling across Africa, Asia Minor and the Arabian Peninsula is a Russian creation; it is perpetuated solely as a political weapon. Soviet-controlled military forces outnumber UN forces two to one; we are powerless to inflict our wills upon the Third World, save for the Indian subcontinent and South America, except as Russia allows. The Great Northern Bear graciously condescends to permit triage judgments rendered wherever and whenever we choose, then points a long propaganda finger and calls us 'murderers of millions'.

"but let us suggest something *beneficial*, such as the Qattara Project, and the Bear immediately exercises his veto. The measure dies without question of recourse."

Cardinal Freneau looked uncomfortable. "I am not familiar with the project," he dissimulated, hoping against hope to divert the old woman's waxing anger.

"Really?" Victoria's eyes radiated pale fire. She spun a tickler file, then touched a series of buttons on the video controller. A full-color map of the Middle East formed in the large tank. "Just southwest of Alexandria, is El Alamein, a town of some historical significance. Near there, Britain's armored forces turned back those of Nazi Germany in one of the climactic land battles of the Second World War.

"Which is neither here, nor there, except that Britain chose that particular site to make her winner-take-all stand for an excellent reason. To the uninitiated, it would have seemed easy for Rommel's *Panzers* to swing out into the open desert, avoiding Montgomery's trap on his drive toward Alexandria and the Suez. Such was not the case; on a larger scale, the area is a corridor much like Thermopylae, and British strategy much like that of the Greeks who stood off the Persian hordes in classical times. You see, Rommel had neither the petrol, nor supplies, to skirt a huge natural obstacle.

"Let your eye drift southward from El Alamein, Louis. See the long crescent marked Qattara Depression? It is a vast sink rather like Death Valley, which lies between the Libyan Plateau and the Western Desert, and is more than four hundred feet below the level of the Mediterranean in most places.

"UNDEP's ecosystems engineers proposed a fifty kilometer-long canal, excavated by use of 'clean' mini-fusion devices from a point east of El Alamein to the depression. A hydroelectric power station was to have been built on the brink: seventy years would have been required for a large, fan-shaped inland sea to form, stretching from Siwa Oasis near the Libyan border to the foundations of the pyramids at El Giza, with a long neck reaching southward along the Ghard Abu Muharik almost to El Kharga. The Qattara Sea would have altered the climate of the Western Desert, bringing rainfall to the parched, rich soil; in ancient times, much of the region was a garden. Egypt could have reclaimed millions of hectares of arable land, helping to alleviate her perpetual famine.

"The Father and Teacher in Moscow vetoed the proposal out-of-hand." With an abrupt gesture, Victoria switched off the video map. "Pardon me; I did not mean to lecture."

Cardinal Freneaux shifted disquietly in his chair. "You make it sound so brave and simple. The situation is much more complex. Visionary schemes, such as this Qattara Project—"

"There is nothing 'visionary' about it," she said in an icy tone. "I could name a dozen similar UNDEP proposals vetoed by the USSR."

The Cardinal ran his tongue around his upper lip. He rose and began pacing the office, hands clasped behind his back. "The Church is not blind." he said "Russia's geopolitical game is far from subtle. Yet the Bear is not to be provoked, Victoria. His Holiness dreads war. Have you any concept of the carnage thermonuclear weapons would wreak among the vast populations of Asia, Africa, Europe and the Americas?"

"I have indeed; a global holocaust would either extinguish our species, or reduce our numbers to something the Earth could once again tolerate. Triage on a grand scale, Louis."

The Cardinal was aghast. "How can you even *think* such a thing?"

The old woman shrugged. "There are wars, and then there are wars. We are engaged in a global war right this instant, and one of the major battles is taking place in Egypt. If His Holiness refuses to recognize this fact, I am hard-put to explain it."

"I've never heard you speak like this before, Victoria."

Victoria sighed. "I suppose my optimism and diplomacy have begun to wear out, like the rest of me." She searched the Cardinal with her eyes. "No, that isn't true. Louise, we are not winning the war just yet. But, we will—must! There are, after all, only three alternatives left: triage, Armageddon, or a sniveling decline that is certain to end in a whimper."

Cardinal Freneaux remained silent for a time. "Our conversation has wandered far afield," he said. "Victoria, do you consider yourself a good daughter of the Church?"

"You know that I do."

The churchman pondered something invisible which had obtruded between himself and the old woman. He cleared his throat. "His Holiness was unusually stern when he dispatched me on this mission. He instructed me to plead immediate reclassification of the four million inhabitants of the Nile Delta. He urged me strongly not to take 'no' for an answer."

Victoria Duiño looked solemn. "Then the stern Father must discover that he has an equally stern daughter," she said. "My answer must be . . . no. Battles are never without casualties; grain shipments to Egypt have already halted."

"I warn you; he has spoken of excommunication."

The old woman grew very pale, very calm. "And do you expect me to be intimidated by such a threat?"

"I do not. I have known you too long."

"I am literally amazed that the Holy Father would stoop to attack me personally, would choose to threaten damnation of my immortal soul in order to destroy me professionally. Were he to carry out this awful threat, it would mean absolutely nothing to the Triage Committee or its works. Doesn't he realize that?"

"I'm not . . . sure."

Victoria fingered her crucifix. "Louis, what have we come to? The Church, our Church, has grown quite permissive on the question of homosexuality, now countenances therapeutic abortion, even condones euthanasia when the pain of life becomes too great for her sons and daughters to bear, yet obstinately faces away from the fact that without triage judgments our planet will *never again* be a fit environment for the human species."

"Discussion is painful to me. I must ask you for a definite answer, Victoria."

"You have had it. Tell His Holiness that the Matriarch of Death considers eternal fire a small price to pay for the work she does, and must continue to do."

The Cardinal's eyes were misted. He bowed. "Then I will bid you good-bye, my dear Victoria. I sincerely hope that our next meeting will be more pleasant."

"I hope so."

The causal chain of the deterioration is easily followed to its source.

Too many cars, too many factories, too much detergent, too much pesticide, multiplying contrails, inadequate sewage treatment plants, too little water, too much CO_2—all can be traced easily to too many people. Dr. Paul Ehrlich, *The Population Bomb*

Monique's package arrived in late afternoon the following day. Dr. Duiño sent two of the suspect birth-control tablets to the UN lab for analysis, receiving a report in less than one hour. Properly stamped with the infertility symbol, the placebos lacked the chop of any pharmaceutical house, and were therefore quite illegal. If found, the seller would be liable to harsh prosecution.

After an evening snack of thin vegetable soup and soya toast, Sra. Duiño retired to her quarters high on the two-hundredth floor, feeling roughly battered by life. She had been attacked from the left and the right, from above and below.

She pondered Monique's problem all evening, sitting alone in the cramped two-room suite. She rarely left the UN Tower nowadays; there would be little purpose in it. Almost everything that remained in her life was here; her meager creature comforts, the small chapel on the twelfth floor where she heard mass and went to confession—more and more infrequently of late—and her work.

Sudden nostalgia spun her mind back to the early days in Argentina when Vicky Ortega, a serious-minded medical student newly risen from the tumbled shacks and endemic poverty of a Buenos Aires *barrio*, had visited the clinic and been lovestruck at first sight of a young doctor named Enrique Duiño. Love had come in the blink of an eye, in the macrocosmic slice of eternity it had taken for the handsome doctor to look at her infected throat and prescribe three million units of penicillin and bedrest.

Oh, she had pursued him; no mistake about that—two months of thoroughly premeditated "accidental" encounters, while her studies went neglected and she lived in terror of losing him.

But she remembered the miraculous day when she had led Enrique up a crooked, debris-strewn alley to the ramshackle lean-to her parents and brothers and sisters called home, the day Enrique had turned his hat brim slowly, nervously in his deft surgeon's hands while he asked her father's permission to make her his bride. Later, mentioning the five children she'd prayed God would allow them to have, Vicky had received the lecture which was to change her life.

In those days, Enrique had been a walking encyclopedia, stuffed with demographic statistics, facts and figures on family planning, on the fantastic rate at which the world's population was doubling, on the coming extinction of fossil fuels, and on and on. They, he had insisted, would have *one* child—two at most. At first, Vickey had been horrified, then resentful, then fascinated.

Their first decade together had been an exciting hodgepodge; the missionary hospital in Bolivia; their studies together in Madrid, and at the Sorbonne, and later in Mexico; finally, the years in America and, somewhat late in life, the birth of young Hector Duiño. That had been the richest, most tranquil period, Victoria reflected. Enrique and she had practiced in San Francisco, and in New York; the boy had grown to manhood almost overnight, so it seemed. And when Enrique's crusading articles won him selection as a delegate to the third International Population Control Convention in New Delhi, she had been so proud, even though her practice had kept her home in New York.

Curiously enough, Enrique had always tended to neglect his own health. When the cholera epidemic erupted, he had refused to be flown home with the majority of other delegates, staying on in India to lend what help he could. The first prognosis from the hospital where they had taken him had been favorable. But Victoria had had an ugly premonition. All her prayers had gone unanswered; her beloved had come home in a plain wooden casket.

The ensuing years of loneliness melted into a blur—long years of struggle and disappointment. She had carried on Enrique's great work, making a nuisance of herself by shouting his message into deaf political ears. But at last—not too late, perhaps; but *very* late—after the Mideast conflagration which all but destroyed Israel and placed the whole of Islam under Russia's thrall, she and the other criers-in-the-wilderness had at last been heard. After much panicking and pointing of fingers, the UN peace-keeping troops had been bolstered and united into a true international armed force. Then—could it be nearly twenty-five years ago?—UNDEP's Triage Committee had been formed. Dr. Duiño had been its first and only chairperson.

The old woman raised withered hands. There were times when she imagined she could see light streaming through the mottled parchment stretched over her bones. Where was pretty little

Vicky Ortega now? Submerged in this twist of exhausted flesh, she supposed.

She rose with the aid of her bamboo cane and shuffled to the window. It was after midnight, and fairly clear. She looked up at the few visible stars for a time, then stood gazing far out over the inky wash of the Atlantic into the depths of night.

Two days later, a preliminary report arrived from the UN Intelligence Agents who were investigating the bogus birth-control tablets. The assistant manager of Gilbert's Pharmacy, thirty-third layer, twelfth sector, northwest quadrant of the gargantuan arcology complex where Monique and her husband lived, had recently applied for parenthood. Pressure was brought to bear—and a hint of amnesty if full cooperation were forthcoming. During the ensuing week, the trail led from the pharmacy to a disreputable retired chemist in Cleveland, to a thrice arrested though never convicted Philadelphia dealer in black market pharmaceuticals, to a drug wholesaler with shady connections in Trenton, and finally to the legman for a prominent Congressman. A second week passed before the UN Intelligence Director called Sra. Duiño and mentioned a name.

"Are you certain?" she asked, stiffening.

"No, madame. There's no way short of a trial to be certain, and I doubt whether the DA would indict upon the sort of evidence we've managed to gather."

"Are you yourself certain?"

"I . . . yes, madame. I myself am quite certain."

"Thank you for all your efforts," she said. "Please make sure your findings remain confidential."

Dr. Duiño snapped off the vidicom and sought her cane. She stumped from the office, startling Harold and three VIP's who were waiting to see her. She rode upward in the private lift, failed to acknowledge everyone who greeted her in the corridor, and spent the remaining afternoon hours closeted with her fellow Triage Committee members behind closed doors.

Late the following day, Victoria entered Bennett Rook's anteroom, breezing past his receptionist unannounced.

The inner office was crowded; Rook was at the chalkboard running over some statistics with a group of underlings. He telescoped the collapsible pointer he had been using. "Dr. Duiño. To what do we owe this honor?"

"I must speak to you at once in private." She shooed them out with her cane, causing a concerted fumbling for notebooks and other papers. The UNDEP employees filed out, studiously avoiding one anothers' eyes.

When the door closed behind the last straggler, she said. "Is this room safe?"

"Quite safe, Victoria."

The old woman inspected Rook analytically. "Well, is it to be 'wroth in death, and envy after'? Or will you bargain?"

"Pardon me?"

"Come, come, Rook; bluffing was never your forte. If for some reason I should choose to step down," she said, speaking slowly, distinctly, "will you allow my granddaughter to bear her child in peace?"

"Why, certainly, Victoria. As I once told you, I'm not a hypocrite."

"No," she said, "merely a . . . !" She choked off the gutter term that came to her lips. "May I ask what I have done to you to deserve *this*?"

"Personalities aren't involved," he said. "It's the job—the job you are *failing* to accomplish. You left me no choice."

The old woman swayed, leaning heavily on her cane. Rook moved as if to help her, but she fended him off, saying sharply, "Please keep your hands to yourself."

Settling herself in a chair, Victoria Duiño looked up at the man, her eyes bright. With measured intonation, she enumerated certain facts concerning an assistant pharmacy manager, a Cleveland chemist, a Philadelphia dealer in pharmaceuticals, a drug wholesaler, and a Congressman's stooge.

Rook was nonplused. "Thorough," he said smoothly. "You've been very thorough, as I anticipated. You realize, of course, that such 'evidence' would never hold up in court."

"No district attorney, judge, or jury will ever hear it."

"Then, how—?"

"Tomorrow morning," directed the old woman sternly, "you will personally arrange official parenthood sanction for my granddaughter and her husband. Spare me the seamy details of how the deed is to be accomplished."

"And . . . if I refuse?"

Victoria's smile was thin, totally lacking in humor—the smile of a canary who has successfully evaded the cat. "I visited with the other seven members of our committee yesterday, Rook. They all seemed quite eager to see things *my* way. Persist in your endeavor, and you will find yourself out on the street, looking in. Discovering another meal ticket might become a serious problem."

Bennett Rook took a moment to digest this information. "Then I suppose you have won," he said at last.

"Yes, I suppose so. As such things are reckoned."

"Do you blame me?" Rook sounded the injured party. "I'm not really an ogre, Victoria. You've lived long, worked hard; you've seen the world change into something ill and decrepit. Was it so despicable to try and force you to lay down your burden and rest?"

"It was," she said, "though I don't expect you to understand why. You are not a flesh and blood creature, Rook; no juices of life flow within you. You are cold and rational—both a superb asset, and a potentially terrible liability to triage activities."

"I'll make the necessary arrangements tomorrow," he said.

Victoria Duiño nodded. "Good. Now that we understand one another, I have a bombshell for you; the Matriarch of Death has at last decided to abdicate. Not, however, because of your foolish blackmail scheme.

"You were correct, Rook: I am indeed old, feeble and used up. And tired—very tired. You strike at me through my grandchild; His Holiness attacks me through my faith; my name is anathema from Antarctica to Greenland, and all around the world."

"You've managed to amaze me, Victoria."

"Furthermore," she went on, disregarding his incredulous stare, "had you refrained from this silly coup, you might well have been elected Chairperson of the Triage Committee next week. As it is, while eminently qualified, you have proved yourself utterly unworthy."

"Bitter gall." Rook grimaced. "That does sting, Victoria. But don't count me out just yet. I—"

"Hear me, Bennett!" She twisted the cane savagely in her hands. "This will be our final encounter, and I intend to have the last word. I want to clarify something, now and forever; something you *must* comprehend.

"You have repeatedly condemned my triage philosophy as

being too leneient, too soft. It is not. Triage is, and has always been, a concession to the inevitable, not premeditated mass-murder. Twenty-five years ago, in the white heat of a new crusade, we set a rather idealistic goal; semi-immediate reversal of runaway overpopulation. We were dismayed to find it not that simple. How can an illiterate Third Worlder, whose single recreation in an otherwise drab existence is sex, be persuaded to remain chaste during his wife's fertile period?

"But now, whether you care to acknowledge it or not, a dim glow brightens the far end of the tunnel. We faced cold facts, long ago, asking ourselves whether it would be wiser to disrupt every socioeconomic system on Earth by seeking a quick solution, or to wage a strategically paced, long-range war. The latter policy is saner, more practical, and far more humanitarian; the ultimate solution may lay farther in the future, but victory is also much more assured.

"I will not live to see even a partial victory; nor, in all likelihood will you, Rook. But my great-grandchild-to-be, whose strange godfather you are, might do so—*if* you and the others make the best possible use of the varied technological weapons we will someday have at our disposal; new bio-compatible pesticides, new hybridized grains, reclamation of desertlands, perhaps interplanetary migration.

"As in any war, we will face mini-triumphs and small setbacks, major victories and hideous defeats; we must bear up equally under good fortune and adversity alike. We must take what we have to take, and give what we have to give to re-create a world where my great-grandchild-to-be can enjoy a noble, cheerful life, a world where a gallon of potable water is not a unit of international exchange, where reusable containers are not an article of law, where food is abundant and air is fit to . . . "

Victoria broke off, shaking her head sadly. "I can see that I am wasting breath. Very well; if you choose to have your lesson the hard way, so be it. I wish you luck; you will need all you can get."

The old woman labored to rise. Though he dared not help her, Bennett Rook came forward half a step despite himself. She did not deign to look at him again, making her way slowly to the door, dignity pulled tightly about her like a cloak.

Her mind at peace, Victoria went to her quarters and phoned St. Patrick's Cathedral. She spent two minutes persuading the young priest who buffered all incoming calls that she was indeed who she said she was. Finally, he allowed her to speak to Cardinal Freneaux.

"Oh, Louis, I'm so glad; I was afraid you had already left the city. I called to invite you to have dinner with me."

"Delighted, my dear Victoria." He sounded pleased and surprised. "I had made other plans, but they can be changed."

"This is an occasion," she said. "A UNDEP news bulletin of some importance will be released tomorrow morning. I want you to be the first to know. May I come by for you in an hour, Louis?"

"Fine! That will be fine. I'll look forward to seeing you."

She dressed without haste—the black gown reserved for formal affairs—and slipped on a diamond bracelet Enrique had given her many years before. She had difficulty fastening the clasp of an emerald brooch at her neck.

When she was ready, she took up a large satin handbag, the fancy black cane with the ivory tip, and called down to the garage. The electric limousine and its driver, accompanied by omnipresent UN Security Agents, were waiting for her outside the tower's staff entrance.

They rode in silence with the windows rolled up despite the muggy summer evening. With keen interest, Victoria watched the defeated multitudes overspilling the sidewalks; four hours, and more, remained until the midnight curfew. They crawled west through dense traffic on East 48th Street, turning right at Fifth Avenue.

When the limousine nosed its way into an enormous queue of hungry supplicants gathered outside St. Patrick's Cathedral, Dr. Victoria Maria-Luisa Ortega de Duiño crossed herself.

Part VI

Afterword

The foregoing discussions and stories indicate and illustrate the problems to be encountered in a world of rapid population growth. It is not our desire, however, to end on an entirely pessimistic note in this regard, so we have included two brief but thought provoking pieces. The first hypothesizes that population is becoming *less* of a problem with each succeeding generation; we ask only that the reader examine critically the arithmetic premise upon which this story is based. The second suggests that the real reason for having children is not linked to social and economic factors after all.

by Theodore R. Cogswell

Probability Zero!
The Population
Implosion

JUST AS more radioactivity is released into the atmosphere by the burning of fossil fuels than by a properly designed nuclear power plant (all coal containing substances other than hydrocarbons, some of which are radioactive), so also is the present world population a mere drop in the bucket compared with what it was only one thousand years ago. In fact, the population of our planet has been shrinking geometrically since the time of Christ. It is true that local urban clusters such as New York, Los Angeles and Chinchilla, Pennsylvania, have been expanding rapidly during the last few decades, but if one considers the entire land mass, a quick examination of available genealogical statistics will show that the average population per square mile is steadily and rapidly decreasing.

The key to the proof of this is the geometrical expansion in the number of ancestors one has as one moves back generation by generation. Assuming no inbreeding, your four grandparents had eight parents, who in turn had sixteen, etc. For purposes of demonstration, assume that each generation produces a new one in twenty-five years. Using 1950 as a convenient starting point, 1850 would see a generation of 16 ancestors; 1750: 256; 1650: 4,096; 1550: 65,536; 1450: 1,048,576; 1350: 16,777,136; 1250: 268,434,176; 1150: 4,294,946,816; 1050: 68,719,149,056; and A.D. 1000: 274,876,596,224.

Now two hundred and seventy-four billion-plus great-great-great-great-great-great-great-great-great-great-great-great-

great-grandparents is a sizable number to have, especially if, as in my case, they were all Anglo-Saxon, miscegenation with Normans and other breeds without the law who slipped over from the Continent during the temporary alien quota relaxation of 1066 always having been frowned on by my progenitors.

I assume that the 50,874-square-mile land area of England proper hasn't changed substantially since the year 1000, so simple division will establish that there were 4,872,913 of my people jammed into every square mile of that little country. This works out to an average of a little less than six square feet per person, or a six-by-six-foot lot for each family of six, with no provision for throughways, supermarkets, jails, churches and other amenities of gracious living. Certainly the population problem then, especially the disposal of sewage, makes that of today shrink to nothingness in comparison. There were certain compensations, however. Nobody ever got lonely. With an average of 7,642 persons per acre, computer dating and singles bars were unnecessary.

Where the other gentry lived, let alone the lower classes and the Scottish, Welsh and Irish servants, I haven't the slightest idea. But with my kin alone, the population density per square mile of all of England was some sixty-six times that of Manhattan today. The only obvious conclusion that can be drawn from this is that there has been a fantastic population implosion during the last thousand years.

Take England alone. If you divide her present population of some forty-four million by the almost 275 billion living there in the year 1000, you'll note that today she has only about 1.6 ten-thousandths of the population she had ten centuries ago, a shrinkage of 6,250 percent. If we assume that some of the original population and I are not related, the latter figure is greatly inflated and the shrinkage becomes even more astronomical.

Since English and American birth rates are roughly the same, we can take the English historical experience as an approximate analog of what is happening in America. So the next time you hear a prophet of doom moaning about the horrible future that awaits us if something isn't done to defuse the population bomb, laugh in his face. Statistics show that you have nothing to worry about.

by George Guthridge

Dolls' Demise

Gentlemen of the press, friends, my dear, dear employees. I have asked you here for an announcement which brings me great sadness. You may have heard rumors about what is to happen. The world will know soon enough. But I wanted to tell you myself, in person.

At the end of the next month the Reznick Doll Company will close its doors forever, as will all doll companies throughout the country. The rubber-mold presses will be shut down; the sewing machines will cease to hum.

You, my dear employees, will be guaranteed comparable jobs in other industries. Yet you will have lost something precious. We were not a large company, but we were a closely knit one. We worked hard. I have come to look upon you as family.

The decision to close was not mine, of course. Nor was it a matter of economics. Sales are booming, and as you know we were about to introduce our revolutionary Rock-a-Betty doll.

Rather, the decision was the government's.

And the decision, I'm afraid, involves more than just the doll companies. Shortly after the companies close, dolls will be banned altogether. The exact beginning of the ban will be announced in the papers. No longer will little girls cradle their favorite dolls; no longer will doting grandmothers stay up all night sewing doll clothes for Christmas or birthday presents.

The reason for this drastic action is both complex and far-reaching in its ramifications. I'll try to summarize as simply as possible.

As you may know, during the last couple of years our industry has come under fire from various feminist groups. It was charged that dolls are a tool of a male-dominated society, that they are used to condition girls to accept motherhood.

Naturally, those of us in management were sensitive to the charge. But we did not merely turn our backs to it. Perhaps we should have—though I doubt if that would have affected the outcome. Only postponed it.

The industry undertook an elaborate and expensive research program. We asked psychologists, sociologists, and, yes, even pediatricians to study the charge. They were given complete freedom. We even allowed representatives of the feminist groups to supervise the research. For we were sure we were right. We were positive that a child's desire for any given toy is a matter of that child's—and not society's—preferences.

The researchers' findings supported our opinions. It was concluded that female children really do prefer dolls over other toys. The feminists were satisfied with our findings, and we thought we were home free.

But unfortunately, the researchers also made a second, even more startling discovery. And some members of the Board of Population Control got hold of the information.

The researchers concluded that girls do not play with dolls as preparation for having children.

Rather, women have children in order to continue playing with dolls.

A